Stronger Than Magic
House of Xannon 1

Copyright © 2012 Melinda VanLone.

ISBN 10: 098874550X

ISBN-13: 978-0-9887455-0-6

Cover Illustration: Carrie Osborne

Cover design and book layout: Book Cover Corner, www.bookcovercorner.com

VanLone, Melinda.
Stronger Than Magic / Melinda VanLone.
Visit the author website: melindavan.com

STRONGER THAN MAGIC
HOUSE OF XANNON BOOK 1

Melinda VanLone

WrittenHouse Publishing

Tallahassee, Florida

For David,

who told me to quit my day job
and follow my dreams.

chapter one

Tarian Xannon lay back on a long, white towel spread over black sand and let the sun soak her body. She inhaled with pleasure the scent of gardenia, hibiscus, and salt. The heady blend soothed her lungs, the inside of her nose, and her mood. Nothing felt better after a long swim in the most beautiful water on earth than to lie here alone, surrounded by lush, tropical trees, caressed by the sea breeze. She sighed, her contentment complete as her body melded with the hot sand. If paradise existed, it was surely a beach in the Pacific.

Her long, hard workouts strained every muscle but were accomplished with the best friends in the world: dolphins. They didn't judge, didn't complain. They seemed happy with life in general and with her, specifically. They bobbed off shore as they watched over her now, chatting with her in clicks, honks, squeaks. This pod, always present, always steadfast, escorted her on countless explorations of the ocean since before she could walk. They were more than friends, at this point. They were a part of her in a way she couldn't explain.

Today, they'd giggled their way over to the Big Island of Hawaii alongside her. She pushed her body to the limit, adding a bit of magical power near the end to be sure she didn't drown. They'd kept pace easily, chittering the entire way. Her workout complete, one of them had given her a ride home by offering a fin. She'd enjoyed images of deep sea and fun sent via the dolphin's special mind-to-mind communication as he rushed her through the ocean back to her own private island. While she touched him, she didn't worry about drowning. She didn't need air when surrounded by dolphins. They provided it, just as they provided a boost of natural energy, which replenished her.

Tarian rose up onto her elbows to look out over the waves kissing the shore to see which dolphin did most of the talking now. As she suspected, it was the one she'd named Roger because, to her ears, every time he saw her he shouted "Roger" both as a name and a statement, and because he sported a scar above his left eye like a detective from an old movie. He wiggled in the water as though tickled by some unseen feather.

"I almost beat you this time!" she called to him. He bobbed, nodded and flipped around. She knew that meant "*Not a chance*" and "*Let's race again.*" If she were in the water with him right now, he'd bump her with his nose to send her an image of him winning their race across to the island on the other side. That's why she had these debates from shore. He couldn't argue back without touching her. Not in a language she understood, anyway.

The sound of sand crunching beneath unsure feet behind her shattered the peace. She knew those footsteps. It was never good when they found her out here. She looked up to squint at Jonus, her mother's chief advisor. He looked stiff with his slick black hair, skinny black suit, and snotty attitude.

"What have I done now?" Tarian raised a hand to shield her eyes from the sun to read his expression. What she saw in his eyes confirmed her suspicion he'd been sent on a mission to fetch her.

Jonus sniffed. "It appears to have escaped the Scion's notice that her presence is required at the monthly leadership meeting."

Two more hated words were never uttered in one sentence. "Leadership" and "meeting."

"How late am I?" She glanced up at the sun.

Probably very late.

"The meeting convened an hour ago, Scion."

Damn.

"May I inform Keeper Marielle that you will attend in a few minutes?" Jonus looked out over the ocean as though he waited for a decision.

"Don't bother. I'm coming." She reached for her towel. Rather than take the time to dry off, she wrapped the towel around her still wet bikini and ran fingers through her soaked hair. It tangled and fought the attention, but she persisted as she walked up the beach with Jonus following after her.

The House of Xannon, home to her family for generations, rose up out of the rock as though vomited by an ancient volcano, clunky and awkward. From a distance, it looked like a jumble of black boulders tumbling down to the black sand beach. Behind the group of rocks, the house's entrance, formed by a natural cave, yawned. She'd heard human sacrifices were once performed in what was now the entry alcove. It seemed vaguely ironic to have visitors arrive and depart from the very spot where people used to be killed in the name of religion, to appease gods who didn't seem to care whether they lived or died. Ironic because the magical Society as a whole honored the power of nature above any mythical being in the sky.

Tarian passed through the open door into the cool, slightly damp air of the entry alcove beyond. Two Sentinels, members of the House of Xannon's elite guard, stood at attention like chess men in all white, their bodies a looming presence in the small space. Two indentations in the walls behind them, created so those traveling by magic arrived directly to the heavily fortified seat of power for the region, waited empty beside them. She thought briefly about using one of them to go somewhere besides the meeting, but forced her sand-covered feet through the entry into the large, welcoming rotunda of the house instead.

Rough rock walls curved to a round skylight to form the cavernous space of the rotunda. It was her favorite room in the entire complex, aside from the beach and the arena, neither of which really counted as rooms at all. Bright, tropical flowering plants adorned any blank bit of space along the walls. Their vivid reds, golds, and purples vibrated against the dark walls which sparkled in the sunlight. A few benches allowed visitors to the house a place to relax or anticipate their meetings. Sentinels stood at all exits from the room, mostly to ensure the magical safeguards embedded within the rock, benches, and floors didn't harm someone accidentally.

To her left, a long hallway led to several bedrooms, including her own. To the right, another long hallway led to the kitchen and, after a few turns, to the arena where the Sentinels trained and where she worked out when she wasn't swimming.

In front of her, with two large doors ajar, the receiving hall beckoned as though it summoned her to a fate worse than death.

Jonus cleared his throat. "I'll inform your mother." He proceeded through the doorway. She didn't hear him say her name, so he must be hurrying to the front to whisper to her mother, rather than shout to the crowd that she'd arrived late and underdressed. Again.

She could simply continue on to her room. Nobody would drag her through the doors. Nobody would force her to interact. She was sure they all wished she wouldn't. Except her mother, of course. Her mother would demand she meet each attendee, a process Tarian found extremely tedious. Then there'd be a quiz later to see if she remembered their names, home towns, and talents. *I should go to my room and change clothes.* With luck, the meeting would be over before she was ready to attend.

Not that I'll ever be ready.

After a long pause, Tarian squared her shoulders, adjusted her towel to be sure it covered all the important bits, crossed the rotunda, and entered the room.

chapter two

Tarian waited inside the doorway of the receiving hall and tapped her foot. Usually the hall stood mostly empty, with only her mother, Advisor Jonus, and maybe a few others sitting at a table on a platform at the far end of the vast space. Today, people crowded the table and several rows of seats in front of it, filling the hall with noise and body odor.

Circus freaks.

She snorted to herself. That wasn't fair. They were people, of course.

Not simply random people either, they were leaders from all the major regions and continents, including North America, here for the monthly Society meeting her mother held as a way to exchange information and solve problems among magic users. Tarian had met most of them, though she hadn't enjoyed the experience. All of them wore disapproving expressions exactly like her mother's. She knew what they thought about her. She didn't measure up as leadership material. The endless droning about trivial details bored her to tears, and the overload of personal power signatures radiating off so many in one spot gave her a headache. Not to mention the different scents of sweat, deodorant, after shave, and perfume, which clashed with the natural floral scents in the air.

It doesn't get any more pointless than this.

Tarian surveyed the room. Same leaders, sitting at the same long table, discussing the same boring problems. Advisor Jonus stood at attention next to her mother. Keeper Marielle led the meeting from the Dolphin Throne, an ornate chair topped by a medallion of dolphins swimming nose to tail in a circle, imbued with magic ancient as earth itself. Marielle's eyes caught Tarian's, and flashed in irritation.

Tarian glanced down at the towel wrapped around her body. A small puddle formed underneath her. She'd thought it better to arrive wet than not at all. Obviously her mother didn't share the same opinion.

As Tarian once again debated going to change her clothes, the meeting ended. She heard muttered conversations as people milled about. Her mother made her way through the crowd, smiling and nodding, ever the gracious hostess.

What a crock.

Her mother was in a far from gracious mood at the moment. Tarian sensed the waves of disapproval as surely as she read the expression written in the small lines around her mother's mouth.

I should have stayed in the ocean. At least I'd feel the waves while I get chewed out. Damn.

She'd been in such a good mood. Until now.

Tarian looked up at the three round skylights currently open in the ceiling, hoping to find balance in the serenity of the outdoors. If the room were quiet, the salt air brought with it the sounds of the sea. She usually loved being in this room.

The thousand-year-old tapestries extending from the high dome to the floor depicted scenes that still mystified her, and her personal symbol etched into the center of the floor made this particular room, the center of the house, feel like home. Unless there was a meeting. The hum of voices overshadowed even the calm of the ocean, and the occasional laugh sent a jolt through her spine, not to mention the small pulses of unintentional power from the guests. Today, she'd rather be somewhere else. Meetings like this one did little to enhance her state of well-being.

Prison would be better. At least they wouldn't expect me to participate.

Clunky footsteps behind her preceded the scent of after shave and a signature that radiated a warm tingle up her arms, followed by a deep, lilting, slightly disapproving, Hispanic voice. "*Chica,* you missed the meeting again?"

"I wouldn't say I missed it." Tarian turned to grin at her friend, Alex. He wore the standard Sentinel uniform, so he must have come from work. "How can anyone miss acting like a stuffy puppet doing the bidding of an invisible puppet master?"

Alex looked into the room, then back at Tarian. "It's a job, *chica.* Like any other. You think I like all the parts of my job? Sitting in the Cellar day in, day out ain't all that."

"You get to go where you want, do what you want, without someone constantly looking over your shoulder or judging every action you take. You have freedom. I have a rock tied to my foot and people spying on me everywhere I go. I'd take your job any day."

Alex snorted. "It always looks pretty on the other side of the ocean, but that don't mean they don't shovel their own brand of shit. Look, when the Keeper is done reaming you, I need a favor."

"Ask now. By the look on her face, it'll take her awhile to calm down." Tarian leaned against the doorway, the carved wood digging into her bare back, and fiddled with the towel to make sure it stayed in place.

"You shouldn't get her so riled up, *chica*. She's your *madre*. You only get one."

Tarian glanced into the room. Her mother had paused about halfway to talk to some tall, blond man with broad shoulders. He gestured with his hands as though they were axes bent on desecrating a stubborn tree. "Are you going to ask your favor or not? She won't be tied up for long."

"Whatever. It's your head." Alex shuffled his feet. "One of the newer recruits lost his snitch. I wouldn't ask, but if the Captain finds out, he'll be booted. It'd be his third strike. This month."

"Sounds like maybe he *should* get booted, Alex."

Alex grinned. "He's a school buddy. He ain't a bad guy, he's just a slow learner. He ain't got your skills."

"Flattery? You must want this pretty bad. Why don't you go?"

Alex dropped the grin. His suddenly serious expression made her pulse jump a beat.

"Tried. Can't find him. The collar's good at hiding, but he ain't dangerous. He's a drunk. It's hard to find a drunk. They don't take logical steps. He'll be an easy snatch and grab for you. Plus, we think he's in Philly. And I know you love Philly, *chica*."

At last, a bit of light at the end of a long, tedious tunnel. He was right, she did love Philadelphia. The grit. The grime. The coffee. Oh, heavens, the coffee. She almost smelled it in the air now. She pictured PJ's coffee shop in her head, along with a mug of glorious liquid.

"Okay. This skip have a name? You have something I can use to latch on?"

Alex nodded and held out a bit of filthy cloth. "The name's Chester. Mark Chester. We got this piece of his t-shirt. Sorry about the smell."

Tarian coughed as the stench of filth, vomit, and decay reached her nose. "Damn, Alex. You don't have anything else?" She held the fabric suspended between forefinger and thumb, away from her nose.

"Nah, that's all Daryl managed to grab in the struggle. He tried to hold him, but this guy is a wiggly bastard."

"Daryl just doesn't have the right equipment for the job." Tarian thrust out her chest.

"And what job requires you to wear a towel, Tarian?"

The stern, feminine voice made her jump. Tarian closed her fist around the rancid piece of cloth and turned to face her mother, putting her hand behind her.

"Catch ya, *chica*." Alex waved, bobbed his head to her mother, and left as fast as his boots would take him back down the hallway. *Coward.*

"Mother. Lovely meeting." Tarian nodded at the people still milling about in the receiving hall. Serving staff scurried in around them, offering refreshments.

Marielle smiled, but it didn't lighten her eyes. "Yes, it was."

Tarian pushed her shoulders back as she looked at her mother. They were the same height, but that was the only thing they had in common. Marielle was a refined, blond, put-together woman who dressed in beautiful dresses and suits. Tarian usually wore tank tops, jeans, and would rather be barefoot. Her black hair never stayed in a bun the way her mother's did. Her blue eyes didn't have the depth her mother's brown ones held. Her face would never wear the mantle of leadership so well. How the woman still had no grey hairs, Tarian couldn't fathom. Dealing with the day-to-day problems would turn anyone's hair gray.

But not Marielle's. She was the very picture of what a leader should be.

And I'm not.

"Anything I should know?" Tarian cleared her throat, gripped the top of the towel, and ignored the water streaming down her back to puddle around her feet.

"Yes. Many things." Marielle closed her eyes and sighed. Her lips moved as though she counted to ten. Twice. When she opened them, the deep brown captivated Tarian, as it always did. Her mother exuded presence, even when not using any of her magic. "The leaders are concerned you do not take your responsibilities seriously."

Tarian shrugged, wishing it eased the tension in her shoulders. "I take plenty of things seriously. They just don't appreciate where I choose to focus my attention."

"They hold power of their own, Tarian. And everyone, no matter where they fall in Society, deserves respect. Showing up late, or not at all, shows them how little you value their presence."

"I forgot the time. It wasn't personal."

"At some point, you'll learn everything you do and say is personal to someone else. They might not mean much to you right now, but you mean a great deal to them. And everything has consequences. Every action causes a reaction. Even something as simple as coming to a meeting late. Or not at all."

"I need to get dressed." Tarian turned, hoping her mother would let the subject drop.

Marielle put a soft hand on Tarian's shoulder. She might as well have bolted Tarian to the floor.

"I know you want to make a difference in the world around you, Tarian. I know you want to use your skills in the manner you think most advantageous. But consider this." Marielle turned Tarian gently around. "With your strength, not to mention your position, comes a duty to do what is right by everyone, not just yourself. You're not a child, and I need…"

Tarian shook her shoulder free of her mother's grasp. "No, I'm not. Yet you insist on treating me like one. Just for one moment of one day I'd love to experience life as it's meant to be lived. To do something meaningful. Not waste it meeting tedious people I'll never understand and who don't like me or want me around. I want a different path, Mother. Why is that so difficult to understand?"

"I do understand, Tarian. More than you're willing to admit. I followed this path before you. I know what sacrifices are required. But I also know the rewards. Rewards you refuse to see, though they are right in front of you. If you looked at it from my perspective, you'd see what I see. Things worth fighting for. Things more worthy of attention than whatever job Alex has asked of you." Marielle took a breath. "You know how I feel about the Scion assisting the Sentinels. They are guards. You're not."

Tarian's fist tightened on the dirty cloth hidden in her hand. "He wouldn't ask for my help if it weren't important, Mother. He needs me to track someone. It's easy for me. And it's Philadelphia, not the gates of hell. I promised I'd help. Plus it'll get me out of this house for a few hours. What's so wrong about that? I'll be back in time for the next meeting."

Marielle arched an eyebrow. "Don't make a promise you don't intend to keep."

Tarian walked down the hallway. This time her mother didn't stop her. She'd make her easy snatch and grab. Haul the guy to the Cellar. Dump him on Alex. Then she'd go to the damn meeting.

Unless something more interesting presented itself.

chapter three

Tarian stood in the shadows of a grime-covered alley, took a long, deep breath, and grinned. Philadelphia wore its own special brand of perfume created by garbage, sweat, hot dogs, exhaust, coffee beans, fried food, and unidentifiable bits of filth. It all combined and infiltrated her nostrils in a full-on assault sure to take down the weak. It certainly wasn't the floral infused sea breeze she was used to. She wrinkled her nose. Compared to that, the city was an ocean of stench. But she still loved it. Nothing wrong with a little grit. It made her feel alive in a way the ocean didn't quite manage.

She waited next to her favorite coffee shop, staring out at a street lined with bars, cafes, suits, and the homeless. None of the people passing by had active magic talent, and they didn't even glance in her direction. None of them was the one she hunted. She leaned against the brick wall and picked at one of her fingernails.

It should be an easy day, no matter what her mother thought. The one she waited for would stand out among normal people, at least to her. Tarian closed her eyes and wrinkled her nose as she pulled on the inner power allowing her to sense someone's magic as it drifted on the air like radio waves, or a special scent only she detected. The tiny hairs in her nose vibrated and tickled, but she resisted the urge to rub. Her tracking ability never erred, and right now it alerted her to the prey only a couple of blocks away. She took another deep breath to focus her energy in case she needed it for defense as well as tracking.

A few minutes more and her target would be here. All she had to do was be patient. *Easy snatch and grab.* She'd be home in time for the next meeting, as promised. She comforted herself with the idea of getting a PJ's coffee to take to the meeting. If she were going to sit through one, she might as well be caffeinated.

"Hey, babe, lookin' for a good time?"

The low voice behind her made her nearly growl in frustration. Distraction didn't help when she was trying to focus magic. She turned to see a praying mantis of a man leering at her. He hadn't been there a minute ago. No magical signature, so she hadn't sensed his approach.

"Oh, sure, it's always been my dream to do it in an alley. Beat it, moron."

"I got whatcha need right here." His hand grasped his junk and wiggled.

"I like men who understand the concept of showering. Get lost." Her gaze moved on to another man, one passing by on the sidewalk. *Shit.* Her target, Mark Chester. He sauntered past, bumped into a garbage can, fell into the street, picked himself up, and lurched forward to the other sidewalk.

Adrenaline kicked into gear, rushed blood to her muscles, and edged her forward. She shoved past the leering man, who let out a growl of frustration and called her a name, which would have horrified her mother. The smelly bum grabbed her arm from behind and spun her around.

"You comin' with me. You got business with my man." He held a knife in one hand, and his eyes filled with a cold certainty she'd do exactly as he said. But the way he held the knife marked him as an amateur. He'd never do real damage with it sideways like that, even if he managed to get close enough to try. He'd watched too many movies.

She took in a slow breath and, with the exhale, pushed a small shield wall of air solidified by magic at him. To him, it'd feel as though a giant hand shoved him backward. To an onlooker, it would look like he tripped. She used only enough to scare him, but not enough for any real drain on her resources. She didn't want to waste energy on this loser. He dropped the knife, his grip on her arm loosened, and his eyes widened in shock as he felt the invisible force push his arms away from her. Tarian grabbed his shoulders and added her body weight to force him back into the alley until she pinned him to a wall, then tied a neat cage around him with strands of air like a spider catching a fly in a web. He didn't fight back, although his hands flapped in the air.

"Hey, they didn't say you could do it too." His protest came out in a squeak. So much for the tough-guy routine.

She tied off the stream, using the man's own residual energy to power it. Everybody had magic energy, even in Philly, but most people couldn't tap into it. Thankfully.

Tarian was rewarded for the effort with a loud growl of protest from her stomach. It took more energy to tie off a stream, but it was worth it. A few extra calories at lunch would replace it, and in the meantime she'd be able to release her focus on this guy and do something more important without worrying about him sneaking up behind her. The whole thing would dissolve on its own over a few hours. Long enough to keep him out of her way but short enough he wouldn't starve to death.

"You in trouble, lady. You already caught, you just don't know yet."

Tarian paused to survey the man. He'd said someone had told him she'd be here and sent him to—what, exactly? Trap her? Take her hostage? Had they lost their minds?

"From where I'm standing, you're the one in trouble." She pointed at the shield which he certainly felt around him even though he couldn't see it.

The man's eyes glazed over. His head dropped as if consciousness had been drained out of him by a siphon. He dangled against her web, a limp dishrag, hanging by invisible threads. Confused, she checked it for anything that might have choked him.

"He isss nothing." The slurred voice behind her instantly tied her stomach into small knots. She spun around to confront the owner. He stood in a fighting stance with feet shoulder width apart, slightly taller than her, blond, and covered in greenish-gray scales on his face, neck, and hands. *What the hell is he, and how the hell did he managed to sneak up on me?* She should have sensed him coming. She gathered focus and pushed another shield out to hold him down. He flicked a wrist and the shield vanished. Shocked, she tried another. He deflected it again.

Her heart thumped hard against her chest. She tried a third shield, this time wrapping it around herself. It held, but she wasn't entirely sure he hadn't simply ignored it.

"And who are you? Or should I say what?" *Keep him talking.* She'd figure out what to do if he kept talking long enough. She forced herself to take a deep breath.

The lizard man licked his lips then flicked his hand. Behind her, she heard a gasp, then silence. She didn't bother to turn around.

"Who *are* you?" She kept her legs loose and her fingers flexed, ready to gather up the water molecules in the air and throw them at this…thing.

"You have something I need." The voice was low and oddly seductive.

"What would that be?" Energy pooled between her breasts and pulsed. Her heart rate matched it, beat for beat. The tiny hairs on her skin stood at attention. She didn't like the dip in her power caused by the shields she'd created, but she still had enough to put up one hell of a fight.

The man-lizard hissed. Liquid dripped down the scales on his face. His hands—claws—darted out and slashed her on the arm before she dodged. The claw sliced through her shield, her leather jacket, and skin as though she were made of thin paper, rather than flesh and blood. The gash left behind rained blood down her arm and onto the pavement. She gasped as the pain hit her, sharp, hot, like a needle. Or poison. No telling what he had in those claws.

Dammit!

His tongue snaked out over his lips then brought the claw up, letting it drip her blood onto the slimy thing. Her stomach churned as she watched. The scales on his face hid expressions from her, but she saw triumph gleam in his eyes.

chapter four

Tarian mustered every spark of energy available to pull molecules of water from the air. When they coalesced around her as tiny, shimmering water-diamonds, she formed them into a basketball-sized bundle of blue water and flung it with one push at the lizard-man. He held up both clawed hands in front of him and pulsed a column of reddish-brown energy. The two forces met, beat for beat, in a tangle of blue and red, dirt and water. In the back of her mind, it registered he commanded a blend of fire and earth, while she favored water and air. They were exact opposites.

The two of them squared off around the center of the alley, the power between them balanced. Dirt met water, created mud, and dropped with wet splats onto the filthy pavement. Bricks around them sparkled as the grime fed the lizard-man's assault, while her own water-based stream drenched his suit, hair, and glistened off his scales. Power cracked and sparked as though a thunderstorm unleashed. The noise bounced off the old brick around them in an assault on the ears, a racket she hoped would blend with the din of traffic outside the alley.

Tarian wasn't ready for a magic fight on the streets of a regular city, and she had no idea what sort of talent this lizard-man possessed beyond the obvious basics. Shields wouldn't hold him, for starters. He was as strong in focus as she was, though he didn't seem to possess ability over a third element like she did. Not that it did her any good, since her ability with fire was fairly weak, especially compared to his. He looked to be a physical match for her, if it came to a wrestling match.

If it hadn't been Philly, someone might have called the cops at the noise they made or the odd scene they created. But in a city like Philadelphia, people maintained their distance, and nobody gave them a second glance.

The loud crunch of metal grinding on metal shattered the air and their concentration. She sensed the lizard-man's hold on the moment weaken and seized the opportunity to push all of her energy into a blended ball of air-based lightning with water, a miniature thunderstorm, which she pulsed outward, aimed right for his head. The lizard-man flicked a look behind her then dissolved into red mist and black dust before the energy exploded. A shower of blue sparks blended with red rained down to create muddy, brackish puddles on cracked concrete.

Tarian sucked in a sharp breath and held it while she stared at the spot. One good thing about a fight: his particular magical scent embedded itself in her psyche. He'd never sneak up on her again. She opened all her senses to test for his magic in the air. All she found were residual traces. Nothing fresh, nothing hidden. It didn't reassure her. She hadn't felt him behind her to begin with.

She let the breath out in a long, heavy sigh, but she didn't release her focus. *He shouldn't have been able to sneak up on me.*

Her ability to track also enabled her to feel magic from anyone or anything. So why not him?

Who are you?

She waited for a few moments, trying to calm her racing heart with deep breaths that refused to do the job properly. He had her blood. *Not good.* He might simply like the taste of it, but somehow she doubted it. He wanted it for something. She shuddered as a chill raced through her core. Her arm throbbed. A hard, sharp knot moved up and down the wound as though looking for a way out or a way to burrow deeper, like the seed of something evil seeking a place to get comfortable. She tried to track the source, but as it left her body it vanished as if it had never been, scattered on air that, for once, betrayed her.

Tarian put a hand over the wound and applied pressure to stop the bleeding. If she couldn't track the lizard-thing by his signature, she should be able to track her own blood. She sent feelers out but met a solid wall of nothing. She tried again. Pain slammed into her skull. Her nose burned as she strained to catch some whiff of his scent, but she found no trace of her blood or the lizard-man. She'd never met someone she couldn't track before.

She turned to check on the stinky bum. His body had vanished, along with her web. Her instincts screamed. The man was gone, the lizard was gone, her arm was on fire, her blood on his claws, and she couldn't track him. He had looked like a monster out of a horror novel, with scales and everything. She looked at the tear on her jacket, now soaked in blood. The cut pulsed.

Tarian took off her jacket and focused her magic on the wound in an attempt to heal it, but after a couple of minutes had to admit she sucked at healing. Even if she hadn't spent a lot of energy fighting the demon, she couldn't have healed this. When she tried to handle something as delicate as skin, she felt clumsy and awkward. The headache wasn't helping, either. The best she managed was a loose scab she wasn't entirely sure wouldn't have formed on its own in a few more minutes.

She surveyed the damage. The angry welt hurt like hell, but at least she'd managed to make it stop bleeding.

Tarian slid one arm into the sleeve of her jacket and winced as the stiff leather brushed against the wound. The torn section stuck out at odd angles. She tucked it in so the rip was less obvious, then searched the alley for any piece of debris the lizard man might have touched. If she couldn't track her own blood, for whatever reason, maybe something he'd touched would help solidify her focus. She found nothing, not even a button or a scale.

"Lose something?"

Tarian raised her head to see a man standing on the sidewalk, surveying the alley. She'd been so distracted she hadn't felt him approach, but now she detected a strong magical signature, cool as an ocean breeze, emanating from him, plus a whiff of some sort of spice. She tested the air, ready to throw every particle of energy she possessed, which wasn't much at the moment. She relaxed as she realized he wasn't attempting to focus power of any sort. Satisfied he wasn't an immediate threat, she took a good look at him.

He had the kind of strong jaw she loved, and his messy black hair soaked up the afternoon sun. He wore jeans, a black wool coat, and relaxed confidence. A shiver crawled down her back and settled in her groin. If they'd met in a bar, she'd have bought him a drink. Or three.

The stranger raised his eyebrows as his eyes passed over the slice in her jacket, then had the nerve to wink at her as his gaze traveled down her leather pants.

"You're in some kind of trouble. Need help?" His smile stretched up and lit a sparkle in his eyes. "I felt the blast all the way inside the coffee shop."

"I'm doing just fine, thanks. I have a job to do, if you don't mind." Great, just what she needed, some Society member thinking he was a detective. She needed to finish her original mission and get the hell out of here.

"You're anything but fine. Whatever job you think you're doing, you need to have that arm looked at first." His eyes didn't lose the sparkle, but his voice took on a serious tone. "It smells wrong, like rancid mud. He's Earth and you're obviously not. If he's done what I think he's done, you need to have it seared and sealed. Fast. And you need to catch the guy before he uses what he stole."

She couldn't stop herself from putting a hand over the injury. He was right. The wound felt wrong, somehow. The cold inside her wove in and around it as though a living, breathing, scaly thing. She didn't want to think about what it searched for. It pulsed in time to the throbbing in her arm. But surely the healers could handle this at home. No big deal.

"Look, I appreciate the concern, but I'll be fine. I don't have time to get it looked at right now." She resolutely put her hand down and pushed past him. Her target couldn't be far. She'd only been here for what, a few minutes? He was probably in the nearest bar.

The man put a hand on her good arm to stop her. The warmth soaked into her bicep and loosened muscles all over the place.

"Make time." The sparks were gone from his eyes. "I'd hate to see the Scion used by something so foul."

"I don't remember meeting you, Mr.?" She pulled her arm away from him.

"I'm disappointed. Though I'll admit it was a long time ago." He put a hand in his back pocket, fished out a card, and handed it to her.

Daric Voltain, Private Society Investigations

The address was the building next to the alley they stood in, the home of her favorite coffee shop. No wonder he'd felt the backlash of spell power. He must live above the shop.

"I told you, Scion, I've had some experience with this. And it's obvious you haven't. That arm is bad news. He's left a mark on you. And if you have some of him, it means he has some of you."

Her skin turned cold as she remembered the lizard man tasting her blood.

"Look, Mr. Voltain, it's no big deal." She put the card in her back pocket and matched his know-it-all stare with a glare of her own.

"Call me Daric. I'll take that as confirmation. The clock is ticking, Scion. Tell me, what'd he look like? Did he have scales?"

Tarian nodded, numb.

"If he's a Laghairtine, which I suspect he is from the smell and the scales, the stronger he is, the faster the clock will tick. If he knows what he's doing, I'd say you have a week, maybe less."

A week before what? Before her arm fell off? She put her hand over the wound again. It didn't feel life-threatening. Her head pounded. Dizziness threatened to drop her on her ass.

It was as if Daric read her mind.

"A week before he has control over you. Your powers. Everything. You'll be his to command. That would be a very bad thing, for you and the rest of us, Scion."

"Tarian." Her thoughts swam as she slumped to the curb. Daric knew who she was. Not surprising, with her position in Society. His comment about her powers, though, pushed at her gut. If someone had control of her power, they could use her to destroy the Throne, her mother, the House of Xannon, everything.

"What the hell is a Laghairtine, anyway?" She wished her head would stop spinning.

Daric sat next to her on the curb. "It's a half-daemon, half-human hybrid. The kind they scare you with as a kid."

"And you know this because?"

"My mother is a teacher. And I have a tiny amount of healing talent. Enough to know you need to get that fixed. Whatever you're here for can wait."

"This should have been easy." She shook her head. "I do this sort of thing all the time."

"Get attacked?"

"No. Not that part." She didn't add most people would never be close enough to attack her. With her tracking ability and power, she wasn't usually in a vulnerable situation. What was different about today? "I was doing a favor for a friend. Picking up a skipper."

"Some friend." Daric pointed to the alley. "They didn't tell you he'd have claws?"

"I wasn't here for him. I was here for…" The hair on the back of her neck tickled. She looked up in time to see Mark Chester falling out of the bar across the street. She watched as he tripped over his own feet and fell to all fours on the broken concrete.

The whole reason she was here was to pick up the drunken fool. But from the looks of it, the task might have been handled by anyone. Alex, her best friend and trusted guard, had asked her to do this quietly, as a favor for his friend Daryl. But why had Daryl asked for help in the first place? The idiot sprawled in front of her couldn't have run from anyone, let alone a trained Sentinel guard. And the bum in the alley had told her he was sent to grab her. The whole thing smelled of setup. And if it was a setup, Chester might know something about it.

chapter five

Spurred on by the thought of finding out what the hell was going on, Tarian jumped to her feet. Vertigo set in, and her stomach roared and bubbled in protest. She needed to eat, but she didn't have time for it. Her tussle with the lizard had drained more than her blood. It had drained her strength as well.

"Hey, seriously, you need to go to a healer." Daric put a hand on her elbow to steady her.

"I know. But I need this guy. He must know something about all this. Look, thanks for your help, Daric, but do me a favor and stay back here. I have a super power for guys like this, but it won't work if you're next to me."

She glanced at Daric and saw the question in his eyes.

"Boobs."

He laughed, and put his hands up in surrender. She took two deep breaths, willing the world to stop spinning. When the ground under her feet felt firm enough, she dodged her way through the traffic and blaring horns. She reached the other sidewalk and thanked the stars Chester hadn't managed to get off his hands and knees. She offered Chester a hand and a smile.

"Hey, Mark, how's it hangin'?"

Chester looked up. His brows furrowed in confusion. His eyes traveled over her cleavage. He beamed.

"Hey, baby! I hope I know you." He attempted to take her hand but missed.

"You're gonna know me real well." She helped him onto his feet and steadied him while he struggled to stay upright.

"Why don't we have a chat?" She offered him a view of her cleavage again. He swayed toward her, his smile even wider. *Men are so easy. Show them breasts and they'll follow you anywhere.* Tarian pulled Chester through a group of suits, away from the bar, toward the alley next to it.

"There's shomthing different 'bout you. You sure I don't know you?" Chester stumbled on some trash.

"Oh, I'd remember if we'd met, sweetie," she purred. Chester let her lead him to the end of the alley. This one hadn't been sullied by a clash of magic energy. It was a normal, average, every day, rat-infested alley. Once she had Chester behind a dumpster, she pushed him up against the grimy concrete wall.

"I know about your little game, Mark. I know you were sent to lure me in. Who sent you? Was it one of the Sentinels?"

"Huh? Shentinels...you?"

"I'm not a Sentinel, you idiot. I'm the one taking your butt to prison unless you start talking. You remember the Cellar, right?"

At the word "Cellar" a spark of recognition appeared in Mark's inebriated eyes. He made a lame attempt to struggle, but she kept a firm grip and leaned her body weight into him.

"I got friendsh, ya know. Po...pow...big friends. And stuff to do. I'm important. I'm doing shomthin' important. For him."

Tarian almost choked on the fumes of alcohol overload escaping from his mouth as he made his pronouncement.

"Who's that, Mark? The garbage man?"

"Him. You know, the demon. He got you. I can shmell it." Chester hiccuped. "My talent. I can shmell it. He's gonna be happy with me." He poked himself in the chest for emphasis.

The pit in Tarian's stomach squirmed and moved up into her throat. She swallowed hard to keep herself from throwing up.

"What do you know, Chester?" She pushed him hard against the brick wall. "Spill it."

Chester started to giggle. "You in such trouble. He wants you, you know. He gets what he wants. And he got you."

"Do you know how to stop him? Do you know who he is?" The words tumbled out of her in a rush.

Chester laughed, his eyes wide and near hysteria. The laughter turned to coughs.

She wouldn't get anything out of him when he was this drunk. She needed to sober him up first. Then she'd force him to talk.

Tarian glanced back up the alley. Daric stood at the entrance, far enough back to avoid notice but close enough to see. She gave him a wave and nodded her thanks.

With one hand, she held Mark in place. She thrust the other out to cast a travel portal spell. Nothing happened. Her focus refused to cooperate, and her power felt like an empty battery in desperate need of a recharge. The alley and Mark's dopey face swam around her in lazy circles. She closed her eyes and took several deep breaths.

The feel of grimy lips on hers popped her eyes open. She drew back in disgust as she realized Chester had mistaken her closed eyes for an invitation. Maybe she'd played up the sex-kitten act a bit too much. She ignored his pursed lips and took another deep breath. Concentrating on pulling together what was left of her strained resources, she tried again to pull her focus together. This time, she felt it coalesce inside her like it always did, a pool of liquid energy radiating from her chest down to her hands and out, connecting her with the unseen energy found in all living things. The first moments after calling power were always the sweetest, and the most dangerous. The trick was to keep complete focus and control over it, even as it threatened to consume her soul.

She pulled on the energy with her mind, wrapping it into a complex web most people would never see. Next to her, the air shimmered and undulated like an ocean wave. At first it looked like a trick of the shadows in the dark alley. The hole expanded to a large oval big enough for an adult to step through. The alley still shimmered beyond it, but overlaid on top of it was the faint image of the small, stark room made of black rock that welcomed criminals into the Cellar.

Chester lurched sideways the moment the travel portal became clear. Debris tangled his unsteady feet, and he fell headfirst into the trash bin before landing in a heap on the ground.

"No point in running, Mark. It'll only make things worse. You're going to tell me what I want to know." Tarian grabbed his arm and helped him stand. She added a small magic push to force him toward the portal as he struggled and made himself deadweight. He gasped and started to retch. Disgusted, she shoved him through the portal, glancing back to the mouth of the alley. There Daric stood, a grin spreading his lips and creating a dimple she'd love to dive in to. She rolled her eyes at him then stepped through after Mark.

chapter six

The travel spell embraced Tarian in an icy hug that squeezed her body then shattered it. The pieces whirled toward her destination, a journey that seemed like an eternity inside a vacuum, but in reality only took a few minutes. Inside a travel portal, there was nothing to see, hear, taste or touch. Enveloped in a white blanket of nothingness, she suppressed the urge to wander into the what-if-the-spell-went-wrong thought process and focused on her destination.

Just when it seemed like she'd remain a jumble of ice cubes forever, the bits and pieces of her body slammed back into place one by one. Her senses returned as the portal opened and ejected her out into the reception area for the detention center of House of Xannon, more commonly known as the Cellar. More than simply a basement, it secured all levels of criminals with magic ability under rock embedded with centuries-old magic power and surrounded by deep ocean.

Chester huddled on all fours in front of her, his body wracked with telltale heaves. She dodged to the side seconds before he threw up on the polished black rock floor then fell into it. The stench of stale beer, cigarettes, and stomach acid greeted her. She suppressed the urge to puke. Her body felt off, as though she'd gone on some sort of alcoholic binge, and the smell didn't help.

Chester groaned, but didn't lift his head. She almost wished to join him.

With everything that had happened this morning, she was glad to see her best friends on duty. Alex had his feet propped up on the desk and a baseball game playing on the laptop. His brother, Frankie, wore his glasses and had his nose glued to his monitor.

"Tari! You're kidding, right?" Alex pulled his feet down and wrinkled his nose. "Damn. What did he have to eat?"

"More like what he had to drink. I don't think travel agreed with the whiskey." Despite the stench, Tarian's stomach growled. She suppressed the urge to gag. It was an odd sensation, to feel like throwing up and still be starving for food.

Alex and Frankie both frowned at Chester. Alex came around the edge of the desk and paused to survey her.

"Nice look you got going there, *chica*. I'm liking the pants. What's this?" Alex tugged at the torn sleeve of her jacket.

"Just a scratch. That a new shirt?" An odd knot of something traveled up and down the wound on her arm in reaction to Alex's touch. She snatched her arm away, running her fingers through her hair to distract him. Her arm throbbed. A needle of pain shot from her forearm into her shoulder. She had to grit her teeth not to curse.

"You know me, a style magnet." Alex modeled for her, turning his body to the side to show off. His coffee-colored skin vibrated against the white shirt.

"Name?" Frankie tapped on the keyboard. He was a lot smaller than Alex, but she'd bet on him to win a fight every time. Not only was he smart and fast, he hid a lot of muscle underneath his crisp uniform.

"It's Mark Chester." Tarian watched Chester roll onto his side, coating his shirt and hair in vomit, and sighed. It would be hours before he'd be sober enough to tell her anything useful.

The wound on her arm jabbed, and again felt like it wanted to escape. Could it travel from her arm to someone else? *Not on my watch. No way is this thing infecting my friends too.* She shifted away from them, hoping distance would help.

"Enjoy yourself? You got some nerve, skippin' out like that." Alex nudged Chester with his booted toe. Chester groaned.

"This is strange. The charges against him have been dismissed." Frankie pounded a few more keys. "Three misdemeanor charges of negligent use of magic, one charge of attempted magical coercion of a non-talented, complicated by drunk-and-disorderly mischief, compounded by evading and resisting, all dismissed. This morning, after you left."

"How is that possible?" Tarian moved around the desk to stare at the computer. As she moved closer to the screen, static obscured the information. "How do you see anything on there with all the interference?"

"It's not normally like this." Frankie put a hand on her arm and pushed it away from the computer. The screen solidified into a solid image again. "It's you."

Tarian winced, resisting the urge to soothe the wound with her other hand.

"What's up with your arm, *chica*?" Alex pointed at the tear. "That don't look like no scratch to me."

Her heart thumped. "Frankie, who dismissed the charges?"

Frankie studied the screen. "Doesn't say who, specifically, but it'd have to be one of the current panel of judges. I can find out. Any commands they put in are registered, so I can trace it back to the source. Go see the healers. I'll have an answer by the time you're done."

"Who says I need the healers?" Her stomach lurched, and she fought the dry heave even as her shoulder sent a searing shot of pain across her neck and into her head. The reek from Chester's puddle taunted her.

Alex raised an eyebrow at her.

"Okay, fine. I'll see a healer."

"The question is, *chica*, why do you need one? Did Chester do this?" Alex glared at the man on the floor.

She'd have to tell them something. Alex would never give up, and since they might be in danger, she owed it to them to let them know.

"The alleys in Philly aren't the safest places, as it turns out."

Frankie looked up and took off his glasses. Alex stared at her.

"Something nasty was waiting for me. If I had to guess, I'd say Chester was bait."

"What was it?" Frankie leaned forward.

"According to someone named Daric…" she fished the card out of her pocket, "Voltain, it was a Laghairtine."

The swift intake of breath from Frankie and the shout from Alex told her more than enough about her situation.

"You get that looked at right now, *chica*. Don't even bother arguing." Alex pointed at the travel alcove. "We'll talk about this Daric guy later."

"In a minute." She avoided looking at him, choosing to stare at the computer monitor instead. "You told me your friend Daryl asked you to hunt this guy as a favor. What exactly did he say?"

Her hand had somehow found its way to her stomach as though seeking comfort. She put it down by her side and ignored the pulsing throb of blood rushing to the fingers on her injured arm.

"You mean other than 'go grab him'? Not much. He asked if I had any pull with you. If I thought you'd use your tracking to find the guy before his super noticed he'd lost yet another collar." Alex sat on the edge of the desk and tilted his head. His eyes searched her face then traveled down her arm.

"Did he seem nervous?" She backed up a bit, leaned against the wall and let the cold of the black stone wall seep through her jacket. Her arm pulsated, but she did her best to keep her face neutral.

"Well, yeah. He'd lost a prisoner, right? Of course he was nervous. It's his head if he's caught being so stupid. Now he's gonna get his ass kicked too. He sent you to get this bum, and now you're damaged. Not cool."

"Did he say anything else?" She gasped the words out as something sharp burrowed into her neck.

"You okay? You don't look so good." Alex jumped up and joined her at the wall. He put a hand on her shoulder and stared into her eyes. "You stubborn mule, go get this looked at. You're worse than *mi madre*."

She closed her eyes. If he was lapsing into Spanish, he must be really concerned. "Did he say anything else?"

"Lemme see. Chester was sitting on his ass in that sorry excuse for an apartment. *No problemo*, except the bum talked Daryl into stopping off at a bar. Which is odd, 'cause Daryl don't drink."

"And that's where Chester cut loose? At a bar? Does Chester have compulsion talent?" She opened her eyes to find Alex staring down at the arm she now cradled with her other hand.

The concern in his eyes nearly made her lose what little control she had.

Alex shrugged. "Daryl didn't really say. Simply handed me the piece of shirt I gave to you, and begged me to ask you for the favor. Not to tell anybody. I'd have said the same thing, if I'd been that stupid. Look, Tari, this can wait. Let us check into all this. You go get looked at."

Her stomach throbbed, and her neck felt as if something spiky and cruel burrowed under the skin. The headache, which had been in the background, blossomed with a new vengeance. She took a deep breath and let it out slowly, willing the pain now wracking her body to subside long enough to allow her to think.

Something wasn't quite right. She couldn't put her finger on it, other than Chester didn't seem capable of escaping from a bathroom stall, much less Sentinel custody. But he probably wasn't drunk at the time. If he had some sort of natural compulsion ability, it might explain his escape. Maybe. It was too hard to tell with him this drunk.

"From the limited information in the database, if that was a real Laghairtine, you need more than a healer. He's a mix of human magic and daemon, with the odd element twisted up around it. He's a freak of nature. They shift into lizard form, can't be sealed or shielded, and can pop into the Between, which means most of us wouldn't be able to follow him."

Frankie stood up and shook her shoulders. "If he took a decent blood sample from you, he can use it to pull your power. Healer or no. When he gets enough, he'll have control over your body. You'll be a prisoner in your own head, while he'll run the show. Tari, to call this a big deal is an understatement."

The cold inside her felt more solid now, and her neck ached as the pain pounded on ligaments. Her blood felt sluggish.

She knew he was right. She'd read the stories. She remembered a history tutor warning her about this type of creature. She'd thought they were stories told to frighten her into staying in bed at night as a child. *So much for fairy tales.* Daric said she had a week before the demon's spell would be complete.

A week.

Crap.

She sagged against Frankie, fixated on her problem. What should have been a normal arrest of an idiot with minor magic infractions had turned into a hellish nightmare. What would happen to the Dolphin Throne if someone took control of her power? What about her friends? Her family? The House of Xannon?

What would happen to her?

She shuddered as she pictured the rest of her life spent looking out through her own eyes but being unable to control her actions. Being someone else's puppet. A vision of the Dolphin Throne swam through her mind. For the first time, she saw herself sitting on it, but instead of looking like the leader her mother insisted she needed to be, she was laughing maniacally as her power incinerated everyone near her. She saw the lizard-man standing in the shadows next to her, hissing in triumph.

Her stomach boiled as her thoughts swirled and the cold knot at the back of her neck pulsed in a strange rhythm of its own. She fought the urge to vomit. She heard her mother's voice in her head. All those lectures about the security of the Throne, the need for an heir, and the duty of the Scion to provide one circled and lodged in her chest along with a healthy dose of guilt and irritation that she'd let this happen in the first place.

If the Laghairtine was able to control her actions and power, everyone around her would be in danger, and they wouldn't even know it until it was too late. *If* the lizard took control.

That was the key.

"I have to stop him from getting control. If Daric Voltain was right, I have a week. I still feel like myself, for the most part." She pushed away from Frankie to find Alex right behind her. She backed away from them both, trying to take back some of her dignity.

Other than being exhausted and starving from her fight with the thing, the strange sharp knot at the base of her neck, which gave her a resounding headache, and the searing wound on her arm, she felt fine.

"I have to figure out where this Laghairtine is, how he's using my blood, and stop it before the week is up. Simple, right?"

The look of doubt on Alex's face said everything.

"How did he even know where I was going to be? This whole thing smells like the garbage in that alley."

"We'll help. We'll follow the trail from the beginning. You, *chica*…"—Alex pointed at her—"get to a healer. We'll let you know when we have something."

The steps solidified in her mind. Block the takeover of her power, find the demon, and destroy him. It sounded like a plan.

Frankie cleared his throat. "Alex, I say we hold Chester in cell #3 'til we sort this out." He tapped on the keyboard a few more times, entering the information into the official record.

"Fine. As long as she gets to the healer." Alex poked her arm.

"As long as you tell me the instant this idiot is sober." She poked him back, but her heart wasn't in it. After giving her a hard look, Alex turned back to their prisoner.

"Alright, brainless, on your feet." Alex pushed Chester with his foot, but he remained on the floor. "Dammit, Tari, you coulda snatched him before he got so loaded."

"I'm not sure he's ever been sober." It seemed easier to grab him while he was drunk, but now she wished she'd grabbed him before he'd managed to get so wasted. She could be interrogating him right now, instead of waiting for the whiskey to wear off. But no amount of magic would make the alcohol process through his body any faster. She'd have to wait.

Alex reached down and pulled Chester up by his pants, set him mostly upright, then guided him roughly to the door leading to the holding cells. He pushed Chester up against the wall and held him with one hand as he pressed the palm of the other to a plate on the wall. The panel above the plate beeped in approval. Alex muttered, a sound more like a growl than actual words. The panel beeped again and lit up green, allowing the door to swing open.

Alex propelled Chester through the door in front of him, but stopped in the doorway to look back at her. "You gonna be okay? You need help getting to the healer?" Alex jostled Chester, who groaned.

"Let me know when he sobers up, okay?"

Alex raised an eyebrow then pushed on through the door.

Tarian leaned against the cool wall and let the pain wash over her.

"You know we got your back, right?" Frankie's face glowed in the light from the computer.

"Yeah." She gulped, willing the nausea to retreat. "And I have yours."

"Don't think I don't know what that means. I know you. You'll be all about trying to protect us instead of asking for help. And you can't do this thing without help. So let us." Frankie looked at her over the screen. His eyes flashed with too much understanding. They knew her too well. Most of the time, she'd have said that was a good thing. But today, she had the sinking feeling all it meant was they were in just as much danger as she was. She'd never forgive herself if something happened to them.

Since the only way in and out of the Cellar was by portal, she opened one to the healer's hallway knowing Frankie would look to see she went directly to the healers. She stepped through, closed the portal, and then leaned against the wall. Exhaustion washed over her.

What if this power she felt circling inside her reached others? Anyone near her was in danger. The thing in her neck writhed, and the wound pulsed, a living connection to a demon straight out of horror stories. She needed to get her arm healed and the demon out of her body. Fast. Or she needed to get out of the house and never come back. Alex and Frankie, along with her mother and sister, Calliope, would want to help her, no matter the danger. She couldn't let them take the chance. Frankie was right. She wanted to protect them and her family, above anything else.

For the first time in her life, she felt alone.

She took a few steps toward the healer's quarters, but the knot in her neck punched her with a jolt of pain, and the pulse in her wound bonded with it in a throb that never quite matched her heartbeat. She fell against the wall, hoping it would support her since her legs didn't seem to want to do the job. The polished stone soothed the flushed feel of her face. She put her burning forehead against it.

She felt a power force from deep inside her neck reach out into the air around her and search for something.

An odd sound filtered through the air and into her ears. She struggled to listen. Clicking, sing-song staccato. She couldn't immediately place it, but it reminded her of the ocean. Surely she wasn't hallucinating already. It seemed absurd, but her energy was low. Maybe she was losing it.

She forced air in and out of her lungs. Each breath renewed the war with whatever it was that struggled to connect with something around her. She tried to pull her focus together enough to form a shield around herself, but she couldn't muster enough energy. She'd spent too much fighting the demon the first time, and the wound constantly drained her. The travel portals had sucked what remained of her strength. Her body simply refused to gather any more. She'd need sleep and food, and she couldn't have either. Too much pain coursed through her arm and head. Too much power that didn't feel like her own circled around her body.

"Tari? Are you okay?" The soft voice echoed down the hallway and reverberated in her head.

Tarian turned to see her sister, Calliope, standing outside the door to the main healer room. She'd tied back her blond hair and held a bundle of cloth like she'd been sewing. She looked so much like their mother that Tarian squinted to be sure it wasn't Marielle. Calliope's forehead creased as she took a good look at Tarian.

The odd force inside Tarian beat against the base of her neck like a child throwing a tantrum, pushing to get out. Startled, she realized exactly what the object was: a piece of claw, left behind by the lizard-man as a souvenir. Tarian clutched at it, afraid it might rip through her skin and attack Calliope, and backed away even as her sister moved toward her.

"Get back." Tarian put her hands up to block her sister. "I mean it, Calli. Get away from me."

She turned and ran. She didn't even care where she was going, as long as it was away from Calliope. The force inside her pulled tight like a string tugged from somewhere outside herself. Her injured arm nearly lifted on its own. If the lizard did this, he did it from thousands of miles away through some of the toughest magical walls ever constructed.

She slammed down on that thought process. It was too fast. Too soon. She had a week. That's what Daric Voltain had said. A week, dammit.

What if he was wrong?

She barreled out of the healers' hall and into the main one at a dead run. She had to get out of the house. It would be easier in the entry. She could use the steady stream of power embedded in the rock and wood always available in the travel alcoves. She pushed toward it, nearly blind in her need to get there before something horrible happened. Focus. She needed to put up some sort of shield between her and her enemy. She needed to put distance between herself, the Dolphin Throne, and the rest of her family. From the feel of things, her shield would have to be a lot stronger than any she'd ever created before. Without energy. Without sleep, food, or help of any sort. Her eyes twitched as sweat dripped into them.

How could she shield against something she couldn't even see, something living inside her own body? How could she shield herself from…herself?

She reached the rotunda at a full run and turned toward the entry. Her boots, covered in vomit and city grime, slid on the polished stone. Her arms circled in the air in a futile attempt to keep herself upright. She landed hard on her butt, and skid out of control across the floor.

chapter seven

The receiving hall doors burst open on Tarian's right as she slid past. Two Sentinels stormed out, followed by a blond man with eyes wide in anger or fear, she couldn't tell which, followed by her mother. Loud staccato burbling filled the air, and a filament of light formed fingers that reached straight for her. Tarian glided to a stop on her behind near a large potted plant, her foot embedded in a bench.

More Sentinels surged into the rotunda with weapons drawn. Tarian knew they'd focused their magic, because the hairs in her nose wiggled and made her sneeze. They looked ready to do battle but, confused about their target, wiggled their weapons at some unseen threat. Tarian struggled to get her feet underneath her and move out of the way. Shouts reverberated off the circular walls. Boots clumped, weapons clicked, and a buzz rang through her ears. Her own name bounced back to her from somewhere. Her mother's name. She saw her mother raise a hand toward the blond, who seemed to have frozen in position.

The Sentinels pointed their weapons at the stranger even as they backed away from the fingers of light that advanced on Tarian. The piece of claw embedded in her neck writhed. It pushed against the skin as though it would cut her neck in two. Her own power, already sapped from overuse in the alley, struggled to respond to needs she couldn't entirely identify. She wanted to lash out, but at what? The glow? Her own body?

Instinct made her want to run away. To dig at this piece of lizard inside her until she'd ripped it from her body. To curl up in a fetal position. In her panic, control over her own energy weakened and the foreign sensation screamed through her body, unguided. An adrenaline rush of magical energy pounded against her nerves, sending her into overdrive. The odd blend of her own familiar current and the foreign power tied to the piece of claw escalated as it circulated with her own blood. It wanted release but had no focus, no purpose, no destination, because she'd given it none. Her head pounded, her heart thumped in time to the clicks of dolphins, her ears roared.

Overload.

Tarian forced her body to back away from the receiving hall doors, but found her momentum stopped by another giant indoor palm. She couldn't escape. Before she dodged, the tendrils enveloped her. Fear gripped her as the claw ripped at the inside of her neck. She screamed and grasped at the knot formed by the struggling claw even as the light from the receiving hall surrounded her.

Warmth flooded through Tarian and she realized the outside power bolstered, rather than drained. She welcomed it, grabbed it with her mind, and added it to her own dismal energy force, tried to wrap it all around the bit of debris in her neck. If she wrapped the piece of claw in her own energy, someone might be able to dig it out and destroy it.

I hope.

It was harder than anything she'd ever done in her life. Her pulse pounded in her ears. She struggled to breathe. The scene around her faded into the background as she fought her internal war.

"Tari!"

Calliope. Dammit. Her sister had followed her. Of course she had. But now Tarian couldn't spare a breath for anything—couldn't warn her sister away. Couldn't move. Couldn't even really see. She squeezed the back of her neck and gasped as the claw stabbed her spine. She focused on creating a cushion around it instead. She'd never tried to shield something inside her own body before and didn't have the slightest clue how to do it. Instinct guided her, but instinct would only get her so far.

"Let me help." Calliope's voice drifted on invisible waves. Her sister put soft hands on her arms, and Tarian drew on her sister's fresh energy. The power from the Dolphin Throne circled them. Her mother's energy gathered it up and joined the flow, almost as if her arms gathered Tarian and her sister in an enormous hug. The strength of the ocean, a gentle wave of power, and a singsong call mixed with joy and determination, wove in and around them. In the back of her mind, she put a name to the sound. Dolphins.

With the added strength of two other women, and the Throne itself, the foreign invasion of power retreated. Tarian used the shield spell she already knew to fashion one around the relic from the lizard-man.

It was like trying to hold onto a grease puddle, but eventually she managed to force the shield into place and cocoon the tiny dagger in a ball of air energy woven tight, with water energy to seal any cracks. The claw didn't break, but the power flowing from it spread into her shield, which reverberated but didn't yield. The invasion contained for the moment, Tarian gasped with relief. Pain receded and her head cleared a little.

Tarian held the focus of power from her sister and mother for another minute just to be sure the claw wouldn't escape. When the shield held, she released the energy from her mother and sister and collapsed as the backlash washed over her. Power always rebounded. Usually it wasn't enough to worry about. She'd normally absorb it back into her body, burning calories, which would cause a bit of a drop in blood sugar, but otherwise she'd escape unharmed. This much, however, was too much. She fell against Calliope, her legs unable to keep her upright.

Her sister's hands on her arms helped ease Tarian's descent to the floor, but the stone still bruised her knees. She fell forward on her hands, discharging the last of the rebounding power into the rock floor. Solid, steady, boundless earth soaked up what she dished out. The energy reverberated outward along the floor and up the walls to the ceiling, dispelling into a portion of everything it touched, including people. It wasn't her favorite way to discharge. Connecting with earth this way always gave her a headache. Water worked best. But it was convenient, and she'd never be able to crawl all the way down to the shore to use the ocean or dolphins as a release.

When the last of the excess power left her, she couldn't lift her head. She stayed on all fours, pushed each breath in and out, and ignored everything else. Bright light flashed through her eyes.

Migraine. Fantastic.

It took a few minutes for Tarian to realize how quiet the rotunda was. The only sounds were the singsong of dolphins and the caress of ocean waves in her ear. The air smelled of flowers, sweat, tension, fear, residual energy, and cheap cologne. She collapsed the rest of the way to the floor and rolled over onto her back, curious.

Sentinels gaped, their weapons down by their sides. Calliope sat on her heels next to her. Tarian was shocked to see the unnatural paleness of her sister's face. Calliope's brows formed one straight line. She looked like she might throw up.

Tarian glanced around the rotunda to see Advisor Jonus standing near the door to the receiving hall, doubled over as though he were about to vomit. She caught the gaze of the blond stranger, his eyes full of something she thought might be fear, his hands balled into fists. Her mother stood next to Calliope with one hand on her sister's shoulder. She looked regal—and pissed off.

"Well, so much for keeping this quiet." Tarian took a deep breath and let it out slowly. Her arm throbbed. Through the stillness, the dolphin call continued. It meant something. Something important. Something she couldn't quite pull out of the recesses of her brain. She was simply too tired.

The blond man looked around as he, too, recognized the sound in the air. He wore a suit, perfectly pressed, but his tie looked as though he'd twisted it in his hands. His eyes widened, and his hands fluttered by his side in clear agitation as he shifted from one foot to the other. He couldn't possibly know the war she'd just been through inside her own body, but he'd surely felt the magic she discharged. Tarian didn't understand why it seemed to bother him so much. It was her body, after all, not his. None of it had been directed at him.

"What are you trying to pull?" the man sputtered.

Keeper Marielle raised her hand toward one of the alcoves in the entry off the rotunda. "You may leave now, Mr. Aiello. As you can see, I have other priorities." A travel portal appeared, but from her position on the floor, Tarian couldn't make out where it led.

"This is not acceptable." He glanced down at Tarian. He hesitated, on the verge of saying more. Whatever it was, he seemed to think better of it. He pulled himself up straight, and relaxed his hands. "Whatever this stunt was, I'm not impressed. You can't brush this aside. You can't sit here in your island paradise, isolated from the real world, and expect to have any grasp of reality. People need guidance. They need supervision. We need the structure to support that. This…"—he waved his hand at Tarian—"only serves to emphasize my point."

"Sentinels, please see that Mr. Aiello arrives safely at his destination. We are closed to visitors for the remainder of the day." Keeper Marielle glanced down at Tarian and Calliope. "Follow me, both of you." Their mother returned to the receiving hall, her footsteps echoing off the walls as she went.

Aiello glared at their mother's retreating back. He took a step as if to follow her, but stopped when the Sentinels raised their weapons. Physically, the weapons looked like small handguns. Magically, they could put a man in stasis and render him unable to move, kill him, or dismember him entirely, depending on the focus of the user. Aiello growled, turned his back on the Sentinels and stared at Tarian.

Tarian sighed and dragged herself to her feet with help from Calliope. "I wouldn't hang out, if I were you. She's not a pretty sight when she's angry."

"Scion." He made the word sound more like a curse than a title. He smiled, although the expression never touched his eyes, straightened his tie, and smoothed his jacket. His eyes traveled the length of her body and stopped as they reached the tear in the jacket. She crossed her arms in an effort to hide it—and the blood.

"Are you feeling well, Scion?" His expression changed abruptly from anger to curiosity and concern.

"I'm fine."

He smiled. "I'm Victor Aiello. Leader for the Eastern region. I had hoped to meet you under more pleasant circumstances. Are you sure you're not injured? That looks like a dangerous cut. Perhaps I was hasty. In my anger, I didn't see clearly you require attention. May I get a healer for you?"

"It was nice to meet you, Victor." She wasn't about to admit how injured she was to a stranger.

He paused for a fraction of a second then nodded. "I certainly wouldn't want to cause any more conflict. Your mother is right. She has other priorities right now. It was a pleasure to meet you as well, Scion."

His eyes flicked to her arm again before he turned away. She watched as he strode over to the travel portal and entered it.

Politician. Has to be. The smile says it all.

Calliope pulled Tarian through the doors and into the receiving hall. She let her sister guide her, too tired to do much else. Her eyes didn't want to stay open, her head swam, and the knot at the base of her neck weighed her down. Warmth from her sister's touch spread down her arm until it reached the wound, where it stopped.

Halfway through the hall, her sister's grip tightened on her arm. It wasn't like Calliope to be tense, but Tarian didn't have the energy to figure out why. It was all she could do to put one foot in front of the other. She stumbled, but Calliope steadied her.

Together they crossed the expansive room toward the platform which held the Dolphin Throne, along with a long table and several normal chairs.

Her mother marched toward the seat of power as though on a mission. Tarian and Calliope followed. Advisor Jonus staggered behind them as though he were drunk. She'd giggle at the thought of him in that sort of state if she had any energy left. Their footsteps echoed off the stone floor and up the walls.

Her entire body hurt. She felt like she'd run a marathon after a bar fight. Her head pounded. She felt decidedly cranky. And she smelled like puke.

Her mother paused at the bottom of the raised platform and turned toward Tarian. Her eyes held anger and some other emotion Tarian couldn't identify. Panic? Concern? She wondered how those eyes would change when her mother found out what had really happened and the danger they were all in.

"Tarian, please remove the jacket. Jonus, please fetch Healer Chloe."

Jonus flashed a look of resentment or irritation, but it was gone so fast Tarian might have imagined it. He bowed and exited through the side door.

"Tarian." Her mother's voice sounded flat. So much for motherly concern.

"Mother."

"Take a seat." Marielle indicated the Throne.

Tarian shrugged out of the leather jacket and let it fall to the floor. She didn't look at her wound, but she saw Calliope's eyes grow into two small moons, filling her face. Tarian's arm throbbed again, one large, pounding jolt that made her gasp.

The Dolphin Throne glowed brighter as she approached. The light pulsed in time to the throb in her arm.

"I'm not so sure this is a good idea." Nobody ever sat in the Dolphin Throne aside from her mother. Nobody. As far as she knew, the Throne wouldn't allow it.

"Now is not the time to argue. The Throne has properties you need."

Tarian glared at her mother. She opened her mouth to protest. But her mother's eyes filled with an expression Tarian knew all too well. She closed her mouth and shuffled forward. She was being stupid, and her mother called her bluff. Without ever uttering a word.

Calliope helped Tarian up the three steps to the platform and over to the chair. As she moved next to the Dolphin Throne filaments of power reached out to her as they had in the rotunda, except now they seemed to wrap around her injured arm. The wound throbbed in response. The claw in her neck, shielded as it was, still jabbed, tightening her shoulders.

Tarian paused. What would happen if she actually sat down? Some sort of war seemed to be brewing and she didn't like how it was being waged inside her. Her body had taken enough abuse for one day. If the claw decided to rip a hole right through her throat she wasn't sure she had the energy to stop it.

"I don't think I should get any closer."

"I think you should. Sit." Keeper Marielle's voice was soft with a steely note underneath.

"I'm not sure what will happen." Tarian turned to face her mother. The look of concern on her mother's face was so unexpected it completely overwhelmed her.

"It's already happened, Tarian. Whatever is going on with you, the damage is done. Now comes the hard part."

"Fixing it?"

She saw her mother's lips twitch.

"Tari, what's going on?" Calliope looked back and forth between them as if watching a tennis match.

"I bumped into something scaly." Tarian clutched at her

stomach as it churned. Her knees threatened to give way. She saw no other option, short of trying to run from the room. She didn't think she'd make it down the stairs now, let alone out the door.

Tarian moved in front of the Throne and sat.

chapter eight

A sense of warmth enveloped Tarian and extended up her arm into the knot in her neck and shoulders. It soothed her body and comforted her soul, wrapping the claw inside her neck in another layer of cushion. She sighed with relief and closed her eyes.

It felt wonderful. She let her consciousness go and drifted. Was this what her mother experienced when she sat here? It was peace undulating in a rhythm, ocean waves caressing a beach in, then out, then in again. She smelled hyacinth, sand, sea salt, and hibiscus. All of it blended into a tropical-scented paradise. Loving hands must have formed each animal on the wood. Dolphins sang it to life. Their cry echoed all around and through her. Happiness. Safety. Serenity.

Tarian wondered briefly what else the chair did besides soothe strained nerves, but it didn't really matter. She was happy to drift. Happy to let her internal struggle go. Happy to enjoy a moment of peace.

Bliss.

A voice intruded in her Zen moment. Harsh edges cut the soothing ocean kiss. She frowned. Why was there so much talking going on? Couldn't they let her rest a minute? She focused on the words. They came to her ears in pulses of sound, which faded in and out and circled around her head. The voice sounded familiar. It belonged to someone kind. Someone she'd grown up with.

"I'm not sure what else we can do, Keeper. I've never seen anything quite like this. There's definitely a foreign object lodged at the top of her spine, and it's draining her energy."

Another voice. Firm. Worried. "Can you remove it?"

The soft voice again. "She's wrapped it in power strands so complex it could kill her if I tried. She'd have to break the web herself, but that would release the object, which is so close to her brain and spine that I'm afraid of what it'll do to her if not cushioned the way it is."

A pause. Blissful silence.

The firm voice. "If she sits here, the magic of the Throne should replace the power she's losing to the object."

The soft voice. "Yes, but if she leaves the house, the power loss might escalate. She needs rest and food, but beyond that I'm not sure how to proceed. I'm sorry, Keeper."

Tarian opened her eyes and found Healer Chloe frowning down at her hands where they rubbed the wound on Tarian's arm. Chloe's spiked purple hair wiggled as she worked on the sore muscle. Slowly, Tarian's brain registered her arm no longer throbbed. She sighed in relief. Her stomach growled, loud enough for Chloe to raise an eyebrow.

"I could really use a cheesesteak." Tarian's mouth watered at the thought of her favorite meal. She tried to pull her arm away from Chloe, but the healer held it down.

"Ah, back with us, I see. Scion, how did you get this injury?"

Tarian looked around. Her mother, Calliope and Advisor Jonus all stared at her as if she had sprouted a horn or a third eye.

She sighed again, this time in irritation. Having to explain what happened to her mother, after she'd been warned about going in the first place, made her feel like a child caught doing something naughty.

"Long story short, a lizard-man took a swipe at me. And now, according to Frankie and some guy named Daric Voltain, I'm a walking time bomb." Tarian looked down at her arm. The wound had changed since she sat down. The large, angry welt was now a faint white scar, about three inches long. "Wow. Chloe, nice work."

How had Chloe even had time to fix her arm? She'd only been there a couple of minutes. *Come to think of it, when did Chloe even get here?*

"Thank you, Scion, but I didn't do this on my own. Calliope helped. Now, tell me more about this lizard-man. What did he look like?"

"Tall, dark, sorta grayish-green and scaly. Claws for hands. You know, like an Amazon woman and a lizard had a baby. Daric called it a Laghairtine." Tarian shrugged. "What do you mean Calliope helped?"

"A real Laghairtine?" Calliope gasped. "In Philadelphia? But I thought they were a myth or extinct."

"Did he know you?" Chloe's voice was sharp. "Did he say your name?"

Tarian thought back. She remembered the smelly bum, who had obviously been sent to distract her in the alley long enough for the lizard to catch her. *Clever to use someone with no magic talent.* She hadn't felt threatened and hadn't put up any defenses. She hadn't felt the lizard approach either, but she wasn't about to admit it.

"No, he never used my name. But I'd say he knew me, yes. I'd say the whole thing was a set up."

"What did he say?" Her mother moved to stand directly in front of her with her arms crossed.

"We didn't exactly have time for polite conversation. The thing I remember most was him hissing at me. Oh, and he said, 'You have something I need.' He clawed my arm, licked some of the blood off the claw and left."

Chloe gasped. "The object in your neck is part of his claw." She hissed in breath as though she'd touched something hot. "Calliope, that's the query we need."

Calliope nodded and ran for the door.

"What did I say?" Tarian watched her sister retreat in confusion.

Chloe cleared her throat. "Scion, it's obvious, both from your description of events and from your current condition, that your attacker was able to obtain a portion of your blood, and in addition, he's lodged a bit of himself inside you. While this hasn't happened in hundreds of years, the medical journals are quite clear about what Laghairtines will be able to do with your blood mixed with his presence within your own power structure should he decide to use it. Which he obviously has."

Chloe patted Tarian's arm. "We were able to cleanse the wound and seal it, but the bit of claw he left behind will act as a tracer. A link."

"A tracer?" Tarian rubbed the back of her neck. It pulsed, but at the moment, the movement was slow and faint, as though it rested. "So he can track me?"

"Not exactly. Laghairtines are one of the few creatures capable of creating Dominion over another intelligent species. Evil, foul mix they are. Ancient daemon blood mixed with dark intentions and human power. They inspired all the demon legends in the non-magical folk tales, long ago." Chloe took a deep breath and glanced at Marielle before continuing. "He's siphoning your power, Scion, using his claw to store it. While you sit here, in this house, in that chair, the effect is diminished. But now he has his trace on you, it's only a matter of time until he can use your blood to complete the bond and finish the Dominion."

Tarian heard Daric Voltain's words echo through her head: *"You have about a week."*

Great.

Marielle touched Tarian's shoulder in a manner meant to be comforting. "While you remain here, the Throne and I can protect you."

"Remain here..." Tarian's voice trailed away. *Stay here? Confined to the house, like a criminal?*

"If I may, Keeper," Jonus stepped forward, his hands clasped together so tight his knuckles shone white. "I think it would be wise to ensure the Scion's safety at this crucial time by increasing the guards both around her person and the primary locations throughout the house and hallways, as well as increase the border patrol."

"Guards?" Tarian couldn't keep the squeak out of her voice. "Are you trying to arrest me?"

Jonus flushed, and a bead of sweat dripped down the side of his face. "Of course not. I am merely suggesting, as Scion, your safety is of utmost importance, and I must agree with the Keeper that you remain within the confines of these walls, with an armed guard, so we can better ensure the safety of you and the Throne."

"Agreed." Marielle's voice sounded firm and final.

Tarian pushed her mother's hand away and stood up. The cold look she saw in her mother's eyes only added fuel to a fire already forging its way through her veins. Words spilled out before she could stop them. "I'm not sitting here doing nothing while everyone else risks their lives to solve the mess I created. Besides, I have the advantage. I can track him. Now I'm rested, I can find him." It was hard to be puffed up with bravado when she couldn't even stand on her own two feet without leaning on the chair for support.

Marielle planted her feet and clasped her hands in front of her. "Tarian, you've missed several important details. Jonus is right. As the Scion, you simply can't go running off after a creature that hasn't been seen in hundreds of years, let alone one who can exert power over you. And as much as you might try to ignore it, something else has been triggered by your arrival bearing that trace." Keeper Marielle lifted her hands, holding them out as if something hovered in the air. She turned and pointed to the center of the room, at the floor.

Tarian looked where her mother pointed, and stared at the rune embedded in the marble as it glowed bright, then dim, then bright again. In the silence, she finally paid attention to the watery, stochastic call of dolphins. When she'd first arrived, it had been pleasant and reassuring, a reminder she was home. But now a chill ran through her.

Its placement in the exact center formed part of the power structure of the House. She'd stood there on her naming day. She was bound to it and to the House in more ways than one because of the magic contained in both the symbol and the Throne.

And now the rune glowed and the dolphins sang. Her stomach sank to her feet.

How had she not noticed on her trek across the floor earlier? She closed her eyes and counted slowly. Her heart pounded. It couldn't be. She wasn't ready. It was too blasted soon.

The Succession Ritual.

"This can't be happening." The dread lodged in Tarian's heart threatened to overtake her panic at a Laghairtine stealing her power. No wonder her mother had rushed out of her meeting with Aiello. She'd been looking for Tarian. She'd known from the very first dolphin call and the throb of the rune. The Succession Ritual had begun, despite the lack of ceremony or the input of the current Keeper, which explained the look on her mother's face when she'd seen Tarian sprawled on the floor, bloody and ripped up. Tarian sank slowly back onto the Throne, stunned.

"I see you now have a full grasp of the situation." Marielle turned to Chloe. "How long?"

Tarian answered before Chloe could say anything. "A week. More or less." Her heart pounded. "It doesn't matter. The ritual doesn't matter. There won't be time for the full ceremony before we're all screwed. Unless I find that lizard."

Her mother's eyebrows inched up her forehead, creating wrinkles Tarian had never seen before. "The ritual can't be stopped, regardless of other circumstances. The call has already gone out to potential candidates. They will answer and arrive here for presentation within three days, according to the rules set forth centuries ago."

"So with everything else going on, you expect me to go ahead with an archaic, ridiculous ritual?" Tarian's voice rose with each word, panic driving the syllables home. "It's insane. It's not right. Women shouldn't be treated this way. I will not simply spread my legs to complete strangers because tradition insists I should. I won't do it. Nobody should be forced to have a child, and especially not this way."

Her mother stood watching her with the calm of a woman who'd heard every protest before and merely waited out the storm. It was an old argument but one never settled. Jonus shifted from one foot to the other. Chloe shuffled back an inch or two as she too stared at the rune on the floor.

This can't be happening.

Tarian had spent most of her life simply ignoring the subject of the ritual entirely. After all, what woman in her right mind, in this day and age, would even contemplate something like this? An antiquated custom which required her, as Scion, to have sex with a group of strange men, with the objective of getting pregnant with a child who would carry a blend of multiple powers and bloodlines. A child who would, in turn, do it all again so the Dolphin Throne remained part of the House of Xannon.

Why now?

The Dolphin Throne had felt threatened by the attack on the Scion and taken action, her feelings on the matter be damned.

Screw you.

Tarian let the thought drift out into the musical dolphin cries. Their tones didn't change, a static reaction to ancient processes already in motion.

She'd always thought the ritual thing would work itself out eventually if she waited long enough. That maybe, at some point, she'd find men she didn't mind having sex with, start the ritual on her own. She'd get pregnant on her own terms, in her own time, and screw the rules and the Throne. The tenuous, girlhood plan was nothing but vapor. Reality slapped her in the face and poked her in the back of the neck for good measure.

The Laghairtine had no idea how well he'd struck when he slashed her arm.

Or maybe he did.

Marielle paced from one side of the platform to the other, obviously sensing the agitation in her daughter. "This magic is ancient, Tarian. It can't be altered and is the main reason the Dolphin Throne exists. It ensures the safety and succession of leadership. It's a duty, a right, and a privilege. One you were born to fulfill. The consequences if you don't will put our entire Society at risk." Her mother's voice, so tight and controlled, told her far more than words. Her mother was scared. Very scared. "As I've mentioned countless times before, if you'd look at it in a different way, you'd see it's not the travesty you imagine it to be. Laghairtine aside, that is."

Tarian let go of a portion of her anger, though some boiled in reserve. Her mother hadn't caused this situation. The ritual was as old as the island they stood on, created by some long-dead ancestor to ensure power remained within the Xannon family, with the women, rather than bloodthirsty men. *But that was so long ago. Times have changed, and surely the ritual can change with them.*

Except now, there was no time to change it. She'd always thought there'd be time. Her heart ached for missed opportunities she couldn't even begin to imagine.

"I know, Mother, I know. But how the hell am I supposed to do all the steps of this farce, get pregnant, and hunt down a lizard who, by the way, will have stolen all of my power before I've ovulated? How is all this supposed to work?"

As Tarian said the words, her mother's face turned a sickly shade. The real problem, aside from the archaic and twisted ritual, was the Laghairtine would have control of her while the ritual was taking place. He could, if he had control of her body, select the Potentials. Hell, he could *be* a Potential. No rules governed exactly who took part or how, apart from her. The main rule was more than two men, so a combination of powers would mix with her own, providing the heir with new abilities and ensuring no one man could claim to be the child's father and therefore, claim the Throne. But if a Potential had control of Tarian's power and her child's, there'd be nothing to stop him from abusing it. Nothing at all. She'd be a puppet, dancing on invisible strings.

Tarian pounded the arm of the chair. "This can't be happening. I can't believe he was able to trigger the ritual like this. Does he even know? Or was this just lucky coincidence?" The horror of what might evolve from one scratch washed over her.

Tarian leaned her head against the carved dolphins at the back of the chair and closed her eyes. Her stomach growled, oblivious to the tension in the room.

"She needs to eat. Then rest. And then..." Chloe's voice trailed off. "Perhaps Calliope will find something useful. I will check the medical archives as well. Maybe there's a way to extract the claw fragment without further damage."

Tarian slumped in the chair. She hardly noticed Chloe leave the room and didn't hear the door shut. All she heard was the dolphin calls echoing through the empty space, mocking her.

Marielle continued to pace but now seemed to be talking more to herself than the room at large. "Perhaps we should ask for assistance from the Sentinels. A squad could be sent to find..."

Tarian snorted. "Exactly how are they going to find him? It's not like he left a calling card."

Except he did. Inside me.

She rubbed the back of her neck. It felt stiff and sore, as though she'd been struck with a heavy object. Within, wrapped in a shield and layers of Throne magic, the claw pulsed in time to her own heartbeat, fueled by her own power. The lizard held a connection to her now just as she connected with others using their own signature. Surely, if he siphoned from her, she could use the same trick to find him. The fact it hadn't worked in the alley in Philly had to be a fluke, no matter what Daric had said about the Between. *When I get my strength back, I'll be able to do it, surely. I'll track him and take him out before this gets out of hand.*

Tarian looked at her mother. She'd obviously had the same thought because her eyes widened and her face flushed.

"No." Marielle shook her head.

"It's the only way, Mother."

"You must remain here. We can't risk it."

Jonus cleared his throat, and Tarian nearly jumped out of the chair. She'd forgotten he hovered nearby.

"Keeper, the cost if the Scion leaves this house…"

"I know the cost if I stay. I will not put my family and friends or this House in danger. I will not allow that lizard to use me to steal the Dolphin Throne. I sure as hell am not allowing him any part of the Succession. I can find him. I'm the only one who can. But I can't do it hiding here in this room." Tarian tried to stand then settled back into the chair. Her legs were in no condition to support her. She ignored the knowing look in her mother's eyes. "I just need something to eat. And a shower. At the moment, he'd smell me coming."

The main doors banged open, making all three of them jump. Alex entered the room at a fast walk. Tarian rolled her eyes, nearly laughing at her own nerves. She was on edge, that's all. The attack had made her jumpy. Chester must have sobered up enough to talk.

Except Alex advanced as if he had something important to say. Tarian narrowed her eyes and studied his face. He looked grim.

Shit.

chapter nine

When Alex reached the platform, he stood at the base, his back stiff and his arms tight by his side. His eyes never left Tarian's.

"Keeper Marielle, Scion, there's been an incident in the Cellar." Alex cleared his throat. It wasn't like him to be nervous, but Tarian saw sweat forming a spot under his arms. *He must have run here.*

"What happened?" She couldn't hold back anymore.

"Tarian…" Alex stopped, looked around the room. The dolphin cries echoed in the stillness.

She hoped he didn't understand what the calls meant, but when he looked back at her, his eyes wide with shock, her heart sank. Heat traveled across her cheeks. *He knows.*

"Did you have something you wished to say?" Marielle's voice, cold and calm, cut through the air.

"The guy Tarian brought in, Mark Chester. He's dead. I found him a few minutes ago. I was checking to see if he'd sobered up any. Tarian, I'm sorry." Alex shook his head. "He never woke up."

Tarian let the information sink in. Her only source of information was dead. *How am I going to figure out who the lizard is now?*

"How is this relevant?" Marielle's voice rang through the hall.

Of course, she didn't know. Tarian swallowed, wishing her mouth wasn't quite so dry.

"It might not be. He's the one I went to grab this morning. I wasn't waiting in that alley to be a victim. I had a reason to be there."

Alex shifted from one foot to the other and rolled his shoulders.

Tarian narrowed her eyes at him. *There's more to this story.* "How did Chester die? Did he choke on his own vomit?"

"Somebody, or something more like, offed him."

"Are you sure?" Advisor Jonus spoke for the first time, his voice so quiet Tarian almost didn't hear him.

Alex nodded. "Oh, yeah. He looked like he'd been beaten by something pretty strong and then ripped apart and chewed into pieces. Maybe set on fire or something. Frankie is checking it out."

Tarian tried to picture the scene then realized she didn't want to. She'd been around enough puke for one day and had no desire to add to it.

"How did someone manage to get into the Cellar, past two guards, into a secure holding cell, and rip a person apart, as you put it, without your knowledge?" Advisor Jonus's voice sounded louder, more confident, and accusatory.

Tarian turned on Jonus. "If you're trying to say Alex or Frankie had anything to do with it, trust me. They didn't. You should be more worried about who or what would have the power to enter the Cellar without permission."

The Cellar was older than the house, embedded in the rock that created the island. The only way to get in at all was via portal and had only one place, the reception area, where that was even possible. The walls were too thick to dig through and were soaked in magic. Prisoners were locked in stasis, unable to move or even breathe and held in suspended animation until released, something only the guards could do. She pitied the idiot who tried to get past Alex and Frankie.

Alex nodded in agreement. "The Cellar is absolutely secure."

"Except for this obvious breach, you mean." Advisor Jonus squared his shoulders, his face impassive.

Alex glared but didn't reply. The two men looked as though they might step into the arena and settle things the old-fashioned way. Tarian almost laughed. Jonus was a scarecrow next to Alex's bulk. Never mind Jonus's lack of magic strength next to Alex's earth-enhanced power.

Marielle turned to Tarian. "You had business with this man?"

"I wanted to ask him a few questions; that's all. I was hoping he knew something about the lizard. He seemed to. I need to take a look at his cell. I might be able to track who did it." The determination she felt didn't translate to any of her muscles, which simply refused to allow her leave the chair.

She wasn't ready for the chorus of protests erupting from all sides. Tarian closed her eyes and ignored them all, even her mother. She was the one with the tracking ability, not them. It had to be her. They'd figure it out soon enough.

She focused instead on the claw the Laghairtine had left buried inside her neck, but she barely felt it. The Dolphin Throne's magic stifled the signal. There was no way she'd be able to track him from inside this room, or from inside the house, most likely. Chester's cell probably wouldn't be any better, embedded as it was in the bedrock, but maybe there was some other clue. *Maybe he touched something or dropped something.*

"Perhaps you should eat first." Her mother's voice sounded distant. Tarian opened her eyes and jumped. Marielle's face hovered two inches from her own, eyes bright and wrinkles in her forehead vivid.

"Okay," she whispered.

The worried look Alex flashed her mother told Tarian more than a few seconds had gone by. *Dammit.* She'd passed out again. *Nothing like having him see me at my weakest.*

Tarian took a deep breath. "Someone bring me a damn cheesesteak. If I'm going to track a Laghairtine and get pregnant, I need a full stomach."

"That's not funny, *chica*." Alex pointed at her. "You're not doing either of those things by yourself."

"I suppose it would be hard to get pregnant alone, but I hear medicine is really advanced these days." She flashed a weak grin at Alex.

He shook his head, his lips tight and serious. "You're not tracking no Laghairtine by yourself. I got this."

Jonus coughed and moved off toward the side door. She desperately hoped he was getting her some food. She might resort to crawling to the kitchen soon.

"I'm the only one who'll be able to find him. I don't want him trapping anyone else. And I don't want anyone around, in case…"

"In case he succeeds?" Marielle's lips pursed. Tarian knew the expression well. It meant her mother was about to lose it.

"I can handle this."

"You don't have to handle it alone, *chica*. The way I see it, all we gotta do is send out a net of Sentinels. A creature like that is bound to show up somewhere. He'd be hard to hide."

"I don't need you to rescue me, Alex. And I don't need you to solve my problems. If Daric's right, he's hiding in the Between and there's no way you or any Sentinel can catch him there." A surge of anger energized her legs. She stood up and ignored her wobbling knees. "It's my job to look after this House and the people in it. That's been pounded into me since I was a child."

"No leader stands alone, Tarian." Marielle gestured to the door Jonus had passed through. "Every good leader has a team behind them."

"You're kidding, right? All this time, all those lectures, all the preaching about responsibility and leadership. Now suddenly you want me to be a team player?"

"Leadership is not always about calling the shots. Sometimes it's about letting others do what they do best." Keeper Marielle's eyes flicked toward Alex.

Tarian couldn't suppress the flash of anger. "And what about me? I'm just supposed to sit here and hope they find him while my power slowly leaks away? Spread my legs for an archaic ritual that has no business being any part of modern life? Sometimes a leader has to take charge if she's the only one with the skills needed to do the job."

The side door opened, and a young boy entered with a tray of fruit, cheese, a cheesesteak, and a chocolate shake. Her mouth watered in anticipation.

"I could kiss you!" Tarian grabbed the sandwich and swallowed three bites before she came up for air. She forced herself to slow down and savor it. Someone in the kitchen was getting a big hug from her. It was the best thing she'd ever tasted.

"Besides, so far the only way we have of finding this guy is locked away inside me." She spoke around mouthfuls of cheesesteak, ignoring the disapproving stares from her mother. "There's no way anyone will find him without me."

She'd find a way to use the piece of claw the lizard left behind, but it would take a lot of concentration, under the best of circumstances. Impossible with guards staring at her as if she might blow up or faint.

I might take Alex, but no way am I taking an army of Sentinels. Idiotic. He'd hear us coming.

She licked the grease off of her fingers. "First thing we need to do is check the cell. Maybe the killer touched something or dropped something. Is Chester's body still there?" Her stomach churned around the newly acquired cheesesteak at the thought.

Alex set his jaw. "Frankie has the cleaners in there. We can't go in until they're done."

"How am I supposed to get any clue at all if they clean up before I examine the cell?"

Alex set his feet in a wide stance and his face became a stone wall. Tarian rolled her eyes.

"Fine, let them pick up the body but leave any object that might have been touched, including maybe a piece of his clothing."

"You don't get it, *chica*. There weren't no clothes. Just bits and pieces." Alex's face paled under his tan skin.

It must have been some scene.

"Fine. No body parts. But don't touch anything else. I'll take a shower and meet you both down there. I need to get this puke off me." She stood up, grateful for the strength surging through her body.

Alex shrugged. Probably the best response she could hope for under the circumstances.

"Tarian." Her mother pointed to the rune on the floor.

"I know. Can we talk about it later? I really need a shower."
She left her mother and Alex staring at the rune. She had enough
to deal with. Getting pregnant was way down on the list.

chapter ten

Tarian arrived in the Cellar reception area grime- and puke-free. The hot shower had washed away most of her aches and pains. She was grateful to find the floor of the Cellar entrance also scrubbed clean. The scent of citrus lingered in the air, clashing with the musty odor of damp rock.

"I'm not so sure this is a good idea." Alex stood with his arms crossed in front of the door to the cells, wearing a stubborn expression.

"I think it's a great idea." She watched a bead of sweat drip down the side of his face. *Nervous? Or had he been in the deeper parts of the Cellar?* "You're hiding something. What?"

"I got nothing to hide, *chica*." Alex unfurled his arms to run a finger lightly over the newly acquired scar on her arm.

An army of goose bumps stood at attention as his fingers traced the mark, and a shiver ran down her back. She should have worn a long-sleeved shirt, but it was summer and, dammit, it was hot in the Cellar. A tank top seemed like the smartest move, plus it was her favorite. Still, maybe it would have been wiser to hide the reminder of her little problem.

Tarian turned away to look for any sign of forced entry around the metal door. She wasn't surprised to find it intact. She detected no magic traces other than Alex, Frankie, and the natural protection of the rock itself.

"So, the dolphin call…" Alex shifted from one foot to the other, but remained in front of the door as a giant roadblock.

"Wasn't your brother playing in Boston today? I thought you were going to the game?" Tarian shoved her hip into Alex to nudge him over to run her hands over the controls. He barely shifted. The security panel beeped in protest. Her handprint wouldn't open this door. Only six people in the world had access to the Cellar, and two of them were in the room with her. The other four members of the special unit assigned to the Cellar rotated shifts later in the day, so they had alibis. She'd trust any one of them with her life.

"Game was rained out in the third. Besides, there are other things besides baseball."

Tarian cleared her throat. "Did anyone come down here after I dropped off Chester?"

"Not until after we found him dead," Frankie said from behind the desk computer.

She punched Alex in the arm. "So, are you going to let me in, or not?"

"You're not gonna go alone, *chica*. And before you argue, nobody goes in without one of us. Not even you. Procedure."

She nodded her agreement, relieved she wouldn't have to get uppity and pull rank, fight him for access, or worse, talk about the call for Potentials. He shifted and looked embarrassed. He'd obviously already responded. For all she knew, he'd planned on it since his naming day. The thought made her cheeks burn.

Damn the Throne. Why'd it have to go start the ritual now? She had enough to worry about. She'd always thought her mother would issue the call after a long period of debate by the regional leaders. There was supposed to be a grand ceremony for which she'd have to be available. So, she'd made sure she never was and avoided as many meetings as possible in case the leaders brought up the subject.

It was just one more thing to add to the list of reasons to kick that lizard's ass. *Talk about timing. A demon attack and the Succession Ritual on the same day. What were the odds? Pretty damn small.*

Now when she most needed to focus, distractions in the form of men vying for her attention were going to loom on all sides. Starting with the giant distraction currently barring her way into the Cellar.

Tarian watched Alex deal with the security on the door. The muscles along his back rippled as he held his hand to the plate. He was loyal and honest, and he'd do anything for her. She trusted him completely. He was everything any girl would want. Passionate, caring, thoughtful, loyal—and built. And she loved him as she would any member of her family.

She'd never looked at him as mating material before. Tarian had never looked at anyone that way. It was a topic she avoided, one she ran from, if she were honest with herself. And Alex had never pushed the issue. He was a good friend. More like a brother than a lover.

She couldn't afford to spend time dealing with hurt feelings. If she told him she couldn't connect with him as a Potential, she knew he'd be more than hurt. He'd be devastated. He had a gentle soul beneath all those muscles and macho Latino lover impersonations. A rift with her best friend was not something she wanted to deal with. Not now. She needed to focus on the real problem: finding the Laghairtine and stopping him. Everything else would just have to wait.

The door opened, and Alex stood aside to allow her to enter first. Tarian paused to let her eyes adjust to the dim lighting in the hallway. When her sight returned, she started down the hall.

The air grew hotter as they progressed. Her tank top clung to her back before they were halfway to the third cell, and the air felt thick with some sort of energy she couldn't name. The black rocks absorbed energy from the inhabitants, but it didn't feel like that. It didn't feel like a protective spell either. It felt…sticky, somehow. Her neck throbbed. She rubbed it with one hand while she walked.

Two cells away from her target, she noticed a red mist radiating through the door. By the time she and Alex stood next to the door, the mist lay on her skin like a thick blanket of foreign magic. She brushed her arms, but it didn't help. She glanced back at Alex.

"You feel that?"

He raised an eyebrow. "What?"

"You can't feel that?" She shivered, and her neck twinged. *What on earth is this invasive?*

"I don't feel anything but the same heat wave I always feel." He looked around. "You're making me nervous—stop it!"

"I can't believe you can't feel this. I've never felt anything like it. And I shouldn't be able to feel much of anything this far into the Cellar. Whatever it is, it's strong enough to pass through the door. I can't imagine what the inside of the cell is like."

She stepped forward to open the door to the cell. Alex pulled her hand away like she was a child near a hot stove.

"You're always rushing in. Let me check it out first."

"You can't even feel the energy already here in the hallway, how are you going to check it out inside the cell?" She crossed her arms and waited for the logic to sink in.

Alex frowned at the door. He put his hand on it and muttered a word that sounded suspiciously like "chocolate." He waited. Then nodded.

"Nobody's been in since the Cleaners. It's clear."

"Silly. Of course it's clear. I'm sure whatever did this didn't stick around after to make nice with Sentinels."

"Call me any name you want." Alex looked at her with a satisfied expression. "Nobody gets hurt on my watch."

"I won't point out the obvious." She gestured at the door. "Can I go in now?"

He focused his own power, which made the hairs on her arms stand at attention. He stood with feet shoulder width apart, both arms tensed, the nodded. Tarian opened the cell door, gasping when a rush of energy knocked her back into Alex. His arms wrapped around her, holding her tight as her knees buckled. She leaned into him, letting him support her until her legs stopped wobbling.

"I gotcha." He squeezed, a reassuring gesture.

Tarian put her hands on his arms and squeezed back, grateful for the support. "What the hell was that?"

"You collapsed. You seem to be doing that a lot lately. Maybe you should go back to the healer." His chest felt hot against her back. His breath traveled along the back of her neck, even hotter where it touched the cold knot where the claw lay embedded underneath her skin.

"I'm on the list." His whisper caressed her ear.

She pushed away from him and pointed at the cell. "I didn't collapse, Alex. Didn't you feel that? It was a huge rush of energy."

He shook his head and glanced into the cell. "There's nothing here. Same old empty hallway, same old empty cell." He turned back to stare at her, his eyes lit by some internal fire.

Tarian avoided his stare.

He's just a friend.

She rubbed her arms, took a deep breath, and pushed past him into the room. The power had dissipated. She barely felt it now. Only the slightest prickle on her skin and an almost imperceptible ripple of the hairs in her nose. She looked around. Like all of the holding cells, this one sported thick slabs of solid black rock formed the floor, bumpy black rock defined the walls, and more black rock huddled overhead. Just the one door. Two glowing phosphorescent rocks above it did little to cheer the place up, but she supposed the last thing prisoners were supposed to feel was happy if they were in the Cellar.

She walked the entire perimeter of the cell. The toilet, which was usually bolted to the floor, lay on its side. She saw a water cup wedged into the rock along the back wall. The rest of the cell was empty.

"Look at this place. It's been tossed. There's no way Mark Chester upended the toilet. He couldn't even lift his head. And that rush of power. It didn't come from him; he's dead. Not that there's any way he flayed himself either."

Alex shuddered. "Be glad you didn't see it."

"This power didn't come from anyone in this House." Tarian paused near the toilet. Some sort of writing peeked out from under it. *Graffiti?* She pushed the toilet over then stared at the word "Scion." Each letter was formed with precision, in what appeared to be blood.

"So this is what you were hiding. Why didn't you say?" She looked back up at Alex.

Alex shrugged.

She turned back to the writing. Was it even blood? She put her hand down on it to absorb any latent signature. Blood always held energy. Even those without magic talent left residue of themselves behind, at least for a little while.

"Did the Cleaners touch it?"

Alex shook his head. "They siphoned up the flesh bits using the tornado technique they have, but didn't touch anything physically and didn't move anything else. They took some of the pieces to the healers but they don't expect to find anything. Too much destroyed, and no blood. That's the thing, no blood anywhere in the body parts left or the cell."

"Except this, you mean." Tarian sat down in the middle of the floor facing the bloodstain and placed both hands on it.

"You hoping for a vision? You should see a psychic." Alex knelt next to her.

"Just trying to figure out what was in here. Whatever it was, it killed Chester, and in a pretty nasty way. Yet nobody heard anything, nobody saw anything, and there's no way it snuck past you guys. So it came straight here. What could come straight into a holding cell?"

"Nothing."

"Exactly. This power? This is different. It's not normal."

"I don't know, Tari. I don't feel nothing. Anyway, why'd he write your name on the floor? Some think he was trying to name his killer."

She looked up at the words, shocked. Someone thought she had killed Chester?

Alex put up both hands. "I didn't say me. Just some people."

"Who?"

Alex shrugged. "It's only gossip."

"Chester couldn't focus on anything but my boobs. And he wouldn't have been able to write neatly even if he'd wanted to. He didn't write this." She couldn't keep the scorn out of her voice. She had no reason to kill anyone, let alone an idiot like Chester. *But it sure looks like someone wants people to think I did. Or they're calling me out.*

She looked back at the word on the floor. Not her name. Her title: Scion. *Why? Maybe the lizard is taunting me.* The power in the room was his. It had to be. She had it firmly in her psyche now, and the claw in her neck seemed to resonate to it. He'd snatched her blood and now he'd killed her only source of information. And he wanted her to know about it. He wanted her to notice how easily he'd invaded her sanctuary. *Pretty effective way to put my nerves on edge, sneaking into the Cellar.* The one place on earth she'd have sworn was impenetrable. Yet he'd waltzed in here with time to leave graffiti.

She'd never felt unsafe before. Never felt vulnerable. She'd trained to fight. She had power most people never dreamed of possessing. Now this lizard managed to get close enough to leave a serious wound, a link to her power, and melt through Cellar walls as if they were air. She suddenly felt as though she were standing in a glass house that might shatter at the first rock thrown.

Tarian closed her eyes and cast about for more latent energy in the cell. When she tried to follow the mist to the source, the signal stopped cold. She cast further, pushing her tracking ability harder. Nothing. On a whim, she focused instead on the claw. It wiggled slightly, wrapped inside the shields still holding firm. She didn't dare loosen them to continue tracking, but she cast out a feeler from the claw, in case the connection to the lizard lay open.

Her head started to ache as she strained to pick up any sign of the Laghairtine. All she felt was a solid wall of nothing. She huffed, opened her eyes, and rubbed her head with the palms of her hands as she looked around. A whole lot of nothing stared back at her. She stood up to go.

"Why can I feel this mist when nobody else can?"

Alex shrugged. "You got me. Maybe you gotta be a girl to feel it?"

"It seems almost like he was leaving a message. The question is, why?"

"The real question is who. I know you know, *chica*. You got it all over your face. Tell me." Alex stared into her eyes as though he'd drag information out of her by sheer force of will.

She left the cell, hitting his arm on the way out. "Let's get out of here."

chapter eleven

Alex locked the cell behind them but didn't move to follow. When she realized he wasn't behind her, she turned back.

"What?"

"You can't pretend it's not happening. It won't go away, Tari." He walked slowly toward her, his eyes riveted on hers.

"I'll figure out who he is, Alex. I'll find him. You know I can do it."

Alex shook his head. "That ain't what I meant, and you know it. I know you don't wanna face it, *chica*. But you got to."

"If I don't find this lizard, nothing else will matter. Let's focus on one thing at a time, okay?" She squeezed his arm, before continuing down the hallway. After a heartbeat or two, she heard footsteps behind her. *I'm not ready for this.* Potentials. Sex with strangers. Pregnancy. Motherhood. Turning her friend into a lover, even if it was only for one night. How would they even look each other in the eye afterward?

She liked things the way they were. She was just one of the

guys to Alex and Frankie. They were the only people who treated her as a friend, instead of the heir to an amazing gift of power from the Ancients. They were the only ones who made her feel real. She liked that and didn't want it to change.

By the time they arrived at the reception area, irritation colored everything. She was pissed off at Alex for making things awkward, the Throne for starting this stupid ritual, the lizard for attacking her in the first place, her own body for letting her down when she really needed her strength, and her mother because, well, just because.

She glared at Frankie, who remained behind the desk, fixated on his computer.

"Frankie, if someone is hiding in the Between, how do I get there?"

Frankie frowned then started tapping on his keyboard. A few seconds later, he shook his head. "You don't. Humans can't go. Daemons can't either. The only ones who can cross the Between, according to my database, is those with a foot on both sides."

Tarian frowned. "What about Chester? Someone should check who fixed the charges on him."

Frankie cleared his throat. "I'm already on it. The charges were logged in by Daryl, except he shouldn't have been able to because he's not the right level. The records are clean on who dropped them. No trace at all." He scratched at the stubble on his chin.

"There has to be something, Frankie. There are only a couple of places people can even access the system, right?"

Frankie nodded. "On this computer here and the one in the admin offices. You might try asking the Archivists. They have all the old records, plus they have a hive mind full of ancient history. They won't let me put their stuff in my database, so I can't search it from here."

"The archives." She groaned. There was nothing more boring than a giant room filled with dusty old books. And she'd never been a huge fan of the Archivists.

Hard to like creatures with so many rules.

"I don't have time to spend all day in the archives."

"Ask Calliope." A faint smile crossed Frankie's lips, and his eyes focused on something not in the room. *Interesting. Her sister and Frankie?*

If anyone could find information in that dusty cave, it was her sister. She'd ask Calliope to do the book work then do the tracking on her own.

"I know what you're thinking, *chica*. You're not sneaking out alone. No way." Alex crossed his arms, and Frankie looked at her with an expression that said he knew her all too well.

"I'm going to the archives, Alex. Leave it, okay?"

"I'll go with."

Alex opened a portal to the rotunda above them and waited, his mouth set in a firm line. Arguing wouldn't change his mind.

Stubborn mule.

She flounced past him and stepped through the portal. She didn't wait for him on the other side but set off at a fast pace down the hallway leading to the archives.

He caught up after a few long strides and grabbed her arm to stop her. "We're friends, right?"

"I've known you my whole life."

"Then why won't you look at me?"

"I'm looking at you right now." She stared up into his dark brown eyes, daring him to argue.

"You know what I mean. *Chica*, it won't ruin things. We'll still be friends."

Her body heated up like she had a fever. *He always seems to know exactly what I'm thinking.*

"You're not the least bit attracted to me?" Alex flexed his biceps.

Tarian couldn't help but laugh.

"I've never thought about it."

"Not once? Not even when I held you back there?"

The flush burned into her cheeks. She must be scarlet now, even under her tan.

His arms did feel nice.

But it didn't matter. The ritual didn't allow for personal feelings. She needed sperm donors, nothing more. She wasn't even supposed to know the Potentials. A few generations back, the guys wore masks so the heir never saw their faces. Just the eyes and relevant body parts of three or more men. In the past, it had been as many as 20.

Ridiculous. I should know the fathers of my child.

But now she had to admit the whole process might have been developed to spare hurt feelings and situations like this one. After all, it had to be awkward for the guy too. He was being used for his sperm, nothing more. He'd never know if his blood was part of the mix that created the child and would never be a father to her. She'd never call him Daddy.

Tarian had the odd moment or two over the years, wondering who her own fathers were and if they knew her. If she saw one of them every day and didn't know. If they even cared. But the gap was usually filled by friends and plenty of male father figures. And she had the dolphins. *I couldn't ask for better friends.* She hadn't felt a serious lack. How could she? She was Scion. Surrounded by people, by the ocean, and by magic.

She hoped, right now, her heart was stronger than her magic, in case it was broken in the whole ritual process. *Hope the dolphins have a cure for heartache.*

Alex stepped toward her, and she backed away until the wall stopped her. He leaned in, his body hot and close. "I know what you're doing in that head of yours. You're thinking of all the reasons why it shouldn't be me. But give me a chance. Right now. If I can't spark passion in you, we quit and I won't ask again. One chance, that's all I ask."

"We can't do it now. We're in the middle of a hallway. I have a lizard to chase."

He nodded to a door a few feet away. "Nobody ever comes down here. And you aren't gonna catch the lizard in the next half hour." He raised his eyebrows until they looked like dark brown umbrellas. "If you gotta do this thing, who better than a friend to see you through? It's the one thing I can do for you that you can't do for yourself, *chica*."

Knots in her stomach made her uncomfortable.

I'm not ready for the ritual-become-a-mother-take-over-the-Throne thing.

The words stuck in her throat. Tarian licked her lips and tried to swallow them. Even if it would be years before she had to take the Throne, the ritual still made it seem closer than it had been the day before.

She didn't want to lose her best friend. But she didn't want to use a group of strangers to father a child either.

If I do this with someone I know, what happens then? Awkward looks, fights, or cold shoulders? Will I lose my best friend?

Alex leaned in, supporting his body with hands planted on each side of her head against the wall. His breath and magic, hot, earthy, and sweet, filled her nose. "It won't change things. I'm your friend. I'll still be your friend. If I act funny after, you have my permission to *try* to kick my ass." His grin lit up his eyes in a way that always made her grin back. "You won't be able to. But you can try."

"I already have. Don't you remember? Arena Games, three years ago?"

He laughed. "I let you win."

"No way. I had you on your ass before you even managed to gather focus. I didn't even have to use magic."

He shook his head, his eyes full of laughter and heat. "In your dreams."

"In reality."

"I just wanted you to land on top of me."

"Sure you did. That's why you were sweating so hard."

Her giggles subsided. She studied his face. Warm, kind, passionate, full of Latino heat and pride. His arms on either side of her, supporting his body as he leaned in toward her. Safe arms. Arms that had comforted her on more than one occasion. Arms that had sparred with her, hugged her, and pulled her out of one fix after another. Arms that had always been there for her. It all generated heat inside her.

Damn it all.

She turned and crossed the hall to the door he'd indicated. The thought of having sex, right here, right now, had a naughty quality that turned her on. The thought of ignoring the tradition of waiting for the vetting of Potentials satisfied the hell out of her; and the thought of the lizard lurking out there somewhere, his claw inside her, added an element of danger that made it all exciting. And Alex, if she looked at him with objective eyes, was more than attractive.

He is damn hot.

Alex followed her into the room. It was a guest room. It needed a good dusting, but it had a bed, a bathroom with a shower and nothing else to distract them.

Tarian stood in the center of the room, suddenly unsure. Alex stared at her full of passion and heat. She closed her hands into fists.

We're really going to do this.

Her heart skipped a beat, and nerves took up a dance in her stomach.

Alex smiled, and it melted her spine. "It's not the way I'd normally seduce a woman. I feel just as awkward as you."

"What would you normally do?"

"It usually involves a few beers, some great food, maybe a relaxing shower or hot tub."

"I'd hate to have beer brought here. It would start rumors, and I would bet there're plenty of those going around by now. There's a shower, but I already had one."

He chuckled. "It's not about getting clean. Go on, take a shower."

She shrugged. *It delays the inevitable, but what the hell.* "I'll be out in a few."

Tarian started the water in the shower and waited for it to get hot before stripping. The steam invaded her sinuses and relaxed her lungs. Even this small amount of water soothed her nearly as much as being in the ocean did. She took slow, deep breaths then entered the shower.

Alex was a good friend and a good man. *I'd rather have his arms around me than some hairy stranger.* She'd heard things about Alex from others. He was passionate in bed and out. She was curious to find out exactly what that meant. Her experience with men in this area was limited to a few one-night stands. She hadn't felt anything for those men. This was more. Much more.

Water coursed over her breasts and tickled her thighs as she started to lather up.

At first she didn't notice the warm hand joining hers in the suds on her shoulder. The touch was gentle, barely there, and she'd been so involved with her thoughts she hadn't felt his energy behind her. When she realized she wasn't alone in the shower, nerves shot back up through her stomach and chest.

"It's okay, *chica*. It's just a shower." Alex kept his voice soothing and low, as though speaking to a skittish horse. He squeezed her shoulder before exploring the rest of her arm.

She closed her eyes, and steadied her breath. *Just a shower.* Just two friends in the shower. Naked. With soap. And hot, steamy water. And body parts touching.

His body radiated heat behind her. She leaned back into it, and he slipped his arms around her in a gentle hug. Bare chest, tight arms, and water all combined.

Holy shit. She took another deep breath.

"Alex…" She wasn't even sure what she wanted to say.

"If you want to stop, just say so. If not, then no more words. No more thinking. Just close your eyes."

She thought about it.

She didn't want to stop.

She kept her eyes closed and squeezed his arm.

He kissed her ear then nibbled. A thrill shot straight to her groin. She had no idea her ear was so sensitive. When he moved on to her shoulder, she was almost disappointed. Until he lifted her hair and began kissing the back of her neck. The piece of claw ensconced in layers of magic pulsed. A small sound of protest escaped her lips, and her hand moved between his lips and her neck.

"Does it hurt?" Alex massaged her shoulders, careful to avoid the base of her neck.

"Not exactly. I just..." Tarian swallowed. "Just don't touch it, okay?"

Alex grunted and, after a soft kiss on the offending body part, worked his way around her back. She forgot he was her best friend. She forgot every issue she'd ever had with the ritual. She forgot about the lizard and his claw. This was delicious and steamy and felt so right.

She'd probably regret it later, but for right now, she let it all go. She relaxed into his kisses and sighed. He squeezed her arms again, and his hands started to knead.

And she'd thought the kisses were nice. They were nothing compared to his hands.

It was the softest caress she'd ever experienced. It had been so long since anyone had touched her this way.

Hell, nobody has ever touched me quite this way.

He traveled down her arms and back up, then massaged her shoulders, this time careful to avoid the base of her neck. He worked on each remaining knot of tension, letting his breath and hands soothe them away. Her stomach melted and her knees liquefied as he worked out the stiffness and worry. The claw remained still and distant.

By the time he was done, Tarian's legs wobbled like jellyfish. Alex reached around her and turned off the water, then pulled her back against him in a tight hug. Every naked inch of him pushed against her. His erection poked into the crack of her behind, wet and hard. The heat and thrill of it made her groin throb.

She turned to face him. The passion and longing on his face and his eyes at half-mast sent a river of heat down her thighs.

She pulled him in for a kiss. He didn't hesitate, and when their lips met he took over.

Her mouth vibrated with the force of his kiss and tongue.

When he finally pulled away, she still felt him. Hard, tingling heat imprinted on her lips and in her mind.

Alex pulled her out of the shower, never breaking eye contact. She let him lead her to the bed. She couldn't get past his eyes to even look at the rest of his body. Black hair plastered to the side of his face led a river of water across his cheeks and down his chest. It was the sexiest damn thing she'd ever seen.

Alex maneuvered her down onto the bed. He pushed her back against the covers, head above hers, hands on either side of her holding him as he hovered above her.

This is really happening.

Alex lowered himself to kiss her again, leaving her lips feeling bruised. He set to work kissing the front of her as thoroughly as he'd kissed the back in the shower.

When he reached her thighs, she spread her legs to let him know she was ready for more than kisses.

He took her up on her offer. Without a word, his hand reached in and caressed her inner thighs. Her groin. His fingers worked their way in between the folds until he touched her clit. It was so sensitive she jerked. He tried again, softer at first, in gentle circular motions.

She groaned.

More. More.

Tarian pushed at his hand, willing his fingers inside her.

"You ready for me, *chica?*" He breathed the words while his hand continued to circle. Every time he touched her clit she pushed down, intensifying the pressure.

"Alex." Her lips forgot how to form words.

He maneuvered his body and legs until he straddled her, the tip of his penis pushing against her. For a moment, he hovered, his eyes so dark the depths extended out of reach. She drank them in, lost in the chocolate brown, heat, and spark of him.

She raised her legs until her feet pulled on his butt and drew him toward her, encouraging him, wanting him, pulling him toward her until he slid inside with a soft groan. His mouth parted slightly and his gaze never left hers.

Tarian closed her eyes, unnerved by the intimacy in his stare. Denied the visual stimulation, every other sense heightened. His scent, fresh moist dirt with a hint of grass, spoke of his earth-based talents. The touch of his legs as they brushed against her inner thighs, solid, steady, smooth as stone. The taste of spice he'd left in her mouth and on her lips from the salsa he'd probably had for breakfast.

More. More. More.

Alex worked on her in a slow, tantalizing tease of motions. In, then slowly out. In, pause, out. Her breath matched the movement of his hips, but her heart raced for the finish line, frantic and eager.

She encouraged him with her legs, helping him push deeper with each thrust.

So good. So damn good.

She ached for release.

He stiffened and leaned down to whisper in her ear.

"Come with me, *chica.*"

She groaned in response.

Alex moved faster, in a steadier beat, racing up an invisible hill. Tarian pushed her hips into every thrust, straining every muscle in her legs and back to meet him, to join him in the explosion she knew was coming. With one hand she gripped his shoulder, with the other she rubbed at her swollen and tender flesh.

As his body tightened, nearly at the top, her own climax washed over her groin, legs, and up into her chest. She rode the wave of pleasure, enjoying the tremors that ran through his body as he, too, released.

Holy shit. Why'd we wait so long?

She opened her eyes to find him staring at her as though memorizing every pore. She offered him a small smile, but couldn't think of anything to say. Instead, she squeezed his arms, and let her legs fall off his hips and onto the bed.

Alex examined her face, his gaze moving from her lips, to her cheeks, to her eyes. She watched the passion in them fade, and some sort of wall rise up, as though he walled away his thoughts and feelings.

She frowned. *Please don't end like this. Please.*

He lowered his gaze and shifted his body until he lay beside her on the bed. They both stared at the ceiling, the tips of their fingers the only body parts touching.

Suddenly the room felt small and awkward, the connection they'd shared a few seconds ago shattered. She felt his withdrawal like the slamming of a door.

I guess that's why we waited so long. Should have waited a hell of a lot longer. This was a mistake.

Her heart ached. She couldn't be any sort of partner to him. She didn't even want to be, not really. She had a job, as heir to the House. He had a job, as Sentinel. She wanted him as a friend, not a life-long lover. She squeezed her eyes shut to stop tears.

Dammit, he knew I couldn't marry, or even be faithful. The ritual demands I screw as many men as possible. At least three. He knew.

The countdown had begun. One down, at least two to go, with no turning back. Alex was right about one thing. She was glad he was the first.

Better a friend than a stranger. I hope. If he can handle it.

She took his hand and squeezed it in silent thanks.

Her stomach growled. In the silence, it startled both of them into giggles, shattering the sadness. For now.

"You should eat." Alex rolled over and propped himself up on one elbow. His gaze remained firmly on her face, rather than her naked body sprawled across the bed.

"I suppose I should. I'll get something after the archives."

"Why is a Laghairtine after you? What started this? Be honest. There's something you're not telling."

"I don't know, Alex. I really don't. It almost doesn't matter. What matters now is stopping him."

"The why of something always matters." His finger traced the side of her cheek, down her neck where he stopped at the base.

She had no answer, so she said nothing.

"Something like this, the usual reason is sex, money, or power." His thumb wiped away a trace of a tear, which, despite her efforts, had escaped her eyes.

Tarian put her hand on his to stop the motion. "Maybe all three? Maybe this guy thinks if he gets my power, he'll get the sex and money? Or is the power the ultimate thing? I don't know, Alex. All I know is I can't let it happen."

She moved his hand away and sat up. "I don't get it. He's more than powerful enough as it is. He had me easy, Alex."

It was hard for her to admit, but she had to be honest.

"He caught you by surprise, that's all. You're not an easy fight. Don't go getting down on yourself."

"It's just…even if I'd been ready, his magic is different. I wish you felt it in the Cellar. It's not just Earth. It's something else. Something I don't understand. And if his combined with mine…" She licked her lips, her mouth suddenly dry. "I don't even want to think about what would happen. How the hell am I going to stop this?"

"One step at a time. It's not you alone, *chica*. You got a team backing you up. He don't. Plus he obviously don't know you at all, or he'd never have let you leave." He squeezed her arm. "I'd never let you leave. That's for damn sure."

She turned to look into his eyes. She'd never noticed the flecks of gold before. "Alex, you know….I can't promise…"

He nodded. "I've known my whole life it would come to this, *chica*. I knew it would be this one moment. It's okay. It's worth it, to me. We're still friends. I still got your back. It's all good."

She saw the tiniest flicker of sadness in his eyes before he looked away. He'd planned it his whole life? And she'd never known. Where did he see this going?

He knew I couldn't marry. Wouldn't marry. He knew. My family doesn't work the way his does.

Alex was one of nine children. Part of a huge Latino family who placed blood bonds above all others. It had to hurt. But he'd done it anyway. For her. She wanted to cry at some loss she couldn't even name.

"I better get going." She was suddenly aware of how naked they both were. Alex nodded and stood up to pull her up off the bed. They nearly bumped heads as they reached for various bits of clothing, dressing in silence. There didn't seem to be anything else to say. When they had put themselves back together, they stood for a moment, staring at each other. *Awkward.*

"I'll have some food sent to you in the archives." Alex looked as though he wanted to kiss her again, but he didn't follow through.

She didn't pull him in.

It was over. She hoped their friendship wasn't.

chapter twelve

Tarian stood outside the plain wood door to the archives, lost in thought. Every now and then her neck throbbed or ached, but so far, she didn't feel any power leaking out. Maybe it was so gradual it couldn't be felt. Or maybe she really was protected inside these walls.

Fatigue settled on her shoulders like an elephant. She closed her eyes and wished she were outside on the beach, that she'd never gone to Philly, and that her world hadn't been turned upside down. For once, she wished she'd listened to her mother.

The most unbelievable part wasn't the lizard attack. It wasn't the siphoning of her power, and it wasn't the obvious plot against her family or the Throne. Deep inside was the fear stirred up by thoughts of the Succession Ritual and the realization she'd just had sex with her best friend.

She was glad she'd stuck it to tradition by having her little session with Alex. Her body still tingled in places, she still felt him inside her, and smelled his scent all over her body. It did make her smile to think of it, even if she had to ignore the awkwardness.

Nobody knew yet, and she liked that too. The Throne might have called the ritual, and she had to participate, but she'd decide who and when and where. It gave her a feeling of power to know she'd already started, without waiting for permission or approval or official sanctions from anyone. She hadn't waited for the kick-off reception, where all the hopeful candidates would be presented to her.

She put her hand on her abdomen. Even now motherhood might be on the way. A chill ran through her at the thought. The faint sound of the dolphin call filled her ears. Did the Throne know? The sound was joyful, as always. Full of life and happiness. It was such a contrast to what was really going on. Her life fell apart around her, but the dolphins were happy. *Good for them.*

She opened her eyes and put her hand on the doorknob, but couldn't make herself open the door. It seemed so solid, like it wouldn't open even if she pushed with all her might. *Just like trying to find someone hiding in the Between, just like this stupid ritual.* Immovable objects. The part that scared her most was she was too tired to fight the Laghairtine. She'd never felt so overwhelmed in her life.

Well, isn't this just a pity party?

Her problems wouldn't be solved by wallowing. She closed her eyes and took several deep, cleansing breaths to initiate a short, calming meditation. For the moment, she was fine. She still had her power. She still had options. *One step at a time.* She opened her eyes, squared her shoulders and pushed the door open.

On the other side, the room opened up into a large hall with row after row, shelf after shelf, of books. She'd never really liked books all that much. Books meant homework and long hours inside when she'd rather be outside, preferably surrounded by water.

Water and books don't mix.

She glanced up at the dome ceiling. It was the only thing worthwhile in this dusty corner of the house. A mural depicted a forest in vivid detail, so real she wanted to step into it and get lost among the trees. She followed the vines that extended from the mural down onto the rough black and brown rock walls and into the carved wood bookcases. One of the books was covered in what looked like luxurious blond hair. She shook her head. *Who makes books like that?*

Next to the blond-haired book lurked a stone creature that looked like a monkey and bulldog made love and had a very ugly baby. Its flat face, squashed by some invisible press, spread into pointy ears and a sunken chin, and perched on a squat, ape-like, hairless body ending in long boney fingers and toes. It waited with closed eyes and a grumpy expression.

I'd be grumpy too if I were stuck in this room.

Tarian glanced around and noted several more of them on various shelves, unmoving. Usually they all waited in the shadows, unseen until called on.

They must have a query.

Calliope sat at a table covered in books, below the closest monkey statue. Her curly blond hair was pulled back in a ponytail. Her sundress looked like a ray of sunshine in a pile of dust. A collection of leaves bathed in light from a floating green orb lay in a pile on the table in front of her. Her sister picked up one leaf, then another, and stared at both. Fascinated, Tarian started toward her, then stopped as one of the carved statues came to life, picked up a book covered in vines, and scurried over to Calliope. It dropped the book on the table next to her, crawled back where it came from, and froze again.

Tarian tiptoed across the floor until she stood just behind Calliope. In a gravelly whisper she muttered "What are you up to?"

Calliope squeaked and dropped the leaf she was inspecting. "Tari! You scared me!"

"Mind telling me what Chloe sent you scampering off to research?" Tarian pulled up a chair next to Calliope and sat down. Several stacks of books lay nearby, one pile so tall it was in serious danger of falling off the table.

Calliope frowned at Tarian, her forehead forming elevens between the eyebrows. "How's the arm?"

"Barely a scratch, see?" She held out her arm for inspection, and avoided her sister's scrutinizing gaze. The back of her neck tingled as though a bee were trapped beneath it. The claw apparently didn't like something in this room.

Or maybe it does. This room is very earthy, after all.

"Why didn't you stay back when I told you to? You could have been hurt, Calli."

Tarian picked up one of the leaves and examined it. It looked like a plain, ordinary leaf. Holding it up higher, the green light shone through it and illuminated scrawled handwriting on the leaf. *Fascinating.*

"You looked like someone slugged you, and you sounded all panicky." Calliope turned to face her. The frown was touched by a bit of something else now. Scorn? "Asking for help isn't a sign of weakness, you know."

"I didn't say it was."

"You sure acted like it." Calliope turned away to examine the leaf again. "I don't scamper."

"You do, too. If you scampered any more, you'd be a squirrel." Tarian looked around. None of the Archivists moved or twitched a stone muscle. She watched her sister read for a moment, exhaustion making her feel numb and slow. She sighed. "I need help, Calli. You know how to research better than I do, and I'm too tired to fight about it."

Calliope turned to face her again, her eyebrows raised.

"I need Mark Chester's address. He was murdered in the Cellar, but there wasn't anything left to track. And I'm pretty sure his death is related to my little problem."

"You could've asked Frankie." Calliope tilted her head sideways.

"There's something else, too. Frankie thought there might be something here in the archives about it. I need to know how to get into the Between." She explained about the strange power she'd sensed, the red mist nobody else saw or felt, her title written on the floor, and her suspicion about where the lizard-man was hiding.

Calliope frowned as she listened.

"I can start a search with the Archivists, but I'd have to stop the one they're running now. They'll only do one query at a time."

"They have such stupid rules. Why can't they do more than one?"

"That's all they promised. And before you ask, no, I have no idea who they promised. I'm not about to waste a query to find out."

Calliope fiddled with one of the leaves, letting the light play on it at different angles.

"What have you been doing?"

Calliope glanced at her then looked back down at the leaf. "Trying to help you. When you passed out, Mother was beyond freaked out. Chloe couldn't wake you. We thought maybe the Laghairtine already had…" Calliope gulped. "Chloe thought maybe the archives would have information on the sort of rituals that can be done with someone's blood. It's not just anybody who can pull them off in the first place. It'd usually have to be someone with an affinity for both water and earth, which is pretty rare. But it should also mean the ritual can be broken. Probably with air and fire."

Tarian though back to her struggle in the alley. The lizard definitely had an affinity for earth, all right. But the red mist and the jolts he shot at her weren't water based. If she had to guess, she'd swear he had a bit of fire in him.

Calliope placed the leaf carefully on the table and turned to face her. "A lot of people spend their lives making sure we're safe, Tarian. It's not a good way to pay them back, risking yourself like you do."

"I never asked them to do it." She stood up and paced, her temper spilling over. "I never asked for any of this. I didn't exactly stand there shouting, 'Victim here, victim here,' Calli."

Calliope watched her pace with calm eyes.

"I don't know why the Throne can't go to you anyway. You'd actually enjoy it." All Tarian wanted was to use her talents in a way that benefited everyone, not sit on a throne in a house all day, away from everything useful. Away from the ocean she loved. It wasn't enough to simply hear it through windows and open ceilings. She needed to be surrounded by it, a part of it, immersed in it.

I'm not meant for this.

She knew it, deep down. She was a fighter, an outdoor girl, not a Keeper.

"That's not the way the rules work." Calliope sniffed in a

disapproving sort of way, making her nose wrinkle.

"It's about time someone else made the rules." Resentment bubbled up and blended with the anger. It wasn't rational, and it wasn't mature, but Tarian couldn't help herself. "It's about time this old-fashioned idea of inheritance was abolished. Why shouldn't you be able to take the Throne if you want it? Hell, why shouldn't anyone?" She paced back and forth, unable to sit still.

"Anyone like the Laghairtine, you mean?" Her sister's quiet tone in the face of chaos stoked Tarian's anger.

"Don't be ridiculous. I mean, sure, keep it in our family; hell, keep it only for women since we're the strongest magically. But why should we be forced to do the Succession the way they say? Why can't the child know their father, or fathers? Don't you wish you'd known yours? Even a hint of who and what he was?" She took a deep breath, building up steam. "And another thing. These Archivists. Why can they only answer one question at a time? I need answers to more than one question, and I don't have time to wait."

Calliope watched her but offered nothing.

"How the hell am I supposed to deal with all of this? Seriously, tell me how?" She threw herself down into a chair next to her sister. Calliope radiated acceptance. Tarian closed her eyes and drank it in, fighting the tears that threatened to spill over.

"What's up with you, Tari? Something's off."

Tarian's eyes popped open.

"What do you mean? I've been attacked by a lizard. Of course there's something off."

Calliope shook her head. "More than that. Something's different. You have, no offense, but a sort of scent about you that's not you. You're…" Calliope narrowed her eyes.

Tarian kept her eyes down, so her sister couldn't read the

truth in them, and ignored the heat in her cheeks.

"Your lips are very red, but you're not wearing lipstick. Your cheeks are on fire. And your hair...you've been messing around, haven't you!" Calliope laughed. "In the middle of all this, you did it. You started the ritual. Like, just now?" If her sister's voice rose any higher she'd break the water glass sitting next to her.

Tarian should have known she'd never keep that particular secret from her sister. Not right after it happened, when her emotions were still all tangled up. Still, it felt good to tell someone. She nodded then looked up.

"Who with?" Calliope's hands flew to cover her mouth.

"Alex."

"Alex? Really? Alex?" Calliope's eyes widened yet another notch until they were giant orbs of white with liquid brown centers. "Alex. Seriously? Alex?"

"Stop saying his name like that." Tarian shifted some of the papers and put them into a neat pile.

"Where?"

"What difference does that make?"

"Just now?"

Tarian nodded.

Calliope giggled. "I've heard stories about him. All the girls in the healer's hall love to watch him work out. How was it?"

"Oh, Calli, a lady never kisses and tells." Her lips stretched in a slow grin that melted the last bit of resentment and anger. She couldn't help it. It was impossible to be in a bad mood around Calliope.

"You're no lady. You're my sister, so tell."

"He was...a friend." The grin faded. "I hope he still is."

"Why wouldn't he be?" Calliope looked genuinely confused, her brows wrinkled.

"Sex changes things, Calli. Especially when it's with someone you spent your whole life thinking of as your best friend, not your lover."

"Don't worry, Tari. I'm sure it'll be fine. He's a good guy, and he knew what he was getting into. He knows the deal. I wouldn't be surprised if he planned on this happening since he was a kid. He's always had a thing for you."

"Really?" He'd never even tried to kiss her. Not once. Until today.

Calliope nodded, the deep look of wisdom back in her eyes. "You just didn't look for it."

"Well, whatever happens, I'm one step closer to finishing the ritual. On my own terms, not someone else's." All she had to do was find at least two more men willing to partner with her. She really wasn't looking forward to it.

Calliope's face lost the giggles and amusement. "Oh, Tari, I'm sorry. This sucks. But you've done more than start the ritual. You've freed up one of my questions for the Archivists. I won't have to stop the query they're on to ask a different one. If you finish the Succession Ritual, then the Laghairtine won't win that particular battle. We can focus on finding him. It's a good thing, even if it doesn't feel like it."

Tarian grinned. "Oh, it felt just fine, at the time. So, explain to me what the Archivists are answering right now, and how we can change it to help me fix this mess."

chapter thirteen

Calliope's mouth lifted in a ghost of a smile. "The query they are working on right now has to do with identifying exactly who attacked you and what his talents are. I thought if we knew that, we'd be able to form a plan on how to stop him using his weaknesses."

The question was a fantastic one. Tarian hadn't even thought to ask it, figuring she'd rely on her own abilities to find the lizard. But if she still couldn't track him, she'd have to find him some other way, a need her sister and Chloe had obviously anticipated. What a choice. Tarian would have asked about how to get into the Between, but what if she were wrong about where he was hiding, what good would the information do? She'd have wasted time and energy, things she didn't have to spare.

Calliope's face softened with concern. "You look like you've been up for five days straight."

"I feel like it too." Tarian ran her fingers through her hair. The burst of energy she'd managed to get from her tryst with Alex had long since vanished. So had the cheesesteak, which seemed a lifetime ago.

As if on cue, the door to the archives opened and a boy scooted through it with a tray. Resting on top were two more cheesesteaks and a steaming cup of her favorite coffee. Alex had followed through on his promise.

Bless the man.

Tarian accepted the tray and placed it on the table next to the leaves. Taking the paper cup in her hand she closed her eyes and inhaled. Next to the salt tang of the ocean, the smell of coffee was the most glorious scent in the entire world.

"Tari." Calliope's soft voice broke through the coffee trance. Tarian opened her eyes, and saw the cup on the floor, surrounded by a puddle of precious brown liquid.

"Crap." Tarian reached for the cup and looked around for a towel to soak up the liquid.

"Tari, you're exhausted. You need rest. Here."

Calliope leaned toward her and placed both hands on Tarian's arms. Warmth spread from Calliope's hands up her arms and into her chest, along with a soothing calm. Tarian took a deep breath and closed her eyes again, opening herself to the infusion of power from her sister. Calliope's talent for blending magic from someone else with her own was unique, like Tarian's tracking ability. As far as she knew, Calliope was the only one in several generations with magical empathy. It tended to bring an emotional empathy with it. With a touch, she could cure depression as easily as she boosted energy.

Tarian let the combined power race through her veins and skin. It energized her and fed her soul. Not quite as good as a dip in the ocean, but still welcome. Her neck tingled as power raced over it, making her pull away from her sister and open her eyes.

"Better?" Calliope glanced at Tarian's neck as though she knew what had made Tarian stop the exchange.

She still felt tired but not exhausted. She nodded and smiled her appreciation, and kept her hands firmly at her side instead of rubbing the back of her head. The claw settled down to a slight ache, and she breathed a sigh of relief.

Calliope frowned, but didn't comment, instead turning toward one of the stone creatures. It sprung to animation, hopped up and down, causing the books to teeter, and placed his paw in Calliope's hand.

Tarian watched her sister's face for any sign of the conversation the two held within their heads, but saw nothing.

Finally, her sister broke the silence.

"They're going to help search for a way to remove the piece of claw in your neck. It's a break of their usual rule, but they say a threat on the Scion is more important and does not violate their promise. They seem more bothered by what happened in the cells than anything else."

"Why?"

Calliope released the paw and turned to her. "He wants to talk to you."

Seeing the concern on Calliope's face, Tarian took the offered paw/hand without comment.

A small chorus of voices immediately reverberated through her head. *"We have been waiting, Tarian A'marie Maitea Xannon. We expected communication."*

"I've been busy. You know, with being attacked and coerced into motherhood." She looked around, but only one Archivist showed any signs of life. Yet it sounded like at least twenty of them talking in her head, some high pitched, some low, all sort of growly. Their hive mind always unsettled her. It was as if a thousand people saw into her soul and every nook and cranny of her mind.

"There is no need to verbalize. We wish more detail. Please show us the events."

She was about to ask how, but her mind was filled with a picture of the archives inside her head, a movie in reverse. She held her breath as scenes rewound in her head and stopped with her standing by the door of the cell. She even felt the warmth of the air. Everything was crystal clear. She felt each stirring of power, again felt it blast through the door and encompass her, Alex's arms around her, and the red mist.

When the event was done playing in her mind, it immediately faded. It was an odd feeling to have her mind suddenly blank. Her communications with the dolphins were never this vivid or as in depth. Then again, she'd never spent a lot of time trying. They seemed content to simply let her be, for which she was grateful. No demands, no judgments. Just happy to see her. Her, not the Scion.

"We sense a tracer within you. Please show us acquisition."

A surge of irritation flowed through her at the words. How did they know? Her mind leapt to the scene in the alley. The encounter with the Laghairtine played back in slow motion. Every excruciating detail, from the bum in the alley to the scrape down her arm to their struggle. She didn't think her memory had ever been this good. The image faded as the lizard-man dissolved. Her thoughts were her own again.

"This we feared. Shield is clever, but will not hold. This results from imperfect understanding."

"Care to explain?" Her stomach tightened, and her hand formed an involuntary fist around the tiny paw. Her brain felt violated.

"The power signature belongs to one type of being only. This requires more study."

"You don't know what caused it?"

"We know the source. We do not know how it was possible."

"Can you tell me who he is or how I can find him?" She had a hard time keeping the frustration out of her voice.

"Youth requires patience. And understanding."

"Yes, understanding is what I seek right at this moment. And I don't have time to be patient."

"The source is Laghairtine. This requires more study."

Her hand around the Archivist's small paw tightened.

"I knew that much! What's his name? Where is he now?"

Mutters filled her head. Some angry, some patient, all mixed and jumbled until she couldn't make complete sense of them. One thought stood out stronger than the rest. They didn't want to answer her question.

"This guy threatens my family, my friends, this House, the Society, everything. I'm trying to protect people. Even if I manage to complete the ritual, the child won't be born before he gains control of me. I need to track him." Panic filled her at the thought of the Laghairtine having control over an unborn child on top of everything else. Her child. The next Scion. Her stomach clenched.

She felt her sister stiffen beside her at this speech. Somehow she couldn't manage to make herself think the words, rather than say them aloud. Calliope heard only half the conversation, but it was more than enough.

"Dolphin ritual has already begun."

An image of her and Alex in the shower flashed through her mind. Her cheeks heated. She hoped Calliope couldn't tell she was blushing.

"Never mind that. Will it harm me to track the creature?"

"His power differs from Scion's. He is Laghairtine. Scion is not. He crosses worlds. Scion could cross, but battle in the Between is not possible. Acquisition of signature is not possible."

No wonder her previous attempt gave her a headache. The lizard must have known about her tracking, and had prevented it by slipping into the Between before she knew she needed to. Score one to him.

How can I defeat him if I can't follow him into the Between?

Her shoulders sank.

"To follow is not the correct assumption. Scion cannot abandon who and what Scion is."

"Hey, I wasn't talking to you." She took up one of the sandwiches and munched on it as she pondered the information. His power differed from hers. That much she'd figured out on her own. But in a fair fight, who'd win? "How is his magic stronger than my own?"

The arguing in her head after such a simple question filled her with curiosity. She'd struck a nerve. *Interesting.*

"Difference and strength are not equal. Strength is measured by more than magic."

"All magic came from daemons. He's at least part daemon. Like you."

"He is not WE. He is other. Daemons are the Source. Daemons belong to the Universe, and the Universe to Magic. All are one. Daemons are magic. Laghairtines are not."

Why can't you all stop talking in riddles and tell me what I want to know?

She didn't say the thought out loud, but they heard it anyway.

"Understanding comes with knowledge and time. Daemons are the Source. Laghairtines are other. Constructs of society and imperfect

understanding, greed, pride, fear. A blend of human, daemon and Ancient which should not exist, resulting in a blend of magic which should not exist. Red mist denotes fire. Claw attack denotes Earth. Understanding requires study."

Her thoughts circled back to the lizard-man in the alley. So he used fire and earth, and he wanted control over her. He wanted the Throne. A Throne based in water. Why?

"Is there a way to capture him?"

"There are possibilities. This requires more study."

"What do they mean it requires more study?" Tarian looked at Calliope.

"I think it means you need to come back later." Calliope shrugged.

"Of course it does." She dropped the creature's hands, which immediately sank back down into a silent statue pose. She picked up one of the leaves and twirled it while she sorted out the situation.

"Are you sure you should be doing this? You need rest, Tari." Calliope chewed on a fingernail then yanked her hand away from her mouth. From the state of the other fingernails, Calliope had been eating them all day.

"I need Chester's address. There might be something there I can use. Some clue, some information, some trace I can follow. Something. If the Archivists here can't, or won't, tell me who the lizard-man is and how to destroy his hold on me, then it's the only lead I have." Tarian stifled a yawn. If she didn't sleep soon, she might fall over where she stood. "What's with the leaves, anyway?"

"It's fascinating, really. Some of the oldest records are on all kinds of material. This one is a journal written by the first Keeper, Serin. I guess she thought it would be easy to keep it from prying eyes if it looked like a houseplant. It has a lot of information on the first Succession Ritual, why she set it up like she did, and how the Dolphin Throne came to be part of the House. She mentions an Ancient, one I'd never heard of before. Lasair. Fire based. There's even a bit about the Archivists. Their presence in the House originated around the same time, almost like they helped build it. But it's not easy to read." Calliope studied her face. "Go take a nap. When I get the address, I'll wake you up."

"Do me a favor? Don't tell anybody you're doing it?" Tarian stood and gave Calliope's shoulders a squeeze. "The boys all seem to think I'm a china doll about to break."

"Well, you do look a bit fragile right now." Calliope frowned.

"Hey, I'm a warrior woman!" She flexed a muscle.

Calliope chuckled, shook her head, then bent down over the leaf again.

"Don't tell anyone about Alex either, okay? I want to do the choosing without being chased around."

Calliope grinned up at her. "I don't think you'll avoid that, now the call has gone out. But don't worry. I won't tell anybody, sister swear."

Tarian left her sister, wondering if research was even worth the trouble. She'd find a way to track the lizard, just as soon as she had a nap. And if she couldn't follow him or fight him in the Between, she'd find a way to draw him into this plane of existence. A few hours of sleep, then she'd sneak out, away from the magic protection of the house, and use the tracer against the creature who'd put it inside her. The lizard had no idea who he'd messed with. She couldn't wait to show him.

chapter fourteen

Tarian lay in bed twisted around cool, white, cotton sheets, lost in a delicious state between sleep and awake where she swam in the memory of a dream. All she had left were impressions, but the lingering blend of muscles, dark hair, and dimples set her body on fire. She had a feeling, from the way her groin throbbed, that those arms had been holding her, and those hands had been caressing all sorts of areas. She kept her eyes closed, trying to hold onto the feeling as long as possible.

A knock at the door jolted her out of the blissful moment. She stared at the mural on her ceiling, a child's garden full of fairies and wildflowers, and tried to bring her mind back to earth. Memory flooded back. Lizards. Tracers. Rituals. Daric Voltain. A shower with Alex. Her heart pounded. How long had she been asleep? Dammit, she'd set a glow ball when she lay down to wake her with a bright light. Why hadn't it gone off? She glanced over at the wall where a ball of blue flame should have been glowing, but the wall sconce remained dark. If it'd gone off, it had since worn out. How long had she been asleep?

Another knock at the door reminded her why she was awake in the first place. She groaned and swung her legs over the edge of the bed. Her feet brushed the cold stone floor. Her muscles felt stiff, like she'd been sitting still for a long time. Light snuck into the room around the edges of the curtains on the window. She yawned and stretched.

The knock came again, louder and more insistent. The door swung open and a head popped through, followed by the entire body of her sister.

Calliope hurried into the room, but before she closed the door, Tarian spotted two Sentinels standing at attention across the hall behind her sister. One of them flashed her a small smile, and the other's cheeks turned instantly red. She glanced down. She wore her usual tank top, panties, and nothing else. She rolled her eyes as the door closed.

Calliope bounced onto the bed, a triumphant expression etched on her face.

"You look like you just won a prize. Spill." Tarian yawned.

"I have the address. It was harder than it should have been, but I got it in the end." Calliope flicked her hand, and the wall sconces flared into life.

Tarian winced at the sudden brightness. "Why?" She escaped the glare by shuffling into the bathroom to get rid of the fur coating her teeth.

"Because all records of Mark Chester had been wiped. Including any arrest records. It's like he vanished. Except whoever messed with the records forgot to check the non-magic ones. Chester was born in a regular hospital in Chester County, Pennsylvania. His parents still live there."

Tarian spit out the toothpaste then poked her head

around the corner to see her sister with a Cheshire grin. "How'd you get those?"

"The only way possible. They're still on paper. I went there and pulled them from the files."

"They let you do that?"

"Well, sure, using a glamour. I made myself look like an employee who was out sick, waltzed right into the records office. After that, it was easy enough to track Chester's parents, and once I had their address I went to their house and told them I was a girlfriend and couldn't find him. They seemed very excited to hear he had a steady girl. Or maybe they were just happy I looked so respectable." Calliope giggled.

"How the hell did you do all that?" Tarian glanced over at the window again. The distinct shade of reddish orange light, which only came with sunset on this side of the island, filtered through. "And in the middle of the night? Philly is hours ahead of us."

Tarian narrowed her eyes at her sister. "How long have I been asleep?"

A sheepish expression replaced the smile on her sister's face. "You're right. By the time I figured all this out, the offices were closed, so I had to wait until they opened the next morning. You were so tired. I told you I'd wake you when I had the address."

Tarian stared at her sister in disbelief. She'd slept a full 24 hours? She'd slept through the alarm?

Calliope looked down at the paper in her hands then handed it to Tarian without making eye contact.

"So you've been to Philly, to a records office, and to Chester's parents' house. Alone? Seriously?"

"Don't be silly. I wasn't alone. Frankie went with me. He was a huge help with the whole thing. He can hack any database. I need to learn how to do that."

From the look on her sister's face, that wasn't all she'd like to learn from Frankie.

"How could you let me sleep so long? Dammit, Calli, I only have a few days and now I've lost one to sleep."

Tarian crumpled the paper in her hand. She wanted to throw it, but she needed the information so, instead, she paced the floor in front of her room. Calliope watched her, but said nothing.

Smart.

After a few laps across the room, Tarian stopped and sighed. She couldn't get the time back, no point in getting pissy over it. She uncrumpled the paper and studied the writing on it. Chester hadn't strayed far from his birthplace. He'd lived in Philadelphia. In probably the worst section of the city. The Mansion District, which, despite the name, contained no mansions. It did, however, have a lot of row houses, a lot of drugs, and a lot of violence. Tarian committed his address to memory. She needed a shower to clear the grogginess and fog in her brain, and she needed to get her ass moving. A whole day, lost.

Calliope followed her into the bathroom and leaned against the sink. "I found a history on Laghairtines. It's a bit of a mess because they didn't actually exist."

"What's that supposed to mean?" Tarian rubbed shampoo into her hair and let the water cascade over her. Memories of Alex and his hands threatened to distract her, but she pushed them out of the way.

"Well, daemons existed before the earth. They're older than old, possibly the oldest thing in existence other than Ancients, who are a pure form of daemon. Ancients were formed from the original magic spark, part of the primordial soup that formed the universe, and daemons came shortly after, a blend of Ancient magic and our own atmosphere. There are four basic kinds."

Calliope held up her hand and ticked off each one on her fingers. "Air. Earth. Fire. Water. And all of them have different levels of magical abilities, like us, but stronger of course. More pure. The Archivists are earth based."

"So what's this got to do with the lizard?" Tarian rinsed the soap off her body, letting the water sink into her pores.

"Laghairtines are a more modern thing. From what I can tell, they're an experiment gone horribly wrong. Someone from one plane tried to cross and mate in the Between with someone from the other side, and it all went haywire."

Tarian reluctantly turned off the water.

Calliope gathered a bit of air energy and held her hands out toward Tarian, letting a soft, warm flow of air circle around and dry away the water.

"It's not even supposed to be possible. And there's something else twisting it all up. Even if he were a blend of pure daemon and human, he shouldn't have turned out like he did."

"Why not? Maybe he's a cross of earth daemon and human." The only earth daemon Tarian knew of were the Archivists. She pictured a human mating with one of them and shuddered.

"No, he can't be. He's definitely able to go into the Between. That means whoever it was tried to mate with someone from air. The side that's been split from us for thousands of years."

"Air. I didn't feel any air." Tarian paused. Something about that statement struck a warning bell but she couldn't put her finger on it.

Calliope picked up a brush and started to undo all the tangles in Tarian's hair. "The claw piece feels different. Like it's part fire. But he's earth. Very earth. The Archivists seem pretty sure of that. But not because of them. His magic is different. They don't understand it, which is scary. I've never known them to have this much trouble sorting something out before."

Tarian mulled over the information as she left the bathroom and set off in search of fresh clothes. She'd lost an entire day. Her heart skipped a beat at the thought.

"What's with the Sentinels?" Tarian scrounged through her closet and emerged with a denim jacket, jeans, and a plain black T-shirt. She needed to blend in with a rough crowd.

"Honestly, Tari, everybody knows you're going to try to hunt down the Laghairtine all by yourself. You didn't think they'd leave you unprotected, did you?" Calliope shook her head. "Especially now. Mother has the Sentinels working up all kinds of extra security. Advisor Jonus filled the rotunda with Sentinels, and all the hallways have a walking patrol. Plus the ones stationed outside wherever you happen to be."

"What do you mean 'especially now?'" Tarian pulled on the T-shirt.

"The call, Tari. Potentials are already arriving. You have to be at the reception. Tonight. It's in a couple of hours."

Tarian groaned. "I don't have time."

"Frankie is researching ways we might get into the Between, and Alex is formulating a plan to catch him on this side. I have the Archivists researching the Laghairtine's magic and how to fight it. With all of us working together, something is bound to sort this out."

She envied the confidence in her sister's voice.

"How many Sentinels?"

"Don't even think about sneaking out, Tari." Calliope's tone held the same warning in it their mother's did when Tarian contemplated doing something her mother wouldn't like.

She thrust her legs into the jeans and pulled them up.

"Thanks for all the info, Calli. And for the address. It helps a lot." Tarian patted Calliope on the arm then opened the bedroom door. She stuck her head out into the hallway. It looked like six guards on each side of the door, plus a few more at either end of the hallway. She shut the door.

"I suppose they mean to follow me everywhere I go?"

"They have orders not to let you anywhere near a travel portal."

Tarian snorted. "Like they could stop me. What are they going to do, wrestle me to the ground?" She moved to a corner of the room that held an old rocking chair.

"They do have stunners, you know."

She pulled the chair out of the way then turned to her sister. "Do me a favor? Cover for me? Tell them I have a horrible headache."

"Tari, what are you up to?" Calliope frowned at the corner.

Tarian smiled. "I need to check out this address." She turned and pictured the address in her mind. She'd been near the neighborhood before. It contained a small park, and a tiny Italian restaurant she'd eaten at once or twice, a block away. She envisioned it all in her mind. Her power jumped at her focus, like always. She was delighted to find her strength back to full. Or nearly full. Something felt a bit off, as if she had a cold, but not enough to worry about. Yet.

She pushed a tiny bit of energy into the special back door she'd created for sneaking out when she was younger and grinned when she felt it open. It wasn't a large hole in the perimeter defenses, but it was enough for her to portal through. *Perfect.* She opened a travel portal to the park near where Chester lived. She'd start there and walk.

A soft hand on her arm stopped her before she stepped through.

"Tari? You're the only sister I have. Please don't rush into this."

Tarian looked back and felt a surge of guilt at the concern in her sister's eyes. She gave Calliope a quick hug. "Don't worry about me, Calli. I'm only checking the address for something I can use. He's not there anymore, and nobody will know I'm gone. I won't go after the lizard tonight, okay? Promise."

Her sister stared at her, disbelief etched on her face.

"I swear. I'll be right back." Tarian ignored the guilt and stepped through the portal.

chapter fifteen

Tarian stepped out of the travel portal and onto a cracked sidewalk in the Mansion District of Philadelphia, so named for a historical landmark of a house, once a grand reminder of better days, now an unofficial half-way house for homeless junkies.

She stood across the street from a small, triangular-shaped park.

Not exactly paradise.

Far from lush, the park contained patches of dirt, a few rusty benches and one street light. A few old leafy trees huddled near the benches, carved with so many initials it was surprising they still lived. Feeble bushes wilted around each tree. Someone had dangled old basketball shoes on the light. A shadow moved around some of the trees. Drug pushers, the late shift. Tarian blended into the shadow of the house behind her. She didn't need their attention.

She took note of her surroundings. Old row houses, looking more like prisons than homes, with bars on the windows and doors. A convenience store crouched nearby, covered in graffiti. Across the park, a couple of abandoned warehouses. A surprisingly graffiti-free church complete with steeple and bell. Trash and bottles and the stench of urine everywhere. Ratty cars that probably didn't run. *Prime real estate.*

She checked the street signs then set off down the one she wanted. The address took her two blocks from the park along an empty street, except for the occasional rat or cat.

Chester's block looked like a war zone, with barred and boarded windows. Torn crime-scene tape decorated the door of several houses. Blank, empty windows stared out at the deserted street. She stopped under a grimy street light in front of a section of house that probably used to be white but now looked brownish-gray. One of the steps leading to the door was missing. A bullet hole graced one window. Inside, a surprisingly feminine flowery curtain valiantly tried to dress the place.

Looking down at the paper in her hand, Tarian scrutinized the address. She looked at the dumpy house in front of her, then at the crooked number on the mailbox. She was definitely at the right location.

A spicy scent, so out of place in the filth, wafted over her a second before a magic signature tickled the hair on the back of her neck and in her nose. She whirled in place, her power focused enough to block any spell coming at her. She relaxed slightly when she saw Daric Voltain.

"We have to stop meeting like this." He glanced down at her arm, but the denim jacket she wore covered the scar. "So your healers solved the problem?"

"How do you know so much about Laghairtines?" She crossed her arms, hiding the injured one underneath.

"My mother was a teacher before she retired." He shrugged,

as if that explained everything.

She studied him. There wasn't enough light to get a good look at him, but she had to admit he made an impressive silhouette against the street light. A remnant of the dream she'd woken up to circled in her head for a moment and heated her face. She imagined those arms belonging to Daric and all too clearly how those arms would feel wrapped around her.

"What are you doing here?" She took a step backward, out of the pool of light.

"I was about to ask you the same question." Daric gestured at the neighborhood. "This doesn't seem like Scion territory. Especially since you're supposed to be somewhere else tonight."

She didn't think it was possible for her cheeks to be any hotter, but she was wrong. *He's been called. He knows about the ritual.* A brief image of him with her in bed flashed through her mind. She wondered how he'd feel, compared to Alex. She pushed the thought right out of her head and ignored the sudden throbbing in her groin. "I'm here on official business."

"In the middle of the Mansion District, on the night of the reception for Potentials?" His eyes flicked to the house behind her. "We have something in common. I'm on official business too."

"What sort of business?"

"I'm looking for someone who's supposed to live here."

"This is Mark Chester's last known address. If you're looking for him, you're wasting your time." She shifted from one foot to the other. *Why do I feel so agitated around this guy?*

"Actually, it's his cousin I'm looking for. Kevin." Daric stepped closer. The light from the street lamp lit him from behind and silhouetted his body, but she still saw his crooked grin.

A faint, jagged scar on his left cheek emphasized his eyes,

his nose looked as if it'd been broken, and his dimple made her stomach twist. *Unbelievably sexy.* It all came together in a way that made her want to kiss him. Or slap him. Maybe both.

She willed her body to stop reacting to pheromones. Her body didn't give a crap what she wanted and let her know by sending her nervous butterflies.

"Did my mother send you?" She wouldn't put it past her mother to have tried more than one way of keeping her under watchful eyes.

"No." He looked at her with a curious expression. "I sent myself."

She glanced back at the house. It was a crime scene waiting to happen. Something in the distance sounded suspiciously like a gun shot. It wasn't a bad idea to have company in this neighborhood at this time of night. She didn't normally shy away from a fight, but her magic was off, and she didn't feel quite like herself. The memory of the lizard attack lived in the forefront of her mind and the back of her neck. *He's out here, somewhere. It would be nice to have backup.*

"Fine. We'll check it together." She turned and marched up the steps. She heard his footsteps crunch on the cement, and a tingle went up her back at the thought of Daric's eyes on her.

A hint of residual magic leaked out through the walls of the house in front of her, faint but noticeable. Enough to tickle the hairs on her arms, anyway. She knocked and waited. No lights flared, no footsteps hurried for the door.

Daric joined her, standing a little closer than he needed to. She felt the heat from his breath down the back of her neck. Tingles. She knocked again. A dog next door barked, the sound loud and deep against the backdrop of distant sirens and city traffic.

She tried the doorknob and it turned easily. Odd, in this neighborhood, that Chester and his cousin had left this place unlocked and unprotected.

The front door opened into a small living area, which connected to a tiny kitchen. Torn wallpaper with gaudy yellow flowers lined the walls. Dilapidated steps coated with stained carpet led to the second floor. Stale beer stench coated the air. The whole place felt dejected. The American Dream, gone to hell.

"Chester lived here?" Tarian couldn't believe a rat lived in this place, much less people. She kicked a few empty beer bottles out of the way.

"I wouldn't call it living." Daric pushed a broken chair aside, but nothing was behind it but a thick layer of dirt. He sneezed three times in quick succession.

Tarian moved into the kitchen. Squalid was an understatement. She wrinkled her nose at the filth and smell of sweat, beer, and old stinky feet, but followed the trail of magic that tickled the hairs on her arms. It led to a narrow door. Steep stairs behind it led down into black nothing. She tried the light switch but, of course, in this dump it didn't work.

"You wouldn't happen to have a light, would you?" She didn't want to float a ball of magic to light her way. Not without knowing what hid in the basement.

"There's probably something we can use as a glow rod. Hang on."

Daric moved off into the front room and returned a few minutes later with an old Popsicle stick. Holding it in one hand, he focused on it. The Popsicle stick lit up and cast a diffused light around them. He handed it to her. Her fingers brushed his as she took the offered light, sending a tiny thrill up her arm. *Hormones.* She really didn't need them tonight.

"Ready?" She glanced at Daric. He nodded, and she held the stick high as she led the way down the steps.

Tarian tested the air at each step for any trace of magic. The dank smell of mold wrinkled her nose and made her sneeze. The residual magic grew stronger and settled on her, but she felt no active presence, human or otherwise. The basement was empty. No boxes or cast off bits of furniture. Odd.

Daric scouted around the corners of the room while she concentrated on the middle. Something had happened here. The magic felt similar to what she'd experienced in the Cellar, but less pronounced. And as far as she saw in the dim light, it wasn't red. But it was so dark, all color faded into shades of gray.

Daric stood in the middle of the empty space. From the expression on his face, his frustration mirrored hers. "Can you track the people who were in this room? I hear you're good at that sort of thing."

"And you aren't?"

"It's not a common gift."

"So what's yours?"

Daric raised his eyebrows. "Can you track them or not?"

"I doubt it. There's a reason they came down to this basement. The earth and walls help block the signal, and earth isn't something I can handle easily. But I suppose it's worth a shot."

Tarian placed the glowing Popsicle stick on a beam that ran along the ceiling where it cast light over most of the basement. She sat down in the middle of the floor and put her hands on the filthy concrete.

"You going to clean the floor now?" Daric looked down at her, amusement playing around the corner of his eyes.

"Sure. I do housekeeping on the side for extra money." She pointed at the corner. "Go stand over there."

"Don't trust me?" He moved to the indicated corner, a full grin turned up the corners of his mouth and caused a dimple on one side. Cute.

"I don't need you messing with the signal." She closed her eyes and took a few deep breaths. Magic focused in the center of her forehead and chest, the hairs in her nose twitched, and her neck thumped. She tried to ignore the ache, which settled immediately at the top of her spine, but her pull on energy out here beyond the protection of the House of Xannon and the Dolphin Throne seemed to excite the claw, even behind the shields she still maintained.

She shook her head, trying to clear the fear gathered in the pit of her stomach.

"Are you okay?" Daric knelt where he stood. In the dim light he formed a dark lump with glittering eyes.

For a moment, panic flared through her. Here she was, a claw inside her, in a dark basement used for the heavens knew what, in the middle of the worst district Philly had to offer, with a stranger. *Not smart. Not smart at all.*

She didn't feel any movement toward her from Daric or any gathering of energy. He seemed a lot like Alex, actually. Concerned and helpful, with a heavy dose of sexy. Plus, she didn't have a lot of options right now.

She took more deep breaths, then a few more for good measure. Calm surrounded her, and from within it she extended her focus out into the stifled basement air in search of any leftover signatures.

The claw jiggled and lurched as something external tugged on it. She rubbed at her neck with one hand and tried to ignore it, but heat descended over her body, as if she suddenly had a high fever. She gasped and pulled her magic back into herself. Something grabbed the other end of her power stream and tugged, as if a rope extended between them and this was a game of tug-of-war. If she hadn't been sitting, she'd have fallen.

Damn him! The lizard felt her and was pulling on her power. Determined, she tried to follow the invisible rope.

Her power hit a wall and rebounded back at her so hard she cursed out loud. A hand gripped her shoulder. She punched out at the owner, just missing him.

"Tarian. Snap out of it, dammit." Daric shook her shoulders.

She opened her eyes and found Daric on his knees in front of her. She hadn't heard him move.

"What happened?" His grip tightened on her shoulders.

"I can't track him." Even to herself, she sounded frantic. "They were right. I can't follow him."

chapter sixteen

It wasn't possible. *How the hell is he blocking me? How is he jumping into the Between so easily? How does he even know I'm trying to follow?*

The Laghairtine tracked her, but she couldn't return the favor. How the hell was she going to find him if she couldn't use her strongest ability? How was she going to stop him when every time she used magic at all, he stole it away? She panted with the effort to control her panic.

Daric's grip on her shoulders grew so tight she nearly cried out in protest. "You have a tracer, don't you? He left something behind. Didn't he?" Daric shook her shoulders. "Are you crazy? You shouldn't be here."

He picked her up off the floor, anger palpable in the feel of his hands on her and in the depths of his eyes, then set her down hard on her feet. She shoved back at him.

"The only way to be free of him is to find him. You told me yourself. I have less than a week to do it. You know it. I can't hunt him from home. I have to be out here, outside those walls. They block too much."

"Why didn't they remove the tracer?" He kept his arms by his side, but his hands twitched as if they'd like to throttle her. "Where is it? What did he leave?"

"Why do you care?" She glared at him.

"Tarian." His voice was a soft growl.

"It's only a tiny piece of claw."

Daric ground his teeth. "Where?"

"What difference does it make?" She rubbed at her neck.

Daric grabbed her shoulders and turned her around. He lifted her hair, and placed a hand on the small bulge created by tense muscles and foreign object. Warmth flooded the area.

He's a healer. Like Calli.

He hissed in a breath and released her.

"They can't." His voice, now flat and unemotional, scared her more than anything else.

"They're working on finding a way." She shifted her feet. Her muscles ached from her tug of war with the demon. She felt drained, weak, and vulnerable. It wasn't pleasant.

Tarian cleared her throat and turned away from his stare. "Something happened in this basement. Whoever did it was bound to have touched something."

"This is the last thing you should be doing."

"I have a mother, Daric." She turned back to him. "If I use the claw to track him, he'll drain me faster. I need something else. There's too much power here for it to have only been Mark Chester or his lame-ass cousin. Whoever was down here couldn't spend much time and not touch something. A button. A light switch. Something."

"This place is scrubbed." Daric stood still for a moment, his face set, his gaze still steady on her face. She stared at him until he broke eye contact, walked over to the corner, and crouched to check the floor.

Tarian started in the center of the room and worked outward in circles. The two of them crawled over the filth, an inch at a time, in silence. Every inch was like a vise around her heart, making it difficult to breathe.

"This might be something." Daric brushed his hands over the dirt in the far corner of the room.

Tarian joined him. As Daric swept away the dirt, she saw it in the dim blue glow of the popsicle light. Neat, red handwriting spelled out the word "Scion."

"Shit." She sat back on her heels. The bastard was taunting her. With fantastic penmanship.

"Can you use it?"

"I doubt it."

"You've tried before?"

She nodded. "He left something like this in the Cellar. I didn't get anything from it."

Daric's mouth formed a line, but he went back to his search.

"Hey." Daric scraped his fingers on the floor and held out something fuzzy. "What about this?"

Tarian scooted over on her knees to join him. "Is that hair?"

"Yes. Can you use it?"

She took the hair from him and shuddered at the thought of what or who it might have come from, not to mention where. But if it was all they had, she'd work with it. She folded it into her hand and glanced at Daric.

"Where's the trust?"

"Go stand in the other corner, and don't gather any power."

He complied, but his expression was unreadable. *Was that*

concern? Or irritation? She seemed to have that effect on people. She didn't want to explain his personal signature intoxicated her and created a distraction she didn't need. His obvious concern for her well-being unnerved her.

We just met. Why does he care?

She closed her eyes and focused on the hair in her hand. She'd never used hair to track anyone before. It might not work.

She sent a light touch of magic along the hair and out into the air. Not tracking, simply reading the residual leftovers or imprints. Her neck twitched, and tugged, but nothing overwhelmed her like it had before.

A few seconds later, her head filled with the image of a girl, larger than life, with her eyes so wide open the whites glowed. *Cold. Horror. Pain. Incredible pain.* Tarian gasped and dropped the hair.

"Holy shit."

"What happened?" Daric crossed the room in a flash. His hands reached out toward her, maybe to comfort her or shake her again—she wasn't sure—then stopped.

"The hair belonged to a young black girl, really young, like 14-ish, with a big mole high on her left cheek and a small scar near her chin. She's…dead. Like Chester." Tarian shivered. The image had been so vivid and the emotional impact of death so real, she might as well have been standing there when it happened. Tears formed in her eyes. *That poor girl.*

"Chester is dead? How?" Daric put a gentle hand on her shoulder. This time she didn't push him away. The shock of seeing the girl's face in what was probably the last moment of her life ran too deep. She'd never felt anything like it. The girl's horror ran through her bones. The bit of human contact Daric offered provided welcome relief.

"He was ripped apart. In the Cellar."

Daric's hand tightened. "Can you track who killed the girl from hair?"

Tarian shook her head. "It doesn't work like that. I need something he's touched. I mean, really touched. I don't think yanking hair out counts. I can't track thin air, there are too many signals. I have to know which is his. I have to have some connection to the person." Her voice shook. Emotion flooded through her. Horror, for the girl. Panic, at her situation.

Had the girl had been conscious when she was murdered? The thought experiencing an arm ripped from your body, or heart torn out, was almost too much. She'd tracked petty thieves and drunks before as favors for the Sentinels, but never something like this. It struck her how protected and cloistered she'd been all these years. *Couldn't risk the Scion, after all.*

"You okay?" Daric's tone was soft and low. He pulled her in close and wrapped his arms around her.

Tarian started to push him away, but instead let the warmth of his arms filter through the cold that had slammed into her along with the image of the girl. She squeezed Daric in silent gratitude, relishing the contact for a moment before moving away slowly to stand on her own.

Daric traced his hand down her arm as she stepped away. "That's the girl I was hired to find. The mole, the scar, fits the description. I thought Kevin might have snatched her. Now I know, and I can tell her family. It's something."

Tarian glanced around. She didn't want to admit to herself how much she needed there to be more in this basement than the hair of a dead girl.

"You shouldn't be here. Don't you have a reception to get to?" Daric's eyes glinted in the flickering glow of the Popsicle stick.

"Don't you have a family to visit?"

"You know, we should work together on this." Daric held out his hands as if in truce. "We're on the same team."

"I'm not a team player." At least, not anymore. Now the Laghairtine had entered her life, she didn't need one more person at risk by being around her.

"You don't like to admit you need help, do you?"

Anger flared in her, mixed with fear. "I have plenty of people trying to help me. But I'm not going to sit around and let others fight the battle for me. I'm not going to allow them to be hurt because I'm tangled up in something I should have avoided."

"You really think you could have avoided this? You don't seem the type."

"What type is that?"

"Martyr."

She glared at him.

"If someone is willing to risk their life to take yours, there's not a whole lot you can do. Besides stop them. Now you know about it, you can plan. But you couldn't have known before the alley, so stop beating yourself up over it and start planning the solution."

He was right, but it didn't soothe her temper any to admit it, even to herself. "Don't you think I'm trying to come up with a plan? Why else would I be here?"

"Seems to me you're trying to run. Maybe from a certain ritual?" Daric shook his head. "Don't you think it's odd that after all these years as Scion you're suddenly a target? Why now?"

"I think it's odd that you keep turning up wherever I happen to be. Exactly why are you here, Daric?"

"Exactly what are you trying to say?" Daric's head jerked on the words, his irritation obvious.

"Why were you so conveniently close by when I was attacked?" She crossed her arms. It wasn't rational, and she knew it. But if this was what it took to get this guy to back off and go away, so be it.

"You're way off."

"You found what you came for. I think your official business is done here. It's time for you to go."

"You first."

"What, so you can follow me again?"

"So I can make sure you don't do something stupid."

"Excuse me?" Disbelief and anger overrode any gratitude she'd felt from his comfort earlier. Had he called her stupid?

They stared at each other in silence. Their standoff lasted until the dust and mold in the basement tickled her nose, and she sneezed.

Daric muttered something that sounded suspiciously like "stubborn."

"I don't get it. Why are you so angry? I'm the one with the problem here."

Daric pointed at her. "You say you have a problem, but you don't really believe it. You have no idea how high the stakes are. You haven't faced facts. You're running around without any help, without a plan. It makes me angry. The people around you care about you more than you care about yourself."

His words hit uncomfortably close to home and echoed Calliope's "it's not weakness to ask for help" advice. She kicked at an imaginary pebble on the dusty floor. "You don't even know me."

Daric stepped closer to her, until his nose nearly touched hers. His breath, and the fresh scent of mint, caressed her cheeks. "What if I said I'd like the chance to get to know you, before some lizard takes over your body or worse, rips you to shreds? You're making it damn near impossible."

"I'm not the one who caused all this. You act like I did it on purpose."

"You take foolish risks. Like now. If every use of magic speeds up the process, why the hell are you here, using your power?" Daric swept his hand through the air.

"I'm the only one who can track him, dammit." Her voice broke with frustration. She backed away from him until her back hit a wall. "I'm the only one with the ability. What am I supposed to do, sit and wait until he wins?"

"I thought you said you couldn't track him." Daric's voice was steely, quiet.

He was right. She couldn't use her tracking. At least, not the way she normally would. "There has to be some way. I'll figure it out."

Daric moved closer to her, leaving her nowhere to run. He stared into her eyes as though he'd drill sense into her. When he spoke, his words were measured and low, almost a whisper. "When you decide to climb down off that pedestal and admit you need help, you know how to find me." He brushed her cheek with one finger. It felt hot where he touched, and carried a hint of power. His signature burned through her skin and into her psyche. He'd touched something she wouldn't lose. She'd find him anywhere now. Shame he hadn't touched more than her cheek.

Damn, what am I, a teenager?

She ignored the shiver that ran down her back.

"Scion." Daric bowed his head slightly, in mock salute.

She didn't like how he said the word. Like it was the lowest title he knew, instead of the highest.

Daric opened a travel portal. She saw her favorite coffee shop in Philly, PJ's, dark and empty, wavering in the glow of street lights. A sudden, intense longing for a cup of coffee and a quiet corner filled her. If only life had a pause button.

He stepped through, and closed the portal behind him, leaving her alone in the damp space.

She stared at the air where the portal had been. Daric left thinking she was a spoiled, selfish brat. *It's for his own good.* But Tarian didn't want him to think that way about her. She wanted him to like her, more than she cared to admit. *You're not allowed relationships, so get a hold of your hormones. You are Scion.*

Scion, a breeding machine for the good of the magical Society. She wasn't allowed to form attachments.

Somewhere deep inside her a voice whispered, *"Why not?"*

"Because it's my duty." Tarian said the words out loud. Even to herself, her voice sounded flat.

She stared at the title "Scion" scrawled on the floor. *What is this, a tease? You want me to come and get you? You trying to blame me for all this? Who are you and what do you want?*

Frustrated, she kicked dirt over the offending word. Her brilliant plan of checking Chester's house had turned out to be a dud. She'd found nothing but the remnants of a dead girl's last moments and lost a bit more magic for her trouble. She had no idea what her next move should be. *If I can figure out exactly what he wants, maybe I can stop his attack from another angle.*

One giant dead end and a ritual pushing her right into another. Daric was right. She needed a plan.

She took one last look at the title now obscured by dust, and made a portal to her bedroom. The back of her neck pulsated as she used the small bit of magic. She rubbed at it, snatched the Popsicle stick down from the beam she'd balanced it on, and stepped through the portal.

chapter seventeen

Calliope stared as Tarian stepped out of the portal into her bedroom. Her sister's frown filled the room with disapproval, but Calliope had never been one to stop at a dirty look.

"I thought you said you'd be right back. It's been two hours, Tari."

"It took longer than I thought." She flicked the Popsicle stick at her sister, who grabbed it and shut off the glowing light.

"You sure know how to make Mother angry. And you got a whole group of Sentinels in trouble." Calliope looked at her. "You look like you rolled in dirt. What happened?"

"Nothing." She put a hand on her neck. Now that she was back in the house, the claw had settled down. And she was starving.

"What's wrong?"

"Let's get this stupid thing over with."

"You aren't wearing that, are you?" Calliope looked appalled at the idea. In her soft blue skirt and white blouse she looked like one of the flowers in the mural above the bed.

Tarian glanced down at her clothes. Dust coated her jeans. Her boots were scuffed. Her tank top had some sort of stain on it. The jacket looked fine.

"What's wrong with it? It's who I am."

Calliope crossed her arms and tapped a foot.

Tarian opened the door and stepped out into the hallway. Twelve Sentinels stood at attention. Two more, along with Advisor Jonus, stood at the end of the hallway. She started toward him, her boots clunking their way down the hallway.

She heard her sister's dainty footsteps behind her and slowed down to let her catch up.

"Really, Tari. You could at least take a shower."

"I'm putting an end to this farce, Calli. I have bigger problems." She rubbed the scar on her arm. *By the time the Potentials are officially chosen it'll be too late.*

"I have an outfit ready, you know."

"You sound hurt."

"I put a lot of effort into it."

"I'll tell you what, Calli. If I find the lizard and kill him, I'll wear it without complaint. I'll even smile."

"Tari." Calliope put a hand on her arm to stop her. "We'll get through this together."

She turned on her sister. "That's just it, Calli. I don't want you to get through this. I don't want anyone to have to deal with this mess." Her voice rose to echo the frustration she felt. "The Laghairtine wants to use me. I might not know exactly why, but I can guess, and it's not healthy for anyone around me. I'm not letting it happen. I need to kill him. Or…" she stopped, seeing her sister's eyes grow wider.

"Or what, Tari?"

Tarian started walking again. She wasn't going to spell it out. If she couldn't kill the Laghairtine, she needed to take herself out of the equation before he used her to hurt anyone else. It was as simple as that.

I have to protect my family.

After a moment, Calliope followed. They reached Advisor Jonus together. She felt Calliope's agitation rolling off her in palpable waves.

"Tari, what would stop him from coming after me? If you... if you weren't here?"

Tarian stopped mid-step. *What would stop him?* No doubt, if Tarian were gone they'd lock Calliope in some sort of gilded cage and initiate the ritual on her, since she'd be the only surviving heir. But the lizard had already infiltrated the Cellar, which she'd have sworn was the most secure place on earth. If he broke into the Cellar, no hiding place would keep her sister safe. Her mother would have the protection of the Dolphin Throne, which might be enough. But not her sister, unless the two were together constantly. Only the Keeper called the Dolphin Throne power.

Her brilliant self-sacrifice rendered inconsequential, just like that. She sighed and started walking again.

Advisor Jonus looked at the state of her jeans, his expression thoughtful, but made no comment.

"I suppose you think I'm underdressed too?"

Jonus bowed his head slightly. She imagined her mother's reaction, as well as the room full of men taking in the dirty jeans and disheveled hair.

She turned to her sister.

"It's an impossible situation, isn't it?"

Her sister pressed her lips together in a tight smile.

"Don't you think it's a bit hypocritical to pretend to be

something I'm not?"

"You're more than your clothes, Tari. I think it's rude to show up looking like this. The Potentials don't know what's going on. All they know is the call went out, and they want to impress you. They'll all be dressed up in their best, and nervous. So be nice; impress them back. Think of it as a deposit in your karma bank account."

Tarian sighed. She'd stood at the receiving hall door just three days ago, dripping water all over the floor, wrapped in a towel. At the time, she hadn't cared what people thought.

What's changed?

It wasn't these men's fault she was locked into this ritual just when her life turned inside out. And she did have to complete the ritual with someone else. Two someones, at least. How would she do that if she never met anyone else? She could pick someone else from her limited pool of friends, but it seemed like a stupid idea to fish those waters twice. She'd rather the next be someone she didn't have to face every single day.

Or Daric Voltain. He might be there.

"Fine. Whore me up."

Calli grabbed Tarian's hand and pulled her back down the hallway. "You head for the shower. I'll get everything ready."

They left Advisor Jonus staring after them. When she glanced back, she saw he hadn't moved. He simply watched.

An hour later, Tarian stood in front of her full-length mirror and saw a stranger.

"I think you worked some serious magic here, Calli. Whoever this girl is, I hope she enjoys herself." She shook her head and watched the girl in the mirror shake hers in response. Calliope giggled behind her.

"I didn't use any magic at all. Well, not tonight, anyway.

You're beautiful; you just don't usually bother to show it." She fluffed a stray bit of hair.

The pantsuit her sister had created looked ready for the red carpet or maybe some intimate Hollywood after-party. A silky black material, it draped in a way that made every feminine curve demand attention. A red sash accentuated her waist, and a sweetheart neckline hugged her breasts. Calli had styled Tarian's hair loose. It spilled in soft curls over her shoulders, looking more like an invitation than hair. Diamond beads sparkled like water droplets against her dark curls. The sleeveless design showed off a silver cuff on her upper arm. The scar was barely noticeable.

"Some model should be wearing this on a runway somewhere." She spun, liking the silky feel of the fabric against her skin.

"Well, who knows? Maybe someday they will." Calliope smiled impishly.

"It's not fair," Tarian shook her head. "You are selling them someone else. I can't live up to this image."

"You already do, Tari. Don't worry. Try to think of it as speed dating or something. A lot of women would kill for this chance to pick and choose. To get to spend a night with a man without complications or commitments."

"Except for the whole motherhood thing, you mean."

"A lot of women would kill for that part, too."

"A lot of women. But not me." Tarian stared at herself in the mirror. Who was she, really? *Lucky. So far, my life has been all about luck.* Born at the right time in history, to the right woman, in the right situation with the right power. Strength and power beyond most people's wildest dreams, and yet what she really wanted was…

I don't even know anymore.

The Laghairtine had forced her to think about her life but taken away the chance to do anything about it, with one swipe down her arm.

"What's wrong, Tari?" Calliope fluffed a stray piece of Tarian's hair.

"Besides the obvious, you mean?"

Her sister turned her around so they faced each other. "Something's on your mind. Something new. So what is it? Is it Alex?"

"No. Nothing like that. I'm just thinking."

"About?" Calliope tilted her head to the side. She had the look on her face a terrier gets when it's eyeing a bone.

"Something Daric said."

"Daric? The guy Frankie told me about?"

"Frankie told you?"

"Don't deflect. What did Daric say?" Calliope folded her arms but maintained eye contact.

Tarian looked down at her outfit. "He seems to think I take foolish risks. I don't plan enough. I'm pretty sure he thinks I'm a spoiled brat."

Calliope smiled, an impish little grin. "So he knows you that well already?"

"You think I'm a spoiled brat too?" She glared at her sister.

"Of course not. You're an independent woman, Tari. One who usually doesn't have to struggle much to get what she wants. I call it confidence, not spoiled. But he's right about one thing."

"What's that?" She turned to look at herself in the mirror again. Calliope's gaze met hers in the mirror.

"You do take risks. But I wouldn't call them all foolish. Everybody makes mistakes. That's how we learn. You're learning, that's all."

"Yeah." She turned to face Calliope. "But can I learn fast enough?"

Calliope grabbed her hand and squeezed.

"We should get going." Calliope led her to the door and opened it. Impulsively, Tarian gave her sister a quick hug.

"Thanks, Calli," she whispered.

chapter eighteen

When they met Advisor Jonus in the hallway for the second time, he smiled as he surveyed Tarian's new outfit, but it didn't reach his tired, puffy eyes.

"Not sleeping well, Jonus?" Tarian fell into step beside him on their way to the receiving hall, with Calliope on his other side.

"It's quite troubling, the current events surrounding tonight's festivities. I've been working with your mother on options, but I'm afraid, so far, we've yet to find any palatable ones."

The news that her mother had been trying to solve the problem warmed Tarian's insides. Maybe having some sort of conference with her mother and Jonus wasn't a bad idea. She thought about it as they walked toward the reception, to distract herself from her destination.

The doors to the Hall stood open, and deep tones of male voices spilled out into the rotunda. Jonus led the way into the room, and continued on through the hall without looking back.

Tarian paused inside the door. A hundred men, each

projecting a magical scent that fought for attention greeted Tarian as she entered. They all stopped talking with each other and stared at her. By the glints in their eyes, most were picturing the ritual as if it were their own private porn movie. She felt like a prize calf on display at a county fair. *Get your meat right here, fellas! Plenty to go around!*

Calliope took her hand, and they started to pick their way through the crowd. They pushed past men on both sides as they made their way down the walkway formed by a red floor runner. Long tables filled the vast space, making it seem cramped and small. Some of the men moved into the aisle ahead of them to either greet her or run her over, she wasn't sure which. The smell of aftershave, ocean, and magical signatures assaulted her from all sides. Tarian brushed her nose with the back of her hand to stem the flow but it didn't help.

"I had no idea." Calliope shook her head, her eyes wide as she was jostled from the left. Tarian helped her keep her balance.

"How did I get to be this popular?" Tarian pushed one man with particularly groping hands out of the way. "Is every man in the region here for a piece of ass? Aren't there any gay men?"

Ahead of them, Advisor Jonus stopped, waved a hand in the air, and several of the Sentinels stepped in to clear a path for them. For once, being surrounded by guards held an advantage.

Tarian couldn't keep the bitterness out of her voice when she reached Advisor Jonus. "You didn't tell me the circus was in town."

"Scion, I assure you I had no idea we would have this many answer the call. Usually it's no more than three dozen or so."

"Oh, gee, only three dozen." She looked around. There had to be a hundred more than that number in the room, at least.

It was a good thing this hall was more like a ballroom, or they'd never all fit.

The crowd resumed their conversations, creating a buzz around her head and in her ears she wanted to swat away.

"I can't believe I agreed to come here." Tarian stared at the rune in the center of the floor as they passed over it. It still glowed. She assumed it would until she managed to procreate. Calliope squeezed her hand.

Through breaks in the crowd, Tarian saw a long table set up at the front of the room. Several leaders, representing all four continental regions of the Northern Hemisphere, plus Hawaii, watched her progress. They looked eager and excited. She'd forgotten they'd oversee the vetting of this initial wave of candidates.

With this many, the whole procedure would take weeks, if not months.

Ridiculous. The whole thing is completely stupid.

"I think I should thin the herd." Tarian smiled mischievously at Calliope. Leaving her sister and Jonus behind, she pushed her way up to the head table. An older leader with a thick nose and gray hair, from the Western Region if Tarian remembered right, rose to greet her then stood dumbfounded as she climbed onto one of the chairs and finally onto the table, being careful not to step on any of the cutlery or empty china plates. She accidentally nudged a crystal goblet too hard and it fell over, rolling onto the floor. She watched it shatter, but couldn't hear the sound over the low rumbling of male voices.

"Gentlemen, may I have your attention?" A few men nearest the table stopped talking to look at her eagerly. A few more noticed her standing on the table, and a general "shhhhh!" went through the audience until relative quiet descended. All of the eyes in the room turned toward her, expectant, eager, lustful and a few other emotions she'd rather not notice. The leaders watched her with their mouths hanging open.

"I want you to know I believe this ritual is antiquated and completely foolish." Her voice rang out loud and clear in the now quiet hall. "I'm not a piece of meat here for your pleasure. If you're imagining some sort of porn scenario in your head where you waltz in and have your way with me, you'd better leave right now. No matter what tradition dictates, I'll be the one picking who I will and won't sleep with. On the day of the so-called official ritual, the first one through the door that wasn't handpicked by me will lose his manhood. Even if I did choose you, I'm liable to bite it off anyway. And I won't pick anyone who can't stand up to me in a fair fight. Arena style. So if you can't fight, don't bother."

Amusement flirted with irritation as she watched several men make for the exit. Tarian climbed down off the table and back to the floor, satisfied with her small effort to regain control of this charade. *Losers. Good riddance.* She looked around to judge reactions and found all of the leaders in a frenzied, whispered conversation. She caught sight of Alex laughing to her right. He winked and gave her a thumbs-up sign. She grinned back. At least he wasn't acting jealous. *So far.*

She looked more closely at him. He looked smug. He'd already been the first man through the door, and he very clearly hadn't lost his manhood. She smiled to herself.

Heat trickled down her back like slow dripping water. She turned to see what created the reaction and discovered the Dolphin Throne casting a glow in her general direction. Soft clicks nudged her ears. Underneath, the gentle sound of tide rolling in.

"What's it doing?" Calliope reached out to touch the Throne but pulled back as the glow reached her. The two of them watched as the glow encircled Tarian for a moment then traveled out into the crowd of men, none of whom seemed to notice.

"I don't know."

Advisor Jonus approached the table with a stiff back and a neutral expression painted on his face.

"Your mother will be here momentarily, at which point dinner will begin."

A gong sounded, followed by a melodious male voice.

"Keeper Marielle A'Tania Erlea Xannon. Leader of the Society in the American Region. Keeper of the Dolphin Throne."

Polite applause broke out among the assembled men. Her mother sailed gracefully through the side door and over to the head table in a cream gown embroidered with gold trim. It was modern and sleek, with one shoulder bare. Marielle looked like Tarian's sister, rather than her mother.

"One of yours?" Tarian asked Calliope.

She nodded and flashed a proud smile.

"Well done. It's fabulous."

Her mother paused next to both of them, greeted Tarian with a tight-lipped kiss to the cheek before placing her lips near Tarian's ear. "You might fight the leaders and tradition, but you can't fight the magic of the Throne. One way or another, the ritual will be fulfilled. The House will have an heir."

"Is that what the Throne is doing? Choosing for me? And exactly how will it get me to follow through with the rest of it?" Tarian looked out over the crowd. She saw a faint glow around Alex.

"I think you'll find, in the end, you'll choose to finish the ritual and that it's not the burden you imagine. In all other ways, the Throne is a tool for us to use. But for this, we are the tool."

Tarian whispered in her mother's ear. "I'm taking care of

things my way. I don't have time to wait for the process."

Her mother drew back, startled. She glanced at the Throne, then out to the crowd.

"I see." A ghost of a smile played across her lips before she turned to greet Calliope with a warm hug before taking a seat on the Dolphin Throne.

Tarian had never felt so resentful of a piece of furniture.

She sat next to her mother and looked around at the dining table. *Everyone talking, laughing and having a good time at my expense.*

The kitchen staff moved swiftly as they served a small bowl of soup. It smelled of pumpkin and spice, and provided a welcome distraction. She raised the spoon to her lips, but paused when she noticed one man in the crowd with his face turned toward her instead of his soup bowl. *Well, well, well.* Victor Aiello had answered the call. Her gaze met his, stare for stare, over the soup spoon. After a moment, he dipped his head as a greeting and smiled. Tarian nodded at him in return.

She looked down at her spoon. It was unnerving, being stared at. He looked hungry in a way that had nothing to do with food. Had the Throne issued some sort of aphrodisiac to the crowd? *As if they'd need one.*

Tarian looked back at the crowd. Victor continued to stare. His lips curled in amusement in a lazy sort of way. She pointedly looked in another direction, hoping he'd take the hint.

"Is that who I think it is? Wasn't he arguing with Mother?" Calliope picked up the bowl of soup with both hands and sipped.

Tarian nodded. "Victor Aiello." She looked down at her soup again. "He keeps staring. I feel violated."

"He's not the only one." Calliope took another sip of soup. "Look to the left, over by the door."

Tarian casually glanced toward the door. Daric Voltain. He'd changed into a black knit shirt that didn't hide a muscle on his chest. When he caught her looking, he chuckled and his dimple winked at her. She raised an eyebrow at him, and in return he raised his glass in a silent toast. Even from this distance, she appreciated the way he was put together. Her thigh muscles tightened in anticipation of spending some quality alone time with him.

"Figures." She looked back down at her soup, making little circles in the liquid with a spoon.

"Who's that?"

"Daric Voltain. He helped me check out Chester's house tonight."

"You didn't tell me he was so hot. He's staring at Victor, I think, instead of you, now. Who, by the way, is still staring at you."

"When did my life get to be so complicated?" She asked the soup, not expecting an answer.

"It always was. You just didn't take the time to notice." Calliope nudged her with a shoulder. "Change doesn't have to be painful, you know. There are worse problems than picking which hot guy to have sex with."

"Really? Like killing a lizard? I agree."

"I didn't mean that." Calliope blushed and took another sip of soup.

A serving girl took away Tarian's bowl, leaving in its place a small plate with appetizers of various types.

"What's the point of this dinner?" Tarian stared at the plate.

"You're supposed to meet and mingle with the Potentials. I think it's so you don't feel so awkward, you know." Calliope cleared her throat.

"It's not working. I've never felt more awkward in my life. This is such a waste of time. I've already started the ritual on my own. I don't have time to wait for leaders who don't know me to pick and choose the next man to get between my legs." Tarian fought to keep the panic out of her voice. The walls inched toward her. The room seemed to swirl lazily, and the smell of fried things turned her stomach. "I only have three, maybe four days left. I can't spend them sitting here doing nothing. I've had enough."

She jumped up, nearly knocking the chair over in her haste.

"Tarian?" Her mother looked up at her, concern and irritation at war on her face.

"I need air."

Tarian almost ran out of the room by the side door, and stood taking deep breaths in the utility corridor to the kitchens. Workers scurried past, carrying plates and pitchers. More than one glanced her way with a mixture of curiosity and awe. *It's the outfit. I'm a fraud in fraud's clothing.*

She might be Scion, and she might have magical power, but the Laghairtine was stronger. Deep down, she knew it. She'd known it since he sliced through her shield in the alley. These people had no idea their Scion couldn't protect herself, let alone anyone else.

The door behind her opened, and Advisor Jonus hurried out. He slowed when he saw her. "Scion, it's time for introductions."

Tarian glared at him. "Are you a robot or something? You can't possibly be human."

"It's not as overwhelming as it may seem right now. Although the room is full of applicants, they won't all be selected. The vetting process begins in the morning, in front of a committee made up of leaders from all across the region. No more than twelve will make it through the process. And you, of course, will select the finalists."

"Gee, that's good to know. Glad I have some input." Tarian pointed at the door. "I don't even know why you bother with this charade. Might as well line them all up right now and have me spread my legs. Don't you get it? None of this matters." Her voice echoed off the walls.

Jonus folded his hands in front of him. "I understand far more than you give me credit for. I know what you are facing, and I know how you feel about this ritual, but the fact remains it has been called and will proceed regardless of other circumstances or desires. We must, by law and tradition, continue with the steps. You must participate. There is no other option."

"Seems to me like there *is* another option. Our House is under attack. I'm under attack. And all you can think about is introducing me to a bunch of strangers?" She turned away from him. "I won't put other people in danger, not even them."

She heard him take in a breath and looked back. Anxiety and frustration competed on his face. What did he have to be so upset about? It was her body!

"Scion, what are you planning?" Jonus held his hands out as though he might stop her.

"Wouldn't you like to know?" She pushed past him and stalked down the hallway. She wasn't going to admit she didn't have a plan.

She turned the corner and entered the rotunda, so focused on her anger she didn't see the man standing in her way until she plowed right into him.

chapter nineteen

Tarian caught a whiff of musk as strange arms circled her in an effort to keep them both upright. Her face planted into a broad chest, and they both struggled for balance. She tried to pull away while he tried to steady her in a clash of arms and feet. By the time she regained her composure, her fingers had curled into fists and she was ready to hit him.

He covered her fist with one large hand, his magic tickling the hairs on her arm and in her nose. The claw at the back of her neck warmed slightly. She'd only met a few men with this much latent power, and Daric was one of them. *This isn't Daric.* She looked up.

Victor Aiello looked down at her. The smile crawling across his face matched the triumphant gleam in his eyes. She jerked her hand away.

"Tarian, I'm glad I caught you." His teeth were perfectly straight and absurdly white. *He should be in a toothpaste commercial or running for government office.* "I was afraid after you rushed out I might not get a chance to apologize for my behavior. How are you feeling?" His eyes traveled down her arm and fixated on the scar.

She covered it with her hand and crossed her arms for good measure. "I'm fine."

Victor raised his eyebrows. "You seem a bit put off by the event tonight."

She shrugged.

"If I can help in any way, you'll let me know? Perhaps we can have coffee, get to know each other?" Victor held out his hand as though he expected her to take it.

She stared at it, then back at his face. "Why?" Charisma dripped off him. This was a man used to getting his own way, probably by stroking the egos of men and flirting with women.

Victor smiled and dropped his hand down by his side. "I'd love to get to know you under less trying circumstances. Even if I'm not a final candidate, you are my Scion. I would like to know my future leader better."

The way he spoke, with his head tilted slightly and his shoulder squared, made Tarian think he had no doubt he'd be a finalist, *and* that she'd select him as one of the ones to take her to bed. Leader of the Eastern Region. Political power. Money. And magical power most men didn't come close to manipulating. She supposed most women would love to bed him at least once.

I'm not most women.

"You don't seem to like how my mother runs things, Victor. What makes you think I'll be any different?"

Victor's face clouded and cleared so quickly she thought she might have imagined his expression. "Parents always seem to think they know what's best for their children, don't they? But even parents can be wrong."

"What about you, Victor? What were your parents wrong about?" She watched his face, but whatever thought darkened his eyes vanished.

"They thought the status quo was good enough, that's all. I'm much more forward thinking. Change is difficult but sometimes necessary, wouldn't you agree?"

"Maybe. If it's the right sort of change." She found herself studying his lips. They looked soft, but a bit twitchy.

"And exactly what sort of change would you like to see, Scion?" Victor's voice, barely a whisper, drifted to her on the air along with his musky power signature. "Would you like to make a difference in the world? Would you like to have a child destined to rule? Or would you like to step back and let someone else take the reins?"

The words hit home in so many ways. Tarian stared, mesmerized by them and Victor's eyes. He'd struck a nerve at the very center of her doubts. She found herself leaning toward him, without consciously trying to. There was something...very... hypnotic...

Behind Victor, the receiving hall doors creaked open; the sound echoed through the otherwise silent hallway and broke the spell. Tarian blinked.

Wow. What the hell was that?

Victor glanced at the doors then turned back with a hand outstretched. "Scion, I'm taking far too much of your time this evening. I know it's been a stressful situation for you." His smile stretched all the way to his hairline and crinkled his eyes as she shook his hand. He leaned in closer to her, both hands covering hers in a familiar grip. "Meet me for coffee. We can get to know each other, and perhaps I can help with your situation." His gaze flicked down to her arm before he released her.

Animated voices and the sound of chairs scraping against the floor drifted through the open doors.

She saw something flicker through his eyes. Anger? No. More like determination.

"I'll show myself out. Tarian, it was a pleasure. Think about my offer. I am available to you whenever you need me." Victor smiled, turned, and strode toward the entry.

Well, he certainly doesn't lack confidence. Or charisma. She stared after him. He was cool composure and fashion, bundled up with a magic string.

Voices behind her erupted into a flood of men. They quickly engulfed her in small talk, each one trying to shake her hand and give his name. Faces, names, body scents, magical signatures and an undercurrent of desperation surrounded her.

It took a few moments to realize the desperation was all her own.

Every time she tried to escape, another man stopped her. She glimpsed Advisor Jonus in the crowd and pushed her way toward him with the thought of telling him off. *He opened the doors on purpose. Probably wanted them to stop me before I did something the leaders wouldn't like.* By the time she made it halfway to her destination, he was gone.

In exasperation, she planted both feet, crossed her arms and painted a go-away expression on her face. She saw a few men hesitate, but most weren't deterred. She was the star of the moment, whether she wanted to be or not. All of them wanted a piece of her. Literally. And the ability to call themselves Potentials. It's not like they were paid. Their only reward was a one night stand and a title. *Men. Is that all they care about, labels? Sex? Does the ability to father a child without commitment turn them on this much?* Resentment burned in her chest. It was one thing to offer herself to a man in the heat of passion. It was quite another to be forced to procreate for the good of the masses. It was a violation. It was primeval.

It's really bad timing.

The tension in her shoulders reminded her of exactly what she should be doing, and it wasn't fending off men rutting around for a chance to spread their seed and call themselves Baby Daddy.

As the crowd thinned, she caught sight of Daric Voltain. He leaned against the receiving hall door with his damn dimple displayed without shame or apologies. She couldn't help looking at him in between each male body that demanded attention, or her hand, or a kiss on the cheek. His eyes danced as he watched her fend off each suitor. When she finally managed to push off the last Potential, she confronted him with righteous indignation.

"I'm glad the whole situation amuses you." She rubbed at her forehead. It ached from maintaining a frown for so long.

"You should see your face. You look like you ate something sour. Maybe you did. I take it from your display in the dining hall the call was not your idea."

"Of course not. What woman in her right mind would have set up something like this?"

"I believe, if you check the histories, it actually *was* set up by a woman. She had her reasons at the time, I'm sure."

"I'd like to give her a few reasons why she can kiss my ass."

Daric chuckled, which made his eyes twinkle in a completely adorable way.

Damn him.

"I'm not sure you appreciate the culture of this area in ancient times. Women picked among multiple partners to join them at night. Marriage, commitment, is a modern affliction. I'm sure the current rules are nothing more than a reflection of everyday life as it was. Which doesn't sound half bad, actually. At least from a woman's point of view." Daric paused. His lips twitched as he surveyed her outfit. "You clean up good."

His eyes might as well have been lasers. They created heat as they studied her body until she was sure her face was scorching red.

"You clean up fast." He did look good in the knit shirt. *Damn good.*

"It's odd timing, don't you think? The call coming after you were injured?" Daric glanced down at her arm.

"Not odd at all, if you think about it." Tarian rubbed the scar on her arm.

"I suppose not." Daric moved until he stood so close she felt the heat from his body blending with her own. "I found something that needs investigating. I was hoping you'd join me."

"I have other things I need to take care of, Daric. Besides, weren't you the one who left in a huff over my risk taking?"

"Unlike some people I could name, I'm asking for help. I'll be there to mitigate the risks, and I think I can help you formulate a plan of attack at the same time." He stood, his eyes burning a path into hers, his breath caressing her cheek and his body heat melting the tight knots in her stomach.

She put her hands on his chest to push him away, but instead of pushing she found herself leaving them to absorb the warmth. He put his hands over hers, and the lower part of her body melted. She wondered if he knew.

I hope not.

"I wouldn't ask, because I know what it will cost. But I need to track a child who's in danger, and you're the only one I know with the skill. And I believe this is tied to your own issues. We might be able to kill a few birds, or maybe a lizard, with one stone, so to speak. And save a girl at the same time." Somehow, he made the entire statement sound like an invitation for something that involved sheets and low lighting.

A cough behind her caught her attention, and she looked back over her shoulder. Alex stood in the middle of the hallway, a stare of pure malice directed at Daric.

Tarian pulled back, but not before Daric whispered "Meet me at PJ's. I'll be waiting."

She stared at him, ready to ask more questions. But he held up a hand to stop her. "Get something to eat because I'm pretty sure you didn't bother. You need your strength. But don't wait too long." He kissed her hand, his lips remaining a lot longer than they strictly needed to for a simple farewell, keeping his eyes on hers the entire time. She found it strangely seductive and tried to ignore the warm wave traveling up her arm. His signature embedded in her skin and tingled private places.

"This outfit suits you a lot better than the leather pants, but I like the jeans the best." He winked at her and walked away toward the travel alcoves.

Is he asking for my help or trying to seduce me?

She pondered what he'd said. He needed a tracker. And a little girl's life hung in the balance. A little girl somehow tied to her Laghairtine problem.

She turned back to give Alex a piece of her mind for being a jealous idiot. Clearly their little adventure had changed things, despite his promise to the contrary. But he'd been replaced by her mother and sister, with several Sentinels lined up behind them. She remembered what her sister had said about extra security and about Tarian not being allowed around the portal alcoves. It wasn't going to be easy to get out of here to meet up with Daric, even if she wanted to. She was a prisoner in her own home.

Frustrated, Tarian turned from them and stormed down the hallway to her bedroom. Heavy boots followed behind her but no clickity-clack of heels. She wondered if Calliope would tell her mother she had a secret way out. When she made it to her room and closed the door, she discovered Calliope didn't have to. Her carefully constructed back door had been sealed with magic that reeked of dolphins.

Damn it! She kicked a chair, hobbled to the bed to kick off her ridiculous shoes and nurse her injured toe. If she stayed here, the lizard won. Sooner or later, he'd have her power and she'd be his.

Don't they see? I have to get out of here. Sitting here will not help me or stop the Laghairtine or save that little girl.

Tarian pushed her shoes out of the way and paced over to the mirror. She saw a trapped princess, all dressed up and ready for market, reflected back at her. *No, thank you.* She ripped the sparkling beads out of her hair, stripped off the outfit her sister had made. She wanted to rip it off, but love for her sister made her slow down and take care with the buttons. Once she had it off, she threw it on the bed.

A soft knock on the door followed by "Tarian?" made her clench her teeth. Calliope.

"Feeling guilty?" She shouted through the door on her way to the closet. She needed jeans. T-shirt. Denim jacket. *I need to be me.*

"Tari? Please. Let me in."

"Go away."

"I didn't tell, Tari. Mother and Jonus found it while you were out."

Like hell she didn't. Tarian pulled on her jeans, shoving one leg through and then the other as if the jeans were fighting back.

"I brought a cheesesteak." Calliope singsonged.

Tarian's stomach growled in response and her mouth watered. Dammit, she really was hungry.

"Look, I know you're mad. But I think you're going to want to hear this. Don't make me shout it through the door."

Tarian snorted. Unless Calliope knew another way out of the house she didn't want to hear it. The thought made her pause. The kitchen used a serving entrance to bring in supplies, and food. The tiny entry was usually guarded, but only by one or two Sentinels. Surely the guard hadn't been increased. It'd be easy to sneak around the few who lingered at this time of night, especially if Calliope helped to distract them.

Tarian pulled on the T-shirt and crossed to the door and opened it, letting her sister in. She grabbed the plate Calliope held and sat down on the bed to eat the sandwich. She hadn't realized how hungry she was until this moment.

"Spill." She took another bite, savoring the juicy beef. *Heaven.*

"When I left, the Archivists were close to an answer. They seemed to be arguing about it actually."

"They know where to find the lizard?"

Calliope hesitated. "Not…exactly."

"This is what you came to tell me?" Tarian took the last bite of the sandwich.

"Why do I get the feeling you're trying to rush out of here?"

"Maybe because I am. Daric needs my help to save a little girl and thinks he might have a solution to my problem. Tonight. The longer I wait, the worse this is all going to get."

Her sister frowned. "Why can't you can take a team with you?"

"Nobody here would go with me, Calli. They're only interested in incarcerating me." She watched as her sister gently picked up the outfit she'd worn earlier and placed it on a hanger. It really had made her feel feminine and beautiful.

Or maybe it was Daric who'd made her feel that way.

"I don't think you should go out alone, Tari. Forget the ritual and all that. I don't want to lose my sister." Calliope turned to put the clothes back in the closet.

"You aren't losing me. And I won't be alone. Daric will be there."

"Can you trust him?"

Can I? She didn't really know him at all but somehow, she did. She trusted him. "I think so. He seems familiar somehow. Like I've known him for years." She crossed to the door, but Calliope stopped her with a hand on the door.

"Tari, wait. I need to tell you this. I checked with the Archivists after you left dinner, to see if I could start them on another query. They told me to tell you 'beware of danger from within' and 'knowledge is key.'"

Tarian turned the words over in her mind. *Danger from within.* Within herself? As in the claw? *Like I need to be told the obvious.*

Knowledge is key.

"What the hell is that supposed to mean?"

"No idea. They wouldn't tell me anything else. They wanted to tell you directly. It sounded like they *have* to tell you personally. I think you should go talk to them."

"I will, but not right now. It'll have to wait. I'll visit them when I get back. Right now what I really need is a great cup of coffee."

She grinned at her sister.

chapter twenty

Tarian stood outside PJ's, trying her best not to have flashbacks. Faint pink on the horizon did little to brighten her mood. Memories of the lizard struggle in the alley next to PJ's tied her blood in cold knots. She'd never been timid, far from it, but being so close to the alley where she'd been attacked unsettled her. *Damn that creature for making me hesitate. I can't afford to be weak. Not now.*

Calliope hadn't wanted to help her sneak out, but in the end, she'd done it after Tarian explained what she'd seen in the basement and how another little girl might suffer the same fate. Calliope loved children and her soft heart relented despite her misgivings. Her sister distracted the guards while Tarian made a portal in the entry off the back of the kitchen and popped through before anyone stopped her. She closed it as soon as her feet touched the sidewalk on the other side.

Her blood and power both trudged through her veins as though moving through an iced-over stream. Maybe the

Laghairtine had already stolen enough power to make a real dent. She flexed her arms. *Not yet.*

She needed coffee, for the routine if not the caffeine. At least it would wash away a bit of the fatigue settled on her shoulders. She stood in line and ordered her usual from a sleepy barista, moved over to the condiment bar and stirred in cream. A decent sized crowd filled the place, mostly tourists or people on their way to work. They occupied most of the small round tables, but she spotted a vacant couch in the back.

"No sugar?"

The deep voice behind her sounded amused, and the touch of warm breath on the back of her neck sent shivers all the way to her groin. *Damn the man!*

"Definitely not." She threw the stir stick away and turned. He had the same grin and dimple on his face he'd worn earlier, like she was a source of perpetual amusement. "So what's the plan?"

"Sit with me for a minute. I'll explain while you drink up."

They moved to the empty couch. She sat in one corner so she faced the door. Happy faces all around. No lizards. *Yet.*

Instead of taking the other corner, Daric sat next to her so their thighs touched. It perked her up in a way the coffee hadn't, and her groin pulsed in response, which she refused to acknowledge. *My hormones need to learn to take a back seat.*

She raised the coffee to her nose and inhaled. *One of life's pure joys, this coffee.* Not only did the aroma promise the delights within, but it temporarily overloaded any magical signatures on the air that might be infiltrating her senses. Like Daric's heady spice. She sipped and closed her eyes to savor it.

"You going to drink that or make love to it?" His eyes crinkled and his dimple deepened as he watched her.

"I might do both."

He laughed before his expression turned serious. He reached into his front pocket and pulled out a necklace, which he laid across her leg. It sparkled against the denim.

"What's this?" She picked it up. A small blue crystal on a silver chain caught and held the light.

"I'm trying to find the girl who owns it. She's about twelve. Been missing for over a week from Chester's neighborhood. No registered magic talent in her or her family."

"So no Sentinel attention." Tarian nodded and ran her fingers over the smooth stone. It gave off a slight vibration, enough to tickle her nose. If the girl didn't have overt talent, she certainly had some latent ability. This thing hummed with energy.

"And no police attention to speak of because of the neighborhood. She's been written off. I've been able to follow her movements up until she was grabbed out of the park in the Mansion. She was walking with her cousin when two men pulled up in an old clunker and grabbed them. They must have used magic, because after the initial struggle both girls entered the car on their own. The description fits Mark Chester and his cousin, Kevin. Chester's dead. Kevin's MIA. Suspect he's as dead as Chester. My leads have run dry, and judging by what you found in the basement, she's running out of time." Daric put a hand on her thigh. "Can you track her?"

Warmth ran up her thigh and onto her back from the contact, but she ignored that and stared at the necklace. *If the girl is alive, sure.* But she'd have to use magic. Magic that felt sluggish and somehow less than the day before. Not by a lot, but enough to make her uneasy. *How many times can I use my power before the Laghairtine gains control?*

"Why didn't you say all this back at the reception? Why not ask Alex or Frankie?"

"I figure they're keeping a tight lid on you now, and Alex isn't exactly my biggest fan these days." Daric narrowed his eyes at her as though he knew exactly why Alex might be so territorial. "I knew if I asked through proper channels, they'd tell me to shove it. I wouldn't blame them. I almost told myself."

She nodded. "How is this related to my little problem?"

"It's just a hunch. The girl who was killed, these girls, you… it's a pattern. Your name on the floor. Call it a gut feeling." He glanced at her arm.

"You think the Laghairtine is collecting blood from more than just me?"

"Can you track her?"

"You're avoiding the question."

"I don't know. What I do know is, if he needs these girls, we might be able to use them to flush him into the open. If she's still alive, he's not finished with whatever it is. He'll have to come back to check on her or to finish up. We save the girls, get backup and wait for him." Daric squeezed her leg. "You, me, and maybe some of your friends."

"You mean Alex." It felt odd, talking about Alex with Daric. It also felt odd to realize how quickly she'd placed the friend label on Daric.

"And anybody like him. Muscle is always useful. So, can you track her?"

Tarian thought for a moment. The horror of what happened to the girl in the basement still lingered. Now another girl, only twelve years old, was in the lizard's hands. The girl, her cousin, and possibly more. *I can't leave them there. Not when it might be my fault they're in this mess.*

Tarian gently removed Daric's hand from her thigh, taking one last sip of coffee. "Let's find out."

Daric followed her out of PJ's. Once out on the sidewalk, she hesitated. She didn't want to use the alley where she'd been attacked.

"This way." Daric led the way around to the other side of PJ's, to a red door inlaid in the brick. Behind it, narrow stairs made a steep climb to the floor above the coffee shop.

"You live here? I'd drown in coffee if I lived here." She smelled the aroma even here in the musty stairwell.

"But it'd be a tasty way to go." Daric opened another door at the top of the staircase and led her into a surprisingly modern, updated loft. It was open, with bright wood floors and very little furniture. It'd do.

"Stand over there." Tarian pointed to the corner of the room.

"Where's the trust?" Daric moved to the corner, his shoulders slumped.

"I can't concentrate with you so close."

He raised his eyebrows, and the dimple reappeared.

"I mean your signature interferes with the signal."

If anything, his dimple deepened.

"Oh, shut it." She closed her eyes and folded the necklace in her fist. Deep breath in, then slowly out. In, then slowly out. She let her heart rate lower and entered a near meditative state. If she did this with only the scent in the air, without actively pushing, she wouldn't have to draw as much power. Her talent was slow to answer the summons and weaker than she cared to admit.

She pushed the thought aside. *It doesn't matter. Finding this bastard and saving those girls does.*

The hair on the back of her neck wiggled, and an ache immediately settled in as her talent focused on the necklace in her hand. Any use of magic seemed to excite the claw. Her heart pounded at the thought. *I need to make this quick.*

It didn't take long to get a lock on the girl who'd worn the necklace. "She's alive." She took a long, relieved breath. She'd been expecting the worst.

"Where?"

"Hush."

She turned slowly, letting her magic drift out along the invisible scent in the air. Her nose hairs twitched and fought as her body rotated until she found the general direction of the source. "Not far. A couple of miles, I'd say. That direction." She pointed at his kitchen.

"What, no address?"

"I'm a compass, not a road map. Let's head that way, and I'll take another reading when we get closer."

"So we need to triangulate?"

She nodded.

Daric thought for a moment, then opened a portal. She saw a large old building in it.

"No security?" She was surprised. Living here in the city, with a Laghairtine attack nearby, and he had no shields on the apartment. *Brave man. Or foolish.*

"No need. Coming?" He stepped through ahead of her. She followed, her fist still tight around the necklace.

When they emerged, they stood in the middle of a broken sidewalk next to a park. Tarian surveyed the area. The park, the row homes…it was the same block she'd landed in earlier, looking for Chester. This time, she stood in front of the larger of the abandoned warehouses.

The warehouse huddled against the sky, a stain on the night sky. It was a cozy spot, with graffiti on every surface and boarded windows with the boards half falling off. Weeds overshadowed the walk to the front door. Broken bits of glass littered the ground,

along with empty syringes and unidentifiable bits of trash. A rat
ran across Daric's shoes as he walked toward one of the boarded
windows. The whole thing shouted, "Go away!"

"You sure can pick the spots. First a dingy basement,
now this."

"Are you kidding? This is perfect for a first date."

"Is that what this is?"

"Take another reading."

Tarian glanced around. Even though a lot of the nearby
row homes looked abandoned, she felt eyes watching them.
"Why here?"

"Can't you feel it?"

Tarian looked closer at the warehouse. "It's subtle, isn't it?"

"Easy to overlook, unless you focus up." Daric pointed to the
windows along the roof.

Tarian opened her senses and felt a distinct magic trace
coming from the upstairs window, along with a small illusion
circling the perimeter. Someone had warded the building against
any non-magical intrusion. It wasn't strong. *No wonder I didn't
notice it before. I was too focused on Chester.* It was enough to
keep those with no magic out without even knowing they were
avoiding the place. They'd simply walk on by. She didn't feel any
other magic trace. No lizard. At least, not nearby.

"Hang on." Tarian closed her eyes and focused once more on
the crystal necklace in her fist. The signal rebounded on her, red
hot, making her nostrils flare. She was as close as she was going to
get without being right on top of the girl.

A bolt of pain hit her neck and traveled up into her scalp,
where a headache bloomed. The lizard made a grab for her along
the open pathway of magic she'd used. A wave of nausea swept
over her. She gasped and shut down her power fast. Energy

rebounded and nearly knocked her right onto her ass.

"What the hell?" Daric grabbed her arms to steady her.

She gritted her teeth, waiting for her stomach to stop flip-flopping. "Lizard."

"Shit. We have to move. I could put up a shield but no telling if it'd work." Daric nodded to the building in front of them. "That's made of steel and cinderblock. Natural signal blockers."

Daric pointed to the side of the building. Tarian followed him down the tight alley between the warehouse and the home next to it. Glass and other debris crunched under her shoes. At the back of the building, a loading dock broke up the brick exterior. Metal steps led to a door to the left of the dock. Rusted locks remained firmly in place on the door. The dock entry also looked rusted shut.

Daric placed his hand on the padlock. He grunted, and Tarian felt a tight pulse of energy as the lock broke apart, raining pieces down on the metal steps. The clang rang through the quiet alley. Skitters and screeches answered it. "Water can be so destructive, don't you agree?" He grinned, and ushered her through.

Inside, they found the entire floor gutted. Empty beer cans littered the floor, strange rusted metal pieces lay at odd angles, and an old metal desk chair with the bottom gone sat alone in the middle of it all like a throne. The stench of decay and urine brought tears to her eyes. Even though they were cracked and filthy, windows set high in the wall let in enough light from the outside street lamps for them to see. One rickety metal staircase rose from the trash on the far right side of the vast space and disappeared through the concrete ceiling to the floor above.

"I'm not climbing that," Tarian said.

"Well, you're not making a portal here. You already have his attention, no sense sending him an invitation to the party. Not until we're ready for him." Daric opened a portal and they jumped to the second floor without taking the rickety stairs.

The second floor housed derelict musty offices. Dust lay an inch thick on the floor. No footprints. No scuff marks. Still, Tarian felt someone in the building. Several someones. She heard nothing, but the feel of a human presence was unmistakable.

Daric stepped ahead of her, checking each office as he went. They found two girls in the last office. They lay inside a red circle drawn on the floor, their heads pointed toward the center. Duct tape kept their mouths shut and bound their hands and feet. Neither one even twitched at their approach.

Red symbols covered all four walls. On closer inspection, Tarian discovered the red was dried blood rather than paint. "Scion" was written in neat red letters in the center of the circle at the girls' heads. She shivered.

Pulling out his phone, Daric snapped pictures of the walls. Tarian moved closer to inspect the girls. The youngest had to be the one who owned the necklace. The child's chest rose and fell in a natural enough rhythm. They still lived, but a spell held them here. *It might just be a simple sleep spell.*

Tarian glanced down at the graffiti on the floor. It was old fashioned, archaic even, to draw a power circle. They weren't really necessary. Magic was innate...something Society members were born with, like brown hair or blue eyes. Circles had been used a long time ago as a way to focus power, but it turned out it was more of a placebo effect. Those with the ability focused power with or without a circle. All it took was belief and confidence.

She'd been taught about them, of course, because it was a part of history. Everyone learned about power circles, and everyone created their own power symbol as part of their naming day. She'd drawn her own over the rune in the center of the receiving hall, the same rune glowing because of the Succession Ritual. But other than symbolic gesture, she'd never needed one to gather more power. She couldn't imagine the lizard did either.

So why draw one?

"These markings make no sense." Daric snapped a few more pictures. "Some belong to a couple of different power rituals I've seen, but some don't. I have no idea what these are." He gestured to the wall closest to him. "They look like gibberish."

"Maybe it's all for show?" She shrugged and pointed to the floor. "Why the circle? I don't feel any power coming from it. So what's the point?"

"No idea. But clearly whoever it is values this location. It's not a full circle yet, but when it is…" Daric's voice trailed off.

"You think he's coming back?"

Daric pointed at the girls lying so still on the floor. "There's only two. This sort of thing needs five, I think."

"What do you suppose he's going to do with them?"

Daric met her look with a grim one of his own.

She thought of the girl in the basement and shuddered. There was no way she'd let the Laghairtine do the same to these girls. "We have to get them out of here."

"Agreed." He turned to look at the circle. "He's calling you out again."

"I saw that. How'd he even know I'd come here?"

Daric moved into the circle and knelt by the youngest girl. "Good question."

The Laghairtine might use a spy, but the idea didn't sit well. It would have to be someone very close to her. Only Calliope knew where she was tonight. No way Calli would have told on her.

"Something's wrong with this girl. She's having trouble breathing. I can't break the spell, either." Daric bent over the tallest girl and felt her wrist, then her neck. "Her pulse is way too slow. Even in a sleeping spell, it wouldn't be this erratic. They might be drugged. We need to move them out of this circle and get this crap off them."

He stood, then pulled the girl up by the arms and dragged her toward the edge of the circle. Tarian stepped toward the youngest girl.

"Tarian, wait!" Daric's shout reached her as her foot crossed the circle.

She realized too late exactly what was going on. Old fashioned or not, this circle contained hidden power, and she'd crossed the line.

chapter twenty-one

Energy radiated out from the center of the circle as though a bomb exploded. The force of it lifted the smallest girl off the floor and tossed her like a dog's toy. It gripped Tarian with icy talons and scraped her insides. The claw in her neck scraped at her skin as though trying to dig its way out.

Daric toppled as the power hit him, taking the oldest girl down with him in a heap.

Pain reverberated through Tarian's body as the force surrounded the claw and attacked the shield protecting it. She couldn't move. If she'd been able to breathe, she'd have screamed. She fell to her knees.

Frantic, she reached for her own magic to solidify the protection she had in place around the evil piece the lizard left behind. Mistake. Bad mistake. The Laghairtine latched onto her power from wherever he was hiding and wove it into his own spell.

In the next moment, the outer part of the shield cracked. It ripped away from the claw as though some unseen hand snatched a bandage off an old wound. The unbound energy stabbed and seared its way through her skin. Power leaked through with it, carried away into the air and out.

Tarian gripped her neck and tried to scream, but the sound stuck in her throat.

Focus. Focus, dammit. Focus!

Something hit her on the head. The force pushed her over onto her side. She kicked and hit something soft. *There. Contact. Take this, you bastard!*

A low moan followed by "Tarian!"

Shit. Daric. Trying to break the spell. She stopped thrashing, but couldn't take her hands off the throbbing, white hot knot of agony at the base of her neck. Daric grabbed her feet and pulled her out of the circle.

Daric left her near the door to the room, away from the circle, and raced back to the center. Tarian squinted through the pain as he did some sort of jig or wild dance. *What the hell?* The youngest girl fell to the floor with a soft thump. The lizard's hold on Tarian stopped with a snap, power rebounded back to the circle with a crack and evaporated. She screamed at the sudden release and headache that flared up behind her eyes.

Clutching her head in shaking hands, Tarian curled into a fetal position and laid still, eyes closed. Her thoughts centered on the pain like it was a beast to be wrestled to the ground.

Noise. Pain. Light. Pain. Pain. Pain. Breathe. Breathe. Breathe.

She chanted the words, and tried to make her breath match the rhythm.

Warmth and spice at her back and neck cascaded over and around her, but stopped at the mound of claw plus what remained of the protective shield. She submitted to Daric's energy, letting it wash away the terror and pain until it was gone. All except the headache that kept sticking the back of her eyeball with a hot poker.

Gently, she felt at the back of her neck and met Daric's hand. She clutched at it then held it in place as she felt gingerly through the skin, letting her awareness sink lower into the shield and claw.

The outer layer of shielding around the claw was gone, leaving the claw plus one last thin layer of defense, weak and hot underneath her skin. Her mouth ran dry. In those few seconds, the lizard siphoned quite a bit of her power and destroyed half of her protection.

Fear coursed through her. The deadline, it seemed, had been moved up. Just like that.

"Shit." Daric breathed. "Shit shit shit."

"Yeah." She couldn't even get to her feet yet. Her eyesight blurred with each pulse of pain. Tarian moaned, and rubbed at her eyes.

"Let me." Daric pushed her hands away and placed his palms over her eyes. The gentle pressure and heat diminished the pain some.

"How the hell do you do that?"

"Hold still." Daric encased the top of her head in his hands. More warmth. Less pain.

He moved around behind her and massaged at her shoulders, sending tiny pulses of energy and heat through them.

Tarian opened her eyes slowly, testing her vision against the light of the room. Everything jumped to crystal clear focus and the stabbing stopped. "You should sell that. It's better than aspirin." Her voice felt harsh against the raw meat of her throat. *I need a drink.*

Daric helped her up and kept her steady with his arms around her. "What did he get?"

"Enough." She forced air in and out in an effort to slow her pulse. Panic wouldn't help this situation. "He cracked the shield. Dammit."

"I'm sorry, Tarian. I didn't get what your title in the center meant until too late. A targeted spell, a blind one. It would only be triggered by you. I didn't think he'd get through these walls. I didn't feel any energy from the circle at all until you crossed the line."

"I don't think he was close. I felt something when we arrived, but nothing like this." She waved at the room. "This was nothing more than a well-placed trap. The basement was probably supposed to have one too. But it didn't go off." She rested against Daric for a moment while she tried to get her breath, and wits, back. The warmth of his chest did more to calm her than anything.

"Can you seal it? The shield?" He rubbed her back in a soft up and down stroke. Every touch helped relax her. *Oh, heavens, he really should sell that.*

Tarian shook her head. "On my own? Probably not. It took three women and the Dolphin Throne to put it in place."

"You should get out of here. Go build another one. Get inside the walls of Xannon."

"Not until we get these girls out. He'll kill them if we don't."

"He might kill you if we do."

She pulled out of his arms and looked into his eyes. "He doesn't want to kill me. If he did I'd be dead already."

It hurt to admit, but there it was. *Truth.*

Tarian looked over at the girls. Both were now back on the floor, unaware they'd been used. "Why did he need them? Were they bait?"

"Not sure. The markings make no sense." Daric stepped back from her but held his hands out as if he thought she'd fall right over.

"I'm fine. Go take care of them."

"Look, we're going to figure it out. Everybody has a weakness. We'll find his."

"So it's 'we' now, is it?" Tarian rested and studied him as he released the spell on the girls. Even the relatively small bit of power he used indicated how much more he had in reserve. His power matched hers in strength, under normal circumstances. *Water based. No wonder he feels so good.*

Daric comforted each girl they woke, making small reassuring noises. He asked each one her name. The oldest, Latisha, pointed at her cousin. "That's Kia. Please don't hurt her, she's just a baby."

"Shush now, nobody's hurting anybody." Daric glanced at Tarian. "Anymore."

Daric worked on each girl in turn, his hands gentle and soothing, making circular motions on their backs. He whispered calm words and smiled. Each girl smiled, probably taken in by his ridiculous dimple. Tarian couldn't help but smile with them. He conveyed kindness and safety in a few well-chosen words and thoughtful hands.

The scent of spice filled Tarian's nostrils as he expended his talent. She detected healing, though not exactly what, and empathy, and something else she couldn't name. And the soft caress of ocean waves. *Surprising he doesn't live closer to water.*

Tarian admired the way his muscles rippled as he tore the duct tape off their feet and hands. He lifted Kia and placed her on her feet, then ran his hands through her braids as he sorted out the butterfly clips holding them in place. All the while he uttered soothing words.

Bet that feels great.

Embarrassed at the direction her thoughts were going, Tarian cleared her throat and went to help Latisha to her feet. Even with the duct tape removed the poor girl struggled to breathe.

"Something's wrong here." Tarian glanced at Daric. He patted Kia on the shoulder, before turning to take Latisha's head in his hands. A second later he moved his hands down to her chest. Her struggle eased almost immediately.

"Asthma." He muttered. "Do you have an inhaler with you, sweetie?"

"I...left it." Latisha sputtered, and started to cry.

"Don't worry, honey, you'll be okay. We'll get it for you." Daric kept his hands still for another minute, and she stopped crying and struggling. Instead, she looked as though she'd lapsed into some sort of trance.

"Tell me what happened." Daric's voice was low, haunting, seductive. Latisha began to speak, while Kia burrowed into Tarian's side and clung as though she held a life-raft in the middle of the ocean. With their bodies touching, Tarian detected the faintest whiff of ozone, like the air after a summer thunderstorm. It matched the residue on the necklace Tarian still had in her pocket.

She has talent. Air. I knew that necklace wasn't lying.

Tarian squeezed the girl's shoulders. When this was all over, they'd have to come back and check on her. How Kia had come by magic in a Philly neighborhood surrounded by regular humans was anyone's guess. But she'd need help as she matured.

After a few soothing words and questions from Daric, it was obvious the last thing either of them remembered was Kevin and Mark Chester talking to them at the park, and climbing into a car. Neither remembered anything after that.

Just as well.

Tarian looked over the girl's head at Daric. "It's not smart to keep them talking here."

Daric coaxed addresses out of them and created a large travel portal. The travel experience would jar them on top of everything else they'd been through, but it couldn't be helped.

They stepped through as a group, with Tarian holding Latisha's hand tightly and Daric holding Kia in his arms. As they stepped out on the other side, both girls gasped, and Latisha coughed, a loud barking sound sure to wake the neighbors.

Daric set Kia down and rubbed Latisha's back, took her face in his hands and stared deeply into her eyes. He looked like he was trying to hypnotize the poor girl. *Maybe it would have been better to leave them in the thrall of the sleep spell until we got them home.*

When Daric took his hands away from Latisha's face, Tarian watched, dumbfounded, as she smiled, turned and walked serenely into her home without another cough, word or backward glance.

"Kia lives pretty close. Let's walk it." Daric took Kia by the hand and the three of them set off down the dark street.

When they reached Kia's tiny row home, they stopped outside the rickety porch adorned with plastic Jesus statues. Tarian took in the decor of crosses, nativity scenes, and general religious paraphernalia with interest. She'd never understood the need for this sort of thing but found it fascinating anyway. Her own beliefs centered on the power in all living things, not some mystical creature in the sky. Still, she supposed to these people, her friends the dolphins or the Archivists with their ancient magic, would seem like gods.

Daric took Kia's face in his hands. Tarian expected the same vacant smile and was ready for her to drift off into her house, but instead, the girl giggled as he finished.

"Thanks for saving us. You don't gotta worry. I won't tell."

The startled look on Daric's face made Tarian smile. So his talent wasn't all powerful.

"Promise?" Daric grinned at Kia.

She nodded. "You're different. I like you. You gotta name?"

Daric chuckled. "I do. It's Daric."

Kia looked at Daric from underneath her eyelashes, a sly smile on her face. "You come round here much?"

"I will now I've met you. I like you too, Kia. Now be good, and no more walking through the park alone. Okay? Promise?"

"Promise." She gave a solemn nod.

He gave her a hug, and Tarian handed the necklace she'd used to track to Kia back to the girl. She took it and fastened it around her neck, then skipped up to the front door of her home. Before she opened it, she paused and turned back. "Don't forget to come see me. You promised." She blew a kiss to Daric, and entered the house.

"I think you have a fan." Tarian laughed.

"Well, I always did have a way with women."

"What did you do?"

"A memory wipe. At least I tried to."

Screams filled the air as Kia entered. Someone inside sounded very excited to have her back. Shouts of "Praise Jesus" drifted through the open door.

"So that's your talent."

"Useful in situations like this. It's not easy with this much trauma. And didn't work on Kia at all. I bet Latisha remembers some of it anyway. Hopefully, it'll just seem like nightmares."

"Would it work on me?" Tarian studied Daric's face in the dim light from Kia's living room window.

"No. You're Society. It only works on non-magical types."

Good to know. "Kia is definitely magical. Air based. But undeveloped."

Daric nodded. "Someone really should come back to see her sometime. She'll need help when she hits puberty."

"Pretty sure she expects you to do the honors." Tarian poked his arm. "You're such a charmer."

Daric flickered his eyes at her. "I have my moments."

"And you have such a small ego." Tarian rubbed the back of her neck. The muscles were stiff and sore, like she'd worked out for hours with heavy weights. "Any idea what those markings on the wall were? Or why the Laghairtine needed these girls in the first place?"

Daric took out his phone and displayed the picture he'd taken.

"Looks like an old-style focus ritual, but I have no idea which one. I've seen some of these markings before, but others make no sense."

Tarian grabbed the phone out of Daric's hand, but static obliterated the image.

Daric snatched it back from her. "Hey, watch it! What are you doing?" He tapped the screen, and the static cleared.

"Let me see the picture." She held out her hand, and her foot tapped a staccato on the sidewalk.

Daric moved the phone closer to her. The static returned. He moved it away. The static disappeared. He shook his head.

"Not a chance. You're some sort of destructive force of nature. No way I'm letting you wipe these images." He held the phone away from her.

"Oh, I am *not*. Don't be ridiculous." Tarian darted to the side and snatched the phone out of his hand. She managed to see the image for about two seconds before even the static disappeared. The blank screen glared in silent accusation.

"Well, shit." Blood rushed to her ears. Tarian handed the useless thing back to Daric without looking him in the eye.

"Great. Thanks." He put it in his pocket. "You go home and catch your breath while I take more photos of the walls."

"Catch my breath? Seriously? Is that code for something?"

"Like what, Scion?" Daric opened a travel portal. She saw the entry alcove in it.

"You trying to handle me?"

"*You* obviously can't go back to the warehouse. Now we've sprung his trap, the Laghairtine will be watching for you. And I need photos of those markings and any trace evidence before he scrubs the place like he did that basement."

"You don't know he did that. You don't know it was him at all." The lizard's signature had been in the basement, but she wasn't about to tell Daric. *Not now, you jerk.*

Daric stared at her as though she'd sprung a third eye in the middle of her forehead. "Your title was on the floor, Scion. The person you were looking for died in your house, Scion. This entire scenario is custom made for you, *Scion.*"

Tarian stomped her foot. "And that's why it has to be me going after this guy. Me. Scion."

"Stubborn. They have a word for women like you where I come from."

Tarian narrowed her eyes at him. "Try it. Just try it."

"I will. But not now. Go home. I'll get the photos and look for clues; you rebuild the shield. Maybe get backup. I'll meet up with you once I have these markings analyzed." He gestured toward the open portal. "After you, Scion."

Tarian glared at him. *Damn the man.* "Who the hell do

you think you are? What makes you think you have any sort of leadership responsibility in this scenario? This is my life. You don't get to tell me what to do."

"All evidence to the contrary." Daric wiggled a finger at her neck. "You have a claw embedded in your neck, and the shield created to isolate it is cracked. If I hadn't been there, you'd be his puppet by now. You're losing magic every minute and the only reason the lizard doesn't have control of you right this second is because I temporarily severed the link. Not to mention you need to complete the Succession Ritual before the Laghairtine gets a chance to do it on his own terms. I think I have every right to tell my Scion she's in over her head."

"Screw you."

"I'd love to but now's not the time. Look, are we going to have foreplay all night? I can think of better locations." Daric indicated the portal.

It wasn't safe for her to be out on these streets. But to admit that Daric was right struck a raw nerve. "I got news for you. It'll take a hell of a lot more than this to get into my bed." She stalked over to the portal and stepped through.

chapter twenty-two

Tarian stormed through the entry and into the rotunda, her thoughts in turmoil. The man was completely frustrating. And right. *Dammit.*

She nearly tripped over the small, furry, gargoyle-like statue in the center of the room, highlighted by early morning sunbeams. The Archivist sprung to life as she reached it. She'd never seen one move so quickly.

"Scion plays a dangerous game."

"I'm not playing games. What're you doing out here?"

Voices erupted to the point she couldn't make out any words. In defense, she pulled her hands away, breaking the contact. She waited for a count of five, then held her hands out again, and the Archivist leapt up. When it made contact, the voices were jumbled but more subdued.

"I can't understand you all at once like that."

"Scion must know. Scion is vulnerable. Scion must beware of danger from within."

"You know, that's pretty cryptic. If you're worried I'll somehow let the Laghairtine have his way with me, don't. There's no way I'm going to have sex with a lizard. Not happening."

Voices jumbled again. She made out "sex," "join," "ritual," but not a lot made sense. This time, she waited for them to calm down. Exhaustion crept up her spine and made a home in her shoulders. *What I wouldn't give for a nap.*

"Scion must beware the ritual and the choices. No treasure is worthy."

Why did they insist on repeating the same phrase? It wasn't helping her understand any better. She shrugged.

"What treasure?"

Silence greeted her. Odd after her head had been so filled with voices.

"Come on, speak up. What treasure are you talking about?"

The voices stopped. One continued in the void. *"One query at a time. Query is already running. Do you wish to abort?"*

"It's not a query. It's just a question."

"One query only."

"I don't care what your rules are. You brought this up; now explain yourselves."

Indignation filled the voices. *"WE are not servants."*

"No, you're not." She pushed. "You live in the House of Xannon. That makes you family. And family helps each other out. Got it?"

The voices muttered. She heard the word "family" repeated several times.

"What treasure?"

"Scion asks the wrong question."

"Scion thinks you're avoiding the subject. Are you trying to say there's something that will help me out of this situation?"

Mutters filled her head. Angry ones.

"But you don't want me to use it?"

A long pause was followed by an actual verbal squeak from the creature in front of her. They seemed pretty upset for such a simple question. *Interesting.* Her pulse quickened.

"What is this treasure? You might as well tell me. If you don't, how will I know what to avoid?" The argument sounded lame to her ears, but still.

She waited. They argued amongst themselves. She caught flashes of images. An old woman. A book.

"What's that book?"

Anger rippled through the thoughts in her head. The creature tried to pull his hands away but she held on tight.

"Oh, no, you aren't running away that easy. You brought it up. Now you have to explain. What book is that?"

A single voice full of reluctance filled her head. *"The Book of Daemon."*

She'd never heard of such a thing. "And what's in it?"

"Knowledge."

She rolled her eyes. *Ask a stupid question.* She tried again. "What specific knowledge does it contain?"

"Daemons. History. Spells." The voice sounded defeated.

The word "spells" made her ears perk up. A book of spells, specifically for daemons? Was there a spell that would stop the Laghairtine stealing her power? Destroy him? Trap him? Something? He was, after all, part daemon. The thought made her almost dizzy with excitement. Or hope.

"Where is it?"

"No treasure is worth the price."

She let out a long sigh. "He'll kill me if I don't get it. He will destroy this House. Is that what you want? You live here too, you know. To me, some things are worth the price. Whatever that is."

They muttered. Finally one voice responded, *"Current location is not definitively known."*

Of course it wasn't. It would be too easy to think the book was sitting here in her archives.

"Scion must understand before Scion makes promises." The voice, urgent, also filled her heart with defeat and sadness. As though the information was painful to divulge or worse, held consequences for them or for her.

She kept her tone gentle. "Understand what?" Tarian knelt beside the Archivist. "Tell me. What do I need to know?"

Mutters. Voices. Arguments. Finally, one voice above the others. *"To receive, one must give. To give, one must understand. To agree is to vow. Vow cannot be broken. No treasure is worth the price."*

"All actions have consequences. Yes, I understand." She nodded. Every step she'd taken in the last few days had dire consequences. Why tell her this now?

Confused, she stood up, letting the Archivist's hand drop. He dissolved without another attempt to communicate.

What about that was so important that he left the archives? I don't get it.

First he told her about a book that might solve all her problems and seemed at war for doing so, like it was something she should not use, then he mentioned making promises as though that were the most important thing. He'd handed a breakthrough of sorts, yet obviously didn't want her to use it. *Odd. Why tell me at all?*

Angry voices drifted through the partially open doors of the receiving hall, startling her from her thoughts. Surprised, she pulled one open further to hear better. Her mother appeared to have the upper hand in the conversation, but Advisor Jonus raised his voice and gestured with more animation than Tarian had ever seen from him.

"Absolutely not. She shouldn't be anywhere near that woman, especially now. I don't care what book she's hiding." Her mother stalked from one side of the platform to the other.

"Keeper, I understand your concern, but Tarian is the only one who is capable of reaching her. All other ways have been blocked. She won't come to us. We must go to her."

"Then I'll go myself."

"Begging your pardon, but that's simply not possible. Sucole lives on the edge of the Between. Only someone with a foot in both planes can even get near her front door, much less go inside. The Scion has the right..." Jonus cleared his throat. "Background. You don't."

What book? Who's Sucole? Curious, Tarian pushed the door all the way open. "Did someone say my name?"

Her mother paused mid-step. The startled look on her face would have been amusing in other circumstances.

"Who is Sucole?" Tarian crossed the room on a direct path for her mother.

"As I was saying to Advisor Jonus, it's out of the question." Her mother shot a look of pure poison at Jonus.

He cleared his throat but didn't look away.

Tarian reached the platform and stopped. *It sure is a long way up.*

"Does this have anything to do with the *Book of Daemon*?"

Her mother's eyes widened. Advisor Jonus coughed.

Her mother turned to Jonus, pure fury in her eyes. Tarian saw the Dolphin Throne begin to glow in response to her mother's anger and spoke quickly to ease the tension.

"He didn't say anything to me, Mother. It's not his fault."

Tarian sat on the bottom step. She needed to rest. Just for a minute.

"Tarian. What's happened?" Marielle appeared in front of her, eyes full of concern.

"I stumbled into a trap." She didn't even bother lying. Her mother would know, anyway. She always did. "The shield…"

Marielle took a quick breath in then reached around to the back of Tarian's neck. A couple of seconds was all it took.

"Get up. Now. In the chair. Jonus, get chocolate. And coffee."

The two of them hustled Tarian into the Dolphin Throne. Jonus ran for the side door and disappeared through it.

Tarian leaned back and closed her eyes. Dolphins sang in her ears, and ocean air revived her senses. "I'll be fine."

"I'm not sure you understand that word." Marielle touched Tarian's shoulder, and power streamed from mother to daughter. Tarian soaked it up as though it were a last meal.

"I've put some cushion on the shield, but not as it was before. We could do more, if we summon Calliope."

Tarian shook her head. "No time, and she's exhausted. Let her sleep. I just need to rest a minute or two. And coffee sounds great." Tarian opened her eyes. "Really. I'm fine. This has to be done, and you heard Jonus. I have to do it. Someday you'll have to explain to me how I came by the right background. But not today."

Marielle's face froze.

"You cannot go after that woman in this state."

"Power doesn't exist in the Between, right? So that's exactly where I should go."

Marielle squeezed Tarian's arm. "It's not that it doesn't exist, it's that it cannot be used in the normal way. But Sucole is not normal."

The side door opened and Jonus returned carrying a tray. He placed it on the table next to Tarian and she took up the coffee with relish.

"Pardon, Keeper, but Sucole is harmless. Her residence is more dream than reality. And perhaps the Scion is right. So near the Between, her own struggle might be diminished."

Marielle glared at him but offered no argument. He cleared his throat and muttered, "The book was last seen in her possession."

Marielle leaned against the table. "Eat the chocolate, Tarian. You need sugar."

Her mother closed her eyes, and the Throne glowed. *What the hell is she doing?*

After a moment, her mother sighed and opened her eyes. The look she gave Tarian was one of exasperation and fear. "Is there any way you can do this from here? From this room?"

Tarian shook her head. "I can't track from inside the house. Too much interference."

Keeper Marielle nodded and stared at Tarian as if she'd never seen her daughter before.

Tarian took her mother's hand and squeezed it. "I've been trained to fight. I control three elements of power, more than anyone has seen in generations. I can do this."

"This woman is…difficult. No amount of magic will make her easier to deal with. The book itself is dangerous. I'm not sure the risk is worth it."

No treasure is worth the price. The price of a daughter's life. Her mother's unspoken words resounded loud and clear to Tarian's heart. *She wants to protect me.* Before, Tarian would have thought it smothering. Now, facing an impossible enemy, it gave her a steady place to stand. To fight.

"I won't point out the obvious." Tarian put a hand on the back of her neck and rubbed at the knot. Next to a Laghairtine, dealing with one difficult woman should be a lot easier. She needed the book. Screw the Archivists. "Who is she? How do you know about this book?"

Her mother gestured at Jonus, who cleared his throat again and stepped forward. He held a coin out to Tarian.

"Sucole Poole was once a powerful member of Society, with a strong base in both Water and Earth. She loved research. She actually worked in this very house when young, with the Archivists."

Tarian took the coin and examined it while he spoke.

"One day, she followed her research down an unfortunate path with the consequence she had to be removed from Society. She's in self-imposed exile near the Between, but she left this as a way to find her in an emergency. I'm not even sure how it works."

Jonus shuffled from one foot to the other, and clenched his hands in front of him. "She has knowledge, and she was the last to possess the book. If anyone knows where it might be, it's her. No daemon would give us the information, even if we asked, since the book could be used against them."

No wonder the Archivist didn't want to tell me.

Tarian studied the coin. It was about the size of a quarter, but instead of a heads and tails it had raised bumps all over one side, and on the other, words etched into the metal.

"There are none so blind as those who will not see."

"Very philosophical." Tarian ran her fingers over the raised bumps. *Braille?* "Is she blind?"

"She is…constricted." Jonus sounded stiff.

"How strong is she?" Tarian looked at her mother, then Jonus. Her mother spoke first.

"It's not a question of power or strength. She can't use her magic to attack anymore, or I'd never let you go at all. She's paying a high price for dabbling where she shouldn't have." Her mother's lips quirked. "A lesson other people should learn."

"I don't dabble." Tarian closed her hand around the coin and let her senses drift along it. A hint of a signal drifted back to her. Wherever Sucole Poole was, it was a long way from the Pacific.

"Tarian if you do this, you should know she's not the most reliable of people. She's been twisted by life and by practicing things she didn't understand. She can't be trusted, even though she can do no direct physical harm to you. I'm not sure the book is worth the price you might have to pay."

No treasure is worth the price.

Her mother's words echoed those of the Archivists so closely, it gave Tarian goose bumps.

"Does anyone have any clue where she lives?"

Jonus shook his head. "No, Scion."

"Guess I'll have to do this the hard way."

"I suppose you'll ignore anything I say, at this point." Her mother frowned.

"That all depends on what you say." Tarian smiled. "If you tell me I should do whatever it takes to solve this threat to our family, I'll listen one-hundred percent. If you tell me I should sit in my room and wait for disaster to strike, I'll find another way out. Again."

"Nobody is saying we should wait for disaster. But there's a time for caution and prudence. A time to plan and strategize."

"So I've been told. This book *is* the plan. I don't know what else to do. And I only have a couple of days left. Everyone else is doing their part to solve this. I have to do mine. You understand that, right?" Tarian rubbed the coin. "I need to complete the ritual and find a way to stop the lizard, or the Dolphin Throne is up for grabs. That's the reality. And it's all sitting on my shoulders. It's not like you can complete the ritual for me, Mother."

Her mother looked at her so long, Tarian's face heated up under the scrutiny.

"You have help here, Tarian. Here, you are protected by the magic embedded in the very framework of the house. Here, you have a buffer against the threat. And the Throne itself is not helpless. Neither is the person who sits on it."

"I don't have the right to call on the Throne's protection without you, and if I don't solve this problem, I'll never have the right. Some puppet form of me will. And I'm not going to let that happen. I'm not."

"Neither am I." Marielle patted Tarian's shoulder.

"Tarian, you are my daughter. Your safety, above everything else, is my concern. Please don't put yourself at risk by rushing in where you should pause and think. Sucole speaks in riddles. Be sure you've solved them before you move forward."

"What harm will a riddle do? I'm not planning on doing anything but tracking her down, asking for the book and leaving. It's as simple as that."

"Life is rarely simple."

Her mother's eyes were so full of pride, frustration, and concern, Tarian felt herself stand straighter. She wanted to be worthy of it in her mother's eyes. "So I'm beginning to understand."

She left her mother staring after her, Jonus beside her as the ever-faithful watchdog.

chapter twenty-three

As she left the receiving hall, Tarian encountered a stone-faced Alex leaning against the wall. The entry Sentinels appeared to have gone on a sudden break.

She held out her hands as if to say "let me have it," and Alex obliged.

"Where did you go, *chica*? What the hell happened? I heard you. The shield is cracked, the lizard got a piece of you and now you're heading out to do God knows what near the Between? Alone? You know the dudes in the kitchen are being disciplined now."

"I didn't mean to get them in trouble, Alex. I had to go out."

"Out where? What's more important than your safety, Scion?" Alex stood in front of her, an immovable mountain.

"How about a little girl's safety, Alex? Two of them, to be exact. Two innocent, beautiful girls ripped away from their lives and their families, because of me. How's that for a reason?"

"That sounds like a job for Sentinels not Scions."

"Sentinels couldn't have found them without my help. And Sentinels couldn't have stopped what happened. It was the right thing to do, no matter what the consequences. It's who I am, Alex. It's who I'm meant to be. I am a shield for my people. And I'd do it again." Though, looking back, she might not underestimate the Laghairtine. He'd left two taunts that did nothing, so she'd expected nothing when she encountered the third. *Very clever.*

Alex shook his head. "How you gonna be the great protector if you're dead, *chica*?"

"He doesn't want to kill me. I'd be dead already if he did." Tarian ran her fingers through her hair. This discussion hit familiar chords. It sounded remarkably like the one she'd had with Daric. *What is it with men?*

Alex studied her in silence. When he spoke, his voice was lower, more like a whisper. Subdued. Very un-Alex-like.

"That why Voltain was hitting on you?"

"He wasn't hitting on me." She caught the glint in Alex's eyes and relented. "Not exactly. But yes, he asked for my help in finding these girls, so I helped. Just like I helped you when you asked for it."

"Yeah, see how that turned out." Alex puffed air out his nose like a rhinoceros getting ready to charge. "You shouldn'ta done it, *chica*. You shouldn't be sneaking out."

"I didn't exactly have time to assemble an army, Alex. We had to move fast, and we had to be quiet. You know what happened to Chester. You know what would have happened to those girls. I couldn't let it. It's because of me they were even taken."

"You don't know that."

"I do. I really do, Alex."

"Explain it to me, *chica*. Make me understand why your life was worth risking."

"Daric knew Chester and his cousin snatched these girls, but he didn't know where they were taken. When we found them, they were under a sleep spell in an abandoned warehouse, surrounded by really old ritual markings, a power circle, and my title written in blood on the floor. We pulled them out and took them home."

Alex shook his head. "That ain't the whole story. I heard you talking to the Keeper. What about that claw thing?"

Tarian rubbed the back of her neck and winced. Still sore. "He'd set a trap."

"So he knows you well enough to bait you. Not good, *chica*."

"I know, Alex. I know."

Alex rubbed his jaw. "So what's the plan? What's this thing you're looking for?"

"We know the lizard will go back. He wasn't done. We need a way to catch him when he shows up. This thing is a book that has information we need."

"What you mean by 'we?' You mean you and Daric?" Alex thrust out his chin. "You mean you and Calliope? You and the Keeper? 'Cause I know you don't mean you and me."

Seeing the hurt look on his face made her pause. "You have a problem, Alex?"

"Yeah, I got a problem. My best friend ain't including me."

"I had to go, Alex."

"With Daric, you mean." Alex clenched his teeth, causing a rigid line along his mouth.

"Dammit, Alex, you knew you wouldn't be the only one. That's what this is about, isn't it? You think I'm going to choose Daric, and you don't approve."

"We don't know him, *chica*."

Tarian stamped her foot. "Hell, Alex, I don't know any of

the others either. I have to do this, and I'm not going to keep apologizing for it. It is what it is." She blinked in irritation, willing her eyes to stop tearing up.

They stood in silence, glaring at each other. A Sentinel patrol stepped into the room then quickened their pace when they saw the storm brewing between the two of them. Tarian waited for the echo of their footsteps to fade before she finally spoke.

"What would you have me do, Alex? Sit in my room? Wait it out? Refuse to do the rest of the ritual? What? If you were Scion, what would you do?"

Alex looked down at his feet. When he looked back at her, his face relaxed and his eyes softened. "I don't have the right body parts for the job."

Tarian thrust out her chest. "Boobs do help, I have to admit."

Alex rubbed the scruff on his chin. "I guess I'd do same as you. But I'd take backup."

She put a hand on his arm. "I didn't go alone. I think that's what's bothering you most."

"Maybe."

"I like him, Alex. He's a good guy. I think you'd like him too, if you gave him a chance. He's a lot like you, actually."

Alex squinted at her. "How so?"

"He's sexy and a pain in the ass."

They both laughed, the tension fully broken.

"Anyway, if you can handle it, I need your help. If you're willing."

"You know you don't even gotta ask, *chica*."

"I need a team to help spring a trap on the Laghairtine."

"How many we need?" Alex straightened his shoulders, making his white shirt ripple along the arms, every inch the Sentinel.

Tarian took a moment to think. "I'm not sure. I don't want to mess this up. There's a lot riding on it. It's not some easy snatch and grab. Somehow I don't think flashing my boobs will get it done this time. This time, I think we need more finesse."

Alex flexed one of his arms. "You mean muscle."

"I mean power. A lot of it."

Alex nodded. "You want me and Frankie, then."

Tarian smiled. "Any little tricks you can come up with that will help keep this lizard occupied while I do my part are great."

"What you mean, your part? What're you up to?" Alex narrowed his eyes.

"For this, we need a little more information. I'm going to get it. You're going to get my backup ready. Daric is checking on the markings to be sure we know what we're facing. When we all have our parts, we'll put them together and the lizard won't know what hit him."

Alex studied her face then shook his head. "That's not the whole story, is it, Tari? Something you're not telling me, *chica*."

She paused and searched his face. Alex set his jaw and refused to budge.

"The shield is cracked. I have two, maybe three days left. If we don't move now, it'll be too late." She swallowed, her mouth unexpectedly dry. "And my future lies in the hands of a crazy woman."

Alex nodded, a gleam of triumph in his eyes. "You should stay here. Let us do this. I promise to let Daric tag along. I don't promise to save his ass though. We'll get this thing you need, you don't gotta worry."

She shook her head, exasperated. "Look, Alex, I know you want to protect me. But the Laghairtine isn't going to come out of hiding for you. I need a way to lure him to me and trap him, and the only way to find out how is in a book Sucole Poole is keeping near the Between. You can't go there, only people with daemon and human blood...can..." She trailed off. *Someone part human and daemon. Like the Laghairtine. And since Mother didn't argue the point, it means I'm like the Laghairtine too. Part human. Part daemon.*

The realization hit her in a vulnerable spot deep inside her heart. *One of my mother's potentials must have been an air daemon. I'm part daemon.*

Tarian shook her head to clear the thought. It didn't matter. Not right now. What mattered was she had the ability to go to the Between. Just like the lizard. And that's where Sucole had the book.

"It has to be what, *chica*? You look like you're seeing an army of ghosts."

She put her hand on his arm and squeezed. "It has to be me, that's all."

"I don't get how you're gonna find her. No human can go to the Between."

"I have my ways. I'm a tracker, after all." Tarian shrugged, and hoped he'd drop the subject. She didn't want to discuss her origins right now.

"Is it safe?"

"Mother seems to think so." Tarian surveyed Alex's face. *I know that tight-lipped look.* He wasn't happy with the situation, but it was more than that. "What's wrong?"

"I was looking for you for a reason, *chica*. Before you rush into things, there's something you gotta see. And something you need to hear."

"I don't have time, Alex."

"You gotta see this." Alex caressed the weapon at his side and licked his lips.

Must be serious. He looks ready for a fight, and not just with me.

She gestured for him to lead the way and followed him down the hall and out into the practice yard.

"They found him this morning when he didn't report for duty."

"Found who?" Alex walked so fast she had to double time her steps to keep up with him.

"The asshole who started all this mess. Daryl."

They entered the Sentinel's quarters and stopped at the first small room. Alex gestured for her to enter and followed behind her.

Daryl lay on the bed. He looked as if he were in a deep sleep. She stepped closer to him and realized his chest wasn't moving.

"How long?" She turned to Alex.

"Frankie found him like that an hour ago." Alex shrugged. "When he didn't show up for duty, Frankie started a search. It seemed odd, him not showing, when he's so connected to this mess. That's when I went looking for you and found out you'd skipped." A bit of resentment hung in the air along with the words.

"So you never asked him anything." She looked around the room. It looked undisturbed. Clothes hung neatly in the closet. The desk looked unused. Just a pair of shoes on the floor. No sign of struggle.

"Have the healers been in?"

"Yeah. They don't know what killed him. No sign of poison, no bruises, no broken bones. *Nada.* They're sending for a guy to check for magic overload or other things before they move him."

She shook her head. "I don't feel anything like I did in the Cellar. No red mist. No big magic trace. Just normal stuff."

"Tari. The guys are getting anxious. That's two in a week.

Inside the house. And both connected to you somehow."

She turned back to face him. "They think I did this too?"

"Well, Daryl was the one said you did Chester, so now some think maybe he was killed to shut him up."

She snorted. "Well, he might have been killed for that reason, but I didn't do it."

"Most of the guys aren't stupid. You're one of us. But they don't know about the lizard attack on you. We've kept it quiet. All they know is nobody should be able to get into the house and do this. It's making everybody edgy. Not sure what this means. Either someone inside the House is a traitor, or someone is able to walk through walls without us noticing."

"Or both."

"What's that supposed to mean?" Alex pulled her out of the room and back into the arena, which stood strangely empty. *Must be mealtime.*

"Nothing. Just thinking out loud." *A traitor inside the House.* Once again, the thought made skin tingle as though dipped in ice. Daryl had to have had help from somewhere. He couldn't access the database on his own. He'd obviously sent her out to be attacked. But he had no reason. Not on his own. It had to be the lizard. Somehow he'd convinced Daryl to do this.

Unless someone else inside the House had done it. Was the Laghairtine working alone, or did he have help?

Beware the danger from within.

The Archivists had warned her. She hadn't understood the message before, but now she knew what it meant. The warm sun which bathed the arena couldn't shake the chill she felt. The thought of someone she trusted cooperating with the Laghairtine made her sick to her stomach.

I need that book.

"Keep the team small, Alex. Just you and Frankie. With Daric and me, that should be enough." She didn't trust anyone else. Not with this. A traitor lurked somewhere.

"Tari, don't do this. Don't go alone." Alex put a heavy hand on her shoulder. She winced at the pressure so near the claw on her neck.

"I'll take Daric with me. You stay here and guard this House, and get ready."

Watching Alex's face cloud over with jealousy sent a stab right through her stomach. "Just because we had a moment together doesn't mean I'm tied to you, Alex. You knew I couldn't be. You said it wasn't a big deal. It wouldn't change things. You knew I couldn't make promises. You knew there'd be others."

Alex worked his jaw again. "Does it gotta be him?"

"What do you have against Daric Voltain, Alex?"

"Just seems convenient, him showing up at all the right times in all the right places."

"He wasn't there when you convinced me to pick you first."

She watched the color brighten Alex's cheeks. *I should have known. He can't help it.* It was his Latino passion talking now. His brain might have understood it was a one-time thing, but his heart didn't agree.

"Dammit, Alex." Tarian stomped her foot. "You promised. You promised it wouldn't change things."

Alex ran his fingers through his hair, let out a growl. "I know."

"I need my friend to be a friend."

"A friend wouldn't let you rush off into danger without backup. Daric should respect that."

"I think he respects it more than you give him credit for." Even if she wanted Alex along for company, she wouldn't do it now. The two men squaring off at each other would be too much of a distraction.

She watched his face. He understood, but he didn't like it. The frown, the crinkled eyebrows, the set jaw, the stiff arms spoke far louder than any words.

"I don't want to lose my best friend." She whispered the words, because it hurt to say them. It felt like her heart might break.

He dropped his defensive posture and relaxed. He swept her up in his arms in a giant bear hug that nearly crushed her rib cage. "You won't. I promised, right?"

He put her back on her feet, and she pulled his face down to plant a kiss on his cheek.

His hand covered the spot, and he acted like he might faint. She laughed.

"I hate to say it, but promise you'll take him. Don't go it alone, right, *chica*? Take backup. It's just smart."

She punched him in the arm. "You and Frankie stay on the Chester and Daryl train. Something shady is going on. I need all the eyes I can get."

"On it." Alex ruffled her hair and took off for the locker rooms. She watched him go. *Men. I'll never understand them.*

chapter twenty-four

Back in the entry, Tarian paused in front of one of the portal alcoves, lost in thought. If she used magic, the lizard would sense it and steal more power from her.

This is a pain in the ass.

Frustrated, she stomped out of the entry and into the fresh air. She made her way down to her favorite beach, sand crunching under her boots. The constant reminder of the lizard's hold on her was really starting to get on her nerves. Her power drifted away each time she used it. If she focused on the implications, she'd lose her mind long before the lizard had a chance to steal her body.

She stood for a moment on the black sand and watched the waves eat the shore. A dolphin wiggled above the waves briefly, extending a greeting with the wave of a fin before plunging back underneath.

This beach, her friends, her home. It would all be lost to her if she couldn't stop the lizard in time. The thought hurt, more than the claw in her neck.

Tarian closed her eyes and took a deep breath of the salt air. The scent of flowers, a roasting pig somewhere in the distance, and the unmistakable tang of ocean filled her with contentment for a brief moment. She let her senses roam. Waves rushed the shore to greet her, and a slight breeze played around with her hair while she let the sun warm her face. Accepting the sun's rays always lifted her mood. For the moment, here on this secluded beach with the sea wind caressing her skin and the ocean licking at the shore, she didn't think about anything.

The image of the dead girl from the basement flashed through her mind and her serenity shattered. She opened her eyes and stared at the water as it moved in and out. The girl had been young. Probably full of hope and plans and dreams. She'd most likely had a family and friends and people who loved her. *The lizard must pay for destroying her life.* Even though he'd killed Chester too, it was the girl that bothered Tarian most. Chester had been in on the whole plan, and he'd not been a stellar example of Society anyway. Most likely nobody missed Chester, or his low-life cousin.

But someone, somewhere missed that girl.

Tarian studied the coin she still held in her hand. Sucole Poole was so far away she couldn't even determine which direction to travel. She'd never been to the Between before, and didn't have the first clue how to do it. She'd have to use her tracking skills. Which put her at huge risk. Every use of magic would send more of her power to the lizard. She'd have to make each use count.

Don't go it alone, right, chica? *Take backup. It's just smart.*

Alex's advice still echoed in her ears. He was right. She'd had no intention of bringing the two people she trusted most along for this part of the plan. If something went wrong looking for

Sucole, really wrong, she needed him and Frankie to look after her mother, Calliope, and the House. She'd tried to explain it to him over the years, but he didn't seem to hear the words. He thought those words included her. Usually, they did.

But not today.

If you decide to climb down off that pedestal and admit you need help, give me a call.

She should swallow her pride and ask Daric to join her. Just as backup. Not as foreplay, despite what he thought. She kicked the sand and watched as a small piece of lava rolled drunkenly along the beach.

Daric could make the portals for her, which would conserve her energy and make it harder for the lizard to follow or siphon any more of her energy than he already was.

Of course, first she needed to find Daric.

Tarian let her mind focus on the remembered feel of his hands on her face, the warmth his healing had generated, and the lingering scent and signature of his talent. Her nose twitched with the memory of spice as she pictured Daric. His eyes, brown and full of heat. His arms, which folded around her as she thought of them. The warmth he generated down her spine when he spoke. His signature, strong and sure and a close match for her own.

Tarian stood on the beach, the wind whipping her hair, and simply drank in the vision of Daric she'd created.

When it felt so real she thought he stood beside her, she let her mind drift out along his wave, an almost palpable, tangible string in the atmosphere, which attached her to him. She fixed on Daric's location within seconds and breathed a sigh of relief. Everything seemed to be going so haywire lately. It was nice to have something work like it should, for once. She knew where he was from the direction. He was either in PJ's, or in his apartment directly over it. She could almost see what he saw, so strong was the connection.

Before she changed her mind, she opened a portal. Ignoring the throb in her neck as the claw reacted to the power use, she stepped through to Daric's apartment.

Late afternoon sun poured through the windows. It didn't surprise her to find him sitting on the sofa, watching her arrive. It did surprise her to find he had two cups of coffee from PJ's on the coffee table. She raised her eyebrows at the sight of them.

"I'm that obvious?"

"Maybe this is for someone else." Daric picked up one cup and sipped, and leaned back. He wore jeans, a black T-shirt, and a grin. Her pulse throbbed, along with other body parts, at the way his body owned the couch. The thought of the two of them on the couch naked rushed blood to her cheeks. She coughed and took the other coffee to distract herself.

She took a sip. Her favorite blend, cream, no sugar. Just the way she liked. How the hell had he known she'd be here? She glanced at him and found a look of satisfaction. She focused back on the coffee.

"You didn't risk making a portal only to have coffee, did you?" Daric took a sip himself.

"How'd you know?"

"You have good friends. Really good friends. Friends very interested in your well-being." Daric's eyes twinkled. "You need me?"

Tarian rolled her eyes. "I need to track down a woman who might have a book I need."

"What book?"

"The *Book of Daemon*." Another sip. Another glance up. He looked intense. She kept her tone casual. "You know it?"

"My mother is a teacher."

"Have you seen it?"

Daric put the coffee cup down on the table and leaned forward, his arms resting on his thighs in a way she found extremely seductive. "Not personally. But I know it's a very dangerous book. Not one humans are meant to have. Why do you think it'll help?"

"The Archivists told me it would. I think there's a spell or power of some sort, which will trap the Laghairtine. If I can do it to him before he does it to me, problem solved."

"How will you know which spell?"

She didn't have an answer, so she deflected. "Does your offer still stand?"

Daric stood up and ran a hand through his ruffled hair. Tarian imagine the silk feel of it against her own fingers, which twitched in response. The dimple reappeared on his cheek. "Are you asking me for help, Scion?"

"I'm asking you to join me. And I'm going to smack you if you call me 'Scion' one more time."

Daric laughed. It was a deep, rich laugh made her grin in return.

"We'll save the smackdown for later."

"Jerk." She took out the coin and showed it to him. Daric reached out to take it. His body radiated heat in a way that made her want to snuggle. *Damn the man, how am I supposed to concentrate with him doing that?*

"Braille?" He examined both sides of the coin before handing it back to her. She might be imagining things but she swore his fingers lingered on hers.

"No idea. Nobody could tell me." With the coin folded into her fist, she let her senses drift out along the signal Sucole had left on it. She'd jumped from Hawaii to Philadelphia, and Sucole remained the same distance away as she'd been on the island.

"Have you ever been to Europe?"

Daric's eyes held confusion and amusement. "I have family in Ireland I visit from time to time, but if you'd like to meet my mother she's in Boston. Why?"

"Sucole isn't anywhere near us, and she wasn't near Hawaii either. We need to start further away. If you know a place?"

"One portal coming right up."

The portal he created shimmered in the living room. Tarian saw a lot of trees in it. Daric gestured toward it. "After you."

Tarian stepped through and out into the most lush, rolling hillside she'd ever seen. The shades of green were different, denser, richer. No hibiscus here, but different flowers with vibrant reds and yellows all the same. *Stunning.*

"Get anything?"

Her heart felt full as she looked at the landscape. A nearby tree leaned over a babbling stream. The air smelled rich with grass and earth and a bit of manure. Somewhere in the distance, a cow called out for food. They stood at the edge of a meadow so full of flowers it made her eyes hurt. It was breathtaking. It felt strangely like home, even though she'd never been here. She saw a house nestled among trees in the distance. "You have family here? It's gorgeous."

"I have family scattered all over, but my grandparents live over that small hill." He pointed to the house. "I'm sure they'd love to meet you, but now's not the time. We go now, we'll be there for weeks."

"Right." Tarian gripped the coin and searched. Sucole remained the same distance away. How was that even possible? "I think we over-jumped. She's still the same distance away."

"Not very precise."

"I told you, I'm a compass, not a map."

"Let's try somewhere in the middle." Daric opened another portal and gestured for her to step through.

She emerged and glanced around. They stood on an isolated stretch of beach, bordered by palm trees and low brush. The ocean smelled different here, somehow, though the calm in and out motion of the waves was the same as home. One thing, though, was very different.

"I need to get out more. Pink sand?"

"Bermuda. Great place for a vacation." Daric took her hand and wrapped his around it.

Deep inside, something tingled and lurched. It wasn't the claw. Her neck remained still. She stared at her hand encased in his. Warmth spread from his touch up her arm and into her chest. Her body reacted to him without her mind even being engaged. It wasn't like with Alex. Alex was comfortable, friendly, safe. Daric was new, exciting, dangerous, raw heat, and something else she couldn't define.

He looked into her eyes. His breath joined the warm breeze across her cheeks. Tarian smelled the traces of coffee, and the spice she'd come to associate with him. Her lips parted, ready for the kiss she felt sure was coming. She leaned toward him.

"Try to track her again." His whisper caressed her ears and cheek.

It took her a moment to process what he'd said. Her body was so ready for a kiss. She quashed the flare of disappointment. Now was definitely not the time, even if the place was definitely very right.

She tried to pull her hand away but he held tight.

"I want to see if I can follow along or maybe amp up the

signal. If you don't mind." Daric's lips twisted in a half smile.

She nodded. It was a good idea. It would be better if her body wasn't betraying her.

Damn the man, why wasn't he affected the same way she was? *He might as well be holding hands with his sister, if his expression is any indication.*

She licked her lips and closed her eyes. It enhanced the warmth of his hands on hers. The feel of skin to skin. The thought of her flesh touching his. *Focus. I need to focus.*

"Relax." His whisper sent a thrill of anticipation down her spine.

He squeezed her hand and sent a surge of power into her.

The shielded claw in her neck turned into a jumping bean of frenzy, and her shoulder muscles seized.

She swallowed and did her best to ignore the churning in her stomach. Her senses drifted out along Sucole's signal once more, buoyed by the influx of power from Daric. Once again, she remained the same distance away.

Frustration built up inside Tarian and made her head hurt. Or maybe it was the lizard deposit in her neck doing it, or the muscles along her back as they cramped. She tore her hand away from Daric and backed away to sever the link-up. He shook his head.

"I have no idea how you do what you do. I couldn't feel anything."

"That makes two of us."

"You didn't get her?"

She sat down on the beach. "No."

"The Laghairtine?" Daric sat next to her.

"I don't think so."

She picked up a rock and threw it, missing the water by at least three feet.

How is this possible? How can she always be the same distance away? Usually Tarian triangulated fairly quickly to narrow in on her subject. The way this was going, she was aiming blind. She'd clutched the coin so tight it cut into her palm.

There are none so blind as those who will not see.

See what? What was she supposed to see? She knew who she wanted to see. But obviously Sucole did not wish to be seen. She rubbed the coin, willing the Braille to make some sort of sense. The raised dots pushed against her fingers. A blind person would understand, but the bumps might as well be pebbles on the beach, for all the meaning it held for her.

She watched the ocean, wishing the waves would send her an answer. They rushed in and out, oblivious. "I don't suppose you read Braille?"

"No. I'm sure we can look it up."

"No time." She'd left the house thinking she had the answer to all her problems when really all she had was another problem.

Daric nudged her with his shoulder. "We'll figure it out."

"It's as hard to figure out as this beach. Why the hell is the sand pink?"

"No idea."

"Why is there Braille on this coin? I don't get it."

"Maybe she only wants blind people to visit."

"Blind people." Tarian repeated the words. They had to be important. Why else would it be on the coin? Why would she even give the coin to someone as an emergency way to find her, if it couldn't be used somehow? Who, exactly, did Sucole expect to come looking for her?

There are none so blind as those who will not see.

"Maybe I should pretend to be blind." Tarian held the coin tightly in her hand and closed her eyes. Once again she rubbed the raised dots with her thumb and tried to understand what they meant without actually being able to read them. She slowed her breath to match the rush of ocean waves and emptied her mind, allowing calm to descend. Birds in the background sang a lullaby that lulled and soothed. The warm salt breeze played with her hair.

Keeping her eyes tightly closed, she focused on trying to see Sucole, rather than track her. It was hard, not knowing what the woman looked like, but she allowed an image to form in her mind anyway. A dumpy, graying older woman, with milky blue eyes covered in cataracts and long claw-like fingers wore an old-fashioned flowered dress with a filthy apron over it. Her fingers were caked in what looked like fungus or something equally foul. She seemed familiar. It was the image she'd seen when she talked with the Archivists.

Sucole. Sucole. Where are you? Sucole. I need to find you.

Tarian pictured every detail of the woman she wanted to meet and set her senses adrift on the air. She added in the phrase on the coin for good measure and continued rubbing the Braille with her thumb.

Nothing happened.

After a while she stopped, feeling ridiculous.

"This isn't working. You're right. Maybe we should find a real blind person." Tarian opened her eyes and was startled to see her surroundings had completely changed. The pink sand was gone. The birds were gone. Daric was gone.

She was alone.

chapter twenty-five

Tarian sat on a patch of soggy ground, bathed in gloomy twilight. Ancient trees loomed overhead. Moss dripped. Small bugs floated through the air, and slimy water lay in somber stillness all around her island, disturbed only by some sort of insect which skated along the surface. The stench of mold, mildew, and saturated earth tickled her nose and made her sneeze. Her jeans were already wet from the soggy grass.

Where the hell am I? Where was Daric? A rush of fear pushed her heart up into her throat as she stood and spun around, expecting to see Daric behind her. She jumped when she saw the woman she had pictured so clearly in her mind. *Sucole Poole herself?*

Tarian stared, at a loss for something to say. The old woman's eyes were glazed over by something milky, making them look like whitish-blue marbles.

"Sucole Poole?" The woman didn't answer or move.

"Ms. Poole?" The old hag didn't nod or even blink. Tarian

looked closer at her. Something else was missing. Sucole Poole wasn't breathing, either. Moving forward, Tarian reached out to touch her on the shoulder and felt her hand pass right through. Either a ghost stood in front of her, or this was an image or reflection. *Not real.*

"Sucole, I need your help."

For reply, several frogs started a chorus and a mosquito bit her on the arm. Tarian looked down at the coin. It lay in her palm, lifeless. It didn't offer advice or anything else useful, like an explanation on exactly how she'd arrived in this place, or how to speak to the image of a blind woman.

"Can you see?" A geriatric woman's voice sounded all around her. Startled, Tarian looked around. Nothing moved except the wildlife.

"Can I see what?"

"Can you see?"

"I can see a swamp and an image of an old woman."

"There are none so blind as those who will not see."

Frustrated, Tarian stared around her. The water, the little patch of dirt she stood on, the frogs, the bugs, it all seemed normal if she expected to be in a swamp. What else was she supposed to see?

She'd arrived her by closing her eyes. Maybe she had to go in blind. Maybe that was how Sucole was able to stay hidden for so long.

She closed her eyes and inched forward with the coin in the palm of one hand and the other outstretched.

"Sucole, Advisor Jonus sent me to you. He said to show you this." She held her hand out. Her eyes registered a change in brightness, but she kept them tightly shut. It wasn't easy when every instinct in her body screamed at her to open them.

Warmth on her skin told her the sun had come out. A bird twittered nearby. There hadn't been any birds in the swamp. She felt the coin snatched from her hand.

Startled, she tried to open her eyes but found she couldn't. Frantic, she tried to pry them open.

"Do you see?" The old woman's voice was close to her ear.

"No. I can't see anything." Panic started to creep in.

A wrinkled hand pulled her own hands down from her face. Suddenly, even with her eyes shut, she saw. She stood in a beautiful garden. The dirt patch now floated in the middle of a pond, rather than a swamp. Trees and flowers turned toward the sun and birds happily tweeted. Beside her, a beautiful young woman with long flowing blonde hair and gorgeous blue eyes held her hand.

"Sucole?"

"Do you see?" The woman's voice was a whisper blending with the chirping birds.

"I see a woman and a beautiful garden. What else am I supposed to see?"

"You do not see." Sucole shook her head, dropped her hand, and turned away.

"Wait!" Tarian followed after her. "Please, I need your help. I need to know about the *Book of Daemon*. I need to know how to stop a Laghairtine from draining my power."

Sucole stopped but did not turn around.

"You look. You do not see. You ask wrong questions. Twenty-four years. You are still a child." The voice never rose above a whisper.

Irritated, Tarian struggled to open her eyes. She pried them apart then wished she hadn't. Everything was pitch black. She blinked and realized the only time she saw anything at all was when her eyes were closed. It made no sense, but neither did Sucole.

"What the hell is this? What have you done?"

"You look. You do not see." Sucole started to walk away again.

Keeping her eyes firmly shut, Tarian followed her. Sucole kept walking, winding her way through flowering bushes.

"What question should I ask?"

Sucole stopped and turned back toward her, a slight smile on her face. "Better."

Tarian thought for a moment. What question did Sucole want to hear? She really needed to know how to stop this lizard. But more importantly, a part of her suspected there was more to this puzzle than a Laghairtine's quest to turn her into a puppet. People usually had reasons for their actions, justifications, excuses. This lizard shouldn't be any different.

"Why is this lizard taking my power?"

Sucole smiled, and beckoned for her to follow.

As Sucole walked away, Tarian hesitated. She couldn't feel the claw here, other than the knot of sore muscles in her neck, but she couldn't feel her own magic either. Not that she'd tried, but it circulated constantly inside her and, at the moment, it was gone. Or subdued. She didn't like the feeling. And it didn't seem like a bright idea to follow a complete stranger, blind, into someplace she didn't know. She felt like a tasty fly buzzing straight into a spider's web.

"If you would see, you must follow." Sucole continued to move away. She didn't so much walk as float, with her long blond hair billowing behind her.

Taking a deep breath, Tarian followed.

She walked with her eyes closed, even though every impulse

told her to open them. Every time she did, a black void greeted her. She stumbled and tried her best to keep her eyes closed. It was like a giant spotlight lit the inside of her eyelids.

The path led into heavy undergrowth. The bushes gave way to tall trees, which seemed to get progressively bigger the further they went. Sunlight filtered through their giant leaves, creating patterns on the path. The earthy scent in the air reminded Tarian of a place she used to visit often as a child. She called it her fairy garden. *Odd, to remember that now.* She hadn't visited the fairy garden in years.

Sucole stopped in front of the biggest tree Tarian had ever seen. The trunk was larger around than a lot of apartments she'd seen. A car could pass through it and not touch the edges. Sucole stepped forward and faded into the tree.

"To see, you must follow," Sucole whispered.

Exactly how am I supposed to follow a disappearing act? Tarian stepped over to the tree and pushed against the rough bark on the trunk. It was solid. She felt along the bark for any clasp or hinge or hint of a knob. Nothing.

"I don't know how to merge with a tree." Silence met her complaint.

"I don't get it. Why are you making this so complicated?"

"Don't look. See." The woman's words drifted on the air.

How was she supposed to see, if she didn't look?

Maybe that was the point. Maybe Sucole didn't want someone coming into her home with any advantage. Maybe she wanted any visitor to come in blind. A safety measure, most likely, for a woman with blocked magic. Or maybe it was being so near the Between that did it. Nothing about this place felt remotely like the earth plane.

A leap of faith. She had to trust she wouldn't run into

anything, trust she'd be safe on the other side of whatever this was, and trust this decision wouldn't lead her somewhere from which she couldn't escape.

It seemed a lot to ask. *But, really, what choice do I have?*

Tarian opened her eyes and faced the black nothingness. Holding her breath, she put her hands out in front of her and took a giant step forward. Then another. Four steps later she still hadn't hit the trunk of the tree. She closed her eyes again and discovered she'd passed through the trunk and now stood in the middle of a good-sized circular room.

Sucole, looking like the young beautiful blonde of the vision above ground, sat in a chair on the far side, teacup in hand. A cheery fire burned in a pit in the middle of the floor. It smelled like incense, although there wasn't a lot of smoke in evidence. Everything around her, shelves in the wall, a table, the chair Sucole sat in, looked as if it had grown there. Even the fire pit looked like a rock bowl formed over centuries. The only thing Tarian didn't see was a door.

She blinked, and her sight righted itself. She almost cried with relief and rubbed her eyes to be sure they still functioned like they should.

Sucole rocked, teacup in hand. Tarian looked for another chair but saw nothing, so she sat on the floor by the fire pit. She felt like a child waiting for a ghost story.

"Do you know why the Laghairtine attacked me?"

"A good question." Sucole smiled.

"Does it have an answer?"

"A stupid question." Sucole snorted.

"You're right. Obviously it has an answer. What I meant was will you tell me why he attacked me?"

Sucole smiled and took another sip of tea.

Tarian took a deep breath. She summoned every ounce of patience she possessed. It felt like a game, but she didn't know the rules.

"Why aren't you talking to me like a normal person?"

"You look. You do not see."

"I really don't have time for this." Frustration drove Tarian to her feet. This was a stupid waste of time. This woman didn't know anything and even if she did, she didn't seem willing to talk. Tarian paced to the edge of the room before she realized she had no idea how to get out.

"You wander a blind woman."

"That's why I came here to get help. So I wouldn't go in blind. But all I get from you is riddles." She clasped her hands together. The urge to hit something nearly overwhelmed her.

"Life is a game."

Giving in to the helplessness of the situation, Tarian sat back down on the floor and started a meditative pose. Ignoring Sucole, she focused instead on her breathing. *In. Out. In. Out.* With her eyes closed, Tarian let her surroundings fade away as she focused. She found calm somehow in the repetitive nature of her breath. She'd need a lot of it to figure out exactly how to communicate with Sucole.

"That is better." A voice whispered in her ear. She saw Sucole in her mind as the beautiful young woman. In the vision, the two stood in a grassy meadow. Sucole smiled and sat in the grass facing her. Tarian joined her on the ground. A cool breeze gently moved Sucole's flowing blond hair in a soft swirl around her face. "I thought you couldn't do magic here. Is this real?" Tarian looked around her.

"Magic *is*. Real is subjective. Can you see?" Sucole stretched out her hands.

Tarian took them both, and the two started to spin. The meadow leapt around them and soon it was a blur of color, blue up top for the sky, green below for the grass, with dots of color of flowers whipping by. Colors blended together. Tarian watched as an image of herself formed in front of them. She stood outside the door to the cell where Mark Chester had been placed. She saw Alex walking away.

She moved closer to peer into the door and saw a red blur streaking around the room. Chester cowered on the floor, still incredibly drunk. The blur dodged this way and that, in and out, and as it went, chunks of Chester simply went missing. His mouth was open to scream, but no sound came out. She wondered if that happened in reality, or if this vision simply didn't include sound. Flesh flew everywhere, until just the core of his body writhed on the ground. His stomach and intestines formed a grotesque trail across the floor of the prison. A giant hole gaped where his heart should have been. Empty eye sockets stared blankly out at her.

She felt like throwing up but forced calming breaths instead. The red blur stopped moving for the briefest moment, and she caught a glimpse of the lizard-man from the alley. *The Laghairtine.* He spun around the room, faster and faster until some type of explosion rocked the cell, shaking the door. Even this remote, Tarian saw the pulse of magic. Then it was gone, and the blur dissolved. The mist remained in the air, tainting everything it touched.

Exhausted, she dropped her hands and the vision ended. The calm meadow surrounded her, and Sucole sat opposite her once more.

"I see." Tarian took several more deep breaths of the sweet air. "You are not a child."

"No. Not anymore." She thought for a moment. The lizard might easily have done that to her during his first attack. Eaten chunks of her flesh until nothing was left. Torn her arms off, like the girl in the basement. But he hadn't. Instead, he'd stolen her blood and now siphoned her power. It made no sense. He was stronger, faster, and filled with a power she didn't understand. Why did he want her?

"I need the *Book of Daemon* to catch him. Do you know where it is?"

"A good question." Sucole held Tarian's gaze. She seemed anxious to say more. Why wouldn't she just speak?

Her mother had called the woman difficult. This was more than difficult. It was impossible. Tarian was beginning to sense a pattern to the answers, though. Perhaps "a good question" meant "yes."

"How do I get the *Book of Daemon*?"

Sucole sighed. Tarian couldn't tell if it was from relief or anxiety or something else entirely. Sucole squeezed Tarian's hands, and once more a vision filled her mind.

Tarian stood…somewhere. At first, the place was a void of white. It slowly filled with grass, trees and a twilight sky. It felt familiar, though she didn't remember ever being here. Hands pushed her from behind into the grass. It was warm, springy, and very real. She marveled at the detail in this vision as she stood up. Sucole had vanished, even as the trees appeared.

"Is this real?" Irrelevant question, really, but she asked it anyway. Her words drifted away on the air, unanswered.

In the distance, a dark shadow appeared, at first a spec, then larger as it came near. For some reason, the shadow didn't frighten her, though it should have. Somehow, this place felt safe. *It was only a dream, anyway. Nothing to fear from dreams.*

The shadow resolved itself into a tall, thin, dark-skinned man with deep, black eyes. There was something enticing and seductive about him. It might have been the five o'clock shadow along his chiseled jaw line, or his fit, slim waist, or maybe it was the way he held himself. Relaxed, both feet planted as though he owned the ground he walked on. Confidence radiated from his hair down to the way he held his arms...one loose by his side, the other casually holding a book. Her heart raced. It was the *Book of Daemon*. It had to be. She stared at it, her mouth dry in anticipation.

The man's lips turned up in a smile, and a gleam of triumph filled his eyes. He nodded, a slow movement that barely dipped his head and never moved his eyes.

"Scion."

"Who are you?" She took a step back. His hungry eyes fastened on her.

"I have what you seek."

"I see." But what did she have to do to get it? Her first thought was to fight for it, but she couldn't feel her magic. This place operated under rules she didn't understand and couldn't control. Her mother couldn't have anticipated this. Marielle would never have let her come here, if she had.

The man raised an eyebrow. "Will you exchange?"

"Exchange what?"

"Join with me, and you may have the book." The man held out his hand to her.

chapter twenty-six

The words tied her in knots. *Join.* He probably wasn't asking her to join a softball team.

"Join as in…"

"Exchange energy. Life force." His eyes smoldered as they drank her in.

Sex.

His lips twitched.

"You're a daemon? An air daemon?"

He smiled. "We would not meet here, were I not."

"You know this Laghairtine? The one who attacked me? Did you send him?"

The daemon drew himself up straight and stiff. "I did not. Another uses him as a tool. You need information if you seek to vanquish him. As I believe you should."

"What the hell do you know?" Tarian started to pace. "Why are you here?"

"I believe I've stated my purpose. Yours is equally clear. The correct question is will you make agreement?"

Tarian paused to study his face. It remained haughty, but neutral. Something was going on here, something Tarian struggled to understand but couldn't. Pieces of the puzzle had been stolen. She had a feeling those pieces were vital to her well-being.

"The Archivists told me no treasure is worth the price."

"They are a noble race, prized for knowledge. Good allies. You have chosen your friends well. The question remains, Scion. Will you reach agreement with me?"

The man didn't make a move while she thought it out. He stood, the book in one hand and the other held palm up.

The book had the spell she needed. All she had to do was...she shuddered. Her stomach flip-flopped, and her chest tightened. She'd stopped breathing. She gasped and forced air in. Sweat beaded along her forehead and dripped down her face. She ignored it.

Join.

Mate.

Sex.

No treasure is worth the price.

What, exactly, was the price? Sex with a daemon? He wanted her to sell her body for a book?

The man laughed, and the sound filled the air before fading away into the trees. "I am not seeking sex as you would define it, Scion. I am seeking a joining. It is a commingling of magic energy, not a physical exchange of bodily fluids. It is how daemon recharge and revitalize themselves. I think you'll find it does the same for you. I sense you are in desperate need of an influx of energy."

"If I...join with you, will I end up like Sucole?"

The man lowered his hand. "You will not. I offer a simple exchange. The book for one joining with you. You will leave here with that which you seek."

"And what about you? What exactly do you seek?" She watched his face for any sign of dishonesty. His gaze never left hers.

"I seek only to join with you."

"Why?"

He spread his hand out in the universal gesture of "it should be obvious."

Of course, she supposed it was. He'd join with the Scion during the Succession Ritual.

Is this what my mother did? Is this why I have daemon blood? She exchanged with an air daemon. Why?

Is this real, or is it a dream? Would it be such a bad thing to give in to a man in dreams if it resulted in obtaining the thing she needed to solve this mess? It might be, if this man were the Laghairtine in disguise.

"Who *are* you? How do I know this isn't a trick? How do I know you aren't the one I'm trying to fight, in disguise?"

The man's expression changed to one of complete disgust. He wrinkled his nose as if something foul had passed under it. "The one you fight is an aberration who shouldn't have been allowed to exist. His very presence causes great pain to all around him, a drain on life forces. My blood is ancient and far greater than something like *him*."

"Ancient? I feel no magic from you."

"In this place, Scion, we are protected. In this place, magic is not sequestered. It surrounds and binds. Lives and breathes. It does not belong to one or the other. All are equal, here. A conquest such as he plans is not possible here. Surely you knew when you came, else why risk the journey?"

Tarian squeezed the back of her neck. He was right. The claw lay dormant. *If only I could wrap the magic of this place around me and take it with me.*

"The Between can't be moved, Scion. We stand betwixt your plane and mine, protected from magic on both sides. Signals are muted. Here, we are able to join. It would not be possible, otherwise. I may not cross the Between to your plane. I offer this information freely, so you may enter into agreement with me."

This all explained why she couldn't track Sucole. How she'd managed to travel here remained a mystery. Tarian wasn't sure she could repeat the journey, even if she wanted to. This was a one-time shot at the prize, so to speak. This man, this daemon, held the object she needed to solve her problem, and he demanded payment for it. She'd never get this book any other way.

She studied him as she worked it through in her head, wondering how the hell she'd go through with it. The feeling she was being tricked settled on her. But she needed the book.

"Scion must understand before Scion makes promises."

"You are worried. I see images in your thoughts. Scion, I reiterate. Joining, for my kind, is not the same as it is for yours. We shall exchange life force, not body parts."

"So you're saying it's not sex. If it's not sex, what exactly is it?"

"If you agree, you'll experience it yourself. Both parties are left with more than they give away. Energy is strengthened, power infused. I sense energy is something you might use in your current struggles. I cannot remove the debris left behind by the Laghairtine. It is too closely connected to your core and is bound to your blood. It can only be removed by the issuer or by his death. I can, however, offer the means for you to fight against it a bit longer."

Tarian felt a rush of hope. *If I do this, I'll have the book I need plus enough power to defeat the lizard. And it isn't sex.*

"*To receive, one must give. To give, one must understand. To agree is to vow. Vow cannot be broken. No treasure is worth the price.*"

The Archivists had known she'd end up here. She'd love to know exactly how they knew, when they never left the house. But they'd told her what she really needed to know. If she promised this, she had to follow through. No backing out. And they didn't think it was worth it.

She thought of her mother, her sister, Alex, Frankie, and Kia. A total stranger, whose life she'd helped to save. It felt right and good to be able to do it. She wasn't ready to lose the ability.

She thought of Daric. How pissed off he must be right now. She'd disappeared right in front of him with no way for him to follow. Was he still waiting on the beach? What would his reaction be if she made this deal? He was a Potential himself. He knew the rules, and he knew what was at stake. Still, she was sure he hadn't envisioned this scenario when he'd suggested she speed up the timing of the ritual.

Don't go it alone, right, chica?

She didn't have a choice. She stood here alone, forced to a decision, without backup. Even if she had it, what would they say?

Did this daemon tell the truth? She'd leave here, intact, with the book? She wouldn't end up like Sucole? Why had Sucole become so twisted in the first place?

"She had no agreement." The man smiled.

A chill ran up her spine at his words. He read her thoughts. Well, why not? This was a dream, after all. Of sorts. He knew everything she'd been thinking. She felt naked.

"And we do?"

"We will."

Why does this feel like a deal with the devil?

"Such a creature does not exist."

"You sure about that? I don't know you, I don't know who or what you are or where you came from, and yet you're asking me to trust you with everything I am, based on the hope you follow through on our little agreement."

"If you agree, Sucole will witness and ensure both sides are met. She will see your safe passage from this place. Agreements are binding for both sides. Consequences for breaking one, for such as I, are severe. You need not fear. I do not enter into agreements I intend to break." His words rang through the air around them. She felt the truth of them. She also felt layers of hidden meanings that would take her a long time to decipher.

"Neither do I."

Tarian studied him. His dark eyes consumed her. His confidence and surety overwhelmed her. Yet something else in his eyes grabbed her attention. Maybe it was the twist of his lips or the tilt of his eyebrows or maybe the way he held his shoulders. She sensed...determination. He wanted this agreement as much as she wanted the book. But why? Was it a trick? A trap? Something more?

"How do I know I can trust Sucole?"

He shrugged. "The choice is yours, Scion. I have that which you seek. You will not be forced to deal. All parties must enter by choice, not coercion."

His voice held the ring of truth. His body language showed sincerity. It seemed so simple. A few minutes with this man and she'd have the book she needed.

No treasure is worth the price.

The Archivists didn't know the full stakes. The treasure was more than the book. It was her own magic, her talent, the very core of her being, which was slowly drifting away into the hands of the Laghairtine. It was the Dolphin Throne, which protected her family. It was her sister, who would be left vulnerable if Tarian failed. It was her mother, who belonged to the Throne in every way and was the heart of their Society and way of life. It was the House of Xannon, which would crumble without her family to protect it.

Some things were worth the price.

The man smiled. He gestured, and Sucole stood beside him. She took the book, and caressed it. She licked her lips, and hugged the book close to her body. Her milky eyes stared into nothing.

"Do you see?"

"If by that you mean do I agree…" Tarian swallowed. She had to say the words. "Yes, I agree. I will join with this man before me one time, in exchange for safe passage from this place and possession of the *Book of Daemon*."

Sucole turned slightly. "Do you see?"

"I agree to the stated stipulations."

Sucole blinked. The book in her hands glowed then vanished. In the next moment, Sucole was gone too.

Tarian took a deep breath and held it. *How am I going to do this?* She had to. She'd agreed. She let out her breath in one long sigh in an effort to relax.

The man held out both hands to her. She couldn't seem to make her feet move. In the next moment, he stood in front of her, although she hadn't seen him step forward. She felt his breath on her face. It smelled of fresh, mountain air. The kind generated by the movement of cool breezes through pine trees drenched with sun.

He took her hands. "You fear. There is no need."

"Easy for you to say." She took another deep breath and realized she'd been doing that a lot. It didn't help. Her nerves vibrated. No amount of yoga or meditation was going to calm them now. "Can you at least tell me your name?"

"You should have stipulated that as part of the agreement." His smile deepened, bringing life to his eyes. His thumbs caressed her hands, a soft movement that did little to relax her.

"Really? It's going to be like that?" Her hands tensed around his fingers.

"I merely instruct for the future. I suspect, before long, you'll need more knowledge of agreements."

She frowned at him. Now he lectured as though she were a child? Who the hell did he think he was anyway?

"My name is Ruarc, of the Mayfanata." He inclined his head slightly, a soft chuckle dancing in his throat. "I do not wish to be your parent. Far, far from it."

He squeezed her hands. Power cascaded from his hands into hers and traveled up her arms. She'd never felt anything like it. Until that moment, she hadn't realized how far away her own magic was in this place. Time, space, and talent held no meaning here. His power surged into her.

The claw inside her neck lay dormant, uninterested. Her shoulders relaxed, the muscles at ease for the first time since the Laghairtine attacked. The rest of her body responded to the additional power by raising goose bumps all over. She shivered. Tingles traveled up and down her arms and legs and settled somewhere in the center of her chest.

Tarian closed her eyes. Whatever he was going to do next, she didn't think she wanted to see it coming. She expected to feel his hands explore her body or his lips touch hers and braced for it.

Instead, magic forged a way through her entire body, but his hands never left hers. With her eyes closed, her other senses heightened and took charge. His mountain-air signature invaded her nose and left the taste of fresh air on her tongue. Energy pushed through her skin and entered into the core of her being. Her groin pulsed with it. Her body filled with pure, raw, power like sunshine on her skin.

It came from all around them. From the trees. From the grass. From the very air. And from Ruarc. It heated her blood, played with the hairs in her nose and the back of her arms, and made her toes dig into the ground. Enticing. Exhilarating. Exhausting. As if she dove into deep water and drifted. Surrounded. Pressure building. Unable to move. Unable to breathe. Filled with life, teaming with power, encompassed by energy.

Deep inside, Tarian's own power responded. Weak, at first. Then stronger, until it surged toward the influx from Ruarc. The two powers met, collided, merged. A lightning show erupted behind her eyes, providing a kaleidoscope of color with forks of white that danced and played over her eyes. Electric pulses covered her body from head to toe, prickling the skin as if a thousand tiny needles stimulated every nerve ending. Her skin, on fire. Her eyes, blinded. Her mind, filled and overflowing with the immensity of it.

She gasped as the pulses reached her groin, her uterus, her heart. Powerful. Omnipotent. Amazed, her heart soared. With this much power, she'd never fear anything, ever. Half of this force was hers. Even after the lizard had stolen so much of it, she held plenty in reserve. Somehow, Ruarc had known.

She sensed he gained as much as she did by this joining of power. This was what he had meant. Not sex. Not as she thought of it, anyway. This was something different. Intimate. Her spirit opened…a flower that had never truly seen the sun.

Tarian ached for more. She groaned with need, but heard no response from Ruarc. No moans or whispers of her name as a man in passion might make.

On instinct, she tried to draw more power, to pull from him the essence he seemed to be taking from her. She thought she heard him chuckle, but no extra surge greeted her. She couldn't pull more than he allowed. He tugged on hers, and she blocked it. They joined as equals, just as he'd promised.

Power built, cascaded, ascended. Her pulse throbbed as it raced through and around her. Her heart felt as though it would explode, and her head filled with pressure. She sensed overload. It was an orgasm created entirely with magic, and it wouldn't take more than a tiny shove to push her over the edge into burnout. She'd heard of it happening, and wondered briefly if Sucole had suffered such a fate. Was this why the Archivists didn't want her to join with a daemon? This surge of power might burn her out forever?

"Stop." She gasped the word. Fear and panic set in as she realized how close she was to losing it.

"Your side of our agreement is complete." Ruarc dropped her hands. When she opened her eyes, he was gone. She stood alone in the meadow, trembling, panting for breath, reaching for control of emotions she didn't understand.

So much energy. She'd never known it existed. Not like this. It scared her, how badly she'd wanted more.

She rubbed her neck. The claw remained quiet. Her stomach, though, shifted and complained. Her uterus felt oddly raw and a bit crampy. *The ritual. If this counts as one of the Potentials…*

She closed her eyes again. If this counted as sex, she needed one more donor. If it didn't, she needed two. How would she know?

This was getting her nowhere. *Focus. I have to focus. One thing at a time. The book. Where is the book?*

"Sucole?" She turned to look behind her and found Sucole. Her eyes, dull, milky, and lifeless, stared into space, and her shoulders drooped. She held the *Book of Daemon* in her arms as if she cradled a baby.

After hesitating and working her mouth up and down as though trying to spit out words that refused to come, Sucole held the book out. Tarian took it and heard a voice say, "The agreement is fulfilled."

It was over. She had what she needed. She took several deep breaths, but it didn't help. She struggled to create a calm void around her, but it eluded her.

The meadow dissolved around them, and the tree room formed once more. Sucole sat in her chair with the cup of tea in her hand, as if they'd been in the room the entire time.

Tarian hugged the book to her chest, her prize for sacrificing...what, exactly? *It had better be worth it.* "Which spell in here will help me destroy the lizard?"

"A good question." Sucole smiled, a small, sad movement of her lips. Placing the teacup on a table next to her Sucole joined Tarian on the floor.

The ancient volume looked like it might have come from the House archives. It smelled old, musty and cloying in an odd, sweet way. Sucole placed her hand over the book and the pages turned themselves, settling on one near the center. Tarian felt a rush of power rise up and wash over her. Not enough to do anything specific, but the book obviously held energy.

"Will this catch the Laghairtine?" Tarian studied the page. The spell was in an ancient, dead, magical language. She'd had lessons on it from tutors, but not enough to read what appeared on the page.

"Banish." Sucole winced as though the word caused her physical pain.

"Thank you." Tarian rose, and on impulse gave Sucole a quick kiss. As her lips touched the cheek, Tarian swore she felt something old and leathery, but when she moved back, all she saw was the beautiful young face surrounded by flowing, blond hair.

She started to make a travel portal but found she couldn't. Closing her eyes, she pictured the clearing where she'd first met Sucole. The swampy one, with the old woman.

"You do not see." The soft whisper followed Tarian as she left.

chapter twenty-seven

"What don't I see?" Tarian asked the empty air in the swamp. Silence greeted her. No frogs, no birds, no flies. Nothing. The swamp was a dead, empty thing, except for the trees and the gross water and the tiny island she stood on. After a moment, she gave up waiting for an answer and turned her attention to the book in her hands.

She needed a quiet, safe place to study the ritual Sucole had indicated. She should probably check in with her mother and Alex and she definitely needed to find Daric. *He must have gone crazy when I disappeared right in front of him.*

She had no idea how long she'd been gone, but surely Daric hadn't waited. He'd probably gone back to his apartment, since it was their starting point. *Or he went to check my place. Oh, I hope not.* She didn't want her family or Alex stirred up any more than they already were. Which they certainly would be if Daric showed up claiming to have lost her suddenly on a beach in the Bahamas.

She tried to open a portal but found her ability still blocked.

Since she hadn't arrived here in the normal way, maybe she had to leave the same way. *Worth a shot, anyway.*

Tarian closed her eyes and pictured the alley near PJ's in her head. She constructed every detail of it, from the scratching of rats in the dumpster to the smell. She added intention—more than anyplace on earth that was where she wanted to be. It wasn't easy. The alley held bad memories and reeked. But it also was usually empty except for the rats and a good place to suddenly pop out of nowhere. Normal people didn't understand and tended to scream and attract unwanted attention.

She imagined the stench so strongly it burned her eyes. She wrinkled her nose in disgust and opened her eyes to find herself staring directly at the overflowing dumpster next to PJ's.

After the initial surge of pleasure at having something new work as planned, she looked around to be sure nobody lurked in the shadows and put her hand on the dumpster to be sure it wasn't a vision.

Nice! Now how the hell did I do that?

It sure was a lot more comfortable than spinning through freezing white non-space. And more efficient power-wise. Traveling hadn't set off the claw at all. She smiled to herself. *Score one for me.*

It was late afternoon, and the rush hour traffic filled the air with noise, which made her smile. It was familiar, expected. *Normal.* And it meant no time at all had passed since she and Daric left. *Odd.*

She held the book close to her chest and went into PJ's. After a minute of studying the few people occupying the shop, she had to admit Daric wasn't in evidence.

He's probably upstairs.

Tarian left the shop and went back to the alley, and knocked on Daric's door, clutching the book like a shield and jumping at every noise and shadow. It didn't feel safe, being here where she'd been attacked, with this book. The sooner she moved inside the better.

The door creaked open, and she stepped through, expecting to see Daric hiding in the shadows. The entry was empty.

The door closed behind her with a loud click. Energy washed over her back as a protection shield shimmered into place.

Her heart pounded until a shadow appeared at the top of the stairs and the scent of spice reached her nose. She smiled and looked up, knowing who she'd find.

Daric didn't look happy. The hard line of his lips and the crinkle in the middle of his forehead made her think he was, in fact, livid. Her smile faded as she took in his expression.

He turned and disappeared into the room behind him without a word. Tarian counted to ten, then ventured up the stairs and into Daric's living room. He sat on the couch and radiated anger from the whites of his eyes, which practically bulged at her, to the twitching muscles on his arms.

"Miss me?" Tarian smiled, hoping to break the ice.

Daric's right eye twitched. "Explain."

He's pissed.

"I found Sucole." She held out the book. "I got what I needed."

"That's not an explanation, Scion." He tapped his feet, both fists bouncing up and down on his thighs.

If he kept this up, she was going to be the angry one.

"If you mean my abrupt departure, I didn't plan it. I asked you to come, didn't I? How was I supposed to know she had some sort of travel spell on the coin?"

Daric looked down at his hands like he expected them to morph into something dangerous.

"Look, believe me or don't. I didn't do it on purpose. I was just as shocked when I opened my eyes sitting in a swamp as I imagine you were to see me vanish."

"Shocked is not the right word." His hands twitched.

"You were worried?"

"Worried isn't the right word." He looked up and offered her a ghost of a smile, though his eyes remained tight and twitchy.

She sat down next to him. "What's the right one?" She grinned.

"Frantic." Daric put his hand on her arm, and frowned at the book. The crease in his forehead deepened as he looked at the cover.

"Sucole had it?"

Tarian hesitated. She didn't want to tell Daric about the joining with Ruarc. *Not yet. Not until I sort out what it means.* But she didn't want to lie. She settled for a portion of truth.

"She showed me the spell I need. Look."

Tarian flipped the pages until she located the spell Sucole had indicated. Daric leaned into her and studied it. He pointed to a word at the top of the page.

"See the word here? Decipi? I'm pretty sure that means entrap. Are you sure this is the spell?"

"I'm positive. Look at the diagram. She told me this would banish the lizard, and the picture looks like someone being encased in something. This has to be what I need. If he's banished, he can't steal my power, right? He can't do anything at all."

Daric grunted and they both continued studying the page. A task made more difficult, in her opinion, by the continued body contact and the heat it generated.

The diagram showed a box, which had been gilded with gold, a person in the middle of the circle, and some words along the side, which she assumed described more about the picture.

"Can you read any of this?"

Daric shook his head. "Some. Not much, though. I never was good at the ancient language. But I know a few of these words from prior experience." He pointed at a word near the diagram. "This one means metal. Since there's a line drawn to this gold box I assume it means you need a metal container. This power focus is based in earth."

Daric glanced up at her. "You don't have any earth, do you?"

"No." Tarian rubbed her neck. "Though the Laghairtine sure does. Maybe it'll rub off on me?"

Daric grunted, and returned to the page.

"I get a few more words. Banish, or entrap, I never could get it right. They're so similar. Power. Rune. Blood. Void. Not much to really go on. We need to get this translated. You should know what you're saying before you say it."

"I don't know anyone who can translate this, do you?"

He tilted his head, thinking. "I'm sure my mother can work it out. But it might take a few days."

"We don't have a few days."

"I know, Tari, I know. What about your mother or the archives?"

"I don't think Mother can read ancient text. She's definitely not one for old spells. I think the better one for this is Calliope. She's always studying in the archives."

"Then that's where we should go. Worth a shot, anyway." Daric pulled her to her feet, and opened a portal to the house entry. "After you?"

chapter twenty-eight

Tarian stepped through the portal and held her breath, letting it out again when she realized Alex wasn't waiting in the rotunda. She needed to check in with him but didn't relish the thought of doing it in front of Daric.

From the light streaming through the skylight, it couldn't be more than an hour since she'd left this very spot.

Relieved she didn't have to make explanations for an extended absence, she crossed the rotunda toward the archives, then paused outside the receiving hall doors.

"Can you find the archives without me?" She pointed down the correct hallway. "It's the only door on the right. If Calliope isn't there, wait for me. I need to speak to Mother a moment."

"I can wait here." Daric smiled.

"I'd rather you didn't." Tarian scrunched up her nose. "You and Alex both like to listen at doors."

"Only because you won't tell us what we want to know up front."

"I might if you didn't want to know so much." Tarian pointed at the hallway again.

Daric's lips twitched then he leaned close to her ear and whispered. "As you wish, Scion."

She watched him go, admiring the way his walk accentuated the muscles in his back. *His behind isn't bad either.* She tightened her hold on the *Book of Daemon* and stepped through to the receiving hall.

Marielle stood near the Dolphin Throne watching Advisor Jonus shuffling papers. She looked up when Tarian entered, her gaze moving to the book Tarian clutched in her arms.

"I see you were successful. Well done, Tarian. How was Sucole?"

"Every bit as annoying as you anticipated." Tarian crossed the room at a fast walk. As she passed over the rune in the center of the floor, a small pulse of energy and the sound of dolphin calls wrapped around her. For a brief second she felt encased in ocean waves. When she passed completely over the rune the effect ended.

"What did she ask for in exchange?"

Tarian reached the platform and looked up into her mother's eyes. How had she known?

Marielle smiled. "Nobody lets go of something valuable without getting something in exchange. The question is what price did she demand?"

Tarian looked down at the book. *How am I supposed to say this? I had sex with a daemon? I'm a prostitute? I whored myself out for a book?*

"I take it the price was steep?" Marielle folded her hands in front of her and waited. Beside her, Jonus's hands stilled, the papers he'd been gathering apparently forgotten.

"You could say that. It…" Tarian swallowed. "It wasn't her price. It was someone else's."

"Oh?"

Tarian glanced at Jonus, who kept his eyes on the papers, then back at her mother. "It turned out the one holding the book was a daemon named Ruarc, of the Mayfanata. I…dealt… with him."

The quick intake of breath from Jonus drew her gaze. He didn't look up but his entire body radiated tension from the stiff shoulders to the way his knees locked into place.

Marielle pursed her lips. "Ruarc." Her voice was flat. "Well. I certainly didn't anticipate that."

"You know him?" A quick survey of her mother's face told her not only did Marielle know him, she knew him well.

"We've met. You would have too, eventually, when you visited the Balance Court during the gathering later this year. It's the only time the daemon ever meet with our side unless there's an emergency."

Marielle sat on a nearby chair and indicated for Tarian to join her. "He is the current leader of the Mayfanata. Very powerful, very important and extremely dangerous to deal with. Every word he utters is full of double and triple meanings. He's worse than Sucole for riddles. If he was with Sucole, I hate to think what that means." Marielle's eyes searched Tarian's. "What is he up to?"

Tarian sighed. There was no way to hide this from her mother, but she didn't have to tell Jonus. "Can we speak privately for a minute?"

Marielle glanced at Jonus. "Would you excuse us for a moment, Jonus? I'd appreciate some hot tea."

Jonus frowned. "Wouldn't the Keeper prefer to have two points of view on something this important?"

"I don't know about the Keeper, but the *Scion* definitely prefers to speak to her mother alone." Tarian stared at him. *He usually does exactly what Mother asks. Immediately. Odd he isn't jumping right to it now.*

"Of course. Excuse me." Jonus laid the papers down and exited through the side door, closing it softly behind him.

"He's a trusted member of the family, Tarian."

"I know. But some things a girl only wants to share with her mother. Is that so wrong?" Tarian laid the book down on the table between them.

Marielle touched the cover briefly with her fingers. "What did Ruarc ask for?"

Tarian took a deep breath. "One joining."

"Oh." Marielle leaned back, her face now an impenetrable mask.

"It probably wasn't the smartest move." Tarian bit her lip. Silence spun a web around the two of them. Finally, she blurted "I needed this book, and some things *are* worth the price. It's not like I really had sex with him. Now I have it and the spell I need, and if all goes well tonight, the lizard will be history." The words came out in a fast tumble as she scrambled to justify her choice, to make her mother see it had been worth it. To make herself believe it, too.

"We'll be safe now." Tarian swallowed the lump in her throat. "I'll be safe."

"Oh, Tarian. If only things were that simple." Marielle frowned at the book. "I question his need for this sort of action at this time, with you. He gained something. Most obviously, he gained the chance to add his essence to any child you might carry from the Succession Ritual. What he hopes the child will do for him in the long run remains to be discovered. Worse, with Ruarc, the un-obvious is the most dangerous part." Marielle rubbed the side of her face. When she spoke again, Tarian wasn't entirely sure her mother wasn't simply thinking out loud. She didn't seem to expect an answer or input. "One thing that never changes is the Mayfanata code of self first. His goal will be selfish and self-centered. It will benefit him directly. That means he wants a child armed with air abilities, even more than she'd already possess. The question is why? How will it benefit Ruarc? Does he have some battle he needs to fight?"

Ice formed in Tarian's veins as her mother spoke. Chunks of it broke away and started stabbing her in the heart. She'd been so worried about the Laghairtine stealing her will and using her power as his own, she'd overlooked what might be an even bigger threat in the future. Her own child, part daemon. More than part, since Tarian also carried daemon blood. *Which is something I should ask Mother about. There's a story there.*

She'd not only gambled with her own body but with her future child's as well.

Her hand pressed her stomach. Was a child coming already?

"Should I…is there any way to stop…" She couldn't voice the words.

"There's always a way to stop pregnancy. But if you do, the ritual won't be fulfilled. We take a risk either way."

Marielle brushed a stray piece of hair out of Tarian's face. "Were I you, I'd choose the future over the present. This child will be more than Ruarc. She'll be you and a part of every Potential you join with, a blend enhanced by our link with the Dolphin Throne." Marielle smiled. "Much like you. You control three elements of power because of the unique mix created during my own ritual."

Marielle glanced away. Her index finger traced the outline of the title on the *Book of Daemon*. "Ruarc plays a dangerous game, one where he cannot control the outcome. It's unusual for him. He must be desperate, to release something so valuable with so little to show for it. Had I realized he had it…" Marielle paused, her finger continuing to trace, obviously lost in thought.

I wish I could read minds. Tarian sat back in the chair and watched her mother's face. She found no information. Nothing to indicate what her mother was thinking or feeling.

Finally, Marielle sighed and put her hand back in her lap. "The important thing is for you to not react in kind. Desperation seldom leads to smart decisions."

Tarian nodded. Maybe all was not lost. Her child would, after all, carry Xannon blood.

"How did you do it, Mother? How did you stand this?"

"Meaning?" Her mother held her gaze without flinching.

"What was this whole archaic ritual like for you? Did you like it? Did you like the men? Did you have any choice at all?"

Marielle took a deep breath. She took another and smiled. "In all the years we've argued over this, you've never once asked me how it was for me."

"I suppose I was too busy resenting the situation to worry about it. And until recently, it didn't really matter."

"You do realize had I not participated, most likely you would not be here? How can you doubt I made a good choice?" Her mother looked out across the room. "To answer your question, yes, I had a choice. All of life is a choice."

Her mother leaned back and folded her hands in her lap. "When I first approached the ritual, I was barely eighteen. I'd been raised for that moment, and it was something I approached with anticipation and excitement. I'd always wanted to be a mother. I used to volunteer in the nursery, and I helped with the healers during childbirths. I found the start of a new life fascinating. Your grandmother thought I should wait, but I didn't see the point. I was more than eager to get started with the next phase of life."

Marielle smiled at her. Tarian was startled to see moisture in her mother's eyes. "The beginning of your life was the most amazing thing I'd ever experienced. I felt connected with you in a way I'd never been with anyone. I wouldn't trade it for anything. And once I had you, I knew exactly why I would put up with the tedious parts of the job, and of life. You and your sister are worth a million tedious meetings and all the day- to-day grind. For me. And I'll admit, I found the ritual itself to be a life-affirming, fun adventure." Marielle smiled again, but this time her eyes danced.

She liked the sex! Stunned, Tarian stared at her mother like she'd sprouted a horn off the top of her head. She'd never thought of her mother as a young girl. As a person, really. She was…her mother. But Marielle was also a human with drive and ambition, desires, passions, longings. All of it.

Tarian realized her mouth was hanging open and hastily shut it.

"Now you have the information you sought, what do you intend to do with it?" Marielle studied Tarian.

"You aren't going to *tell* me what to do?"

"Part of being Keeper is making decisions. Choosing a course of action to solve a problem. I won't be Keeper forever. I'd like to hear your plans to solve this particular problem."

Tarian thought about it. Until now, she hadn't exactly made plans. She'd been reacting to events as they happened. It was the main difference between her and her mother. Keeper Marielle strategized, examined a problem from every angle. Tarian pushed her way through and winged it. So far, all that'd gotten her was attacked by a lizard and sex with a daemon. Perhaps planning wasn't a bad thing.

She cleared her throat. "Well, first I need to get this page translated. I can't do the spell properly if I don't know what the words mean."

Marielle nodded her agreement but said nothing.

Tarian looked at the book cover. *Book of Daemon* emblazoned on the cover like a taunt. "I need to do the spell it describes so I can trap the lizard before he hurts me or anyone else. And I..." she looked at her hands, folded in her lap not unlike her mother. "Need to finish the succession, so the Throne and our family are safe."

"Do you intend to perform the spell alone, Tarian?" Marielle picked up the book and started flipping through the pages.

"To be honest, I hadn't thought that far ahead."

"Perhaps you should." Marielle continued to flip idly through. "Though I often find a little knowledge goes a long way. Once you know the words of the spell, then you'll know how to proceed, I would imagine. Unfortunately, I can't help you with translating this. Ancient text is difficult and complex, and since it's no longer used, I never felt the need to learn. A weakness, in hindsight."

"That's not weakness. That's common sense. Why learn a dead language?"

Marielle stopped flipping the pages. "So I could assist my daughter in a moment like this."

"Daric knows a few of the words, and I'm hoping Calliope knows more. Surely we can figure enough of it out."

Marielle nodded. "Yes, Calliope is who I'd ask for help with this. Your sister's affinity for languages has always astounded me."

Marielle closed the book, setting the cover down gently.

"Consider carefully the location. If it were me, I'd perform the task here, in this room."

Tarian looked out at the room, at the glowing rune on the floor and the tapestries. Her home. "Not here. No way am I bringing him here."

"The House is powerful, Tarian. The Dolphin Throne can help. I wouldn't even attempt something like this without it."

Tarian shook her head. "No. The best thing to do is split up. I don't want the lizard getting both of us near this Throne. I want him far away from here and far away from you and Calli. Just in case. And I think we already have the perfect spot in Philly. It's a place the lizard won't expect us to be." The warehouse, still ripe with the Laghairtine's power, provided a direct link to him. Combined with the relative privacy, it was the perfect place.

"If we try together…"

Tarian bolted out of her chair, too restless to sit still any longer. "Don't you see? That's what he wants. I'm not going to give him the chance to take us all. He already took my blood. That's all he's getting. Don't they say never put all your eggs in one basket? Well this House is the basket. And this egg is not staying here with all the other eggs."

Marielle pursed her lips. "I don't suppose someone else can do this? A team of Sentinels perhaps? Our best people?"

"No, Mother. It has to be me. I'm the only one with a close connection."

"But you don't have to be alone."

Tarian thought about it. "No, I don't. And I won't be. I'll take backup. Alex and Frankie are already getting geared for it. I'm sure I won't be able to stop Daric from joining in. Four on one, plus I've had an infusion of energy. That should be enough." *Who am I trying to convince? Mother or myself?*

"Remember one thing, Tarian. The Succession cannot be stopped. The rune is dimming. Do you understand what that means?" Marielle pointed at the rune in the center.

"I figured it would stop glowing when I'd finished the ritual."

Marielle's lips twitched. "Well, yes. But why is a vital piece of information. It started glowing when the ritual was called, which can only be done when you're a week away from ovulation. It gradually fades until you ovulate, at which point the glow stops. Every time you pass over it, the power infused in it on your naming day blends any seed you've accepted into a unique mix which will create the next Scion, should implantation occur."

Tarian stared at the rune. It emitted a faint glow, nothing like it did a few days ago.

"I knew there was a ceremony. I didn't know there was a deadline."

"Any woman trying to conceive faces a deadline. Ours is simply more obvious than most." Marielle stood and put an arm around Tarian and squeezed.

"If part of your plan is to accomplish the ritual, you must not only be here tonight for the reception, but you must act immediately to complete it. By the glow, I'd say you have about twenty-four hours, give or take, before it will be too late."

Tarian swallowed and turned to pick up the *Book of Daemon*. "Then I guess I better get my ass moving."

chapter twenty-nine

Calliope sat exactly where Tarian expected her to be when she entered the archives, the *Book of Daemon* a heavy weight in her arms. She held up one of the green leaves for Daric to inspect, who looked fascinated.

Tarian watched them, her thoughts swirling. *Translate. Sex. Lizard. Throne. Baby.* All of it muddled together, creating a giant wall with no footholds and no door. *How am I going to get through this?*

Daric's eyes twinkled as he caught sight of Tarian.

"How's Mom?"

Tarian raised her eyebrow. "I think the Keeper would be disturbed to hear you call her that."

The dimple in Daric's cheek winked at her. She kept her eyes focused on it as she crossed the room.

"I see you two are getting along."

Her sister's eyes widened as Tarian handed her the book.

"Where did you get this? Daric said you were bringing me

something to translate but he wouldn't say what. Oh, Tari. Look at it. It's amazing!"

Calliope set it down on the table on top of two other open books and studied the cover. Her hand flew to her mouth.

"Oh. *How* did you get this?"

"Never mind how. The real question is can you read it?" Tarian opened the book to the page she needed. "Specifically this page here?"

Calliope sat and studied the page. "I've never seen anything like it. Even the *Book of Society* isn't this...look at the gold tipping! And this drawing, hand inked. It's beautiful."

Tarian glanced at Daric and shrugged. Daric pulled a chair from the next table and sat down.

They waited, Tarian silently willing Calliope to move beyond her obsession with beautiful books and on to more important things, like the instructions on the page.

After a few minutes, Tarian cleared her throat. When that didn't work, she touched Calliope gently on her shoulder. "Calli, I don't have any time. Can you read it?"

"Oh. I know, Tari, I'm sorry. It's just fascinating." Calliope ran her fingers over the words on the page. Each one glowed as she touched it. "It doesn't like us reading it, but I can make out some of it."

"Can you make out enough to tell me what it says?"

Calliope nodded. "I think so. See this here?" She pointed to a block of text at the top of the page. "I don't have to translate this part. I've seen it before."

Calliope rushed off into the stacks of shelves to return a minute later with a very large, very red book. Before Tarian read the title, Calliope opened it and started flipping through the pages. She made a small noise when she found what she was looking for. "Here it is. It says:

'In accordance with policies established among the Ancients, and by the Benata and Mayfanata Courts and the Court of Balance, be it known that any being, magic or otherwise, whose source of power includes absorption from another, shall henceforth be entrapped and charged with protection of earth until such time as there is balance among the planes, and the Courts deem the aforementioned being no longer a threat."

"What is that supposed to mean?"

Calliope moved the book aside to study the *Book of Daemon* again. "It's one of the founding laws when the planes were split. Some daemon were charged with protecting...well, I haven't quite figured it out. Pillars? Something to do with the planes. Anyway, some did it willingly and some were forced, as punishment, for stealing magic. I only know because this is one of the books the Archivists never wanted me to read. Which made me want to read it even more."

Calliope traced more words on the page. "It's definitely a recipe or old-fashioned spell for focus. Really old-fashioned. This part means power circle. A real power circle, created with the seeker's blood."

Tarian groaned. "Do I really have to?"

Calliope nodded. "Yes, definitely. And you have to draw your own power symbol in the center. But I don't get this part." Calliope indicated another block of text. "Too many words I don't recognize."

"Can you make out anything at all?"

Daric leaned forward. "We can probably figure it out if you can get the basics."

"Well, this word means entrap or banish, but I can't tell which because the way it works, I need to know the surrounding words. And I don't recognize these."

"Sucole said banish." Tarian offered.

"Earth. A container, solid with earth." Calliope pointed to part of the drawing. "Metal, I assume. That must be where you banish them to? I can't tell. And you need to be close to the person or being you want to banish."

Tarian rubbed her neck, where the claw lay still for the moment. "Well, I'm definitely close."

"I'm not sure it means that sort of close. It might mean physical proximity. Or it could mean emotional closeness, or maybe it means you need some object that's personal to them. Then there's the spell itself. You say these words three times. If it's like other ancient rituals, you say them once while drawing the circle, once while gathering focus, and once more to cast."

"I know how a circle works, Calli. I did study *something* in school."

Calliope looked away from the book. "All I'm saying is you don't necessarily need to know what the words mean word-for-word. You just have to say them correctly and understand the intent. I can help a bit with the pronunciation even if I can't translate them. They follow basic rules like any other language."

"You're quite the book worm." Daric grinned. "I like it."

Calliope blushed. "I like to read."

"I don't know how we're sisters." Tarian laughed. "Okay, so we need a metal container. Any ideas?"

Calliope leaned against the table, one hand protectively over the pages of the book. "I have something that should work. It's with my sewing kit. One thing, though. We shouldn't leave this book alone."

Tarian frowned, confused. "Why not?"

"Because the species books were only meant to be seen by the species they're written for. I'm shocked you were able to bring it home. This is the *Book of Daemon*. It belongs to them, and it'll return to one of them as soon as it's released. I bet the only thing holding it here is we've never left it alone. Someone should keep their hands on it until we're done with it."

Daric stood and leaned over the book. "Will it fly away?"

Calliope laughed. "I don't know. All I know is it's not ours to keep. The Court records say so." She pointed at the big red book next to Daric.

Of course she's read Court records. Tarian couldn't imagine anything more boring. Reading dusty old books when she could be in the ocean? *Sacrilege.*

Tarian leaned over and put her hand on the open book. It felt like touching a dormant volcano. It spoke of power, infinite possibilities, and energy beyond her wildest dreams. Like the joining with Ruarc. But sleeping, dormant, or at least unfocused. Waiting. *For what?*

"Plus, it's definitely not a good idea to leave it alone here in the archives." Calliope gestured to the nearest fluffy gargoyle. "The Archivists are, after all, daemon. As the closest daemon they stand the greatest chance of taking it from you. I bet they are not happy you have it."

No treasure is worth the price.

"No, you're probably right. They're probably seething." For once, Tarian was grateful they wouldn't speak unless she took their hand. *I don't want to hear the lecture I'm sure they're giving me right now.*

Something brushed her hand, and she glanced down to find Daric's thumb casually caressing the back of her hand. Tarian watched his thumb move, her cheeks burning. *Those hands could touch other parts. I wouldn't mind. Not at all. And I do need Potential Number Three.*

Calliope coughed. "I'll go get the container."

Tarian heard her sister's footsteps cross the room, and the door shut. She looked up into Daric's eyes. They spoke of heat and mystery and raw lust. Her lady bits instantly responded.

"I should study," Tarian said.

"You should." Daric ran his finger over the back of her hand and up her arm, tracing the scar left by the Laghairtine attack. She barely felt it. Something as mundane as breathing was almost impossible with the way his eyes boiled. He leaned against the table as though it were his own private stage. *Show for one, please.*

"How'd you really get the book, Tari? Nobody gives up something like this for nothing, and Sucole is not daemon. Who really had it?"

Disarmed by the feel of his hand on her skin, she nearly answered him with the truth. But the truth was the last thing she wanted him to know. Not right now. "She handed it to me herself."

Daric narrowed his eyes. His thumb continued to caress the scar. Trickles of heat traced up her arm. "Just like that?"

"Basically."

"You keep a lot of secrets, Scion."

"Everybody keeps secrets."

"Tari, it could be important. Really important."

Tarian shook her head. "Not for this."

"You sure?"

"Pretty sure. And if you're trying to do the hypno trick on me like you did with those girls, knock it off."

Daric grinned and his dimple winked at her. "I'm not doing anything but touching your arm. Do you feel something else?"

Holy shit. If a touch on her arm did this, what would the rest of his body do?

Before she knew what she was doing, she stood and leaned into him. His hands moved up to her face, and one stroked her hair. His fingers worked at a few tangles, which melted her legs and heated up her nether region even more.

Her hands found their way to his arms and squeezed his biceps. *Damn he's stacked. This is a man who can hold his own in a fight.*

The thought of fighting him in the arena flashed through her mind. *Wouldn't that be quite the turn on? Adrenaline, exertion, all those body parts touching...*

Daric pulled her closer, and his lips brushed hers. Heat, like lava, with a tiny burst of sea scent and the promise of waves.

The door opened, Daric released her arms, and Tarian flopped back down into the chair. Her lips burned, but she tried her best to ignore it and didn't turn around.

Footsteps paused, and Calliope's hesitant voice broke the silence. "Uh. I...can come back?"

Daric beckoned her over. "That looks perfect, Calli. Now we just need to help the Scion here learn the words."

He moved away from the *Book of Daemon*, which he'd managed to keep in touch with by sitting on it while they fooled around with body parts. Tarian swore she heard him utter the word "tasty" as he shifted aside.

She didn't look at him. The heat already in her cheeks embarrassed her enough, no need to add to it.

Calliope crossed the room, and handed a metal box to Daric. "I use it to keep enhanced thread. Spell thread gets all knotted up if I let it run loose."

"Perfect." Daric examined the box. "Silver. Nice. You sure you can part with it? I'm not sure you'll be getting it back."

"It's not a family heirloom or anything. I found it in an

antique store on the Big Island. I can get another." Calliope moved to the other side of the table, pulled up a chair, and sat down. "Okay. Time to memorize?"

Tarian pulled the book in front of her, glad her cheeks felt just about normal. All the same, she avoided Daric's eyes. *Damn it.* Didn't her sister have perfect timing? The kiss was delicious, but not enough. *Not nearly enough.*

"Okay, any idea what these words mean? I should know, right? To focus my intention?"

Calliope nodded. "Let me see it. I'll write out what I think it says, and then you can memorize the words while thinking the English translation. I think."

Calliope turned the book around, pulled a piece of paper from a stack near her and a pen from behind her ear. She went to work writing words, scribbling them out, writing others. Tarian watched for a minute or two, still avoiding Daric's gaze. When that proved difficult, she occupied them with looking around the archives instead.

Three of the Archivists now huddled in front of the stacks of books. They exuded a sense of purpose, even stationary.

When did they move?

Startled, Tarian realized one squatted barely a foot from her, though now it didn't even twitch. Obviously, they wanted to talk with her.

It's the book. They want the book.

"You can't have it." She told the nearest one.

Daric shifted his chair slightly, closer to her. "Have what?"

"Nothing."

"Oh, I hope I can have more than nothing." His breath against her ear tickled.

She grinned. *Me too.*

Whatever it was, pheromones, lust, fear, need, she had to admit her entire body wanted more than just a kiss from Daric.

"Anything?" Tarian turned back to Calliope.

"Enough, I think. I'm not sure of a couple of the words, and this is pretty rough."

"It's close enough, Calli. If I know the basics, I'll learn the real words and it'll be enough."

Tarian took the paper from her sister and read the words out loud, careful not to assign any magical intention to them.

I call upon Ancients, and the Power of Nature
To help me banish my foe
I call upon Water, Flowing Song
I call upon Air, Freedom Long
I call upon Fire, Chaos Reigns
I call upon Earth, Solid and Strong
I bind with Spirit, with the power in me
Five points of protection, three times three
I weave this spell
I call this power
To Bind, To Seal, To Banish thee

"Okay. So now it's my turn." Tarian said the first line of foreign words out loud. Calliope laughed.

"No, not like that. The things that look like C and H are silent, but they make the next part a long vowel sound."

They worked back and forth, Tarian stumbling with the words, Calliope correcting her pronunciation, until she perfected them. Daric took the book and quizzed her. In an hour, she recited the whole thing from memory.

Calliope yawned. "I think you've got it."

"How long since you've slept, Calli?" Tarian examined her sister's face. Dark circles. Pale skin. *Since the attack I bet.*

"Oh, I'm fine."

"Get a nap. I need to check in with Alex. Time to get this ball rolling." For the first time since the attack, she felt great. *Probably Ruarc.*

Tarian scooped the book up off the table and held it tightly to her chest. Daric took the silver box in one hand and opened the archive door with the other.

Tarian looked back before she closed the door and saw all six Archivists lined up in front of the stacks.

"Later." She promised them, and shut the door.

We'll talk later.

chapter thirty

As they left the Archives, Tarian turned right toward the bedrooms with Calliope. Her sister glanced at her, but said nothing, leading the way down the hallway. When they reached Calliope's door, all three of them paused.

Calliope smiled at Daric. "Was nice to meet you, Daric. Tari? When are you doing this? I should be there, just in case."

Tarian hugged her sister. "You get some sleep. Thanks, Calli."

She turned away and walked quickly down the hall, not daring to look back. Daric said something Tarian couldn't make out then hurried to catch up. He fell into step beside her.

"In a hurry?"

Tarian slowed down. They reached the door to her bedroom and she stopped. Sentinels stood at attention on either side.

Well doesn't that just kill the mood.

Tarian glanced back and saw Calliope's door still open a few inches.

Daric reached over and brushed a loose piece of her hair out of her eyes. The warmth of his fingers against her skin sparked a fire somewhere in her stomach. His eyes met hers, and she found herself unable to breathe for a second. "Something wrong?"

The soft click of her sister's door as it closed spurred her into action. Tarian grabbed Daric's hand and pulled him into her bedroom and slammed the door, before she made eye contact with the Sentinels on duty.

Won't this start the rumor mill working overtime!

Once inside, she let go of Daric's hand and set the book down on her dresser. She turned and stood, uncertain, in the middle of the room. Daric's eyes burned a hole right through her. Her heart thumped inside her throat. The Laghairtine, the Throne, both could go to hell. She'd have done this even without those things.

Maybe not this fast.

She pulled Daric toward the bed. When they reached it, she pushed him onto it. He sat, but he seemed reluctant to do more.

"You sure about this?" He studied her face.

She pushed his legs apart to stand between them.

His eyes smoldered. She saw desire. He wanted her. A thrill raced through her at the thought. Anticipation and fear blended together until she couldn't sort out exactly which caused her to press in closer. Warmth radiated out from his legs and chest.

Still, he didn't move a hand.

She tilted her head. "No?"

"Why now?" A slight frown forced his eyebrows down.

"Why not?"

He shook his head. "Answer the question."

"Because I damn well want to." If she was going to donate her body for the good of the Throne and the region, she was going to enjoy it. She'd already been with Ruarc and Alex. Her ovarian clock was ticking. And she liked Daric. A lot.

This moment might be the only one she'd ever have. Tomorrow didn't come with a guarantee. And maybe, just maybe, this would keep the Throne safe. At least long enough for her to banish the Laghairtine.

She pulled back far enough to get her hands underneath her shirt then lifted it up and over her head. His nostrils flared as her shirt hit the floor. His hands twitched against his thighs. He wanted to touch her; she sensed it in the way the muscles on his arms tensed. What held him back?

She put her hands on the button of her jeans and worked the button, her fingers sliding easily underneath and pulling down the zipper. His eyes widened at the sound. He put his hands on hers, holding them in place. She felt the heat from him against her bare stomach. She was anxious for him to do more than sit.

"Tarian, wait. I need to understand."

Her shoulders slumped. Obviously, she needed lessons in the seduction department. Usually all a girl had to do was flash a little skin and a willing smile. *Damn the man for being more honorable.*

"What's to understand? Girl meets boy, girl lusts after boy, girl wants sex with boy."

"I get the lust part, and the feeling's mutual. But why right now?"

"I only have right now, this moment. Tomorrow might never come for me. You've been flirting ever since we met. Now you're telling me you don't want this? That you won't…help me?" Anger flooded her. "What was all that earlier, a tease?" She stepped back from the comfort of his thighs.

Daric grabbed her hand, preventing her from getting very far. He pulled her back until she was close again, and his hand cupped her face. She saw compassion, lust, and uncertainty in his eyes and the worried way his eyebrows joined together. Her anger evaporated.

"That's what this is? Part of the ritual?" His thumb gently caressed her cheek. "I'm going to help you get rid of this creature, Tarian. You don't have to do this now. Let's wait until after we've solved your problem, and if you still want this…"

"This can't wait. And if you're trying to save my virtue, don't worry about it. I never had any. My family doesn't work that way. It was up for grabs the minute I was born." She didn't want to go into the physical reasons why it had to be now, this moment. More than anything, she wanted this to satisfy a need to live dangerously. Just in case tomorrow never came.

She traced the side of his face with her fingers. Rough stubble gave way to the smooth scar. Battle wounds or childhood trauma? She'd love to know. She'd love to find out more. But she couldn't. "Look, I realize this isn't ideal. I can't marry you. I can't promise you a relationship or a long-term commitment other than friendship. I can't even promise you I'll be faithful, because we both know that's not in the cards for me. But I can promise I want this. With you. Right now." She moved her face closer to his with each word. "Can you please just kiss me?"

She waited, her lips an inch from his, for his answer.

He quirked a grin. "Yeah, but will you still respect me in the morning?"

"That depends."

He raised an eyebrow.

"Are you going to kiss me or not? A girl has to have standards."

He smiled and caressed her cheek with one hand while the other brushed a stray hair away. He leaned toward her and brushed her lips with his own. Every nerve in her body tingled as his lips traveled, leaving behind a gentle caress of her mouth and cheek.

He shifted his hands from her face to the small of her back

and drew her in closer. His fingers fumbled at the clasp on her bra, and it was free. He slid the straps over her shoulders and down her arms until the bra fell away.

She held her breath, willing him to explore further. She wanted to feel his hands on her breasts, his lips on hers, his body pushing into her. She wanted it with an urgency that wasn't completely sexual. She wanted to feel. Not just an exchange of power that left her wanting more, and not just a sexual release, but to really feel a connection. A physical, emotional, psychic connection.

His lips brushed against the top of her left breast. She threw her head back, presenting her chest for him to play with. She thought she heard him growl, but it might have been her imagination.

His lips trailed along the top of her breast and over to the other. Her nipples hardened as his mouth teased first one, then the other. His tongue flicked the tip before locking on, seeking, sucking, kissing and massaging while his hand caressed the other. He explored each nipple in turn.

He tortured her with the slow, methodical movement until she couldn't stand it.

Impatient, she shoved him onto the bed and crawled up beside him. She lowered her body onto his, relishing the soft touch of his knit shirt against her nipples and stomach.

Daric watched her as if half afraid she would do something dangerous to some part of his anatomy. She couldn't take it anymore. She put her lips on his. His touch was soft, pliable in return. She moved into it, drawing his lips apart with her tongue.

His tongue met hers, and they tasted each other in a delicious quest of exploration. This close, she smelled spice and musky sweat and fresh shampoo. She smiled against his lips.

Daric drew back from the kiss, a question in his eyes.

"You smell good."

He laughed and rolled her over until he had the upper hand. She lay back against the bed, delighted. She found she didn't have to convince him to play along anymore. Whatever his objections were, he must have decided they didn't matter.

"You're overdressed." She tugged at his shirt.

Daric shook his head. "No, no, Scion. Ladies first."

His hands made a slow, exquisitely soft trail down between her breasts, her stomach, before moving further down to the open top of her jeans. He pushed the zipper the rest of the way down, and his hand snaked inside.

She lifted her hips to make things easier for him, helping him push the jeans down past her butt and to her knees. Cool air greeted the heat on her inner thighs and made her shiver. Or maybe it was his fingers as they explored their way down her legs in an effort to get the offending piece of clothing out of the way.

By the time he pushed the jeans down to her ankles, she craved his touch so badly she nearly did it herself. She vibrated in all sorts of fun places.

He took one boot off, then the other. She heard them thump to the floor; each thud made her veins pulse. The jeans followed, inched slowly off her calves and over her foot by his determined, slightly calloused hands. She lay exposed, aching and more than ready for those hands to find their way back up her body.

As if he read her mind, his fingers traced a path up her calves. His lips followed, soft, warm with his breath, gently exploring inch by inch. When he reached her thighs, she groaned. This was torture. She willed his hand to stop and caress her clit. To relieve the pressure he'd built. She moved one leg to the side, a clear invitation.

His hand brushed her panties exactly where she wanted him to, but he didn't linger. He continued on up to her breasts.

"Daric." She grabbed his head and pulled him up for another kiss.

This time, he took command. His tongue explored hers. One hand formed a fist with her hair, while the other massaged her breast. Her lips tingled with the force of his efforts. Somewhere in the kiss, her panic left, to be replaced by intense longing for more. More kisses, more of him touching more of her…just more.

She raked her nails along his back. His muscles felt tight and powerful and made her feel safe. There was no lizard, no ritual, no responsibility. Only this.

Daric lifted from her and cold air rushed in. Her nipples stood at attention, excited by the sudden chill.

His hand moved slowly down her stomach to her panties. His fingers pushed them aside and slid between her lips.

She could have told him she was ready, but she enjoyed the rush, the flare of lust in his eyes when he discovered she was wet and more than willing for him to explore every inch of her body, inside and out.

He kept his eyes focused on hers, a deep connection that shook her, as his fingers worked their way inside her. He dipped into the liquid that had pooled then moved up to stroke her at the very tip of her folds. Her back arched, and she couldn't stop the small sound that escaped her throat.

The dimple appeared on his cheek. He stroked again, and his fingers worked at her in earnest. She pushed her hips against his hands. Her eyes closed. His breath warmed her face. His lips kissed her mouth, her nose, her eyes. The pressure of his hand on the groin and his finger inside her took her breath. She was so close to the edge…

He stopped and moved away.

She groaned and opened her eyes. *What now?*

The look she saw on his face should have been accompanied by devil horns. He'd stopped to tease her. Make her wait.

"Daric."

He stood and took off his shirt, tossing it aside like a rag. The pants came off a bit slower. She wouldn't have missed this show for anything.

She couldn't stop a grin when she saw he wore boxers. The convenient hole in the middle left little to her imagination.

"You seem to be enjoying yourself."

"Immensely." His voice and his eyes held promise. He pushed his boxers off without ceremony.

She couldn't help but stare. She'd seen men naked before. Alex, in particular, was a fine specimen, one any woman would find worthy of excitement. Alex hadn't been her first, either. She wasn't innocent. But this felt different. She wanted Daric on a deep level she couldn't even explain to herself. Maybe it was the fear and uncertainty of what lay ahead. Maybe it was the remains of her power mingle with Ruarc. Maybe it was something else altogether. Whatever she told him, this felt like a commitment. More than her little stunt with Alex. More than her deal with Ruarc. She licked her lips.

Daric must have noticed the shift in her mood because concern replaced the delight and lust in his eyes. A crease formed in the middle of his forehead.

"Tarian?"

She held out her hands. When he took them, she pulled him down next to her.

"I don't want to think. Don't think." She took his face in her hands and looked into his eyes. The warmth banished all butterflies in her heart and stomach. She pulled his face to hers and kissed him softly. "I want you."

His hand on her hip tightened, and he responded by kissing her quite thoroughly.

Daric shifted until his body was over hers. His hand gently moved her legs apart, wider, until he slipped between them and moved so his hardness brushed against her. Her mouth watered. No more nerves. Just longing and need.

"Don't tease." She moaned.

He grinned, reaching down to let his fingers play with her once more. She felt them, slick against her skin. The apex of her groin jumped at his every touch. She was right back on the edge of the cliff so fast she gasped.

He slipped inside her, warm, hard, demanding, possessive. She arched her back to receive him and wrapped her legs around him to keep him anchored inside her. He filled her so completely.

For a moment, he didn't move. She closed her eyes and took in every bit of him. His scent, the feel of his arms beside her shoulders holding himself above her. Her hands drifted along his biceps to his back. It felt so right. *He* felt so right. She squeezed, and he shifted his hips slowly, pushing further inside her.

She opened her eyes to look at him. He watched her, his eyes traveled over every inch of her face as if reassuring himself she was ready and not regretting her actions.

She tightened her thighs around his hips and pulled him deeper. He didn't hold back any longer. His hips started to move in, out, in, out. Her breath matched the rhythm and her legs joined in, helping him move.

If she thought she'd been at the cliff's edge before, it was nothing compared to what she felt now. He moved faster. Her heart raced to keep up.

He shifted again and his motion quickened. Her body responded; every nerve in her groin tingled. She couldn't keep her eyes open anymore. She let go and lost herself in the moment and the rhythm of two bodies joined as nature intended. A soft moan from Daric blended with her groans. More. More. Faster.

Now, dammit, now!

When she climaxed, her magic joined in to push her out into a void of nothing but pure sensation and energy. His mixed and blended with hers. More than the raw strength of Ruarc, this time power mixed with passion, lust, trust, and a blend of fear and unvarnished need.

Her body shook with release, arms and legs trembled, head exploded. The claw stirred in her neck. Energy from it raced along her own magic, buoyed by Daric's, out of her body into the void.

She tried to pull it back, but it was too late. The claw established a solid link, as though it were a thick rope around her neck tied with a thousand knots. She couldn't sever it. Desperate, she pulled herself back from the brink of climax and opened her eyes.

chapter thirty-one

Daric's ragged breath and sweaty body hovered over her. His arms shook with the last of his own climax. His eyes opened and fixated on her. She couldn't tell if he'd felt the lizard or not.

She grasped Daric's arms and tried to steady her breathing.

"Tarian?" He moved off her. She instantly missed the warmth of him inside her. Why did the Laghairtine have to intrude now?

The blend of power had called the lizard to her. Even here, protected by the house. She'd ignored the fundamental rule. Power called to power. With every bit of magic he stole, he solidified his link to her and his ability to sense even the slightest magic use.

Part of her slipped away, already owned by the Laghairtine.

"Talk to me. What's going on?" Daric stood up and picked up his pants, shoving his legs in them so fast he nearly fell over.

The Laghairtine tugged at her. With such a solid link, the connection felt intimate. Almost like they shared a body. He was doing…something. Whatever it was, it took a lot of energy. She wasn't even sure he was aware she'd connected to him at last.

"It's time to trap a lizard; that's what's going on." She put on her shirt and stood to get her pants.

Daric let his shirt fall to the floor again. He took hold of her arms and pulled her close so she was forced to look him in the eye. "We can't go into this with less than all the facts. What happened just now?"

She closed her eyes so she didn't have to see his expression while she explained.

"At the end, the claw joined with the lizard and linked us. I can still feel him, but I don't think he's aware of me." She didn't like the way her voice quivered and cleared her throat to make it stop.

Daric squeezed her arms. "You're tracking him right now?"

She opened her eyes so to glare at him. "Not on purpose. I don't know why it happened. But now I can feel him. I can find him. He's doing something that takes a lot of concentration and energy. If we do the ritual right now, he'll be easy to find and easy to catch."

She pulled away and finished zipping her pants. "I know the words. We have the container. Alex and Frankie will back us up. Let's do this."

Daric picked up his shirt and put it on. She struggled to get her own clothes sorted, her legs still numb and stretched from being wrapped around his body.

What if this doesn't work? The thought chilled her.

"Daric, if this doesn't work. If the lizard gets control of me." Tarian swallowed. Her mouth was suddenly bone dry. "If that happens, I need you to promise you'll end it."

Daric paused, his pants still unbuttoned. "Exactly what do you mean by that?"

"You know what I mean." She couldn't look at him.

"If you mean you want me to kill you, forget it. Not happening."

"I need to make sure my family is protected. You can't let the lizard send me back to this House under his control. The Throne will fight back. Or worse, it'll let him take over." Her pulse throbbed along the side of her neck. "You can't let it happen. Promise me."

Daric shook his head. "I won't make that promise."

"If you won't, I'll ask someone else."

"I doubt you'll find anybody who would agree."

Her instinct was to say Alex would do it. *He'd do anything for me. Anything. Except that.*

Daric took her in his arms. "It's not going to come to that, Tarian. This will work, and if it doesn't we'll think of something else. I won't abandon you. You aren't alone."

"I should be." She buried her face in his chest. "I should have run the second that asshole stole my blood."

Daric hugged her, his hands soothed and comforted. "If the Laghairtine wants the Throne, he'd find another way to get it. One thing I've learned is there's no good way to stop someone who is willing to risk their life for something, except to end them before they succeed. You didn't do this, Tarian. It's not your fault."

"It is. I was sloppy."

"Someone betrayed you. It doesn't make you sloppy."

She pulled away. "I can't believe someone in this House would do it."

"Betrayal only works if it's someone close to you. Who knew you'd be in Philly?"

Tarian thought about it. "Alex. Frankie. Daryl. That's it."

"There's your answer."

"There is no way Alex or Frankie would do this. No way." Anger at the thought rushed through her. He didn't know Alex. If he did, he'd never accuse him of something like this.

"You said another name."

"Daryl? He wasn't the one. He's dead." She thought about it. He was a junior Sentinel. He was nobody. She shook her head. "He was silenced. A bit player. Someone else is pulling the strings. So to speak."

"Everybody has their button. Everybody has their price. If he's dead, it's because he knew something he shouldn't, and someone else didn't want you to know about it. Someone who has a lot to lose if you find out they have one foot in your House and one somewhere else."

"Maybe the lizard is the one pushing the buttons? He did get into the Cellar. Who's to say he couldn't roam the rest of the halls?"

She noticed the slightest hesitation before he answered. His eyes shifted away from her.

"Maybe."

"But you don't think so. You think someone inside this House is in on this…whatever this is. You think there's more than the Laghairtine and Daryl."

Daric nodded, looking her in the eye. "I think a plan this elaborate has a lot of hands. I think something like the Laghairtine would be noticed with so much power embedded in this house. He'd find it pretty difficult to hide out here for long."

"You're hiding something, I can tell."

"Not hiding. Just not certain of facts."

She nodded. "Next time you think I'm holding back something, remember you said that. Come on. Alex is probably pissed off I haven't checked in by now."

She tucked the *Book of Daemon* into a dresser drawer and pulled underwear over it. Her room was guarded by Sentinels and a lot of special wards. It should be safe enough. She picked up the silver box from the nightstand, and the two of them left the room. One last glimpse of the disheveled bed and the door closed.

Hopefully not for the last time.

chapter thirty-two

Tarian nearly ran down the hall to the rotunda. Daric's boots pounded the floor next to her. His stride created strong, sturdy beats echoing off the walls until it sounded like an army followed them, an army which tripled when they reached the round walls of the rotunda.

They discovered Alex and Frankie waiting in the rotunda. Both wore guns, daggers, enough gear to take out a small town, and grim expressions.

"It's been three hours." Alex held up three fingers as he saw her approach.

Tarian slowed to a walk, noting the way Alex's eyes flicked from her, to Daric, then down at the floor. A flush rose on her face. *News travels fast. He knows.*

"Can you track him from here?" Daric surveyed the room.

"What's going on?" Alex glared at Daric. "What'd you do?"

"Nothing any grown man wouldn't do." Daric stared calmly back at Alex.

"Can you two measure testosterone later? I need to concentrate." Tarian closed her eyes and focused. She felt the lizard now as an extension of herself. It wasn't tracking. It didn't involve her power at all. His link to her prickled her skin as if stabbing it with a thousand tiny toothpicks. It was all over, as though the signal were confused or blocked. She couldn't tell what direction she should go.

"What's wrong?" Alex kept his voice low this time, concern rippling through the words.

"The Laghairtine established a link with her. A solid link. He's doing something, most likely harvesting more blood." Daric's voice matched Alex's. The tension in the room changed from competition to concern.

Frankie's voice joined in. "Can you track?"

Tarian opened her eyes. All three men stood shoulder to shoulder, staring at her. "Not without shouting to him we're coming. He feels it every time I use magic. If he feels me, he'll head straight for me and he's crossed these walls before. I don't want to bring the fight here."

Alex frowned. "I don't think we should be handing him any more weapons than he already has. We need a safe place to do this. I don't know of any safer place than this house."

Tarian crossed the room toward the entry. "I will not allow the jerk access to my House or my family, and that's final. We take the fight to him. Now, while he's distracted. He won't expect it. We'll be four on one and have the element of surprise." Tarian stopped and looked back the men. "The only question is, are you with me or not?"

Daric nodded. "Always."

Alex set his shoulders. "You don't even gotta ask."

Frankie glanced down the hall. "We should warn the

Sentinels, just in case." He tapped on a wrist device. She immediately heard boots in the distance as men gathered into assigned positions.

"How you gonna take the fight to him when every time you track he steals power? That ain't a good idea." Alex spoke with patience, as though pointing out the obvious to a child.

Tarian glared at him. "How else are we going to find him?" If she couldn't use her normal tracking, and she didn't want him to know she was coming, how else could she travel to him?

Travel.

"I'm going to try something. All of you stay close." She glanced around. "Maybe we should hold hands, just to be sure."

She took in the perplexed looks from all of them. "If we travel the same way I did to reach Sucole, he won't feel us coming. The last time I used it, the claw didn't even jiggle."

"The last time you used it didn't work out so well." Daric looked at Alex and Frankie. "She disappeared right in front of me, left me standing there feeling stupid."

Alex snorted.

Frankie held out a hand. "She's right. If we're touching each other, we should travel together. That happens even in portals."

Tarian took Frankie's hand. "It's worth a try." Daric took her other hand immediately, but Alex crossed his arms instead.

"What if it don't work? What if you disappear? How we gonna find you?"

"If we don't go now, we'll blow the chance. If I end up there without you, I'll portal back immediately."

Frankie held out a hand to Alex. "It should work, bro."

Alex uncrossed his arms and slowly walked around Tarian until he stood behind her. He placed both hands on her shoulders and squeezed.

"I got your back," he whispered in her right ear.

She felt Daric squeeze her left hand, so she knew he'd heard. But he said nothing. Thankfully.

"Okay, boys, here we go."

She closed her eyes and concentrated once again on the connection with the demon. Without using magic, she tried her best to picture him. The image she came up with matched the one she saw in the alley, but she didn't want to travel to the alley. She let her mind drift. *Where is he? What is he doing? What can he see right this moment?*

For a heartbeat or two, all she saw was the lizard-man. His claws extended toward her as they had in the alley. A room solidified around him. It looked like a living room of a typical house in the suburbs. She grabbed the image and focused on it, willing it to appear around her like she'd done with Sucole. She painted every detail of the room in her mind. Curtains with ruffles around a picture window, a rug made of some sort of rags on the floor, a fireplace with a marble mantle. A smell greeted her, one of must or mold, and something metallic. Wet. Acrid.

Tarian opened her eyes.

She stood in the middle of the scene she'd imagined. In front of her, the Laghairtine, with his half-man, half-lizard body, loomed larger than life. His eyes blazed red, his claws dripped with blood, and a human arm dangled from one of them.

Time faltered, slowed down, and circled the room. The demon's eyes widened and lit up with recognition.

Tarian sucked in a quick breath and squeezed the two hands she still held. Their answering squeeze told her all she needed to know.

Time snapped back and rushed forward. Daric stepped in front of her, his arms thrust out wide in some sort of manly display of chivalry. The lizard responded by throwing the arm at them. She and Frankie both ducked, leaving Daric to take the brunt of a swipe from the creature. The force threw Daric across the room and into the marble fireplace and knocked Tarian off her feet. The silver box flew out of her hands and into the hallway. Frankie drew his gun and fired powered bullets at the Laghairtine.

The lizard deflected each one with tiny burst of earth-powered rock. Ricochet sent them careening around the room, igniting bits of wallpaper or collapsing furniture.

Tarian tried her best to stay low while gathering her focus to her. With Daric down, she wouldn't have time to draw the circle. How well the spell would work without the power circle she didn't know, but she had to try. Frankie couldn't hold the lizard off forever.

In the back of her mind, she realized something was missing. Something important. But she couldn't take time to figure out what.

She started to recite the words she'd memorized, adding her magic to it.

The Laghairtine growled, licked his lips, and held out a hand. He drew on dust in the room, forming a fist-sized stone, which he flicked at Frankie. It knocked him across the room and into the window. Glass shattered as Frankie sailed through it and out of sight. The lizard flicked again, this time toward Daric.

A melon-sized rock struck Daric square on the chest. He slid down the marble fireplace and collapsed, his body slack. The Laghairtine turned back toward her. His eyes gleamed with triumph, or maybe he was hungry. Whichever it was, she wanted no part of it.

Tarian backed away from him, her feet scrambling to get a grip on the slick floor. She managed to stand then run from the room. *Follow me, you bastard. Get away from my friends.* The vision of Daric, Frankie, and Alex all torn apart spurred her onward.

Alex.

Where the hell was Alex? He wasn't with her, and he wasn't in the room. She hadn't felt him behind her when they arrived, either. The realization hit that he hadn't come along for the ride. Her heart pounded. Without Alex, without the guys to contain and distract the lizard, she wouldn't be able to complete the ritual.

Think. Think!

She had to lead him away from Daric and Frankie. If they weren't already dead, distance might save them.

She ran down the hall. A door stood open in front of her and she raced for it, not caring where it led. Anywhere that gave her half a second to gather her power was fine.

The door turned out to be to the kitchen. As she reached it, every window in the room shattered. Glass shards tore at her clothes. Something sharp smacked her in the cheek, and blood oozed down. Something else slammed into her back and she landed on the floor, the breath knocked out of her.

While she struggled to breathe she heard a low laugh that chilled her. A kick sent her skidding across the floor. She slammed into the cabinets and felt one of the handles crush into her back. Gasping, she managed to look up. The lizard flicked his tongue and hissed. He advanced on her with arms flexed. The claw danced in her neck.

She pushed to her feet and kicked his chest, joing the kick with the strongest magical pulse she'd ever managed in her life. It was enough to push him backward, colliding with the wall with enough force to knock a hole in it.

It didn't slow the Laghairtine down. He seemed more eager to get to her than he had been before. She knew she'd never get in another kick. He was in fighting stance now and ready for it. Instead, she sent another pulse, this one aimed at his head. It glanced off him and ricocheted, shattering another window behind her.

She had to do something different. Something unexpected. She laughed, a raucous noise that sounded foreign to her. She said the first thing that came to mind.

"You think you have me exactly where you want me. You're a fool. You can't kill me. You need me."

It was all bluster, but the lizard paused. Sweat poured across the scales on his hands and face. He seemed almost disoriented. His reaction surprised her, but she wasn't going to waste the moment. She gathered a combination of energy, some air, some fire, and sent a ball of flame toward him. He deflected it at the last second, and it exploded the wall behind him. He was covered in an avalanche of daggers made of wood. His clothing caught fire, fueled by her magic. A backlash of power hit her. She staggered, desperate to stay on her feet. Her stomach boiled, and her head swam through thick, stifled air.

For a moment, the lizard stood watching her, his clothes in flames, shards of wood sticking out of his body everywhere that wasn't covered in scales.

"Truth has ssssting." His words, absurd in the middle of the chaos. The lizard disintegrated into a puff of red mist as he had in the alley, blown away by a wind she hadn't created.

Tarian doubled over in pain as her neck and shoulders seized against the claw. Her power flowed out at an alarming rate, pulled along an invisible cord to the Laghairtine. Just when she thought it was all over, he'd taken the last of it, the flow cut off. She collapsed from the sudden release.

She rolled over onto her back, glass and rocks poking into her back. The room spun. *Breathe. Breathe. I can't pass out now. They need me. Daric and Frankie. Alex. Where are you Alex?*

After a few deep breaths, the room righted itself and she managed to get to her feet. She stood in the ruins of the kitchen and gasped. Why had the lizard left so quickly? Why hadn't he simply taken control of her? Wasn't that what he wanted?

Truth stings.

What truth?

She wracked her brain for the words she'd said to distract him.

"You think you have me exactly where you want me. You're a fool. You can't kill me. You need me."

You need me.

She'd like to think she had the upper hand in the fight, but she knew it wasn't true. He'd been kicking her ass. Again. He had to have known he would win this fight. He could have had her. But the timing wasn't right. He needed her for something besides the Dominion. What?

She saw bright daylight through the hole in the wall. She waited, ready to strike at anything that moved.

Silence.

As she released her muscles, both physical and magical, parts of her body started to protest all the abuse. Her back stung, and she'd definitely twisted her ankle. She glanced down and saw new scratches along both of her arms. Blood dripped from them, and her cheeks were sticky and stiff with caked blood. Her eye felt swollen.

The Laghairtine hadn't expected her here. That was clear. He'd been as startled when they showed up as she'd been when he'd tossed two powerful men aside like play toys. He hadn't expected to be caught ripping people apart.

Confusion rippled through her thoughts. He'd attacked her, but when it came time to finish her off, he didn't. Or couldn't. He'd sweated blood, taken a beating, and vanished as though called somewhere in a hurry. He disappeared into the Between, she had to assume. That's why no signal now. *Why?*

The simple answer? He'd been told not to. Something, or someone, wasn't ready for him to finish with her. Yet. Everything from the way he'd let her live, twice, to the way he hadn't finished the Dominion shouted another called the shots. If the Laghairtine didn't call the shots, then who did?

And when would they be ready?

chapter thirty-three

A distant whimper grabbed Tarian's attention. Daric. Or Frankie. She couldn't tell which. And where the hell was Alex? She limped down the hall toward the sound.

A lingering trace of red mist drifted from the living room to greet her. She stopped at the entrance and leaned against the wall. She hadn't really seen the room before. All she'd noticed was the lizard with a body part in his claw. Now she had a chance to survey the situation.

It was pure hell on earth. A nightmare. Small chunks of human flesh spackled the room from floor to ceiling. Body parts littered the floor. She saw a finger, a toe, so many pieces. At least a dozen people. Maybe more. An eyeball stared at her from the middle of the room. It still had the ligaments attached to it. Bile rose from her stomach and burned her throat.

Daric balanced on his hands and knees by the fireplace. Relief surged through her as she realized he was alive and moving, even if he was badly hurt. She limped over to him and helped him stand. He looked dazed, but he wasn't whimpering or even moaning. So what made the noise?

Another whimper drew her attention to the far corner. She left Daric to help whoever it was. A naked girl, or what was left of her, lay at an awkward angle with her head shoved into the corner and her once pretty blond hair now dripping with blood. She must have been the last one to join the party, as she still had most of her body parts attached. Her entrails spread across her stomach, and her legs had been ripped off at the knees. Her eye sockets were both empty, wide, blank holes. Her arms lay at awkward angles, and her hands were missing.

As she watched, the girl's body twitched. One final convulsion and it lay still.

Tarian turned her back on the room and threw up.

She heard footsteps, and a hand touched her back.

"You okay?"

She wiped her mouth and turned to Daric. She noticed an impressive bruise already blooming on the side of his face.

"I'll live. You?"

"Better than her." Daric looked around the room, his mouth set. "Where're Frankie and Alex?"

"Frankie went through the window. Alex…I don't know."

Daric started for the window, but seemed to think better of it and turned for the front door instead. She couldn't blame him. Tiptoeing through the bodies was not high on her list of things to do.

She followed Daric out, anxious to get away from the room of horrors before she threw up again.

Frankie lay on a small section of grass in front of the window. One arm was twisted underneath him, and one leg lay at an awkward angle.

She stood on the front step and watched as Daric assessed the damage.

"Might have a broken leg here and a dislocated shoulder. I can do minor stuff, but this is going to need a real healer."

She nodded, numb.

"Where's Alex?" Daric looked around.

"I don't think he made it through with us."

Daric stood and opened a travel portal in the front lawn. Tarian winced with each breath as pain shot down her back and around her ribs. She looked at Frankie. Her ribs throbbed.

"Should I go for help?"

"We can do it, if I boost a bit. I'll lift." Daric gathered power and levitated Frankie off the ground on a bubble of water. Tarian held him steady, and between the two of them, they pushed him into the portal and out the other side into the rotunda. The water bubble lowered Frankie slowly to the ground and released with a splash onto the floor.

Alex sidestepped the water, looking so angry it was almost comical. Almost. If she hadn't just seen a girl gasp her last breath and two of her friends get the crap kicked out of them.

She held up her hand to stave off the rant she knew was coming. "I didn't know you wouldn't come with us, Alex. Save it. Frankie needs help."

"What's going on?" Calliope's voice echoed down the hallway. "Why are the Sentinels..." Her voice trailed off when she saw the four of them. After a quick look at Tarian, then Daric, she immediately knelt next to Frankie. Calliope's eyes closed, and she began to hum a tune. It sounded suspiciously like "I've been working on the railroad."

Tarian watched as her sister worked. Alex uncharacteristically stayed silent. It took a moment to realize Daric had disappeared.

Frankie groaned and opened his eyes just as her sister sat back, a smug look on her face.

"He'll be fine. Just some small cuts, bruises and one rib. Clean break."

Tarian knelt beside her sister. "When did you learn to heal?"

"I've been studying for years with Chloe. It's why I can sew so well. A body's not so different from a dress, really. Who do you think healed your arm before?"

"I thought it was Chloe."

Calliope shook her head.

"Wow. Nice work." Tarian shifted the wrong way and winced. Calliope took her by the waist and again closed her eyes and hummed.

It was like plunging into a soothing warm bath, with sharp needles at the bottom. "Ow!"

"Hush. You have two cracked ribs, no, three." Calliope hummed louder.

The strangest sensation, feeling her ribs right themselves deep within. When Calliope stopped humming and removed her hands, Tarian ached all over but the stitch in her side was gone, as were the cuts on her arms. She sank onto a nearby bench, grateful but exhausted.

Daric returned a few moments later with Healer Chloe and two other healers. Following close behind them, her mother entered with lips pressed firmly together and wrinkles on her forehead.

Nothing like making a scene.

Marielle watched in silence as Chloe and her helpers patched the wounds Calliope hadn't attended to. Tarian avoided her mother's gaze the entire time, sure if she made eye contact a stern lecture on responsibility was sure to follow.

Two serving girls arrived with trays of glasses containing a green shake plus cheese, fruit, and peanut butter, followed by Jonus.

Well, well, the gang's all here.

Jonus fluttered to Marielle's side, wringing his hands and motioning for the servers to distribute the snack.

"Eat. Healing takes energy from both sides." Chloe instructed each one, making sure everyone took the shake. Tarian grimaced. "What the hell is in this?"

"Drink it, Tari." Calliope put her hand on the bottom of the glass and tipped it toward Tarian. She swallowed. It tasted like apple, pineapple, and maybe some sort of berry. *Not bad.*

They ate and drank in relative silence, the only sounds the slurps and crunching. Marielle stood with her hands folded in front of her, Jonus at her side. Tarian chanced a look at her face and found Marielle staring straight back at her. Tarian grimaced.

That's definitely not happiness on her face.

Her gaze moved to Jonus. His hands still, his back stiff, and a shocked expression on his face. His gazed moved from person to person, almost frantic.

What's he all fussed about? We're the injured ones.

When the silence became too heavy, Tarian cleared her throat. All heads turned in her direction. "Time for Plan B. We can pull the Laghairtine back to the house of horrors; his essence is all over it." Her words echoed off the rotunda walls.

"Yeah, because that worked out perfectly." Frankie muttered. He ran a hand through his hair. Dark circles rimmed his eyes. "Our brilliant plan wasn't so brilliant."

"What are you talking about? You tried the ritual without me? Tari. You said..." Calliope stood up and frowned at her.

"I didn't. You assumed." Tarian forced herself off the bench and paced in front of the group. "I didn't want my sister there in case things went wrong. As it turns out, that's the only thing I did right."

Calliope helped Frankie to his feet. "Well this time you aren't doing it without me. You need me. We both know the circle will be stronger with another woman to help form it."

"No." Tarian stopped pacing to glare at her sister. "N. O. No."

"You don't get to tell me that. You lost the right when you turned up with the Laghairtine scratch in the first place. You're my sister, Tarian. My family. And I'm not sitting here while you fight battles I could help you win."

The two faced each other, the tension thick as molasses after a cold spell.

"My sister needs to be as far away as possible. If this goes wrong."

"Too late." Daric muttered.

"You'll be the Scion. You have to be protected."

"Gee, sounds an awful lot like what everyone tells you. Do you listen?" Calliope put a hand on her hip and tapped her foot.

Despite everything, Tarian almost smiled. Almost.

"That's beside the point."

"No. It *is* the point. I'm going with you."

"All I know is we don't do it some new fangled way. This time we all go through an old fashioned portal." Alex thrust his chin out, daring her to argue.

"Perhaps you'd care to explain what happened to Plan A?" Marielle's disapproving voice interjected in the chaos, ending their arguments. Everyone stopped talking. The men each stared in different directions. Alex and Frankie stood at attention but didn't speak. Daric studied the walls.

Guess it's up to me.

"We didn't exactly have a Plan A. It was more a spontaneous sort of assault."

Marielle raised an eyebrow but said nothing.

"The Laghairtine managed to establish a link to me." Tarian rubbed her neck. She felt the claw but not the lizard. *He's hiding.*

"And through it, I could feel him attacking someone. Like he did those others. Horrible. I could feel it, and I couldn't let it happen. Plus I thought if he were so absorbed in the task, a sneak attack would take him by surprise, and we'd get him before he'd killed again. It seemed like a win-win."

Jonus surveyed the group. "This is what winning looks like?"

"Of course not." Tarian snapped. "This was a complete disaster. I know what it looks like."

Marielle held up a hand to stop any further discussion. "And yet you've managed to walk away from the fight. I'd call that a victory. What about the person the Laghairtine attacked?"

Tarian held her stomach. "Don't remind me."

"They didn't make it." Daric said quietly. "Impossible to estimate how many."

Frankie shook his head. "I counted six heads before I went through the window."

"However did you get away, Scion?" Jonus appeared out of breath, like he'd been running.

"He let us go." Tarian muttered. It hurt to say it, but truth was truth.

"Why?" Calliope's voice squeaked. "Why would he? Doesn't he want to control you? Why not just do it?"

"I've asked myself the same question." Tarian sat down heavily on the bench.

"Did you have an answer?" Marielle crossed to sit next to her on the bench.

Tarian nodded. "You won't like it."

"Try me."

"I don't think this lizard is acting alone. There's someone in the shadows who's using him. And someone in this House is a traitor. They might the same someone, or two different people. But this is a lot bigger than taking down one Laghairtine. After we get him, there's likely to be someone doing battle right behind him."

"Who could control a creature like that?" Calliope wrinkled her eyebrows. "He's so strong."

"He's part daemon. They don't have to control him. They only have to make a deal with him." As she said the words, Tarian realized how true they were. "Someone's offered him something he wants."

"Shame we don't know the deal he made," Daric commented.

"Or who with," Alex added.

"There's one way to find out," Frankie said. "Take out the Laghairtine, and whoever it is will show themselves. They'll have to find another way to act. And we'll be watching for it."

Tarian held up her hand to stop Frankie as he reached for his wrist communicator. "Wait. Don't send out an alert. We don't know who the traitor is."

Frankie paused.

"Let them think we're still after the lizard. When we take him down we'll act like he's still out there. Someone's bound to start sweating."

Daric nodded. "Agreed. If we put up a fuss, will know they must act on their own and might step up their timeline. If we act normal, they must act normal, and wait for a good time to strike. Gives us time to get ready. And provides the best measure of safety."

"Keeper, perhaps we should cancel the reception?" Jonus rubbed his hands, worry etched in every line on his face.

Marielle glanced at Tarian, a question in her eyes. Tarian shrugged.

Daric spoke, his eyes on Tarian's face. "If you cancel, everyone will know something's up. Even the Laghairtine. If we hope to surprise him, everything should remain as usual."

Marielle leaned closer to Tarian. "Tarian, you know what's at stake. Are you sure this couldn't be done by someone else? Here in the House?"

"I'm positive, Mother. He hides in the Between. I can feel him now. But this time, instead of us showing up on his doorstep, he's going to come to us. And it has to be me calling the ritual; I'm the only one with ties close to him. We'll have the trap set and waiting for him." Tarian put a hand on her stomach. Her sister's healing hadn't taken away the slight cramping in her uterus. "But one problem is solved." She whispered the words so quietly only her mother heard. She noticed Daric's sharp eyes on her hands and quickly folded them in her lap.

Marielle pressed her lips together in a quick line. "I don't like this. It doesn't feel complete. There's something we're overlooking."

"There's definitely *someone* we're overlooking. Someone in this House is a traitor." Tarian paused significantly.

"It seems we both have purpose. I will investigate here. But this ritual you're doing. Take your sister." Marielle's lips twitched. "While I understand your need to protect her, she has power you'll need. The two of you together are far stronger than you are alone. You always have been. Use that strength."

Tarian squeezed her mother's hand, and stood.

"This time, we portal. All of us." Tarian turned to Alex and gave him a stare. "The box should still be in the hallway. We get it, I draw the circle, we get ready, and then we'll pull him to us."

"How?" Daric's eyes narrowed as he looked at her.

"We'll use his link to me."

"And this time you take a little more girl power." Calliope stood up straight, her shoulders square.

"You'll also have this." Marielle took Tarian's head in her hands, and suddenly Tarian was plunged into an ocean of water so real she thought for sure she was outside, playing with dolphins. Their calls surrounded her, their energy infused her, and the salty air drove into her pores. She drank it in, a lifeline. It infused her own power, leaving her refreshed, rejuvenated, renewed.

When Marielle released her Tarian stumbled a few steps before regaining her balance. *Right now, I can do anything.* "Thanks," she breathed.

"Take care. All of you." Marielle nodded to the rest of the group, gave Calliope a hug. Tarian felt ocean ripple over her and realized Marielle had donated some power to her sister as well. *We'll need it.*

Marielle left, taking Jonus with her. Tarian watched them leave. Her mother, proud and strong. Jonus, shaken. *He's more scared than I am.*

Tarian turned to the group.

"Daric, please open a portal. I don't want him to feel me moving until absolutely necessary. Let's go to the backyard." She hoped he'd understand she didn't want her sister seeing the room of horrors. He nodded and did as she asked.

"Tarian, you can't be serious." Frankie looked more frantic than she'd ever seen him. His eyes darted back and forth from her to her sister and back.

"What about you? Aren't you going to protest?" She turned

to face Alex, who'd remained strangely quiet.

"I know that look. I ain't even gonna try to stop you. This time, I go first." Alex brushed past her and into the portal.

She turned to Daric. "Together?"

His eyes danced, and the dimple flashed at her in a way that made her want to run with him to the bedroom. He took her hand, and they stepped through the portal.

chapterthirty-four

Alex stood at attention in the center of the backyard, his weapon drawn and his magic focused more than Tarian had ever felt from him. "All clear. For now."

"We should use the kitchen." Tarian led the way into the house. The kitchen was a mess, a giant hole in the wall, rubble and glass everywhere. But she felt the Laghairtine's power here, a red mist coating the floor, the walls, and settling on her skin like a musty damp cloth. She wrinkled her nose but accepted it.

"Not much room in here. Shouldn't we use the living room?" Calliope started for the hall.

"No!" Daric, Frankie, and Tarian all said at once.

Calliope paused. "Why not?"

"Trust me. You don't want to see the living room." Tarian pulled her sister away from the hall. "This is better. I fought him here, and the power is still here. Feel it?"

Calliope shook her head. "No. I feel you but not him. Are you sure?"

"Positive." Grim, Tarian kicked some of the bigger shards of glass out of the way. The claw throbbed in her neck. *He's back.* "We need to speed this up."

Daric rummaged in the corner and came out with a broom and began sweeping a path through the rubble.

Tarian held out her hand to Alex. "Can I borrow your dagger?"

He handed it to her slowly, as if trying to come up with a reason he shouldn't. She smiled as she took it from him and ignored the hiss of breath as she drew it across her wrist. Blood bloomed, running down her arm to drip on the floor. Pain blossomed a moment later. "Do me a favor, Alex? Get the box from the hallway. It should be by the front door."

Tarian traced the outer edge of the circle first, chanting the spell as she went. She tried to get the edges exactly right, but noticed the circle wasn't quite perfect. Bits of glass, grout lines in the tile floor, and cabinets made the edges bumpy and uneven. It should work, but it wasn't pretty. The real power lay within her and her blood anyway, not the shape of the circle. *I hope.*

When she finished the outer edge and a five pointed star within it, she etched her personal symbol in the center with the dagger. Once the tree with three branches and two leaves graced the dirt, she added her own blood to the tree trunk and branches. The tree symbolized the Xannon family bloodline and her mother, the solid base of the tree, and the branches represented her and her sister. Around the tree, a shield…a special touch she'd added as an inside joke. Not many knew her name, Tarian, meant "shield". She finished the last words of the spell as she placed the last drop of blood, finishing the shield and the circle.

The others waited outside the circle while she worked.

Alex returned with the silver sewing box in his hand. He'd used his shirt to wipe it off, but it still had a few red smears of blood. When she finished the circle, Alex handed her the box. She opened it and placed it gently on the ground in the center of her symbol. Satisfied, she stepped back to examine her work. It wouldn't win any art awards, but it would do.

"Ready?" Tarian checked with Alex, Frankie, Calliope, and Daric in turn. All nodded in the affirmative. Frankie and Alex took up a soldier's fighting stance. Daric tensed, and Calliope set her face in grim determination.

Tarian stepped into the circle. Power vibrated when she crossed the line. A ripple of wind lifted her hair slightly. It reassured her she had the strength necessary for capturing the lizard, no matter how powerful he was. No matter how much of her magic he'd stolen. This time, she held the boost from Ruarc and Daric, and she'd used her own blood to seal it. The spell she'd studied was meant for exactly this. It would work. *It has to.*

"Everyone take a corner. Calliope, I'll need you to help pull him. Be ready to cage him, guys. A strong stasis should work long enough for me to finish."

Tarian waited as they spaced themselves out within the circle. Everyone stood with their feet spread slightly, hands to the sides, palms out. Each focused power and radiated it outward until the circle contained a combination of all four. Earth, Air, Fire and Water—all were represented in some way. They were ready.

Tarian stepped forward and stood on her power symbol. Her body responded both to the circle and to the joined energy of the people who stood in it with a rush of adrenaline that made her skin crawl and the tiny hairs on her arm stand on end. Power swirled around her. She closed her eyes, and cast through the air for the Laghairtine. Her link to him glowed, inside the circle a vibrant, glowing filament of air and water, bluish-white and thin, which snaked away from her. Through it, she felt the creature, tense and ready. He knew.

Tarian whispered the first line of the ritual. She cleared her throat, held her palms out, and said the next line strong and firm. Power from the circle swirled around her and through her. The tracer in her neck squirmed, her shoulders tensed, and her head ached. Through the connection, the Laghairtine squirmed too. He moved and pulled on the link as he went. His abrupt movement made her stumble. She worked to get her feet back under her before she crossed outside the circle.

Through the link, thoughts invaded her mind. *You don't need to stand right here. You should move. So easy to drift away. You don't have to fight. Everything will be all right.*

Tarian stomped her foot and screamed in frustration.

You. Will. Not. Have. Me.

She marched back to the center of the circle and gathered the power around her like a cloak. She used every speck of power in her body, latched onto the link with the Laghairtine, and said the third line of the spell, gasping with the effort. She and the lizard played tug-of-war with their connection a taut rope between them. Neither gave an inch.

Sweat beaded up on her forehead, ran down the sides of her face, and pooled at the small of her back. Flecks of multicolored light darted through her vision.

She forced the air she'd been holding in her lungs out, took another deep breath and shouted the fourth line. The rope gave a bit, the lizard struggling harder. Tarian leaned on the power inside the circle. She needed more. Much more. She reached a hand toward Calliope, who shifted to direct her energy directly to Tarian, rather than to the circle. Dust motes rose into the air. Panting, Tarian screamed the fifth line.

The lizard shot through the ether toward her. She stumbled from the sudden release of force on his side. She screamed, "Watch out!" and braced herself on her symbol as she said the sixth line of the ritual. Only five to go.

With a roar, the Laghairtine appeared in front of her. But here, in the circle of power, he looked like a man instead of a lizard.

Startled, she forgot the next line of the ritual. But she'd come too far to stop now. Frantic, she said the sixth again then memory took over. Words tumbled out even as the Laghairtine tried to hit her. Calliope set a shield to surround her before he struck, his spell and hand bouncing off it.

Tarian's skin sang with the concentration of energy her sister generated. *Mother was right. I need Calliope.* Tarian continued, bolstered by Calliope's power and confidence, and as she reached the last line of the ritual, the dust on the ground swirled around until it created a black mist, obscuring everything, even the Laghairtine.

At the very last moment, it dawned on Tarian it should be him surrounded by black, not her. The thought flitted through her mind, impossible to hold, as she felt herself sucked down into a vortex that spun out of her control.

chapter thirty-five

Musty, black, nothingness. Pain. Throbbing. Pounding. Insistent. Pain reverberated through her skull and behind Tarian's eyes. Something sharp and hard poked at her back. She blinked several times to clear her vision. It didn't help the pain at all, so she closed them again and waited.

Soft skitters to her right popped her eyes open again. A faint red light flickered in the distance. She tried to force the room into focus, but there was nothing to see except the wobbling red glow, which did nothing to illuminate her surroundings.

Tarian struggled to sit up. Black dust fell like a veil to the floor around her, which turned out to be some rough type of rock. The walls curved in on her. As she blinked, tiny lights danced in front of her eyes. *My head is going to split in two if this pounding keeps up.*

Looking at the wall sloping upward and the faint outline of rough rock, she realized it was a cave. A cave created out of black and brown, musty, dusty, cold, sharp, unfriendly rock. Soft drips made her instantly thirsty. She licked her lips. The heaviness of the air made her nauseous. She gulped back the urge. Bile sat at the back of her throat and taunted her.

Her eyes adjusted enough to the dim light to make out sharp rocks jutting out at odd angles. The glowing orbs in the distance resolved into eyes that seemed to absorb the darkness. The bodies attached to the eyes were familiar. They looked like the Archivists.

Her head pounded in time to her heart. The creatures stared at her. Odd they didn't huddle like statues. They moved freely and blinked a lot. She tried to summon enough power to create a light. It didn't answer. Perplexed, she pulled again but found nothing. She didn't feel blocked, exactly. The well was empty, as if the magic had simply dried up. Fear settled in and made a home in the pit of her stomach, next to the queasy part. She rubbed her neck, but although the lump of tense muscle was still there, she couldn't feel the claw's pull on her either. *Did it work? If it did, why am I here?*

She wasn't sure what to think. The eyes continued to stare at her. Why were the Archivists here? She hadn't been anywhere near them when she did the ritual.

She pushed her body up onto wobbly legs and shuffled toward the opening of the cave. The creatures watched her go, not trying to stop her but not helping either. When she reached the mouth of the cave, she found another cave. The light emanated from a craggy rock column on an island in the middle of a small, moldy pond. The rock column vibrated a shade of red she'd never seen before. It hurt her eyes, and even with her eyes closed, it throbbed and pulsed. It made no sound, not like fire would. The closer she was, the colder the air. As though it sucked every ounce of energy, whether magical or heat, out of the atmosphere and used it to sustain itself.

She backed off to regain a bit of warmth and study it. The column rose from the ground as though sprouted like some twisted beanstalk with the edges rough and sharp. Tarian craned her neck to see it rose up into a vast expanse above eventually fading from view. Even with the glow, she couldn't discern the ceiling. She'd never seen a cavern this big. Water dripped from above to form small ripples on the pond that glowed in reflected glory from the pillar. A thousand more eyes stared back at her.

"Will one of you please explain what is going on?" Her voice came out a lot higher than she liked and echoed back at her from every side. Refusing to panic, Tarian returned to the smaller cave and sat down on a rock that jutted from the cave wall. Cold soaked through her jeans and made her shiver. The creatures continued to stare at her.

She couldn't remember a time when she hadn't felt magic pulsing deep within her. She'd been born with it. It was a part of her, like blood. Essential. She hugged her arms for warmth and stamped her feet to wake up her toes.

The creatures moved closer to her, and she tensed. Their legs and arms wove in and out in some kind of group hug. The one in front put out his arms, his tiny, childlike hands held out palm up toward her.

She took the offered hands. A chorus of voices bombarded her. Thousands of voices, all talking at once. It overloaded her mind with a kaleidoscope of sound.

"Stop, just stop. One of you. One. I can't understand you if you all talk at once. My head. Shit." She gasped as her skull throbbed. The cacophony died down to a whisper, and one voice stood out above the rest.

"We seek an answer."

"You and me both."

"Scion, holder of air, fire, water. Please tell us why you came?"

"I didn't mean to. I meant to banish a lizard."

Several voices erupted in furious conversation. Trying to make out some of it, all she managed to pick up was "Scion" and "intrude."

"We seek information."

Blink. Blink. Blink.

"I used a spell from the *Book of Daemon*. You told me it would help. But now I'm here instead of the Laghairtine. How are you here? I left you in the archives." As she spoke, images of the power circle and herself struggling with the lizard filled her head.

Mutters. From somewhere in the mix she gathered the name "Sucole," which sparked a frenzy of vocal activity, along with the image of the *Book of Daemon* and the Laghairtine himself.

A chorus of responses echoed in her head.

"We do not leave this place. We are not Archivists. We are Carraig."

"Carraig. I know that name." Through the haze and pain she fished for something to explain the name. Something in history class. Something ancient. Ancient, with a capital A.

"Earth daemon? As in, *real* earth daemon? *The* earth daemon?" Her thoughts slugged through what little she'd managed to hold on to from class. Ancients, like the dolphins, but with power based solely in the earth element. Manipulators of stone. Usually guardians. They disappeared thousands of years ago. She hadn't realized the Archivists were Carraig. They seemed more like stuffy librarians than guardians.

"The one you fight is not Carraig, yet carries earth talent. Born to one blinded by greed and lust, who wields air, who craved union with a creature based in fire, without agreement. He must kill to survive. He will not stop."

Blinded. "Sucole?"

An image of Sucole flashed in her mind along with the general chorus of "yes."

"Why did the spell backfire?"

"Ritual worked." Several voices wove the answer. *"Scion does not belong here."*

"I know I don't belong here. What do you mean it worked? Where is the lizard if it worked? I was doing the banishment on him, not me."

"Scion sent Scion here."

"No, I didn't. I sent..." she paused. She'd said the words. She knew what they meant. *But did I really? What if the translation was wrong?*

Realization tackled her, punched her in the gut and kicked her teeth for good measure. Daric's first reaction had been the correct one. *Decipi.* Entrap, not banish. And Sucole had known. She'd fed Tarian just enough information to make it all seem credible. She'd pointed at the spell and uttered the word banish.

The realization Sucole had given birth to the Laghairtine made it all suddenly clear. Of course Sucole wouldn't want her own son banished or harmed. *Of course not.*

The vein on the side of her neck pulsed as the puzzle pieces fit together. She dropped the daemon's hands and stood up. The sudden silence in her head filled quickly with the roar of blood rushing to her ears and the pulse throbbing in her throat. She held her head in both hands, to stop the pain.

You do not see.

Sucole was right. She didn't see that she'd been lied to, and now she'd led her friends and her sister down the wrong freaking path. She'd banished herself, leaving them to deal with the damn lizard. Alone. She didn't see how to make any of it right while stuck here in this dark, cold, musty place.

The daemons blinked furiously at her. One of them reached out and touched her thigh.

"Scion does not belong here. Scion must not remain here."

"Why can't I feel my magic?"

The eyes blinked slower.

"In this place, no magic. In this place, all are without. Scion must be summoned, to experience life magic once more."

"Excuse me?"

"We protect the Stulos. We stay. To leave, we must be summoned, or the Stulos must fail."

"Stulos." The word sounded familiar. The daemon in front of her gestured toward the red, glowing light.

"You're telling me the light in here is a pillar? *The* pillar? The thing that holds the planes apart?" Nobody had seen these things for thousands of years. She hadn't thought they were real. Not many did, anymore. Certainly nobody had seen one. Not on this plane. And anything not seen was bound to be forgotten or discounted as untrue.

"One of four. Stulos must be protected, must be maintained. Stulos takes power. Stulos does not return power. We guard Stulos."

"How the hell did this happen? How did one banishment spell send me here?"

"Knowledge is power. Book of Daemon contains all knowledge."

"All this time…" Tarian let the words drift off as she thought about what it meant to be stuck in this dark, musty cave for what amounted to eternity. She'd never given these creatures a thought before. They'd passed from awareness so long ago; they were nothing but myth and legend. A history lesson, nothing more. Even the dolphins had lost their Ancient status in most modern minds. Tarian and her family were some of the few who knew what they truly were.

She sat down on the rock again, maintaining contact with the creature's hand. He stood in front of her not moving and blinked occasionally.

"I'm sorry." She finally managed.

Blink. Blink. Blink.

"I didn't realize...I hadn't really pictured what the earth Ancients actually looked like."

"*Earth based spell sent Scion here. Sent Carraig here. Elements protect Stulos. Earth, air, water. All elements exist, though not in harmony. Balance does not exist with planes separate. Fire waits.*"

"Waits...for what?"

"*Freedom.*"

A loaded word.

She sought the same thing. Freedom from this cave. Freedom from the asshole who hunted her and stole her power. Freedom for her family.

"You said I must be summoned out. How does that work?"

"*Summoned acts at the bidding of the summoner.*"

The words, so simple, but so crammed with meaning. She'd experienced the very thing she fought so hard to avoid. Her will, subverted by another.

"*Scion is correct. Scion can then be released. As happened with Carraig in the archives of the House of Xannon.*"

"Is there any other way out of here?"

"*Death.*"

To get out she had to be summoned, and she'd be under that person's control. Sucole knew. Which meant the Laghairtine knew. And she had to assume, whoever the Laghairtine worked for knew as well.

She wouldn't have long to wait. Right now, the lizard and his boss must be getting ready to summon her. Instead of trapping him, she'd landed herself in an even worse position than when she'd started. She wouldn't have thought it possible.

She wrapped her arms protectively around herself. Daric, Alex, Frankie, Calliope…they'd all seen her vanish. They held the lizard in semi-stasis as she left. Maybe they'd managed to defeat him. Maybe they held the upper hand. All she had to do was wait. They'd figure out a way to get her out of here.

Unless they couldn't. Unless the creature had finished them all off. What had happened after she left? Were they okay? Were they lying on the ground, torn to bits? Tarian closed her eyes against the thought, but all she saw was the room with pieces of human flesh and blood everywhere. Her stomach turned.

No. I can't think that. I have to get out of here.

"And how exactly are you going to do that? You're good and stuck here," she whispered to herself. She was completely dependent on someone else to fix her problem.

Tarian rubbed her arms to stimulate the circulation and stood up to stomp from side to side. She swallowed against the dry lump in her throat. It refused to budge. Added in to the equation was the tiny person about to grow in her uterus. She risked herself, her sister, the Dolphin Throne and a possible child who didn't deserve any of this.

A child who would be a blend of Ruarc, Alex, and Daric. What powers would the child have, and what consequences would she suffer because of Tarian's foolish choices? Would such a child forgive her mother for being human?

She sat and reached for the daemon's tiny hands. "Will you tell me why I shouldn't have joined with a daemon? What will happen to the child?"

"Such a thing is not knowable. Possibilities are endless, and conception has not yet occurred, though it is near. It remains to be seen."

"So you're saying I have to wait and see." It sounded trite, but what choice did she have?

"With time, all things are knowable. Scion is daemon. Child would be too. With or without joining another. There is much to know, much that remains unseen on this plane. Such things were lost when planes separated."

She dropped his hands again and paced, unable to keep her body still with her mind in such turmoil. Daemon. She was definitely part daemon. No wonder she saw the red mist when others couldn't.

A rush of adrenaline coursed through her as she remembered how she'd joined with Ruarc, how much she'd wanted more and more power as they fed off each other. The desire to control, to extend, to reach past what she should hold.

Ancients held so much more than humans. *I'm one of them. Sort of.* It felt strange, wonderful, and terrifying all at once. The weight of it settled on her shoulders like a blanket.

Perhaps that's why the Laghairtine attacked. He'd known, somehow. Or his controller did.

Truly, controlling the power of the Ancients would be an enticement for anyone seeking to exert their will over others. The lure, like treasure. She'd been giddy with it herself, in those few brief moments with Ruarc. And if someone couldn't join with a daemon, where would they turn for a fix?

Why didn't Mother tell me?

She and her mother had a lot to discuss.

If I get out of here.

She took up the daemon's hands again. "How do you know all this?"

"We crave knowledge. We learn. We share. We grow through learning. We live through learning. Scion will learn. Scion will see. Good and bad exist in all things."

She sat down, leaned back against the cave wall and closed her eyes. The Archivists really were a spy network. Right in her own House, little spy creatures. They probably knew a lot more than anyone had ever guessed. Even Ruarc had praised their skill. After all, nobody paid any attention to them. And they shared it all via their odd little communication system, so what one knew, the others knew. A pretty useful skill. And they'd tried to warn her.

Beware of danger from within.

Once more she had to wonder what the hell they meant. Danger within her own body? Her own House? Within the Archivists themselves? Within the pages of a book? Only the Archivists knew the answer. They knew a lot more than they told. And they kept it under lock and key by allowing one query at a time. She liked the Carraig better. They didn't seem to live by the same set of rules.

She didn't see a clear way out of this mess she'd created. She needed help. She needed someone to summon her out of here before the Laghairtine did. For once in her life, she was willing to beg for someone to help her, but she had no obvious way to do it.

Tarian reached for her interpreter's hands. He blinked and took hers.

"I need to get a message out. How do I do that?"

"We cannot speak to other than We. You are We. You cannot speak to other."

"There has to be a way. There has to be. Everything depends on this. I have to get out of here. I have to destroy the Laghairtine, and I can't do it sitting here."

A muttering began in her head, a lot of it words she didn't recognize.

"What about the Archivists? They're one of you, aren't they?" The muttering grew louder, and died down abruptly.

"They were We once." The voices didn't sound happy at all.

"Why do you say it like it's in the past? They look and talk just like you."

"They are not We now. They are released." The daemon's eyes blinked slowly.

"How were they released? Why not the rest of you?"

"They were summoned. They made agreements. They were released. They are no longer We."

"Can you talk to them anyway?"

"We…can."

Complete silence.

"Do you not like them anymore because they're free?"

The eyes blinked furiously. It had the odd effect of a thousand flashlights going on and off.

"We are not small minded."

"What is the problem?"

"It is painful. Sacrifice is required."

"It's worth it."

"They may not accept. They are no longer We."

"Can we at least try? They are my Archivists. Surely they'll listen."

Tarian waited while voices murmured in her head and images flashed. They went by so quickly she couldn't even determine what they were. Finally, one voice answered.

"We will help. Will Scion help We?"

"What do you mean?"

"We would enter agreement with Scion. We will make possible a message, if Scion offers in return."

It sounded suspiciously like the deal Ruarc had engineered, but without her side of the bargain.

"What can I offer?"

Voices cascaded over one another in her head. Excited, elated voices.

"Hey, one at a time. My head!" She dropped the creature's hands to rub her ears. Even though the sound hadn't really come through the usual method, her ears still reacted with an odd buzz, and it didn't help the pain either.

The creature extended his hands. She took them, grateful the chorus now seemed solidified once more.

"Freedom."

Such a simple thing, yet complex in execution. She had no idea how to free them. All she could truthfully promise was to try. If she agreed to try, what mess would she fall in to? She needed more time to figure it out, and she didn't have it.

The voices in her head remained silent. Still. Expectant. Hopeful.

If she did not enter into this deal, what would happen?

"True results cannot be seen."

She imagined the possibilities. The Laghairtine or his boss might summon her; game over. Her friends saw her vanish; they might figure out how to get her back on their own. Maybe. She might simply remain here, forever. Calliope would become Scion, and the lizard would go after her. *Maybe. If she's the same blend of daemon blood that I am.*

None of the possibilities sounded good. But making a deal like this, like the one with Ruarc, without all the facts, seemed foolish in the extreme. What loopholes were in this deal?

"We do not deceive. We offer the ability to communicate, though time will be limited. If Scion attains freedom and, in return, offers

freedom to Carraig, then Carraig offers fealty to House of Xannon until released by Xannon blood. We offer knowledge and protection to the Xannon, in exchange for freedom. Penalties shall be forfeiture of freedom, if either party fails."

Stunned, Tarian absorbed both the words and the meaning behind them and the images the Carraig sent along with them. Allies. Free to roam, as they used to do. Control of their earth power once more. But bound to her and her family. Bound to protect them, or lose their freedom.

Freedom for freedom. Simply put. She would ensure they remained free and, in return, they would ensure she and her family were protected. They allied with earth, the one element she couldn't wield herself. They would help her get out of here.

No treasure is worth the price.

"If I can't find a way to free you, what happens then?"

"Penalties shall be forfeiture of freedom, if either party fails."

They waited, like statues. Like Ruarc. No coercion. They'd presented a choice, and it was for her to agree, or not.

You chose strong allies.

Strange, Ruarc's approval of the Archivists swayed her decision. She didn't know him. He did things for purely selfish reasons. Yet, in this case…

"I agree."

"It is agreed."

The words reverberated around the cavern as though Tarian changed something with far-reaching consequences with one small statement. It didn't feel wrong, exactly. It felt… monumental. And somehow, somewhere, she felt like she'd missed an important piece of the puzzle. Something vital she hadn't considered. She shrugged. Whatever it was didn't matter. She'd done the deal.

No turning back now.

A group of the daemon gathered around the pillar on the island the instant the words were whispered in her head. The group formed a tightly packed, giant gray wrinkly ball with arms and legs protruding at odd angles. She almost laughed at the absurdity of it.

The Carraig in front of her pulled on her hands to lead her over to the mass of creatures. They sloshed through the water, which turned out to be about knee deep and cold. Her toes froze in her boots. The water soaked her jeans almost up to her crotch by the time she stepped foot on the island. Scratches on her arm stung every time water splashed them. She scrambled up onto the island next to the ball.

The creature behind her shoved her into the group, which reformed around her. She found herself in the middle of large eyes that blinked in unison, a lot of arms and hands and feet, and a blanket of craggy body parts. Something in her brain shifted, and suddenly she felt as if an antenna had been shoved into her head. The entire world felt like it was in the room with her, and all of it was talking, singing, humming or shouting. It blended together to create a deafening noise.

In the background, one particular sound grew louder as the rest faded away. Humming. She'd know the sound anywhere. Calliope. Her sister must have survived!

"Calli!"

"Wait," a voice said.

The hum grew so loud, it nearly hurt her ears. Pain bloomed in her body, deep within her bone marrow. Panic set in as she realized how trapped she was in this mass of semi-hard stone creatures with no magic and no way out.

"We listen," a voice came.

Tarian struggled to speak through the pain. "I need to talk to Calliope."

"That is not allowed. She is not We. She is allowed one query only."

"Are you kidding me? She doesn't know to ask! I need her help!"

"She is not We. She is allowed one query only. We seek an answer. We seek to understand how Scion is now We."

"Scion did a ritual that trapped her here, that's how. I need help!" In an effort to reinforce the idea, through the pain she pictured the lizard and the room he'd left in Philadelphia. All the gore, the eyeball, the fight, Mark Chester, Sucole, her power circle, the men and Calliope standing in it, all of it.

"Scion has not listened. Scion does not see. Scion joined with daemon. Scion does not heed warnings."

"If you'd been a little less cryptic, I might have." Tarian gritted her teeth.

"Scion makes agreements. No treasure is worth the price."

"I had to. I tried to fix it." A brief picture of her with Daric flitted through her mind. She clamped down on it immediately. She didn't want to share every detail of her life with these creatures. She had no idea how she was supposed to close off part of her mind when they filled it so completely, but she was going to try.

"Scion does not see."

"See what, dammit? What exactly would you have me see?"

"Know yourself. Know the enemy. Know the why behind the what. No trap is greater than knowledge. No knowledge is greater than that which is yours by right of birth."

She thought about it for a moment, trying to see through the pain that jolted her with every word. None of it made sense.

"There is strength in yielding. Yielding grants knowledge. Knowledge grants power stronger than magic."

Their words circled in her head. They thought they were helping, but really they lectured and chastised as a parent did a young child. And like a parent, they didn't fully explain exactly what they meant. She couldn't see how to use it. Not right now, locked here with no magic, with no way out, and with every bone screaming at her.

"Help." She gasped as the pain threatened to tear her apart. She imagined this must be what bone cancer felt like or maybe having your skeleton ripped out of your skin. This wasn't going to work. Disappointment settled in with the pain. She wasn't sure if it was hers or the Carraig's.

A pause. Mutters filled the spaces in her head. A word here or there. Agreement. A reluctant acceptance.

"Knowledge grants power. Scion must seek it. Scion has entered agreements without knowledge or understanding."

"I know…screwed myself." Words. So hard. Pain rolled. Brain. Fuzzy.

"Scion deceived. Such is the way of humans."

"All creatures." She filled her mind with an image of Ruarc and his agreement. Pain threatened to overwhelm her. "Family. Helps. Family. Always. Name. Price. I'll deal."

Silence echoed louder than any words. She'd told the Archivists they were family before, but the Carraig hadn't been present. She felt them shift around her, and heard voices within. Awe, excitement, and a sense of honor filtered through the pain. Somehow, calling them family meant more than anything else.

"What information shall we give?"

"Tell her…where. I'm…in trouble. Book…my dresser… bring me back."

Complete silence reigned. Endless seconds stretched to an eternity of agony as she fought to keep her wits, her sanity, and the pain at bay.

Through the pain she realized the humming had stopped. She felt the connection through the link with the Archivists.

With a shock she realized it wasn't her sister she linked with.

"Mother!"

The Archivists delivered her message. She felt the concern, the alarm, the panic as it was received. Thoughts filled her mind, thoughts that didn't belong to her or the Archivists or the Carraig. Overwhelming fear.

"What if I can't find the right spell? What will happen to her? How can I solve this? How can I leverage the Archivists to free her? Or the Mayfanata? Ruarc did this. I should never have let her go after that book. My fault. All my fault. I should have warned her about Ruarc sooner. I should have warned her. Too late, too late."

"Mother…it's not your fault!" Tarian shoved the words through her head, hoping her mother would hear them. But the thoughts faded away, replaced by reverberating pain and a sense of loss.

"By ancient agreement. Message sent and received. Help delivered. Scion grows weak. Scion must break link." The connection severed, and the ball flew apart as each daemon body broke free. She lay in the center of the island next to the freezing bonfire and panted.

A creature—the same one?—took her hand and pulled her onto her feet and away from the fire. The pain vanished with the link, but the aftereffects felt like the worst hangover ever. She staggered behind her guide, unable to really see where she was going since she had to focus so hard on getting one foot in front of the other. They sloshed back to the small outer cave. Blissful darkness and comparative warmth enveloped her. She shivered and her teeth chattered.

"*Our side of agreement is fulfilled.*" The Carraig stepped back away from her.

She collapsed on the floor, curled up in a ball, and surrendered to the dark.

chapter thirty-six

Tarian rolled against something hard and moaned. Everything hurt. Every pore, every joint, every particle of her body. Beyond that, her heart hurt the most. She'd connected with her mother's innermost thoughts and in them she'd found a frightened girl who worried about her daughter. Tarian had never thought her mother suffered doubt of any sort. Now she knew the truth. Her mother doubted; she just hid it. From everyone. Tears rolled down her cheeks as she realized what grief she'd caused her mother. She hadn't meant to. Her mother was a rock, a pillar, a person she leaned on when she needed to and ignored when she didn't. And it wasn't fair. *When I get out of this. When, not if. When I get out of this I'll go to those meetings. I'll learn who and why and how, so Mother doesn't have to face it all alone.*

Tarian started at the touch of a soft hand on her arm. She pulled back, ready to fight, then saw the giant eyes and remembered where she was.

"Scion goes now."

"I do? I am?" Something pulled at her core, as if whatever it was sucked her entire body into a tube. Her skin tried to get away and hide. Her soul ripped from her body, and her body followed as a black cloud of dust formed around her.

"Remember agreement!" The thought followed her into black nothingness.

She drifted, feeling lazy. It was nice. No pressure, no responsibility, no fear, no regret. She had something important to do, didn't she? What was it? Something vital. She almost remembered. She tried to concentrate, but the thought flitted away. A butterfly in a meadow. Never settled.

The black veil fell away to reveal a yard. She knew this place, but couldn't name it. Grass. Benches. Sky. Tang in the air. A memory teased her. A fight with…someone.

A man stood in front of her. Her body yielded to him. She was a puppet, and he pulled the strings. She'd do anything he asked. Anything at all.

The man walked toward her. She knew his face, but she struggled to remember his name. It danced around the edges of her mind. He looked angry, but his chin rose in satisfaction as he looked at her.

She tried to ask him his name, but no words escaped. She tried again. Stars danced in front of her eyes. Some force held her upright, and she had a feeling if the force dissolved she'd be on the ground. That force allowed her to breathe. It did not allow her to speak.

Something was missing. Something important. Something she needed and wanted desperately. What was it?

The man crossed his arms and glared. His lips moved, but she couldn't hear anything. Her ears heard no sound at all. Her heart raced. Why couldn't she hear?

A woman joined him. Blonde. Tall. Familiar. She frowned. Her lips moved. Tarian couldn't hear the words. Something about this woman…important. Very important. The woman looked at the man, who faced her and moved his lips.

"Tarian."

The sudden sound of her name put her entire body on alert. She was ready. She would do whatever this man asked. She waited for the next words with anticipation and dread.

"Can you hear me?" The man looked worried. "Can you hear everyone?"

"Yes." The word came from her lips but she hadn't thought to say anything. Her mouth was not her own. Her body was not her own. It was his. Deep inside her, a part of her mind pounded at her. This wasn't right.

"What's wrong with her?" A high voice behind her. Soft. Pleasant. Familiar. She knew the voice. She knew it well. Once again, the name escaped her.

"It's part of the summoning. She can't answer unless I ask a direct question." The man smiled. "Is that right, Tarian?"

"Yes." Once again, her mouth moved without her being in control. She pounded inside the cage in her mind. She wanted to scream at this man, but she couldn't. He hadn't asked her to.

The woman next to him pursed her lips. "I'm not sure this fits the definition of saving my daughter."

Daughter. The word flitted past.

"When you summon someone, they are bound to your will. But the bond can be released. It's better to do it one step at a time." The man leaned in close to Tarian, his lips next to her ear. "You have to do anything I tell you to do, yes?" he whispered in her ear.

"Yes." She stood, unmoving, while inside she seethed. She tried to grasp at the pieces of her mind and will them back together.

"I'd rather have a willing partner." He kissed her cheek.

A name danced through her mind, but was gone before she caught it.

He stepped away from her and another woman joined him. A smaller one, though she looked like the taller one. She knew this woman too. Her name hovered around the edges of her mind. Inside she screamed, *"Let me out!"* But outside, her body stood motionless.

The man spoke, and black descended over her once more.

The black filled with pain. Throbbing, pounding, reverberating pain. Tarian groaned and tried to roll over, away from it.

"Shhhh, don't move. Here, drink this." The voice was kind, and deep, and familiar. Something warm and soothing poured onto her lips. She swallowed reflexively, which set off a wave of pain in her jaw and around her head.

"Take another sip."

She tried to push the thing away. It hurt. But the voice insisted, and her hands refused to work, and it was easier to do as she was told. With each sip, some of the pain lessened. It occurred to her this was an improvement over something. She'd had no will of her own. She'd been trapped inside her own mind. Did she have control now?

"Let me try something," a feminine voice said. From somewhere far away she fished out a name. Calliope. Relief joined it. Her sister, alive and well. For some reason, that was important.

Tarian felt herself being shifted slightly. Her body lay on something soft. Had she been drinking? What the hell? The pain seemed endless.

A soothing sensation passed over her arms as if they were dipped in a warm bath. Relief from the intense pain in her bones followed. She felt it receding from her legs next, until it all became a dull ache. Except for her head, which still throbbed. She reached up with her hands to hold her head in a useless attempt to get it to stop throbbing.

"Headache?" Calliope asked.

"The caffeine will help. She needs to drink more of it," the deep voice answered. She knew that voice. It was…it was…

The cup was placed against her lips again and she drank a few more sips. The pain bubbled. Tentatively, she tried opening her eyes. A pair of deep brown eyes stared back at her.

"Welcome back." Daric smiled.

She moaned.

"I can try to help the headache, Tarian, but I'm not very good with that area yet," Calliope said. Tarian looked over to see her sister sitting on the bed next to her. She looked up. The familiar mural of her own ceiling smiled down at her.

"What…" Tarian murmured softly.

"There's always some pain after a summoning is released. I'm not sure why you fainted. Maybe it was my dashing good looks." His dimple winked at her.

She rubbed her head with her hands. Her jumbled thoughts circled and solidified. The ritual. The cave. The Carraig. She'd made a deal. Then black. Then outside somewhere with Calliope and her mother. Now here. Everything felt disjointed and awkward. But her body was her own again. She almost cried as the realization struck.

"Here, another few sips." Daric held the cup up to her lips again and she drank deeper. Coffee. Bless the man, he'd brought her coffee.

"It usually isn't this bad." Daric took the cup away again.

"How would you know?" Tarian tried to sit up.

"I've been banished before." He put his hand on her back and helped push her into a sitting position. He pushed the coffee cup into her hands and she cuddled it.

"You'll need to eat soon. All your body processes shut down when you're banished, but they start up again when you're released. You need to replace the energy."

"I ate this morning." She sipped more coffee.

"That was yesterday," Calliope said.

"Oh." She couldn't think of any other response.

She tried to get up, but fell back down onto the bed, toppling into Daric. His arms immediately went around her.

"Give it a few minutes. It'll wear off soon. Keep drinking the coffee."

"I have to get out of here. The Laghairtine. I have to go."

"No, Tarian. You have to stay. Mother is furious. She won't let you out of the house again, that's for sure. And the reception has already started. You have to be there. We have to keep up appearances." Calliope paced the length of the small living room. She'd never seen her sister look so worried.

"Reception?" Everything was so hazy.

"The reception to meet the final Potentials. Don't you remember?"

"Of course I remember." She glanced at Daric. "I'm not sure I need to go now."

"What do you mean?" Calliope stopped pacing.

"I may have already completed the ritual." She took a deep breath. "At least, I tried to. Just in case."

Calliope's mouth formed an O. She looked from Tarian to Daric then down at her hands.

"I know...well, I hate to ask, but..."

"Yes, Calli, more than two."

Daric's arms tensed around her.

Knowledge grants power stronger than magic.

"I still think you should be there. Mother will have a fit if she doesn't see you walking around with your own mind intact soon. She only left to arrange food and a healer for you. She still doesn't know who the traitor is. You have to go."

"I can't go. Most of my magic is gone. I can barely feel it now. He can take me anytime he wants. I don't even know how you all escaped. He's ridiculously powerful, and with my power added to his…" She gulped then took another swallow of coffee. "I've had firsthand experience of what that would be like, and I can't let him do it. I won't." She used Daric to steady herself as she stood up. Her legs shook but held her upright. Her head still hurt, and her neck throbbed as though the claw tried to work its way out through her skin. She stumbled to the dresser and yanked open the drawer. She pulled every piece of underwear out, throwing it all behind her until the drawer was empty. "Where's the book?"

"I don't know. Where'd you leave it?" Calliope looked around, as if expecting a book to pop off a shelf somewhere.

"The book is gone?" Tarian swayed then sat back down on the bed. Daric's hands moved to hold her arms, probably to keep her from falling off. She waited for her head to stop spinning.

Did Mother take it?

"How did you get me back here without the book?" She turned to study Daric.

"I've known the summoning spell for a long time. It's useful."

"It's illegal."

Daric shrugged. "Arrest me."

She glared at him. "Forget it. You'd enjoy it too much."

Daric's dimple reappeared.

"Is there any way to block the Laghairtine? Any way at

all? The *Book of Daemon* probably has a way." She stood again, stronger this time, and joined her sister in pacing the floor. With every step, her body felt a bit better. The headache receded. "I obviously can't use the spell Sucole pointed out. Damn her."

"So that's what happened? She told you the wrong spell?" Calliope stopped so abruptly Tarian nearly knocked into her. "How do you know?"

"I figured it out. Landing in a dark, smelly cave was a giant clue." Tarian walked around Calliope and continued to pace. "The Carraig confirmed it."

"Carraig?" Calliope's voice squeaked. "You...Carraig? *The* Carraig?"

Tarian nodded, distracted. *Think.* Her mind refused to focus. *Fuzzy. Everything so fuzzy.*

"Well I'll be damned. Your mother said as much." Daric stood in Tarian's way, forcing her to stop. "I don't like this, Tarian. There's a lot more going on here than a Laghairtine trying to control your power. A lot more."

"You think I don't know?"

"What's going on?" Calliope stood next to the two of them, her eyebrows crinkled in confusion.

"Everything. Nothing." Tarian shook her head. "I'm glad you're okay. Why are you? Okay, I mean?"

"The Laghairtine left just as you did. You dissolved, then he poofed out. He didn't touch us. It was like he suddenly had somewhere important to be." Calliope touched Tarian's shoulder. "Are you sure you're okay? You don't look right."

"Good. That's...good." Tarian frowned. Something important. Something...vital. Something she had to...fight.

"Tarian? Look at me." Daric took her face in his hands.

Tarian studied him, her hands limp by her side. His lips, so close. No. That's not what she…she had to fight…something. What?

"Something's wrong. She's free of the banishment. She shouldn't be reacting this way. Calliope, can you reach her?" Daric's worried eyes continued to stare into hers. Her sister's hands touched her forehead. Cool. Soothing.

Something. Important. "Calli…"

"I don't know. Something is off. I can't…I don't know how." Calliope's voice, high, frightened, trembled.

"Get help." Daric ordered. Calliope ran for the door. She screamed at someone on the other side.

Tarian watched her, bemused. Something was wrong. Her eyes clouded. Everything coated in red mist. She blinked. More red mist appeared.

Her blood turned to ice shards that cut her from the inside.

"Time's up."

chapter thirty-seven

The Laghairtine reached for her through their link and coated her in red mist. He took absolute control of her body. Her magic answered to him. Her heart beat an unnatural rhythm as she watched Daric and Calliope talking. Watched their eyes widened. Watched Daric jump. Watched Calliope wave her hands. They shouted her name, but she couldn't answer.

"Scion, at last, we truly meet." The voice whispered in her head, filling her ears and mind with a soft, snakelike hiss. *"You have something I need, Scion. Meet me in your receiving hall. There's someone who would like to see you."*

"Get out of my head! Let me go!" She shouted at him, but the words never escaped her lips. He didn't respond, and neither did her body.

She watched from inside herself, horrified, as her body turned toward the door. Calliope and Daric shouted at her, but their words were incomprehensible. The only voice she needed to hear was the whisper inside her head, which told her to leave.

Calliope grabbed at her arm.

The room spun.

Tarian tried to clear it, to shake it off, to gather her own power. But she had nothing to fight with.

She watched her own hand rise and cast energy at her sister. She watched as it hit her sister square in the chest, knocking her into the door. She watched Calliope land in a crumpled heap, unconscious.

She watched but did nothing.

Inside her head, she pounded at an invisible wall that kept her will locked away from the rest of her.

The door opened, and Sentinels pushed Calliope's body aside as they fought to get into the room. She saw, as if from a distance, all of them draw weapons and aim at Daric. Once again she screamed, but once again the words failed to leave her mind.

She turned to Daric. Even as she fought against the movement in her mind, shouting inside herself to turn away from him, her body lashed out. Force exploded against him and threw him back onto the floor and into the wall. He lay dazed as realization spread over his face. He knew. In the locked-away portion of her mind, she celebrated the small victory. He knew the lizard was in control.

She turned away from him and pushed the Sentinels out of the way. Inside, she cringed at the thought they might try to fight back. Part of her hoped they would. Part of her would rather they didn't, for their sake as well as her own. As she left, she heard them argue, but no footsteps followed her.

She moved down the hallway, her steady pace making it seem more like a walk in the park than a death march. She was positive when she reached the receiving hall and the Throne was in view that someone would die. She just wasn't sure who.

Alex appeared at the end of the hallway.

"Alex, run!" The words didn't come out but danced around inside her head, mocking her.

"You belong to me, Scion. Your attempts are amusing but futile. Where is the book?"

Without even thinking, her mind answered the question. *"I don't know."*

"I can see the opposition ahead of you. Continue to me, Scion. We shall deal with any who stand in our way."

Her hand came up. Her power gathered. A bolt of water shot at Alex. He crumpled, even as she sent another jolt toward the Sentinel.

She stepped over both men and continued down the hallway.

Tarian tried to focus her thoughts. The red mist obscured her vision and made everything hazy. Her hold on reality slipped. It wasn't like the summoning, when Daric had pulled her out of the cave. This felt like the Laghairtine drained her essence. He didn't simply control her, he owned her. Everything but the small bit of mind she used to analyze the situation.

Terror.

She scrambled to take hold of her own body. It continued as though she didn't exist, locked away inside.

She'd lost. It was over. The Dominion, once completed, was permanent. The Laghairtine had achieved his purpose, and now all she could do was watch as he destroyed everything. Her family, her home, Society…everything.

She'd never been so afraid. She had no way to fight back, no way to even communicate with anyone. She cast about with her mind, trying to find anything to latch onto. A sliver of power he didn't control. She was terrified of what would happen when she reached him. Her mind shouted at her body to stop, to turn around, to leave. She beat against the invisible wall that divided her small prison from the rest of her.

She watched through her own eyes as she entered the receiving hall and found it crowded with men she didn't know. Potentials, all anxious to meet her. Guilt stabbed at her. She should have called it off. Told them she'd already completed the ritual. How many of these men would get hurt, just by being here?

She watched their faces as she walked by. Some of them glanced at her filthy jeans and torn tank top, questions in their eyes. But none approached her. She couldn't blame them. She must look like death. And they didn't know yet. They had no idea something was really wrong or that in a few minutes she might start shooting at them. They probably figured it was another of her stunts, like showing up to a meeting in a bathing suit and towel. Another way of pushing people away.

Advisor Jonus stood near the side door. Tarian didn't see her mother, but she couldn't turn her head or even shift her own eyes. She was forced to look exactly where the lizard wanted her to look.

In front of her, the Dolphin Throne glowed, but she wasn't sure if anyone else saw it. It reacted to her presence or the Laghairtine's. She was sure the power built, ready to defend or strike. She couldn't warn anyone.

The lizard must be in this crowd. She hunted for him in her limited vision but didn't see him until she pushed through a large group near the side of the platform closest to the Throne. The Laghairtine faced her, in human form. No scales, no claws. Just an oily smile and triumphant gleam in his eye. Another man stood with him, his back to her, punctuating the conversation with hand gestures.

Tarian crossed the rune etched into the center of the floor and continued. From the corner of her eye, she thought the faint glow pulsed as she passed over it. A spark of hope flared as she detected clicks in the air. Dolphins chittered excitedly about something. They were hard to hear, with all the other noise from conversations, but she'd listened for them all her life. Her friends. Ancient. They'd know, through the Dolphin Throne, what happened here. They'd help if they could. It was a small comfort.

Tarian reached the Laghairtine's side and stood docile, expectant. A drone waiting orders. At first his eyes shone in triumph, then he glanced behind her and they narrowed. He licked his lips.

"Scion. I sense a change in you. I sense…" His pause made her heart thump in her chest. He glanced at the rune, at the Throne, and then back at her, his gaze pointed down toward her abdomen. *He knows I've done the ritual already.* He didn't look pleased, but since he hadn't asked a question, she couldn't speak. "You join with air. This is…unexpected."

The Laghairtine's companion turned to face her. Shock waves rippled through the small portion of mind she controlled. At last, she stood face to face with the one who really attacked her. Victor Aiello. *You asshole! Stay away from me and stay away from my family!*

She pounded against the walls in her head, so frustrated she could cry. If only she were allowed to let the tears flow.

With no other option, her thoughts spun out of control. Aiello. He didn't live in the house; he didn't put in the arrest order for Chester. Aiello wasn't allowed anywhere near the terminals. He'd have been noticed. Someone else, inside the House, had to have done it. Who? Why?

"What did you say?" Victor turned on the Laghairtine. "You said she'd be mine. What does this mean?"

"Our agreement detailed only that I arrange domination of her will through Domini and pass control to you. I have achieved a portion of the agreement."

"You were supposed to do this *before* the Succession Ritual. Before, not after. I was supposed to be the only one she mated with. Me, you idiot. And not," he slammed the table next to him with his fist on the word, "in a room full of people."

"Such detail was not part of the agreement."

The Laghairtine's calm voice seemed to infuriate Victor. Part of her was happy Victor had been thwarted, at least in this. She'd been right to push up the ritual. Whatever else happened, at least she'd stopped that. Even if it meant joining with Ruarc. Between the ache she'd had in her uterus over the last 24 hours and the fading glow of the rune, she knew the ritual was over. *Too late for you, sucker! Even if you try you won't be a part of her. Not now, not ever.*

"I was supposed to be the one to produce a child with her. Me. I wanted me and my child on the Throne. It's vital. I've made agreements with others. You knew that. Don't pretend you don't understand."

"I understand more than such as you can fathom."

The Laghairtine flicked his hand at Victor.

"Fool! What are you doing?" Victor's eyes widened.

"As you requested, I have delivered. My portion of the agreement is fulfilled."

The Laghairtine waved a hand, and the red mist that clouded Tarian's vision lifted, hovered in the air, and then settled on Victor.

Control over her body shifted. It wavered for a moment then snapped together. It felt different but still hopeless. Victor's essence flowed into her, invaded her, commanded her will and her mind. It was the worst kind of violation. The lizard had been clinical and cold. Victor was demented, evil. It made her wonder which was worse, Laghairtine or human.

"And now it is time for your part of the agreement, Victor Aiello." The Laghairtine waited, exuding calm patience at complete odds with the tension in the room. Only his red eyes betrayed his mood.

"You haven't fulfilled your portion. I do *not* have the Throne. You'll wait until I do." Victor smiled his politician's smile, the same one he'd used with her.

"Is the item in your possession?" The Laghairtine sounded as though he discussed the weather.

"It is. Now give me what I asked for. Give me the Throne. Then you'll have what you wanted."

A tiny spark of flared in Tarian's mind. Victor lied. He used that smile when he lied. Whatever it was the Laghairtine wanted, Victor didn't have it. If they had a deal, he was about to break it. She stood between them, watching like a helpless puppy, surrounded by people who did not understand anything odd was happening. Yet.

"Tarian!" She heard Alex's shout from behind her. She couldn't turn to look or respond.

The Laghairtine raised a lazy hand and a blast rushed past Tarian; she heard a grunt followed by a thud behind her, along with exclamations of shock and surprise from several sources. *Alex!*

"Where is the book, Victor Aiello? Our agreement is not complete."

"I take the Throne first." Victor pointed at her. Her entire body snapped to attention. "Scion, order the Throne to pass to me. I have won the right by controlling you."

Her body turned to the Throne but did nothing. As far as she knew, that simply couldn't be done. Calliope had told her as much. It had to be won in battle, and at the moment, its place in her family was solidified by her completion of the ritual. Controlling her wasn't enough. He'd have to kill her mother to put it up for grabs.

She hoped he wouldn't ask her that question. She'd be forced to answer.

"Why isn't this working?" Victor turned on the Laghairtine. "I feel nothing. Why can't I control the power of the Throne?"

"The power that lies in that object is not one I command and is not something I can provide. You must discover it on your own. The book?"

In the smallest portion of her mind, the part that was still uniquely her, Tarian realized what the lizard sought. The *Book of Daemon*. He'd dealt with Victor to get it. She couldn't fathom how Victor convinced the Laghairtine he had it to give. Ruarc was the one who really held it. Why hadn't Victor dealt with Ruarc directly? The whole thing made no sense.

During the exchange, crowd noise behind her died away to shocked silence. For a moment, everything hung in disbelieving silence as the Potentials absorbed the situation. She sensed movement, tension, disbelief, outrage. Murmurs turned to objections which turned to shouts. Several men stepped forward into her field of vision and a barrage of magical attacks commenced. Power whizzed by her head. It wasn't enough. Not nearly enough. The Laghairtine didn't even notice it.

"Victor Aiello, do you possess the item for which we had an agreement?" His words hung in the air above the noise of the crowd. She sensed the consequences of a negative answer. But Victor seemed beyond hearing.

"There's no book, you moron. There never was. And now she's mine, and there's nothing you can do about it." Victor snarled at her. "Tarian, pass the Throne to me."

She couldn't, but he hadn't asked her a question so she couldn't explain. All she did was stand. She cheered for the small blessing. The less he knew, the better.

"Victor Aiello, you will be given one chance. Atonement for attempted dissolution of agreement will begin now, after which our agreement will be forfeit if you do not produce the item, per agreement." The Laghairtine placed a hand on Victor's chest. Victor convulsed before dropping to the floor in apparent agony.

The Laghairtine turned to her. His eyes glowed red, but otherwise he appeared calm. Deadly. "I think you'll discover your joining was a mistake. But I commend the attempt. It is...surprising." The Laghairtine stood close to her, his mouth at her ear. "I'd have you myself, but I sense it is too late. Pity. Your lineage combined with my heritage would have made for a powerful weapon against certain fiery entities. But now, I think perhaps your offspring will provide a much more interesting opportunity, particularly to a certain Ancient being. The outcome of your actions will be extraordinary. It presents possibilities I will enjoy exploiting. I can be patient." He licked his lips.

Tarian struggled against her bonds, but they held. His threat to use her unborn child made her boil inside her cage. She hadn't wanted to be pregnant but she'd protect the child with every force available.

Behind the lizard, Victor gained control of his body once more. He stood, his face red and tight with anger.

"Tarian, kill him." He pointed at the Laghairtine.

chapter thirty-eight

Tarian sent a ball of fire at the Laghairtine, then another. Shocked and horrified, she watched them sail toward the Laghairtine. They would kill him. She was sure of it. She'd never been able to gather that much fire at one time. Never used her power to kill. She couldn't. But with Victor calling the shots, she would.

The Laghairtine formed a shield that blocked the two balls of fire. They exploded on impact and ricocheted. Smaller bursts of flame struck several men around them who crumpled.

"Kill him!" Victor screamed the words behind her.

Tarian sent another fire blast. Inside, she cringed.

Why fire? Fire will kill everyone, not just the target.

Flames which landed on stone died out quickly. The same wasn't true for the clothing they struck. Screams and the hiss of water meeting fire filled the air. Steam rose around those afflicted.

Water talents. Thank Nature and all her minions!

Please stop, please stop, please stop.

Her power, used to kill. Blackness threatened to steal her mind. She'd wanted to destroy the lizard. Imprison him. Banish him for all time. Not burn him alive. Even after all she'd seen, she couldn't bring herself to do it willingly. Death by fire would be as bad as ripped limbs and body parts.

Doesn't he deserve that? Worse, even? Think of that girl.

A glazed eyeball stared at her in her mind. The room, bathed in red mist and blood. Those people. The girl in the basement. All torn apart. Her stomach churned.

That's not me. I'm not a killer. I don't want to burn him to death. Not if it means others will die too.

But still, her body obeyed intentions not her own.

"More! Get past that shield!" Victor's voice behind her, frantic, possessed, insane. So power hungry he didn't stop to think what Tarian's main element was.

Thank Nature for small favors.

Already, her body failed. Calling fire made her weak faster than calling water or air. The next fireball she sent measured half the size of the first. The Laghairtine deflected it with ease.

Men shouted. Waves of energy from all sides struck everywhere but their intended target. Tarian sensed the movement. Sensed the power directed at the man standing in front of her. They didn't know Victor controlled her. They only knew their Scion fought with someone, and they leapt to her aid. Even as they caught the reflected fire. Even as their clothes burst into flames. Still, they tried to save their Scion.

What happens when Victor turns on them? Tells me to kill them too? They don't know, they don't know, they don't know.

Sweat trickled down the Laghairtine's face. Fatigue set in around his eyes. His muscles strained to keep the shield up against the assault.

Which will last longer?

"Tarian. I said kill! Something stronger."

She paused. Gathered power. Focused it into something different. New. A combination of water, fire, and air. A ball of molten liquid, a blend. Silver, with a bright red center. It erupted from her hands and surged toward the Laghairtine.

The Laghairtine screamed as it struck his shield and dissolved it.

The chandelier above them exploded. Showers of glass cascaded down over the crowd. Everyone threw their hands over their heads. The Laghairtine dove to the center of the room, his arms burned, his hair on fire. His suit, tattered.

Panic coursed through the room. Men shoved. Yelled. Tables crashed. Through it all, she stood, unflinching. Glass cut into her arms. She didn't feel pain. If she'd been further to the left, the debris would have killed her. Victor hadn't thought to order her out of the way.

He had, however, ordered her to kill.

No no no no no. Too many in the way. I can't kill him without killing others. Too many. Stop. Stop. Stop!

Tarian turned. She sent another fire and water blended ball at the Laghairtine. It melted around him, like lava.

No shield. He's not shielded. He'll die. Die. Die.

The Laghairtine roared. His arms flailed. Men nearby scrambled to get to their feet and away from the flames. Then the Laghairtine stood. Slow. Deliberate. Power focusing, so much power. He spread his arms out wide. Stretched. Tore. His face split on the side. Scales erupted to cover his head. His arms grew, and grew.

The Laghairtine changed in front of them from human, to the half-lizard she'd fought and beyond. A tail formed, long, powerful. He thrashed, and his tail swiped three men up against the wall where they crumpled.

Horns erupted down his back. He flexed, and they glistened. Red sweat dripped from the scales on his face.

He roared, and it filled the room. Tarian stared. For a moment, everyone stood transfixed as the human became a beast.

When he finished, the Laghairtine stood at least three feet taller. His biceps bulged, and his extended hands ballooned and exploded into claws.

I can't beat him.

Despair. Frustration. Her family would die. The House would crumble. These men would die. They couldn't fight this thing. She didn't have enough strength left to combat something like this.

Knowledge grants power stronger than magic.

"Kill him! I command you to kill that thing." Victor's unhinged voice, frantic, sailed past her. The Laghairtine turned to face Victor, even as he casually threw up a shield around himself.

"Our agreement isssss not fulfilled." The Laghairtine's voice, rough, deep, came out more snake than human. "Agreement with Lasssaaiiirrr isssss concluded. I. Am. Free."

The Laghairtine turned toward Tarian. A long forked tongue snaked over his scales. "Such power deserves a strong masssssster."

"Kill him, you idiot girl. What are you waiting for?"

"I cannot kill him. He is stronger." Tarian's voice shook with effort as she sent yet another bolt of molten water at the Laghairtine. It dissolved when it touched his shield with a loud hiss of steam and sparks.

He asked a direct question. I answered the truth. What else will I say?

The Laghairtine laughed.

Fool. Damn you. Fire isn't enough. I'm not strong in fire. Order me to send water. Water, you idiot!

She railed against her brain, but it was no use. Victor's element was fire, and in his panic, he must not be thinking of anything else. His intention shaped her efforts. Wasted them. Guaranteed they'd all die. Right here, in this room.

Daric ran through the door. Relief he was alive gave way quickly to fear he'd die in this room with her.

Get out! Get out!

"Victor, stop it! You'll kill her." Daric pushed past the Sentinels gathered near the door.

"She has the power we all want. She never uses it." Victor yelled. "Now she uses it for me. I command the most powerful creature in existence."

"You don't, you fool! She's human. He's not. Snap out of it!" Daric shouted. He worked his way across the room, stumbling over bodies and debris, until he stood next to Tarian.

His spice filled her nose even as she sent another ball of energy at the Laghairtine.

Get out. Daric, get out. Don't do this. He'll kill you. I can't stop it. I can't stop.

In her head, tears fell.

Through the confusion, the dust, the steam, and the haze, Tarian saw the side door open and Advisor Jonus run through, pulling her mother along with him.

No No No No NO! Get out! Mother, get out!

Jonus stopped just inside the room and pointed at Tarian as though he knew exactly where she was. Her mother stopped short, stunned.

Terror at what might happen to her mother overrode everything.

Stop, stop, stop. Dammit, stop!

Her body didn't listen. Tarian fired again on the Laghairtine, drenching him in water gathered from the pregnant Pacific air.

He's figured it out. He's using my strength.

The tiny hope the thought provided disintegrated as Tarian saw her mother's hands reach out and the glow around the Dolphin Throne join with her. Marielle was going to fire on the Laghairtine.

She doesn't know. Mother, get out! He'll make me kill you too. Get out! We can't fight this. Get out!

Inside, Tarian dissolved. Tears, screams nobody would ever see or hear filled her own ears and mind.

Advisor Jonus shuffled to the side of the room, away from her mother. Toward Victor.

That's it. Stop Victor. Stop him. Kill him.

Her mother lofted a glowing ball at the lizard. It struck him in the head, and he staggered back. Her next ball struck his shield, which shattered with a loud popping sound. He roared, turned toward her mother. He glanced up then flicked a claw, and the roof over her mother collapsed.

No No No NO!

Mother!

Inside her mind, Tarian raged. Parts of the ceiling cascaded down on her mother. Shouts, groans, and screams filled the air. Marielle fell underneath the weight of stone and rock. Tarian beat against her prison. Her heart ripped open and her soul cried out, but nobody heard.

She didn't shield. The Throne didn't save her. Why? Why didn't it save her?

Agony washed over the tiny portion of mind she controlled. Daric shoved Tarian hard. She adjusted and sent another volley of fire at the lizard.

Without his shield, it hit him full force. He staggered back a few feet and roared. His claws lifted and the shield reformed. The fire along his scales died.

"Victor, dammit, stop it! She can't fight this battle for you. He's too strong," Daric shouted from somewhere behind her.

It's over. It's over. Mother, I'm sorry.

Tarian melted. Stopped the struggle. An empty space claimed her rage and locked it away. She didn't care. She couldn't win. They'd all die. Despair. Acceptance.

So this is what death looks like.

Not some sweet, flowery, ocean side funeral filled with torches and prayers and good wishes for the life Beyond. A fiery hell where the soul was torn to shred and everything she cared for demolished before her eyes. Death did not give a shit. Death ripped her heart out and ate it for dinner.

All my fault.

In front of her, the Laghairtine paused. Behind her, voices carried above the carnage.

"Brother. Nice of you to join me. Didn't I tell you I would one day call the Throne my own?"

Her mind whirled around the word brother.

The Laghairtine's eyes glinted. "I ssssense surprise from your captive, Victor Aiello."

"Look at me, Tarian."

She turned to face Victor. Daric stood between them, a human shield.

Brother?

"That's right, Tarian. Didn't Daric tell you we are brothers?"

"No." Since he'd asked a direct question, she had to answer.

"Still keeping secrets, eh, Daric? Didn't show her the family skeletons? Thought you'd jump into her bed like all the others, just to spite me? Well, you're too late, little brother. She's mine. The Throne is mine."

Her heart was having trouble wrapping itself around what her head was telling her. Daric and Victor. Related. Victor, who called the Laghairtine.

Did he know?

A whisper of doubt colored her thoughts. *Was Daric in on this with his brother, Victor? Is that why he was in that alley?*

Daric shoved Tarian aside, his face a mask of determination, anger, and concentration as he faced the Laghairtine.

Tarian's legs buckled with the force of the blow, and she fell to her knees.

The Laghairtine watched, his eyes flashing. He waved a hand at her, as if dismissing her existence. "Enough. Victor Aiello, you sssshall pay the forfeit pricce now." Power raced over her head, brushed Daric hard enough to knock him backward, and struck Victor.

Victor's scream died in his throat. He stood for a moment, stunned, then crumpled to the floor.

His eyes stared out, already glazed.

The hold on Tarian's body lifted so suddenly, she collapsed the rest of the way to the floor. The claw in her neck ripped at the skin. She screamed and clutched at it as it tore a hole and squirmed out through her fingers. It rose in the air above her, dripping blood and fluid, then raced toward the Laghairtine.

It melted into his claw as though it had never left.

Tarian lay panting as the pain and blood pulsed underneath her fingers.

Pressure. Keep pressure.

She groaned, her body weak. Lying on the ground, she shook.

Her body. Her mind. *Free.* Exhausted, but free.

Loud crunches. The ground shook as the Laghairtine advanced on her. He paused directly over her.

He's going to kill me. I can't stop it. He's going to kill me. Mother.

Tarian closed her eyes.

chapter thirty-nine

Tarian tried to pull power, but couldn't. Pain. Adrenaline. No focus. When the Laghairtine didn't immediately kill her, she opened her eyes.

He stood over her. His tail thrashed and tossed debris aside with each swipe. His gaze examined her body as though it were a science experiment. Something he needed to figure out.

Tarian tried to get up but couldn't make her legs work. They refused to move or support her in any way. Her head rang from the overload of power in the room. When she'd been under the lizard's control, she hadn't felt them. Now she dealt with the after effects of not only the hits, but also the ones she'd dealt.

Drained. Exhausted. She couldn't fight back even if she wanted to. She put her hands to her head and tried to squeeze the pain into nonexistence. All she did was cause more stars.

Behind her, the scent of hibiscus and sea salt.

Calliope.

Tarian turned to see her sister run through the door, stop as she took in the scene, her eyes widened in shock.

There is strength in yielding.

Tears streamed down Tarian's face.

Not her too.

The worst thing would be to scream Calliope's name. The worst thing would be to tell her sister to get out. To call attention to Calliope.

Tarian did both things, unable to stop herself. Her voice came out raw and full of gravel but loud enough for Calliope to hear.

Calliope's gaze met hers.

"Get. Out." Tarian mouthed the words, unable to scream anymore.

The Laghairtine turned, examined Calliope, then turned back to Tarian. "I am free. No longer bound by blood to sssurvive. Ssshe isss not the one Lasssair wants. Amusssing. So much sssstruggle for a human. And....thisss...." The Laghairtine walked forward, each footfall making the floor shake and rubble fall from the walls and ceiling. As he passed Tarian, his tail caught her and pushed her several feet toward the wall. The force knocked the wind out of her. She coughed and rolled to her side, clutching her stomach.

"All of thisss trouble for a trinket?" The Laghairtine sounded confused.

Tarian looked at him. The horns along his back still dripped with some sort of liquid. His claw gently traced the dolphins etched in a circle above the chair.

Tarian turned to her sister and beckoned.

Calliope crouched down and moved quickly, dodging tables and the ruined chandelier. She reached Tarian's side and took her hand. Tarian squeezed, and felt the familiar sister bond take hold.

"It holdsss no power. Ssstrange." The Laghairtine sounded bemused.

Tarian's body shook as she pulled herself up onto her side. She shifted to face the lizard.

He turned to stare at Victor's lifeless body.

"I sssensed his hunger for this object. I sssensed need and longing. But not purpose. It contains no power." He sounded confused.

He can't see the magic of the Dolphin Throne. Just like most people can't see his red mist.

The realization struck her and filled her with hope. This might be the information she needed. She swallowed the lump in her throat. The Dolphin Throne, steeped in water, created energy hidden from this creature of earth and fire. He could not use it. Could not sense it. And since he couldn't, he might leave it alone, thinking it useless. It would give her the advantage, if she called on the power herself.

Knowledge really is power.

She tried to pull enough energy to call on the Dolphin Throne. If her mother really was dead, it was hers to use. If not...

She pulled on it, the two needs conflicting and sending her stomach into turmoil.

Please don't respond. Please.

Her head exploded in pain with the effort.

Through it, the thought her mother must still be alive planted a seed of hope.

Then she saw the glow, a feeble light at first, swirling around the dolphins on the Throne. It grew in strength and size until it filled the room, mingled with the remaining red dust of Laghairtine magic. It blended and circled around all of them.

The power waited to be called, to be used.

"You have to let it in." Calliope whispered. "It's waiting for you to claim it."

There is strength in yielding.

But if she did that, it meant her mother...

Tarian swallowed. Only the Keeper could call the dolphin magic. Only the Keeper.

The Laghairtine raised his hands. Red mist coalesced around him. He shaped something, and she didn't want to find out what. He'd held her once. She wouldn't let him do it again. No scratches, no blood, no rituals, no banishment. If he destroyed the Throne, she'd have no magic to call on save her own.

Knowledge grants power stronger than magic.

Tarian squeezed Calliope's hand, closed her eyes, and opened herself to her sister. With the influx of strength, she opened further. She accepted the Throne, the responsibility, and her position as Scion in her heart, allowing its power to fill her as the opportunity it truly was, not the burden she'd once thought it to be.

Her strength and resolve grew, solidified, and became something more. Calliope's own power joined Tarian's to create a new blend of air, water, fire, and earth. It startled her to realize how much earth Calliope actually possessed. She'd thought her sister purely air.

She glanced at her sister and saw for the briefest moment a gargoyle-like creature with his hand on Calliope's shoulder.

Synergy. Two, together, are greater than one, alone. There is often strength in yielding to the bond of another.

The creature vanished, as if it never had been. The Archivists, it seemed, weren't above passing along their own messages.

Tarian let go of her fear and anger and cast her mind into the glow of power surrounding her. The Dolphin Throne waited. It was hers to command. It greeted her, a long-awaited union.

In her heart, she apologized for avoiding her place, her destiny. She was born for the Throne, and in return the Throne would guide and protect her. It wasn't a bad deal. It was an honor.

She accepted it in her heart and mind.

With acceptance, warmth from her sister and power from the Throne infiltrated every part of her body. It restored her enough to add her own power to the mix. The three combined to become something that one alone could not.

Synergy.

Tarian lay, gathering her strength, bathed in power. Her sister poured energy and healing into her, accompanied by a soft low hum. It healed the muscles along her legs and arms. The open wound in her neck scabbed over. The pain subsided.

"Thank you," she whispered to her sister, to the Throne, and to those who'd stood to protect her. Tarian slowly struggled to her feet. Calliope stood with her and maintained the link of their hands.

The Laghairtine turned, alerted either by their movement or the strands of power Tarian already pulled together.

"You think to defeat me? Your magic isss ussseless against me. Your kind can't even fathom the power I hold."

"If you mean the red mist, you're right. I don't understand it. But I understand this. We have each other. And you stand alone."

History said the genetic makeup of women made them able to hold more power naturally, and to utilize more. But Tarian wasn't sure that history wasn't full of crap. In this moment, she realized what made women stronger in magic power was their ability to let go of ego and join with another. To work together as a group.

She saw a slight smile on Calliope's face. For the moment, they were one. Whatever came their way, they'd face together.

Calliope squeezed her hand. She squeezed back.

Ready?

She thought it in her mind. Calliope nodded. Together, they sent pulse after pulse of power at the lizard. Tarian used a torrent of water, which sang with the dolphin song, while Calliope sent an earth-based jolt of rocks. Both slammed into the Laghairtine. He staggered against it but didn't fall. His answering rage engulfed them in misty-red fire that burned. Tarian closed her eyes and kept firing, trusting the dolphin's magic to guide her. She and her sister sent pulse after pulse, each one doing a bit more damage, though not enough. Not nearly enough.

We need more than this. We can't keep this up.

Tarian stopped the pulses, then opened herself wide and poured every ounce of power she possessed into a flow that stretched across the room and met the Laghairtine. He managed to deflect so the stream didn't quite reach him. His red mist floated around her gold stream in a shower of sparks. Her body drained. *Too fast. Losing power too fast.*

The Laghairtine's chest rose and fall in labored breathing, but he stood tall and strong. He didn't falter.

"We have to do something else. This isn't working. We can't keep this up," Calliope gasped. "Reverse the flow. Extraction."

"Reverse the flow?"

What does that mean?

Calliope gathered the power from Tarian and sent out something she'd had never seen before. It wasn't fire, it wasn't light; if anything, it was the absence of light. It was a black beam of nothingness, almost like a sponge. It reminded her of the banishment when she'd been summoned by Daric and the absence of magic in the cave, combined.

It rushed through the red mist, swallowing it into nothingness as it went. It struck the lizard, melted over his body. He staggered, then roared.

Trying to figure it out, Tarian sent a pulse of water down along the stream only to have it swallowed by the void her sister had created.

"Reverse it!" Calliope gasped. "Pull, don't push!"

Calliope collapsed down onto the floor as Tarian took the stream of magic from her. The black bar of absorption rebounded on her while her attention was diverted, and for a moment, she thought she'd burst from it. Calliope's magic mixed with the Dolphin Throne's, combined with the Laghairtine's odd red rage, combined with her own power.

Her head split in blinding pain. Every pore on her skin hurt, and her stomach churned in revolt. Her eyes held their own laser light show. Lightning struck through her vision, blinding her to almost everything else. Rainbow colors flared every time the lightning in her eyes struck, waves of pain reverberating through her head. Dry heaves made it impossible to breathe, and her ribs shot pain through her with each dry hack.

Not thinking, not even considering what it might do, she closed her eyes. She took a ragged breath and pulled on the Laghairtine's strange red energy. Relentless, she pulled through the pain, through the heat. The acrid smell of burning hair filled her nose and she gagged. She opened her eyes. The lizard moved silently toward her, his eyes wide and terrified. She now had more power than she could hold and had no idea what to do with it. Panic gripped her. Not knowing what else to do, she released the gathered power all in one shot, directly at the lizard.

He gaped at her, throwing his hands up to ward off the blow

as it struck him. The force lifted him fully off the floor where he hovered for a brief second, then exploded. His body turned to red dust that rushed forward, obliterating everything in its path. Tarian ducked, throwing herself down over Calliope.

When she was finally able to look up, the Laghairtine was gone, rubble covered the black marble floor, and her hair was on fire.

chapter forty

Tarian pulled up her shirt to smother the flames in her hair. Fire touched flesh, and pain shot through her hands up her arms. Her stomach heaved at the acrid smell and the crunch of burnt hair on her fingers. She beat at the fire until it went out, and fell onto her back.

Not enough air. She coughed. Rolled to the side to ease the pressure on her stomach and lungs.

Mother. Daric. Alex. Calli.

A lightning show behind her eyes prevented her from seeing the room. Next to her, Calliope lay in a crumpled heap, her breath ragged but steady.

Another fit of coughs wracked her body. Other coughs and moans issued from different corners of the room. She had no way of knowing who they belonged to and didn't care. Her mother needed help.

"Healers! We need healers in here!" She tried to yell the words but couldn't be sure if she managed above a whisper. Everything hurt.

After a moment, her eyes settled down so she only saw flashes of light when she blinked, and the room came into focus. Her stomach churned as the room spun around her for a moment.

Calliope groaned. Tarian turned to her sister and placed a soothing hand on her arm. Her sister opened her eyes, gasped, and closed them again.

"My head." She moaned, and put both hands up to her temples.

"I know, me too," Tarian whispered and softly brushed back some of her sister's hair. "It goes away. Breathe deep and be still."

Reassured Calliope was fine, Tarian pulled herself to her feet. Daric lay with part of his body supported by a piece of table. Victor sprawled next to him, dead.

"Mother." Tarian crawled to the mound of debris in the corner where she'd last seen Marielle. Her head knew what she'd find, but her heart refused to accept it.

"Mother!" She pulled herself around chunks of fallen ceiling and broken tables. When she reached the corner, she pushed at the black stone which pinned her mother's lower body to the floor. Blood coated the side of her mother's face. Her eyes were closed. Her chest didn't move.

"Mother." Tarian tried to move the stones, but they were too heavy and her body too exhausted. She couldn't use her magic. She couldn't even lift her arms. She was spent, in every way imaginable. "Help. Someone, help."

She looked around. Calliope attempted to get to her feet. Daric stood, a hand clutching his side, swaying slightly.

Jonus appeared through the dust and steam as though summoned. He knelt beside her mother and laid a hand on her forehead. "Oh, Keeper."

"Get help! Get a healer, Jonus."

He obeyed without a word, rushing through the side door and into the hall.

Tears burned the corners of her eyes. Tarian blinked them away, but more followed.

"Someone help me move this rock." She tried to shout but couldn't tell if anyone heard. She pulled on the smallest stone and it rolled off her mother. She tried another. Her arms couldn't do it. So tired. So heavy.

Calliope fell to her knees next to Tarian. She lay against Marielle, her hands on her mother's head, and hummed.

"Calli, can you fix it? You can heal."

Calliope closed her eyes. The knuckles turned white, and her face paled. She couldn't have much magic left, either, after the fight they'd had.

Tarian put her hand on her sister's and tried to add what little strength she had. The energy from the Dolphin Throne surrounded them to create a strong, enduring, tireless stream filled with the magic of the sea and the dolphins that created it. Tarian leaned into it, letting her senses open to pull on it, and gasped from the headache that bloomed.

"I can't. Tari, it's too late. I can't."

Tarian looked at her sister. Their eyes met. Tears spilled onto Calliope's cheeks.

"We have the Throne's power. It will work. It has to!"

"Tari. It's too late." Calliope sobbed. "You have the power because she doesn't."

"No. No." Tarian shook her head, frantic. "No, dammit. Heal her. You can heal!" She shook Calliope.

Calliope sagged against Tarian; her high-pitched wail filled the room.

Tarian pulled her sister to her and held her with weak arms.

The two of them leaned into her mother's dead body for comfort and strength that would never come again.

A faint breeze moved Tarian's hair, like the gentle touch of a hand. A mother's hand, saying goodbye. Seconds slowed down into long moments. Time lost meaning. The world dimmed.

A warm hand on her shoulder made her look up. Through her tears, she found Alex with Daric right behind him.

Running footsteps echoed down the hall and into the room. Sentinels, armed and ready for battle, followed by Jonus and Chloe.

Chloe hurried to Marielle's side and gently tried to shift Tarian away. She refused to move. She wouldn't leave her mother alone. Not here. Not ever again.

Alex took her arms and lifted her away. She gave up protesting. Her body wouldn't let her. Daric took Calliope in his arms and carried her a few feet away, holding her against him while she sobbed.

Chloe touched Marielle's head, then her chest. She placed a hand over Marielle's eyes and muttered, "Nature take you and protect you, your energy will surround us all."

The world shattered.

Words drifted by. Calliope sobbed. The room spun. In the midst of it all, dolphins cried, and the ocean waves, which usually soothed her, instead sent wave after wave of grief coursing through her body.

Tarian had no idea how long she sat in the rubble. Did it matter if she stayed forever? Did it really matter if she kept going? Life wasn't supposed to be this way. She wanted to rewind the past few days and start them over. She'd never go to that alley. She'd listen to her mother and stay here and sit in meetings. She'd do it all better. Different.

Would I? Really?

Somehow, she knew she wouldn't. Even if she had the chance to do it all again, it seemed like every step she'd taken was the right one at the time. She'd followed this path to this moment, and now…now her mother was dead.

And it's my fault. My fault and the person's who planned this whole thing. Victor Aiello.

She clenched her jaw and fists. Victor Aiello, insane in his lust for power. He'd caused this. He'd sent people to trick her, to attack her, to steal things and manipulate her. He'd found a traitor in her own House to lure her away and start this roller-coaster ride.

A traitor in her own House.

Beware the danger within.

She looked up. Advisor Jonus stood over her mother's body, talking with Chloe. Making arrangements, no doubt. Planning the funeral. Planning Tarian's ascension to the Throne. Planning next steps.

His clothes were remarkably clean. He didn't have a scratch on him. He obviously hadn't been in the room when the ceiling collapsed, though he'd definitely been there before. She'd last noticed him advancing on Victor. She hadn't seen him since. Not until now.

He wasn't going to attack Victor. Anyone who had been in the room during the fight was covered in dust, dirt, scrapes and bruises. Jonus had pulled her mother into this room, received instructions from Victor, then vanished. Why else would he leave? Why would anyone leave when the Keeper and Scion were threatened?

Unless he had something to hide. Unless he wanted to be out of the way when the Keeper was killed. So the Scion would accept him as Advisor.

Beware the danger from within.

Tarian stumbled to her feet and pushed Alex out of the way to get a clear shot at Jonus. She tried to gather power, but nothing responded at first. She cried out in frustration.

Daric set Calliope on her feet, but kept an arm around her shoulders. "Tarian? What's wrong?" His gaze followed hers to Jonus, then Victor's lifeless body.

Tarian balled her hands into fists. The need to act overwhelmed her. *Power. I need power.*

The Dolphin Throne pulled her toward it like a beacon of safety. She went to it and sat. Dolphins called, circled, encased her in warmth and power. Warmth enveloped her as though she rode the ocean waves. The salt in the water, the air, and her tears combined to fill her. *Jonus betrayed my family.* He'd betrayed the magic of this place and their way of life She knew it, deep down she knew.

She lashed out, pouring every ounce of power available from the Throne into a bolt of air and water she sent hurtling toward Jonus.

chapter forty-one

The bubble of power exploded around Jonus and encased him in a sphere of webbing secure enough to hold an army. Jonus froze in place, trapped.

Tarian panted and sagged against the back of the chair.

"Tarian!" Alex's jaw dropped as he looked from Tarian to Jonus.

"He's the traitor." She rubbed her forehead, wishing the pain between her eyes would go away. "He's the one."

"Tarian!" Calliope covered her mouth with her hands and stared wide-eyed at Jonus. "He can't be."

Tarian closed her eyes, willing strength back into her legs. When she opened them again, the entire room stared at her. Daric, Calliope, Alex, Chloe...all watched, breathless.

"The Archivists told me to beware the danger within. Daric told me someone inside this House is a traitor. And they're right. Someone sent me to Philly. Someone who knew me and my habits, who had knowledge of the databases and the people who live here.

Someone who knew the Sentinels and which one would be likely to earn a favor from me." Tarian glanced at Alex, then back at Jonus. "Someone who sent me to get a dangerous book and knew I'd most likely follow the spell pointed out to me. Someone who knew I'd already fulfilled the ritual without waiting for this reception because that someone saw the Dolphin Throne react."

She forced herself out of the Throne and over to where Jonus hovered immobilized.

"That person dragged my mother into this room during the heat of battle, a battle most didn't even know was taking place, it all happened so fast. Even the Sentinels showed up too late to help, as ready as they are.

"But not Jonus. He knew everything. Knew Victor was here, knew the Dominion had succeeded, and knew exactly when to get my mother. My mother would have told him everything."

Tarian glared at Jonus. "You knew the second the Keeper entered the room during battle, the Throne would be up for grabs to anyone who defeated her and her heir. And I'd already been defeated. That left only one person standing in the way. Didn't it, Jonus? You knew, because you helped plan the whole thing."

Jonus closed his eyes and didn't answer.

"Did you plan on taking it yourself, Jonus? Or did you think Victor would give you something in return for stealing it for him? I paid my price for keeping the Throne safe. What was your price for betrayal? How far does this conspiracy go?"

Jonus remained silent.

Anger welled inside her. Tarian screamed in frustration. "How far does this go?"

Jonus opened his eyes. No longer the faithful sidekick, he'd lost the demure attitude. His eyes, at first defiant, now filled with another emotion she couldn't read.

"Further than you could possibly imagine, *Keeper*." He smiled, a slow, snake-like thing that made his eyes crinkle into half-moon disks of hate. When he spoke, his voice was barely a whisper. "You want to kill me right now, don't you, Keeper? You have the Throne. There's nothing in your way now. What's stopping you?"

Tarian clenched her jaw.

"You need me." Jonus breathed the words. "I know everything. There are pieces of this puzzle older than life itself. You'll never solve it without me."

"Want to bet?" Tarian moved until her nose almost touched his. "Want to make an agreement, Jonus? If you know everything, then you know I'm able to make deals. What is it you want, Jonus?"

He squinted, unable to focus on her so close. "Freedom."

Tarian stepped back. "No deal." She turned her back on Jonus. "Alex, take this traitor to the holding cells. Let's see if some time on Level Three will make him more willing to talk." Her voice had never sounded so like her mother's: calm, collected, and absolutely in control, though exhausted.

"You got no proof, *chica*." Alex kept his voice low. "The leaders are gonna want solid proof. How we gonna prove Jonus was in on it, now Aiello is dead?"

"By following the breadcrumbs." The voice behind her sounded grim and determined.

Tarian tore her eyes away from Alex to see Frankie, his uniform disheveled and his hair singed, stepping over the rubble.

"I found the digital trail Jonus left, just before all the noise broke out. He'd tried to wipe it, but it was still there, if you knew where to look. It matched up with traces of code we found when we checked into Mark Chester."

Alex and Frankie each put a hand on the sphere containing Jonus and pushed him out of the room on a cushion of air.

Tarian turned to face Daric. He clutched his side, and blood dripped down both arms and the side of his face. Her first instinct was to clean him up, to take care of him, to make him whole. But her head swirled with thoughts of conspiracies and traitors. She didn't know who to trust anymore. Her current list would fit in one hand. Her sister. Alex. Frankie. Did Daric fit on the list?

"What about you?"

"What about me?" He lifted his chin.

"Your brother?" She pointed to Victor's lifeless form. "This… is your brother? Did you plan it with him? Was this all a trick for the two of you to get into my bed? To put a child on the Throne? Are you in on it?" Her voice quivered on the last few words.

She'd have done anything for her mother and her sister. Anything at all. Would Daric be so different? They grew up in the same house. They must have learned the same lessons, experienced a lot of the same things, just as she and Calliope had. Daric had been near the alley. He'd known how to summon. He knew some of the words in the *Book of Daemon*. Doubt pounded at her.

"What would it take to prove to you I'm one of the good guys?"

"An explanation, Daric. The truth. The full truth." She sagged against the chair. "Make me feel like less of a fool for trusting you."

"What exactly do you want to hear?"

"All those theories you refused to give voice to. What did you know, Daric? Why didn't you tell me about your brother?"

"It's not something I'm proud of."

"Why were you in the alley? Why have you been shadowing me?"

"I never lied. I told you, I was getting coffee and felt the spell go off." His lips formed a white line.

"Were you part of this?"

"No." Daric's face turned to stone.

"Are you lying to me now?" She watched for any shift on his face, any flash in his eyes.

"No." Daric maintained his stone posture. His eyes never flinched, and they never left hers. Her heart softened. Not enough to forgive. Not yet. But she'd listen.

"You knew the spell. You've obviously seen the book before."

Daric clenched his teeth. "I hadn't seen the book itself. But I *have* seen a journal, which contained notes from it. It was my uncle's. He died trying to keep his hands on the *Book of Daemon*. Every time it slipped away, he hunted it down. He beat me when I found the journal as a kid, but that only made me want to read it more. The spells were useful when dealing with a psychopathic older brother."

Daric stared down at Victor's body. "Victor's always been ambitious. He never hesitated to do whatever it took to get what he wanted. But lately he's been worse. Pushed by something. Insane with a need for more of everything. I tried to stop him, but he was driven to more and more insane bursts of power."

Daric turned back to Tarian. "I didn't know he was plotting against you until the reception. I saw it in his eyes, but I had no proof. It was a hunch. Like I told you."

"You could have said something, Daric. You could have hinted."

Daric rubbed his forehead. "He's always been charismatic. I saw him with you. Would you have believed me?"

She thought about it. "Probably."

Daric raised his eyebrows.

"Maybe." Tarian thrust her chin out. "You should have tried a hell of a lot harder than you did."

"What I did was be there, Scion. I thought if I stayed near

you, I'd find out exactly what he was up to and protect you at the same time."

"Well a fat lot of good that did." Her fist hit the arm of the chair. "This is the result of your protection. My mother is…" Tarian swallowed, her rage gone as quickly as it had arrived.

Daric pressed his lips together and said nothing.

Tarian drew a deep breath. Words tumbled out, almost on their own. "You should have told me. You kept a secret that shouldn't have been kept. Damn you!"

Daric glared at her. "You've been keeping a few secrets of your own."

"This isn't about me."

"I know I wasn't the first to help you with the ritual. That's why you pushed so hard. That's why you wanted me so badly. You'd already been with someone, and you needed at least three. So was that all I was to you? A tool?"

"That's what the ritual is, Daric. That's all I am, a tool for the Dolphin Throne. You knew it. Hell, you all know it." She couldn't even deny it. She had, indeed, used him. But it was more than that. Much, much more. *It's what makes all this so unbearable.*

"Who was it, Tarian? I know Alex is one, but who's the other? That's how you got the book, wasn't it? Who did you deal with?"

Tarian pressed a hand against her stomach.

Flutters at the thought she'd completed the ritual played against her nerves.

If she was pregnant, it would be a long time before she knew the real consequences of her deal with Ruarc.

"I see you still keep secrets. You are aptly titled, Keeper."

"Get out." Rational thought abandoned her. All her anger and fear had to unleash somewhere, and Daric stood right in front of her.

Without a word, he left.

"You know, Tarian, he really is a friend to you," Calliope said, her voice soft in the stillness.

"I know." She stared at the spot where Daric had stood, as if it would bring him back.

I can't handle any more. Not one more thing.

The loss of her mother loomed over her. But she had to hold it together for the sake of the House. A lot of people, just on this island, depended on the stability the House offered.

"Scion…er, Keeper," Chloe said.

"Just Tarian, Chloe." She couldn't keep the defeat out of her voice.

"Tarian, dear, let me do for her now. Do what you have to do. I will have the arrangements made. Your mother was very specific on what she wanted to happen when…" Her voice trailed off as she choked on a sob. Tarian nodded.

"Thanks, Chloe. Please, will you tell Calliope about it all? She's so much better at this sort of thing."

Chloe nodded.

Tarian crossed the room to kneel beside her mother one last time. A hollow place in the center of her chest consumed her, making it difficult to breathe. "I can't do this without you," she whispered.

Calliope quietly sobbed behind her.

"I know you don't like displays, but I do." Calliope pulled Tarian up into a hug. The two of them stood entwined in a hug that dulled the ache in Tarian's heart.

An eternity later, she looked around at the room. The clutter, debris, shambles of a solid life torn apart. It looked how she felt, ripped apart, barely held together by stone and determination. Above it all, the Dolphin Throne remained untouched, serene and strong.

Alex strode into the room, bringing with him a group of people who immediately started clearing rubble. She watched him, setting order, righting her world. A true friend.

Her sister watched with her. "You have a lot of people behind you, Tari."

"I know. Right now, though, it doesn't feel like it." Tarian squeezed her sister's shoulders. "I'll be okay. I'm just exhausted."

She loved their Society. She loved the feeling of magic that flowed through all of them, and into the very rock that formed the House of Xannon. It was her home, and she was willing to defend it against anyone and everyone. Shame it took all of this destruction for her to see the House as it truly was: a home. And the Throne as it truly was: a friend. Not a burden. Not shackles on her freedom. A path to much more than she ever dreamed possible. All it took was a change of attitude.

Alex approached and cleared his throat. "Transitions are touchy, and this one's got everybody spooked."

"What do you mean?"

"With the rumors Daryl started and all the mess, all anybody really knows is you were in the middle of it. They don't know the real story. All it takes is one bad apple, and suddenly you got a bunch of jerks trying to push you around. You have to take the Throne officially, Keeper." Alex drew himself up straight. "As your advisor, I say you do it now before anybody gets any stupid ideas."

At the word advisor, she smiled.

"Set it up, Advisor Alex."

chapter forty-two

A few hours later, Tarian and Calliope stood next to the Dolphin Throne in the disheveled receiving hall. Alex stood beside her. His face was a mix of sadness and awe, and something else she couldn't quite put her finger on. She squeezed his hand before he took up a watchful stance.

Tarian waited while people gathered. Some tried to clear rubble around them. Others simply stood on it. Some looked angry or even hostile. Some looked sad. All looked anxious. She couldn't blame them.

Sentinels lined the room on all sides. This many people gathered in one place, all with some magical talent, made the air vibrate. It circled around them and singed her nose hairs.

"Can you feel that?" she whispered to Calliope.

"Feel what?"

"Magic."

The muttering of the crowd died down as Tarian moved to stand in front of the Throne. From behind her, raw power licked at her back and moved her hair slightly as it caressed her body. She looked uncertainly at Calliope, but her sister stared out at the assembled people, apparently unaware of the sensations Tarian felt. She looked back at the crowd and cleared her throat.

"Uh," she said. *Way to go, Tarian, nice way to begin.* She mentally kicked herself.

"It's with great personal sorrow that I tell you Keeper Marielle…my mother…that the Keeper has died."

She heard gasps and a few startled shouts, and general talk started to rise as people started asking questions.

"Please…have patience. Everything will be explained. I will send out a formal announcement so all in the region may receive the news. She died protecting me and this House"

Tarian turned and stepped to the Throne. She felt the warmth of the power surround her as it invited her in. She sat down, and immediately the dolphin symbol rose up and started to spin. As it spun, it shot out beams of light into the crowd. The glow settled over Tarian, and she felt one with the chair.

She traveled along the beams of light and saw each person in the room as clearly as if they stood next to her. She felt their intentions. She felt their needs, their desires, their hurt at the loss of her mother, and a variety of other emotions she didn't want to feel. They weren't all kind. She followed the light and found it extended out past the walls of the house. For a moment, she traveled along it across the ocean and into the heart of the Region. As she went she saw faces, each one a member of the Society, each one with magic in their very soul. Each one her responsibility.

The sheer enormity of it overwhelmed her. Panicked, she tried to pull back and found she couldn't. The Throne had her and would not let her go. She struggled against it. She tried to push away or stop or reverse the flow but found it impossible.

Finally, she gave in and followed the light.

There is strength in accepting the bond of another.

Across the region, she touched face after face and witnessed families in their everyday lives. Some simply watched TV, some made love or studied or even gardened. Others commanded attention in bars or meetings or casinos. All facets of life. She started to cry as the beauty of it and the weight of the responsibility crushed in on her. Life. All of it precious. She'd never felt so outside of herself before. She surrendered to it, letting the light completely consume her.

As she came back to herself, the crowd in the hall stared at her in awestruck silence. The dolphin emblem shone above her head, a beacon above and separate from the Throne itself. Tarian stared up at it. She'd never known it could be removed from the Throne, but here it was floating above them all. It slowly descended and became part of the chair behind her once more. Alex, who stood on one side of the platform, fell to a knee and bowed his head. She watched as a ripple went through the crowd and each one of them also took a knee.

"Let this moment be for my mother. For Keeper Marielle," Tarian said. Her words traveled throughout the hall in the solemn silence.

chapter forty-three

It was several weeks before the receiving hall was in any kind of shape fit for humans. While Alex, with his skill with earth and stone, worked on repairing the damaged parts of the exterior walls and ceiling, Tarian worked on repairing the damage to her own psyche.

They celebrated her mother's life in a traditional style of the Pacific. Tarian crafted the platform of wood and twine herself, with help from Calliope. At sunset, they stood on the black sand beach outside the House of Xannon, placed her mother's body on it, set the whole thing ablaze with a small, combined pulse of power, and pushed it out to sea. The raft carried her mother on the waves. Dolphins splashed and nodded a salute, each one taking a turn to leap over the funeral pyre, until the last ember died and her mother's ash joined the sea. A void in her heart ached, and no amount of tears filled it.

On impulse, Tarian ran into the surf and threw herself into a wave, letting it wash over and around her. The dolphins joined her, her friends, her childhood, her future, all wrapped up in bodies flowing with the waves. One in particular, Roger, winked his scarred eye at her. He nudged her with his nose, the contact radiating comfort and timeless friendship. The image he sent along the touch was of her mother, at home in the waves. She'd live on here in their collective memory forever. Theirs, and the Archivists, whose strange hive mind never forgot anyone or anything.

Tarian hugged Roger as much as possible with the waves and surf bobbing them both up and down. He remained remarkably still for the encounter, seeming to sense her need for physical touch and reassurance. Her tears joined the ocean water, but this time instead of bitter or angry they cleansed a tiny bit of the hurt.

"Thank you." She let the thought ripple through her touch to Roger, who clicked. A happy thought returned. *"Baby."*

Tarian nodded, not trusting her voice.

Joy colored the water. All around her, dolphins leapt and did somersaults.

"Life. Hope."

She managed a small smile. *Hope, indeed.*

Reluctantly, Tarian turned for the shore. Calliope waited, tears streaming as she leaned into Frankie, who held her in protective arms. Alex stood next to them, stoic.

She searched the gathered crowd. The one person she wanted to see most in the world at this moment was absent. It hurt more than anything else.

She'd sent him an invitation to the funeral. Daric refused to even speak to her, much less return the many messages she'd sent.

It'd been a few weeks. It felt like months. Longer, even. She stood on the shore, took the towel Alex offered, and dried herself automatically. They walked silently through the rest of the crowd gathered for the service, mostly regional leaders all wishing to make a good impression on the new Keeper. When they reached the rotunda, Tarian walked past the doors to the receiving hall, dripping water on the floor, and continued on to her bedroom without a word. She left a trail of sand and water behind her. Nobody followed her.

When she reached her room she shut the door and leaned against it. The power-infused wood did little to comfort her. The room felt empty and bare, though nothing had changed. She sniffled, and moved toward the bed. She'd thought to take a shower but now exhaustion claimed her and all she wanted was to lie down and sleep for an eternity.

Tarian peeled off her wet shirt and paused. The air smelled of lingering spice and coffee. She examined the room and found the source next to her bed.

A single red rose lay on her pillow, and a steaming cup of coffee in a paper cup labeled PJ's rested on the table beside her bed.

Tarian took it in her hands and held it, absorbing the warmth and scent she loved, pretending it was Daric's arms around her and his lips on hers. Tears welled up and cascaded down her face.

He came but he didn't stay. He didn't say anything.

But he left a piece of himself. It was something to work with. A beginning.

Tarian sat down on the bed and caressed the petals. She sniffed it, but now her nose was too stuffy to detect any scent. That tiny loss, of something so inconsequential, made the tears fall even harder.

I miss him.

She pressed a hand against her stomach. Butterfly flutters overtook her whenever she thought about the state of her uterus. There was nothing to fear anymore. Nothing but impending motherhood.

I should tell him.

The next morning, she woke to the stare of an Archivist. He huddled on the table next to the empty coffee cup, an immovable statue of patience.

She sighed and held out her hand. He sprang to life and touched her.

"Keeper. We propose an agreement."

"What is it about these agreements?"

"All daemon are bound by agreement. By such bonds is life ensured, peace and knowledge advanced."

"So you want to make a trade. For what?"

"We know of the promise made to our brothers. Keeper's agreement with Carraig did not specify a time limit. We propose an agreement. The Book of Daemon will be yours for study as long as the promise to Carraig is not kept."

"You have it?" She sat up so abruptly, she dropped his hand and knocked over the coffee cup. She quickly put her hand back out. "*You* stole it? You're the ones?"

An angry chorus of voices circled in her head. *"We do not steal."*

"Still playing word games. How did you get the book?"

"The Book of Daemon belongs to daemons. It returns to nearest daemon."

"You mean I was never going to be able to keep it. He tricked me."

An image of Ruarc flashed in her head along with mutters from the Archivists. *"No trick. Agreement. Precisely worded."*

They were right. Ruarc never promised she'd be able to keep the damn thing. Only that she'd leave with it. It would take a lifetime to master the art of deals with daemons. And a lawyer.

But now she'd been fooled once, she wouldn't be fooled the same way again.

"Why don't you want me to keep my promise?" She'd promised to release the daemons in the cave. She saw no reason not to fulfill the request. And the consequences of *not* keeping it were pretty damn severe.

Silence filled her head. Followed by more silence.

"So this is how you want to play it? You want to give me only the bits and pieces you're comfortable with? Well, I'm not falling for it again. You either give me all of the information I ask for, or we're done with this discussion."

"Keeper has learned well."

"I have good teachers." She waited for them to answer.

"We live under agreement, carefully worded. They would not. There are consequences, seen and unforeseen. Many possibilities, many negative scenarios. Keeper already has in motion one such consequence. There will be others. To release Carraig requires summon or destruction of Stulos. This we would avoid. Our agreement involves the protection of this House and all within. This we do."

"Who was your agreement with?"

"Serin Alaisa Xannon, the first Keeper of the Dolphin Throne."

Tarian knew the name. Her sister had told her the leaves in the archives had belonged to Serin. The sheer age of these Archivists astounded her. They'd been here literally since the foundation to the house was laid. The number of things they'd seen and experienced here made her skin tingle. There was no better source of information, and they had been here under her own roof, since before she was born. They heard her thoughts, but she didn't care. She honored this connection and wanted them to know.

"Do you know for sure that freeing them would cause irreparable harm?"

The lack of voices in her head was enough of an answer. "I'll take that as a no."

"Keeper seeks the impossible. The future is not knowable. Possible scenarios are. Outcomes change as choice changes."

"Well, maybe you should look into all the scenarios. As you said, knowledge is power. If you don't want me to keep my promise, I suggest you give me specifics on exactly why I shouldn't. I will not dishonor a promise using a loophole I didn't realize existed when I made it. That's not who I am. So you'd better have a damn good reason for me to break my word."

Her mind exploded with images and voices. She took her hand away to give them time to discuss her proposal. When the Archivist reached for her again, it was a very subdued voice that filled her head.

"We are bound to assist."

She found it fascinating that even though she had no idea what the agreement was, they felt honor bound to keep it.

Still, she had to ask: "Did you have a part in any of this with Victor or Ruarc?"

"We belong to no court. We are Ancients. We are bound to the House of Xannon." The indignation coloring the words did more to convince her than the words themselves.

"Bring me information, and I'll consider your request."

"We are agreed." The Archivist vanished.

Tarian studied the space where the creature had been seconds before. Some daemons had the ability to travel through walls without really calling to power. The House of Xannon was vulnerable to anyone or anything that was like the Archivists. The Laghairtine had exploited the fact to get into the Cellar. Anyone else like them could come and go at will. It didn't instill confidence.

Alex would fix it, she had no doubt. He and Frankie would find a way to fortify the House against this type of travel.

Tarian picked up the rose and held it gently in her hands. She still held it when she went to sleep, pretending she laid next to Daric. It helped, somehow.

She hadn't told him about her promise to the Carraig. There hadn't been time. She owed them, she'd promised them, and she kept her promises. But she needed help to make it happen. She might even have to make more deals in order to get it done, something she simply wasn't equipped to handle. Daric might help, if we would at least talk to her.

The ache, which filled her when she thought of him, was too much to bear. In her heart, she knew he was much more than just a friend.

Time to grovel.

chapter forty-four

Tarian stepped through a portal directly into the middle of Daric's living room in Philly. She found him sitting on the sofa, staring at the TV.

"You know, you really should put some sort of security on this place."

"No need."

She stood watching him, uncertain. He continued to stare at the TV. *Bad sign.*

"You say that a lot. This isn't exactly the suburbs here. And the Laghairtine attacked right outside your door. I know the building is warded but still, he found a way into the Cellar. This place wouldn't be an issue."

Daric blinked, but his body remained still. Only his hands, resting on his thighs, twitched.

"Still pissed?"

"What can I do for you, Keeper?" His tone was worse than angry. It was cold. He turned off the TV but continued to stare at the darkened screen.

"You can look at me, for starters. And you can stop calling me Keeper."

He balled his hands into fists but continued to stare.

"Fine. Be childish. It's not like I haven't been the same." She sighed. *This isn't going well at all.* Her stomach churned.

"Do you have any crackers? My stomach isn't happy today."

He looked up at her, then his eyes flicked down to her belly and back up. It was enough to encourage her to keep going.

"You don't have to talk. Just listen." She sat down next to him. "The thing is…well, the thing is I stink at apologizing. But that's what I'm doing. I know you weren't in on any of…what happened. I know you are, or were, my friend. And I didn't treat you like one. I'm sorry."

He started to speak, but she put up a hand to stop him. "No, hear me out. I wanted to tell you thank you for all your help. And for the friendship you showed me and my family."

She saw at least his face wasn't set in stone anymore. He listened, even if he didn't forgive. Yet. "Calliope told me what happened after I banished myself, and the Archivists filled in the rest. How you cast the spell to bring me back. All of it. The Archivists are quite the spy network. I'm pretty sure there's nothing that happens in connection with the House of Xannon they don't know. Kind of creepy to think about, but comforting too."

She took a deep breath. "I guess if Victor Aiello were my brother, I wouldn't have advertised it either. Family. You can't pick them. You're stuck with them. But you can choose your friends. And, for what it's worth, I choose you."

She fell silent, unable to figure out anything more to say.

"He was my half-brother," Daric said. His quiet tone still had a hard edge. "His mother died in childbirth."

"So he started young." She nudged Daric with her shoulder. He snorted.

"Anyway, I wanted to thank you for the coffee. And the rose. I wish..." She gulped down the lump in her throat and pushed on. "I wish you'd been there. On the beach. But I know why you didn't come. It's my fault. All of it. And I'm sorry. I hope someday you can forgive me."

She sniffled and waited for Daric to join in the conversation. Nothing. But his back was a little less tense. Maybe.

The silence spun out to fill the room and make things uncomfortable. It was a trick she'd learned from her mother. Most people couldn't stand silence.

She shifted on the sofa then picked at a nail. When Daric didn't fill the void and she'd torn the nail down to the quick she gave up. She stood, disheartened. *He hates me.*

She started to open a portal when Daric finally spoke.

"My mother wants to see you."

Tarian turned to face him. "Your mother? But not you?"

He stared at the blank TV.

"Tell her she's welcome to visit anytime."

She couldn't keep the depression out of her voice. Most people didn't know how to handle her new role, and neither did she. She hadn't been able to go out by herself. She didn't dare leave the House unattended for long. She hadn't heard from Daric at all, which was the part that hurt the most because it was entirely her own fault. "Anyway, that's all I wanted. To say thank you." She sniffed.

Daric glanced at her.

"I'm getting a cold," she said, and sniffled again.

"Right."

Daric patted the sofa next to him. She sat, and struggled

to force words out from between quivering lips. "It's been over two months, but I still feel like she's going to walk through my bedroom door at any moment and yell at me about something. I wish she would."

"She's only dead if you stop looking in the mirror." Daric turned slightly toward her.

"Mirror?"

"You have her smile, Tari. Her nose. Her confident posture. You see her every time you look in the mirror. She's a part of you. Always will be."

Tarian nodded, and looked away. A tear spilled out and worked slowly down her cheek. She didn't wipe it away, afraid it might start a tidal wave.

"If you're up for it, I'll tell Mom to stop by next week. She has plenty of stories you might not have heard about your mother."

"I'd like to meet her." Her heart skipped at the words and at the touch of his hand on hers.

"You already have."

"When?" She searched her mind for the name Voltain. She couldn't remember anyone other than Daric with that name.

"I told you, she's a teacher. She used to tutor you in history. Don't you remember?"

"I hated history." She thought back to her tutors. There'd been several over the years. History reminded her of dusty old books in the archives. An image of a tall woman with sparkling eyes surfaced. Eyes like Daric's. "You mean Miss. V.?"

He chuckled. "You do remember. She'll like that."

"I never knew her real last name. She was Miss. V. to me. Why didn't you tell me?" She punched him on the arm.

"You never asked."

"I slept through a lot of those lessons."

"I know. I heard all about you. You know, we met once. Long time ago. Mom brought me with her for a play date with you."

He flashed a smile, and the dimple peeking out from his cheek warmed her heart.

"I don't remember it." She frowned. *How could I forget?*

"You nearly drowned me. You challenged me to a race in the ocean and you were so fast I couldn't keep up. The dolphins had to help me back to shore. By then you'd gone off to do something else, and I went home. Bruised ego." He grinned.

"Sounds like something I'd do." She smiled back. They locked eyes, and something in his—concern? friendship? something else?—made hers spill over in tears. Sobs wracked her body. Daric took her in his arms and rocked her back and forth. She sank into the warmth of his arms and cried. He rubbed her back and said nothing.

She ran out of tears but remained snuggled in his arms. She felt safe. But she couldn't stay. She was Keeper. She brushed the remaining tears from her eyes and sighed.

"Well, that's definitely going to tarnish my image."

"Not in my eyes." He kissed her forehead. "When are you due?"

"You can tell?" She sniffed. "I do feel fatter."

"You're a puddle. You wanted crackers. Yes, I can tell." The dimple appeared as she spoke. It, more than anything, erased her tears and lifted her mood.

"End of the summer."

He put a hand on her stomach. The heat from his hand spread into her belly.

"I can feel her." He looked up, his eyes wide. "She's so strong."

"It might be a boy. It's happened before."

"Not this time. It's a girl."

"Is it normal to feel the signature this early?" It was yet another question she wished she could ask her mother.

"I'll ask Mom. I'm amazed they let you out of the house. Does anyone know?"

"There's no hiding it. The damn Throne announced it by sounding dolphin calls for an entire day. And didn't ask permission."

"Keeper, I think you should go home. You shouldn't be out where you may be attacked. Not now. I'll go with you."

"Told you to stop calling me that."

"It's just a name. It doesn't change who and what you really are."

"I suppose it's stupid to worry about. But it feels wrong, somehow. My mother was Keeper. I'm just me."

"I'm sure she thought the same thing when she was your age."

Tarian nodded and lapsed into silence again for a moment.

"What's on your mind, Tari?"

"Nothing."

He laughed. "Even the Keeper does the typical female response."

"Bite me."

"Okay, maybe not completely typical. Seriously, what's wrong? I can tell something's up. You have that faraway look in your eyes, and you're tensing your right hand."

She glanced down at her hands, startled. Her right hand had formed a fist without her even being aware of it. She uncurled the fingers, deliberately placing each one separate on her leg.

"I don't want to talk about it."

"Why'd you come here?"

She looked up into his eyes. They held exactly what she needed. Concern. Friendship. Love. "For you."

He leaned into her and kissed her, his lips tender and soft. "You already have me."

"Is that all I get? A kiss?"

"What else are you looking for?" His eyes crinkled.

"I'd like to have sex without a lizard butting in and a ritual hanging over my head. I'm taking volunteers."

He laughed. "Why'd you really come here?"

"I need help. I made a deal with the Carraig. I promised to free them. They kept up their part, now I need to do mine. But the Archivists don't want me to. It's a big mess, and I need help figuring it out. And I think there's more to the Laghairtine attack than Victor's little power play. You said yourself he wasn't always so unhinged. Something pushed him over the edge. There were things the lizard said before the end...someone else is involved. Something else is going on. Question is what?"

"Sounds like you need a therapist. You're seeing conspiracies where they may not exist."

"I need a strategist. And someone to help me do this right. Someone to make sure I'm seeing everything as it is, not as I wish it to be. Maybe your mother could help, since she knows the histories so well. This time, I want to do things right." She put her hand on her stomach. "I don't want her to pay for another of my mistakes."

"Another?" Daric narrowed his eyes. "What aren't you telling me?"

She hesitated. She hadn't told anyone other than her mother. Did she dare? Would he think less of her?

"There's nothing you can tell me that would change the way I feel about you." Daric took her face in both hands and turned it toward his. "Trust me."

She stared into his eyes and realized she did trust him. Completely.

"It's just...to get the book, I had to..." She took a deep breath and tried again. "I joined with Ruarc, of the Mayfanata.

From what mother told me, even though it wasn't physical sex, the results are the same. He's a part of the child."

She closed her eyes and put both hands on her stomach. The life inside responded with a wiggle. Strong, vibrant, and unmistakably happy.

"Tarian." Daric's voice was barely a whisper. She didn't want to open her eyes. She didn't want to see the expression buried in his.

Daric leaned in, and his lips softly caressed hers. "She's you, and me, too. And Alex. I'd say that makes her more than a match for anything life throws at her."

Tarian opened her eyes. Daric's were inches away. What she found in them made her want to cry again. It wasn't disgust, disappointment, or anger. It was love.

And that was definitely power stronger than any magic.

More in The House of Xannon

FINDING FLAME
All that has been is written on the wind. But
will the past save the future or destroy it?

PROMISE OF MAGIC
Some promises are deadly to keep.

TAKING EARTH
The whole world can change in 24 hours.

ELEMENTS OF MAGIC
Balance is hard, and sometimes deadly.